SWEET DELIRIUM

As we entered the copse there was a change in the atmosphere. It was achingly sad within that small enclosure. The sadness seeped into my heart. And it was dark, strangely dark when there were so few trees to cast any shade. And it was quiet . . . and eerie. Somehow my hand found its way into his.

"Afraid?" he murmured, giving my hand a reassuring squeeze. "Don't be."

"I'm not afraid . . . with you. . . ." I turned to face him and strange emotions were unleashed within me as I met his gaze.

His arms went round me and I melted into them. With no thought to the future I gave myself up to the sweet delirium of his kiss. It enveloped me completely—my heart, my mind, my body, my soul.

GOTHICS A LA MOOR—FROM ZEBRA

ISLAND OF LOST RUBIES
by Patricia Werner   (2603, $3.95)
Heartbroken by her father's death and the loss of her great love, Eileen
returns to her island home to claim her inheritance. But eerie things begin
happening the minute she steps off the boat, and it isn't long before
Eileen realizes that there's no escape from *THE ISLAND OF LOST RU-
BIES*.

DARK CRIES OF GRAY OAKS
by Lee Karr   (2736, $3.95)
When orphaned Brianna Anderson was offered a job as companion to the
mentally ill seventeen-year-old girl, Cassie, she was grateful for the non-
troublesome employment. Soon she began to wonder why the girl's family
insisted that Cassie be given hydro-electrical therapy and increased doses
of laudanum. What was the shocking secret that Cassie held in her dark
tormented mind? And was she herself in danger?

CRYSTAL SHADOWS
by Michele Y. Thomas   (2819, $3.95)
When Teresa Hawthorne accepted a post as tutor to the wealthy Curtis
family, she didn't believe the scandal surrounding them would be any concern of hers. However, it soon began to seem as if someone was trying to
ruin the Curtises and Theresa was becoming the unwitting target of a
deadly conspiracy . . .

CASTLE OF CRUSHED SHAMROCKS
by Lee Carr   (2843, $3.95)
Penniless and alone, eighteen-year-old Aileen O'Conner traveled to the
coast of Ireland to be recognized as daughter and heir to Lord Edwin
Lynhurst. Upon her arrival, she was horrified to find her long lost father
had been murdered. And slowly, the extent of the danger dawned upon
her: her father's killer was still at large. And her name was next on the
list.

BRIDE OF HATFIELD CASTLE
by Beverly G. Warren   (2517, $3.95)
Left a widow on her wedding night and the sole inheritor of Hatfield's
fortune, Eden Lane was convinced that someone wanted her out of the
castle, preferably dead. Her failing health, the whispering voices of death,
and the phantoms who roamed the keep were driving her mad. And although she came to the castle as a bride, she needed to discover who was
trying to kill her, or leave as a corpse!

*Available wherever paperbacks are sold, or order direct from the
Publisher. Send cover price plus 50¢ per copy for mailing and
handling to Zebra Books, Dept. 2871, 475 Park Avenue South,
New York, N.Y. 10016. Residents of New York, New Jersey and
Pennsylvania must include sales tax. DO NOT SEND CASH.*

THE BLACK WIND OF PENROSE ISLAND

KATE FREDERICK

ZEBRA BOOKS
KENSINGTON PUBLISHING CORP.

ZEBRA BOOKS

are published by

Kensington Publishing Corp.
475 Park Avenue South
New York, NY 10016

First printing: January, 1990

Printed in the United States of America

Chapter One

I should not have come. The moment I stepped down from the rickety conveyance that had brought me across the waste of Bodmin Moor to Port Zennoc and heard the warning cries of the gulls wheeling and dipping all around me, I knew I should not have come.

"Go back! Go back! Go back!"

They fixed me with evil eyes and, assailed by an unaccountable feeling of dread, I half turned to obey—but it was no more than a half turn, for I knew I could not go back.

Fighting down my craven fears—they only grew out of uncertainty—I looked about me with determined interest at the whitewashed walls of the hostelry, the array of tightly packed cottages clustering round the harbor, proliferating upwards and clinging limpet-like to the rocky hillsides above; at the sea shimmering in the noonday heat; at the dark mound marring the horizon.

Penrose Island!

Gray and forbidding, it lounged like a giant slug upon the calm waters and, in spite of the sun beating down on my back, I felt a sudden chill. What did it hold for me, that dark and distant place? Would it grant me the haven I was seeking? How would I adapt to the new life awaiting me there? Had I done the right thing in leaving all that was familiar to me and venturing

5

into the unknown?

I looked out across the sea at Penrose Island and tried to still my anxious heart. Right or wrong, I had chosen to take this path with my eyes wide open, driven by my need, my desperate need, to get away, as far away as possible, from a life made untenable for me. But oh! if only my stepfather had not been the kind of man he was. If only I had not needed to take this step.

I had seen the advertisement in the *Morning Times*. "Penrose Island, Cornwall. Secretary required. Ability to live in quiet seclusion essential. Apply Pedlar's Employment Agency, High Holborn."

Quiet seclusion! The answer to a prayer! With no further thought than this, I set out at once to answer the advertisement.

Mr. Pedlar was a dapper little man. He peered at me from above the rimless spectacles sitting on the end of his nose and said, in a tone of astonished disbelief, "You wish to apply for the Penrose Island position, Miss Wentworth?"

"Yes, Mr. Pedlar."

"Hm . . . Yes . . . Well . . . Er . . ." He appeared to be at a loss for words, but then he drew out a folder from a drawer in his desk and opened it. He perused the contents in silence for a few seconds, then began again. "Ah, yes. Good. . . . Now then . . . shorthand?"

"No, I'm sorry. I don't do shorthand."

"Oh!" His spectacles almost fell off the end of his nose in his surprise. "That's most unusual . . . in a secretary. Still, it probably won't signify. The situation is getting desperate." He leaned forward confidentially. "Between you and me, there's not been a rush of candidates for this particular job. You typewrite, of course?"

"Oh, yes, I typewrite."

"Hm . . . Ah . . . good. Speed?"

"I don't know." His face creased anxiously. "But I'm quite fast," I added swiftly.

He leaned forward with his elbow on the desk and his chin in his hand. "Miss Wentworth, have you done this sort of work before?"

"Oh, yes . . . for my father."

"That's not quite . . . You're very young . . . pretty . . . you don't look as though you need the job."

"Oh, but I do."

"It will mean cutting yourself off from the world. You will, of necessity, lead a completely different life from the one I feel you have been used to. Penrose Island lies way out in the Atlantic Ocean. Do you think you could adjust to such a change?"

I assured him I could.

He eyed me for a further moment's consideration then, albeit with a certain amount of reluctance, said, "Very well. If you'll wait a moment, I'll wire Mr. Penrose straight away."

Mama's eyes had widened in horror when I disclosed my intentions.

"What!" she exclaimed, dropping her embroidery in her surprise. "Nonsense! It's quite out of the question even to consider such a thing."

I picked up her embroidery and handed it back to her saying, "It's not unusual for young ladies to take up employment these days, Mama. It's nineteen hundred and twelve. Things are changing fast."

"And not for the better, in my opinion," she snapped. "Your father would be horrified if he could hear you speak so."

"I don't think so, Mama. He was quite progressive in his views."

"Progressive or not, he would not have agreed to his only daughter seeking and *accepting* employment. Really, you astonish me! But I blame myself. I should never have allowed you to attend those lectures on 'The Modern Woman' given by that disgrace to her sex, Mrs. Ida—What's her name. However, I can't believe you're serious."

7

"I am, Mama. Very serious. I leave in the morning."

"But where are you going? And who is your employer? You've never even met him. He could be a man of most infamous character."

"Mr. Pedlar assured me he's a man of impeccable character."

I hoped she would not pursue her enquiry into my employer's name and background, for I had no intention of giving it. I breathed a sigh of relief as she retorted, "Well he would, wouldn't he? No. You must write at once and tell him you've changed your mind. If you really feel you must take a job, then take one in London so that you need not leave home."

"I can't do that, Mama. I've signed a contract."

"Then you must unsign it."

"It's legally binding, Mama."

She had turned then in appeal to her new husband. "You tell her, Ted. Tell her she can't go. She'll listen to you."

I had glared fiercely at the man who had taken my dear dead father's place. He had glared back, his eyes that had once been hot and eager, cold and narrowed. We gazed at each other in mutual antipathy and his lip curled back in a sneer.

"Let her go. It's the only way we'll ever be rid of her. At twenty-three, she's firmly on the shelf, destined to be an old maid. Have we seen any young men beating a path to her door? No. Let her go, I say. An old maid burdening us with her presence is not something I can envision with pleasure."

His words were hurtful, intentionally so. But they cleared the way for me. There would be no further argument from my mother. He had made the decision and she would defer to it, as she deferred to him in everything. She might be deaf and blind where he was concerned. She idolized him and could see no fault in him. She had quarreled with and lost friends of a lifetime when they had warned her he was a libertine and a fortune hunter. He had turned her head with his charm and undoubted good looks, and her ears and eyes were closed to his untrustworthiness.

8

I had quickly discovered his worth.

They had been back from their honeymoon less than a month when he started making advances to me. Shocked and revolted, I had rebuffed him angrily, but it only seemed to add fuel to his desire, and I grew to be afraid of being left in a room alone with him. I threatened to tell my mother of his behavior. His reply, accompanied by jeering laughter, had been the recommendation, "Tell her. See if she believes you. She won't. And she'll hate you for it."

He was so sure of himself, and I knew he was right: she would heed me no more than she had heeded her friends. No matter how much I longed to open her eyes to his true nature, I could not do it. To do so would drive a wedge between us, and I should not be able to bear that. I could never tell her where his absences from her side at night took him. Did she ever question him about them? If she did, he must have managed a plausible excuse, for she seemed to accept them calmly enough. But I knew the truth of the matter. There were many willing to tell me about it, scandalized.

But he was right. There was nothing I could say that she would believe. She was living in a fool's paradise—but she was happy in it. What right had I to try and spoil it for her? Much better to let her continue in blissful ignorance of the true facts than see her world fall to pieces around her, as it had after my father's death.

But I could not sit idly by and watch Ted Gibbon making a fool out of her—and I was afraid for myself if I did.

I shied away from further remembrance and cast about me wondering why no one had yet come forward to greet me and take me to the island. The little bustle of activity generated by the arrival of the antiquated carriage had dwindled away. The vehicle had departed, my traveling companions dispersed, and I was left standing alone, a solitary figure amidst the squawking gulls.

But no—not quite alone. A young man, a fisherman by his garb, was standing in the doorway of the inn. He appeared to be

9

searching for somebody. Me? I hastened toward him and was surprised to see a light of recognition spring to his eyes at my approach. It was quenched immediately, as it must be, for he could not possibly have known me. Nevertheless, it sent a strange thrill of foreboding through my already nervous frame.

"Excuse me," I said. "I'm waiting for someone to meet me and take me to Penrose Island. I'm Mr. Penrose's new secretary and I wondered if . . ."

I broke off. He was scowling furiously. "You'm a woman!" he exclaimed. "'Tis a gentleman I'm to meet. Mr. Wentworth."

"I'm afraid you must be mistaken," I said with a shaky laugh. "I am Miss Wentworth."

Blue eyes squinted disbelievingly at me in the bright sunlight.

"I can prove I am who I say I am," I added quickly, fumbling inside my handbag for my copy of the contract I had signed.

Still scanning my face, he took no notice of the document I held out to him, and the deep penetration of his glance provoked further apprehension to rise in me. Then, muttering to himself and motioning me to follow him, he went to pick up my suitcases.

I trod his heels along a narrow, cobbled street leading down to the harbor and through the busy throng of people crowding the quay. The noise was deafening, with skippers selling their catches, shouting prices at the tops of their voices, and buyers, haggling, equally loud. Deft-handed women, slitting open silvery bodies with razor sharp knives, their fingers bandaged against any slip of the blade, and flinging slippery entrails into tubs, laughed and chattered and flirted with the broad-shouldered young men loading the gutted fish into crates and stacking them onto carts waiting to trundle them away. My stomach churned with revulsion at the gory operation and the all-pervading smell—so different from anything I had been used to before.

"Here us be, Miss."

My guide came to a halt, and my heart quailed within me as

10

he indicated that I must cross a swaying rope ladder straddling the water between the quay and the deck of a trawler whose name was emblazoned in large white letters on its side, *Island Queen*.

The ladder wobbled alarmingly as I set foot on it, and I gripped the thick side ropes in fear and trembling, hardly daring to place one foot in front of the other and trying not to think of the drop to the murky water below. After what seemed like an age, to my great relief, strong hands grasped mine and I was hauled aboard. I looked up into eyes cradled in deeply lined sockets and stammered my thanks. Did a flicker of recognition enter them? If so, it was fleeting, so fleeting that I dismissed it as fancy born of fatigue after my long and wearisome journey.

"Miss Wentworth, Cap'n Pascoe." My young guide introduced me. Unnecessarily, he added, "She'm a woman."

"There seems to have been some confusion," I started to explain, and hesitated as I became aware of men gathering round, scowling, muttering among themselves. When they saw me looking at them, they turned away and went back about their business—but I noticed they kept casting surreptitious glances in my direction. Their attitude disturbed me. I sensed something was wrong. But what?

Tales of white slavers leapt to my mind. Ships that transported young women, kidnapped from their homes, across the seas to foreign lands, never to be heard of again. Had I been brought aboard such a vessel? I looked back into the captain's weatherbeaten face and staunched such wild thoughts. I saw only kindness written there, puzzled kindness, to be sure, but nothing to suggest he might be involved in evil practices. I must indeed be tired to allow such lurid imaginings to enter my mind.

He suggested I make myself comfortable down below, but I said I would rather stay up on deck in the open air. He left me to myself, and I leaned against the rail and watched boxes and crates being swung aboard. They were labeled Tea, Sugar, Oranges . . . Stores for the island? How large was the island?

11

How many people lived there? Till now I had not given a great deal of thought to such things, being concerned only with the fact that I was getting away from Ted Gibbon. I had vaguely supposed there might be a small population, had even wondered whether Mr. Penrose might be a hermit, with only a servant or two to minister to his needs. He was a writer, after all—an historian. That conjured up in my mind a dried-as-dust professor immersed in the past and its dead heroes, eschewing anything that had to do with the present. But the sight of so many crates and boxes set me thinking along different lines. There would be fishermen living on the island. Farmers, probably. There would be wives and children. I began to feel quite happy at the prospect.

The *Island Queen* put out to sea, escorted by the vociferous gulls. I was to learn there was no escaping those great, golden-beaked birds. They nested on Penrose Island and followed the ships to and from the mainland. I grew to tolerate them, even admire them, but for the present they were my enemies who did not want me on their territory.

"Go back! Go back!" they screeched at me, flashing back and forth, swooping low as if to attack. This fostered my anxiety, my fear of the unknown, of the island, that slug-like mound out in the ocean, which still looked gray and forbidding to me.

Yet surely, soon I should be able to make out its distinctive features, see its grassy slopes richly green in the sunlight, its houses white and crowded like those surrounding the harbor at Port Zennoc . . .

But the island remained decidedly, determinedly, gray. If anything, it had deepened in hue. Or was I imagining it? My father always said I had a vivid imagination. But was it only my imagination that showed the waves, lately necklaced with gold, now wearing collars of dirty white foam? And was it an imagined wind penetrating my light summer clothing? And was the light fading?

I glanced up at the sky and my heart gave a nervous jump. While I had been lost in thought, the puffy white clouds that had lain so indolently in their blue heaven all day had lost their innocent purity and turned a sour yellow. With a menacing burst of energy, they now raced across the sun to rendezvous with a black, spiraling mass of cloud in the distance.

The ship started to roll as the wind gained in ferocity, lashing the waves into a passion. The hat was snatched from my head, my hair torn from its pins.

It started to rain. Hard, slanting, icy rain.

"Get down below! Get down below!"

I heard the captain's shouted order and could do nothing about it. I was too busy trying to keep my footing on a deck suddenly awash as the mountainous waves leapt aboard. How could I withstand their furious onslaught? They knocked my legs from under me, wrenched my hands from the rails, and sent me slithering along the deck wildly trying to grasp at something, anything, to prevent myself from sliding into the boiling sea.

Bruised and battered, nausea welling, I wondered how long I should be able to hold out against all the forces suddenly ranged against me. Was I destined for a watery grave? Had I escaped one danger only to face another from which there was no escape? Even as these thoughts sped through my mind, I found myself slipping toward the death waiting to claim me. Then I felt myself being raised up and propelled down a narrow, steeply stepped gangway into comparative warmth.

I was thrust onto a bench, groaning and gulping. A bucket was placed on my lap, a blanket thrown over my shoulders, and from then on I was aware of nothing but the wild rocking of the ship, my heaving stomach, and the longing to curl up and die. Then suddenly, blessedly, the wild plunging and surging ceased, giving way to a gentle, cradle-like motion, and relief came to me.

I hardly had time to savor the relief before I was hailed from above. I climbed up into an icy deluge and was soaked through in seconds. The seamen were smothered in oilskins and appeared strange, outlandish creatures in the gloom of this

13

unseasonable June day. My teeth were chattering, it was so cold. Belatedly, an oilskin cape was thrown over my shoulders and a sou'wester placed on my head.

I was helped ashore, clinging desperately to my waterproof hat, and above the roaring wind I heard a rasping voice exclaim, "What? A woman? You're joking!"

"'Tis no joke being snatched by the Black Wind."

"'Tis bad luck to take a woman on board."

"Aye. 'Tis bad luck 'er's brought us, that's certain sure."

"'Tis a wonder we'm in safe harbor."

One by one the seamen voiced their resentment to the gigantic figure on the jetty—at least, he seemed gigantic to me, though it was probably only his thick oilskin coat, boots, and hat that made him appear so. I understood now the reason for the resentment I had sensed from the first and had been unable to comprehend. They believed I had brought them bad luck, and blamed me for the wind that seemed to have risen from nowhere, whipping the sea into a frenzy. How ridiculous! What superstitious nonsense! I wanted to disclaim any such responsibility to the man in front of me, but my lips were stiff with cold and I could not form the words.

The wind whipped my cape back, leaving my lightly clad body exposed to the heavy downpour, and I let go of my hat in an effort to bring it round me again. Immediately it was whisked away and my hair was plastered to my head. I caught the gleam of the man's teeth as he snarled an oath. My errant sou'wester was re-clamped to my head and, with one hand trying to keep it there and the other endeavouring to maintain mastery over my oilskin cape, I was roughly and unceremoniously steered to where a drenched pony waited patiently between the shafts of a hooded gig. I was bundled in, and with my baggage strapped to the back, we set off at a pace that horrified me.

The road was steep and grew ever steeper. Round every bend sheets of towering granite greeted us; beyond every curve was a sheer drop to the sea which surged below. We were traveling

14

much too fast along such a tortuous road and I turned to my escort with a request to slow down, but one look at his beaky nose and thrusting chin, every bit as unnerving as the grim rocks bearing down upon us, dried the words in my mouth. I released my hold on my oilskins to grasp the sides of my seat and immediately the cape flared, allowing the icy rain to cut through my clothing again. My sou'wester sailed away on the wind.

At last the wind leveled, and we drew to a halt. Through the gloom I saw a great stone edifice confronting me. A castle! its battlements etched against an angry purple sky, its windows dark, shrouded, mysterious.

I shuddered as I gazed, transfixed, at the grim, forbidding monument. I recalled the warning cries of the seagulls at Port Zennoc, and knew I should have heeded them while there had yet been time.

Now there was no time. It was too late—or it would be, once I had entered that grim fortress.

Fortress! Yes, that was what that great stone edifice was, a fortress. But I should not have been brought here. I had been brought here by mistake. I should have been taken to Penrose House.

Complaint rose to my lips, but my escort was already out of the gig and wrenching me from my seat.

"Inside! Quick!" he yelled above the roar of the wind.

I did not move. I did not wish to enter that grim fortress. I had the strange feeling that once I did I should never leave it again.

"Get in, woman!"

I was shoved in the direction of a great wooden door which opened suddenly, magically, to send a stream of golden light into the gloom. There stood the figure of a little scrap of a woman, surely no more than four feet high, clad in a dark dress and a voluminous snow-white apron.

"Welcome!" she cried. "Welcome to Penrose House!" Two black hounds leapt from behind her and sped past me, almost

15

knocking me down in their haste to reach the man who was now busy untying my bags from the back of the gig. I heard his voice, low and gentle, as he spoke to them, greeting them affectionately.

"Lordy, lordy," the woman continued—she was, I noticed now, quite plump beneath that voluminous apron. "What a day to arrive on. I knowed we was in for a storm when the wind veered to the west, but I didn't 'spect the Black Wind to come ragin' 'cross the sea."

"The Black Wind?" This was the second time I had heard the name and been intrigued by it.

"'Tis a whirly wind that comes in off the sea," she began explaining as I squeezed past her into the warmth of a rug-strewn hall, where a fire blazed brightly and candles burned in sconces round the walls. "It doesn't usually come in so far, but when it does it brings the darkness with it and . . ."

The lilting Cornish voice faded as I removed my cape and shook out my fair hair, and I saw recognition enter her eyes and resentment follow. Puzzled by something which had happened once too often to be dismissed as fancy, I prepared to question her about it.

A rasping voice interrupted us from the doorway.

"See that *Miss* Wentworth gets out of her wet clothes immediately, Carty. We don't want her catching pneumonia before she leaves in the morning."

"But I'm not leaving." I swung round to face him. "I've got a job here. I'm Mr. Penrose's new secretary."

A hard, unyielding visage met my indignant response. Unshrouded by the sou'wester which he now held in his hand, his sharply molded cheekbones and craggy brow joined company with a beaky nose and square jawline. It was a hard face, not exactly handsome, but attractive in the power of its strength and determination. It was the face of one who would brook no argument, as grim and forbidding as the castle I had just entered, and I did not expect it to hide the same inner warmth.

16

Eyes as cold as steel surveyed me and proceeded to travel slowly from the tangled mass of my hair down past my clothes, which clung damply to my body like a second skin, to my shoes oozing with water, and up again. I flushed scarlet beneath his insolent gaze, reminded of my stepfather's ogling. But then I had to admit that this man's stare could in no way be compared with Ted Gibbon's. It was uncomfortable, but it was not shaming. There was nothing lewd about it, only a contemptuous disregard.

"She'd better have a bath, too," he added tersely.

"Just leave her to me. I'll see her be properly looked after," the woman assured him.

He nodded, and with the two black dogs, which I now saw were Labradors, in tow, he strode away and disappeared behind a door leading off the hall.

"What a rude man!" I exclaimed, finding my voice at last. He had not addressed one word to me, apart from ordering me indoors, and it rankled. I was not used to being ignored.

"Not at all," the woman said. "He's just wet and tired, that's all."

"Tiredness is no excuse for impoliteness," I said. "I'm tired, too. I've been traveling since early this morning and . . ."

I broke off. Her eyes were snapping with dislike.

"What comes with the Black Wind, goes with the Black Wind," she said mysteriously, ominously.

Her cryptic remark carried echoes of the seagulls' dread warnings, and I pondered it in silence as I followed her diminutive figure up the wide, uncarpeted oaken staircase, our footsteps eerily reverberating round the lofty hall. A gallery encircled the hall. It was not lit by candles but was dark and secret. Mrs. Carty, the housekeeper, I had deduced, approached it with a candle she had removed from one of the sconces below. Shadows were cast on portraits lining the walls, giving the men and women depicted an appearance of movement. I walked past them nervously, avoiding the watchful eyes which followed my progress with silent suspicion.

17

It was nonsense, of course. Painted eyes could not see. Painted figures could not move. Nevertheless, I was glad to leave the shadowed gallery, turn down a corridor, and thence enter a room bright with firelight.

The housekeeper lit an oil lamp which stood on a table by the wall, and blew out the candle. "'Tis not a room I would have chosen for a lady," she said, "but 'twill serve one night."

I pursed my lips and bit back a retort. I was going to be here for more than one night. Having come thus far, I was not going to be turned back on the say-so of an odious man like . . . like . . . Whom? Who was he? The estate manager? How much influence did he wield? No matter. My contract was with Mr. Penrose. He would be the one to decide whether I left or stayed—and I had every intention of staying, even though I might wish to obey the seagulls' cries and go back home. I could not go home. I must stay here for a while, at least. I had a contract in my possession and I was determined to hold Mr. Penrose to it. I could be stubborn when I liked, as my mother was often wont to say.

The housekeeper had opened a door and I glimpsed sparkling white tiles, blue paint, a large bath standing on tapered legs with a copper geyser above it heating the water. There was a mahogany washstand, soap, towels, sponges. I looked forward to a long, hot soak.

"I'll run the water for 'ee," she said.

"Thank you, Mrs. Carty."

"I'll thank 'ee not to call me that," she said coldly. "My name's Mrs. Carthew."

"Oh, I'm sorry. I thought . . ."

"Will 'ee be needing help with your dressing?"

"No, thank you. I can manage."

She gave a quick nod. "Don't be long," she said and left me.

I bathed, not soaking as long as I should have liked after the housekeeper's strict injunction, and dressed myself in a pretty frock of pale blue silk sprigged by dark blue daisy-like flowers. It suited me perfectly, bringing out the blue of my eyes and

18

setting off the silvery-gold fairness of my hair. I had chosen it to boost my confidence and to make a good impression on Mr. Penrose.

I sat in front of the mirror and pinned up my hair. Being fine, it had dried very quickly, and was easily smoothed into bunched curls at the back of my head. Unfortunately, perhaps the rain or sea water had something to do with it, it would not stay in position, but kept slipping out of my pins so that curls and tendrils framed my face and straggled down the back of my neck.

In the end I gave up trying to make it look neat and turned away from the mirror. Then I turned back again and gazed thoughtfully at myself, trying to glimpse what these Cornish islanders had seen in me to cause them first surprise and then resentment. The seamen said I had brought bad luck with me. They blamed me for the wind, the Black Wind, that had blown across the island. So did the housekeeper. So did the man who had driven me so recklessly up to the house—this strange, castellated house. Very well. I could accept that superstition might lead them to this conclusion, but was this sufficient reason for disliking me so, when they did not even know me?

I searched in the mirror for an answer and could find none.

A light tap came at the door. I opened it to Mrs. Carthew. Her quick glance took in every detail of my changed appearance and something flickered behind her eyes, but her only comment was, "The master will see 'ee now."

"What's he like?" I asked as we descended the oaken staircase.

"'Twill not matter to 'ee, either way," she replied. "You'm leaving in the morning."

"Oh, no, I'm not," I declared. "I have no intention of leaving."

"'Twon't rest with you," she said, tapping on a door at the bottom of the stairs.

"Miss Wentworth," she announced, and left me standing inside the doorway to face Mr. Penrose alone.

My heart dropped like a stone. The man facing me across the carpet was the same man who had met me on the jetty.

Justin Penrose!

Yet why was I surprised? Deep in my heart I had known all along he was Justin Penrose. The near hermit of my imagination, old and pliable, easily persuaded, did not exist. This man with the cold, sea gray eyes could not be cajoled as my hermit could have been. This man, having made up his mind, would never change it. This man was remote, stern, and unyielding.

"Please sit down, Miss Wentworth."

Justin Penrose indicated one of the two soft, leather armchairs placed opposite each other in front of the blazing fire made necessary by the advent of the cold Black Wind. We were in the library: books lined the walls, and a huge mahogany desk dominated the middle of the room. He remained standing. I was aware of his brooding glance and grew rigid. The interview I was dreading was about to begin.

"My housekeeper will bring us tea in a few moments."

"Oh!" I gulped in surprise. These were not the words I had been expecting to hear.

He lowered himself into the chair opposite me. "You did not have a very good crossing, I'm afraid."

"It was rather grim."

"You are not a very good sailor?"

"Not on a sea as rough as that."

"Hm. The Atlantic can be pretty daunting at times."

Daunting! Yes. A word that could very well be used to describe him. Facing him was almost as fearsome as the journey I had had to endure. His glance never changed or moved from my face, and for one fanciful moment I was seized by a premonition of something so terrifying that it took my breath away. I felt that nothing on earth would induce me to stay on this island, working for him—nothing at all.

I transferred my gaze from his unsmiling visage to the logs burning cheerfully in the grate.

A silence developed between us and I soon found myself wishing he would say something, anything, to break the long, uncomfortable interlude. I wished I could say something, but my mind seemed to have atrophied, and I remained as silent as he. Then Mrs. Carthew eased the situation by bringing in the teatray. She set it down on a table beside me—and departed.

I was to pour.

This simple task, so easy to perform, became a mammoth trial for me. My hand shook as I reached for the teapot. The cup rattled ominously in the saucer as I held it out to him. He leaned forward to take it from me. Our fingers brushed. I drew back quickly. The tea slopped into the saucer. My eyes flew to meet his in sudden fear.

He frowned. "What are you afraid of?" he demanded harshly.

"Nothing!" I declared.

But I was afraid—afraid of him, of his touch. Would I always be afraid of the touch of a man's hand? My dear friend Hetty had said I would not. She had said it would take time to adjust to the natural way of things again, but that I would. Not all men were like Ted Gibbon, and I would come to recognize the fact. *I must believe it.*

"Tell me about yourself." Justin Penrose spoke again.

"There's nothing to tell."

His eyebrows lifted mockingly.

"Mr. Pedlar must have given you my qualifications," I added swiftly. "I was honest about the fact that I had had no previous secretarial experience, but that I had helped out in my father's office on occasion and could use a typewriting machine." His eyebrows were still high. "Mr. Pedlar must have written you all this."

"He did not tell me you were a woman."

"He told you my name. Nicola Wentworth."

"The cable read simply, N. Wentworth."

"You can't blame me for the misunderstanding."

"No, but . . ." His eyes narrowed, condemning me.

21

I knew what he was thinking. A woman's place was in the home. Most men thought so. I accused him of it.

"Most certainly," he admitted readily.

"What if she needs to earn her own living?"

"Do you?"

"No. I mean, yes."

"Are you in need of money?"

"No, but . . ."

"But what?"

I could not answer that.

"A woman like you," he said, "should be content to lead the role you were cut out for—that of wife and mother."

I have many faults. I am stubborn. I am overimaginative. I am impulsive. I was impulsive then.

"A typically masculine attitude," I retorted, echoing a platitude I had heard used at one of the lectures on "The Modern Woman." "Well let me tell you, Mr. Penrose, women will not stand for that any longer. Housework, the raising of children, are all very well, but a woman is capable of more than that. Women are seeking careers for themselves. They are going out into the world, working side by side with men. It is still difficult. There are too many men like you about. But the time is coming when . . . when women will get the vote and then—"

"Good grief!" He gave a derisive laugh. "You're not one of Mrs. Pankhurst's lot!"

"I believe in what she is trying to achieve. Women should have the vote. They should be allowed to have a career—if they want one. They should be allowed to work in an office typing someone else's letters. . . ."

"Which is what you want to do."

"Yes."

I was annoyed with myself for caving in. Momentarily, I had been carried away, not caring what he thought of me, not wishing to stay on this island and work for him. But I did want to stay. It was the perfect hiding place for me; Ted Gibbon would never find me here. So I assumed a more humble attitude.

"I think I'd make a good secretary. I can typewrite. I helped out in my father's office. He was a merchant banker."

"Was?"

"He's dead."

"I'm sorry."

"He was a far-seeing man. He was not averse to employing women. He . . ."

Justin Penrose's eyes narrowed into slits and I realized this was not the way to achieve my aim. Like most men, he expected women to be meek and subservient. I was neither of these things. However, when the devil drives . . . I continued in a less belligerent manner.

"Mr. Pedlar told me you insisted on good typewriting and an orderly mind. I am capable on both counts. You accepted my application, on his recommendation, without question."

"It was the only one I had received and I was getting desperate. Had I known you were a woman, however . . ." He rose, indicating the interview was at an end. "I'm sorry, but you appreciate my dilemma . . . I was under the impression you were of the masculine gender. Nothing Mr. Pedlar said led me to believe otherwise. If I mis-heard your name, I apologize."

"But that's not good enough." I rose to face him fiercely.

"Naturally, I will reimburse any expenses you have incurred."

But my blood was up. "I signed a contract. The fact that I am a woman is neither here nor there. It does not affect the legality of the document one little bit."

"Maybe not, Miss Wentworth." He frowned. "But does it not weigh with you that I was in ignorance of your sex, and that, had I known the truth of it, should never have agreed to employing you?"

"The point is," I stated firmly, "it was signed by your representative and, under its terms, a month's notice is required, on either side, before it can be terminated."

"Or a month's salary in lieu, which I shall be happy to give."

I blanched at his quick riposte. "In lieu? I don't remember seeing anything about that."

"Then I suggest you read the contract again, more carefully."

I did not need to. He was so sure of himself I knew he must be right.

So that was that. I would leave the island in the morning and . . . and what? What would I do? Where would I go? Back to Hetty's? Had I not already strained her hospitality enough? Besides, weren't she and Dickie going up to Scotland to stay with his parents for the summer? There was no one else to take me in, no one I could rely on to keep my secret. I was utterly dejected. Just when I thought I had found a safe haven, this man had wrenched it from me. I glared at him in sudden anger and was surprised at the puzzlement on his face.

"Is the job so important to you?" he asked.

"No," I declared at once, chin up, unwilling to admit my despair.

"Then go home, Miss Wentworth," he said, "you're not the sort of girl who should be out on her own in the world."

I bridled. "I'm quite capable of looking after myself."

Then, puzzlement clouding his face again, he asked, as if the thought had suddenly occurred to him, "You have a home? Your mother's not—"

"Dead? No. . . . But I can't go home."

"Why not?" Another of his quick-fire questions rang out, demanding an answer.

But I had said too much.

The fire spat. Logs slipped in the grate as they burned through. I withdrew my eyes from his searching gaze, lest he read the answer I could not give in their depths, see mirrored there the nightmare that haunted me still. It was engraved on my soul. It rose to torment me again.

The image of my stepfather clad only in his nightshirt,

24

entering my room, pressing his loathsome body against mine, stifling my screams with his mouth, his probing tongue, possessed my mind. I fought against him all over again, struggled frantically to escape from his roving, clutching fingers as they raised my nightgown and touched every part of me. Revolted, sickened, frightened out of my life, I tried to push him away, hit out at him, but his strength overcame mine and he laughed at my puny attempts to evade him. So I bit him. As his mouth slackened with laughter, I caught his lip between my teeth and bit into it as hard as ever I could.

With a yelp of pain he leapt away from me. "You hellcat!" he breathed. "I'll teach you!" And before I could take advantage of the brief respite and scramble from my bed to the door—as in my mind I was doing, screaming for help—he dealt me a blow that set my head spinning. In the moonlight coming in through my window I could see the blood pouring from his lip and dripping onto his nightshirt as he stood over me, and, in spite of my terror, I found myself wondering what tale he would tell my mother to account for it.

I waited for him to hit me again—or worse, the scream gathering within me unable to voice itself through my fear. Then, cupping his hand over the flow of blood, he aimed another vicious blow at my head and muttered. "This isn't the end of this. I'll make you pay for what you've done."

I could not believe he had gone. I lay sprawled on the bed, robbed of movement, yet panting with relief. He had gone. He had gone. My head ached, my cheek was painful to the touch, my skin crawled with revulsion, but he had gone. I had escaped a vile and degrading fate. But for how long?

I sprang into life, ignoring my pain, and locked my bedroom door, something I had never done in all my twenty-three years. I did not think he would attempt entry again tonight, but I was taking no chances. Then I climbed back into bed, sore and in pain and feeling colder than I had ever felt before, and sat there considering what my next course of action should be.

I had to get away. That much was certain. But where? How?

25

When? I thought of Hetty Townley, my lifelong friend, whose bridesmaid I had been six months ago. She lived in Highgate now. I would go to her and throw myself on her mercy. She would take me in. She would listen to me and keep my secret. She would understand that my mother must be kept in ignorance of what had happened.

The decision reached, I wasted no time. By first light I had packed a suitcase and was letting myself out of the house, having left a reassuring note for my mother.

The moment Hetty saw me, she knew something was wrong and proceeded at once to worm the story out of me—not that it needed much worming, for I was only too ready to let it tumble forth. Telling it eased my mind a little, but it did not—could not—erase the terrible nightmare from my soul.

"You must stay for as long as you like," Hetty said. "But don't you think you should tell your mother what has happened?"

"No. No. I must never do that. I know it sounds absurd, but it would destroy her. I doubt she would believe me, anyway. You don't know how that man has her twisted round his little finger. She will believe anything he says against me. He will tell her I am lying and she will believe him and hate me. I couldn't bear that." I choked on a sob. "Promise me you'll never tell her. Never tell a soul. . . . I'm so ashamed. . . ."

She said I had nothing to be ashamed of, but gave me the promise I desired.

I stayed with Hetty for over a month. The experience had disturbed me greatly, and the horror of it remained with me day after day, night after night. I saw all men as Ted Gibbon and recoiled from them—even Dickie, Hetty's husband, the mildest, kindest man one could ever wish to meet. Both he and Hetty saw it as a natural reaction and declared I would get over it in time. And with their help and sweet understanding, the memory faded and I began to see things in perspective again.

But I could not and would not go home.

"Are you all right, Miss Wentworth?"

26

Justin Penrose's voice brought me out of my nightmare. I looked into his face and felt bitter toward him. Fearful as I was of the future, I was more fearful of the past and could not return to it—yet he was denying me sanctuary.

"I cannot go home," I whispered, only half-aware that I spoke aloud. "I dare not."

I was trembling uncontrollably. I thought I had recovered from the harrowing incident. Now I knew I had not. Every detail was as fresh in my mind as ever it had been, and I felt my newly won equilibrium slipping away from me.

"Sit down." He was assisting me into my chair. "I'll get you a drink." A moment later he handed me a glass. I eyed it suspiciously. "It's only a mouthful of brandy. You'll feel better after it." I sipped a fiery mouthful. "Now, tell me what it is you have done that makes you so afraid to go home."

"Nothing! I've done nothing! But I can't . . . I can't go home!"

His brows were drawn together, but I thought his eyes softened a little. On impulse I said, "Let me stay, Mr. Penrose. Please let me stay, if only to work out a month's notice."

"I'm sorry." He grew stiff and stern again.

"Oh, please . . . let me stay . . . you must let me stay." Tears threatened and choked my voice. I drained my glass to steady myself. My mind was working fast. I had to persuade him to grant me time to recoup my energies and plan for the future, and realized I must play the supplicant, the woman unable to fend for herself, in need of a man's strength to rely on. "I appreciate the fact that you were under the misapprehension you had hired a male secretary," I continued humbly, "and accept that the position will not be permanent, but if you could see your way to granting me one month, to give me time to find another post, I should be most grateful. . . ."

My plea petered away. It would gain me nothing with a man so narrow-eyed and granite-faced. Under his silent observation, I rose.

"I'll leave in the morning," I said with an attempt to regain

27

my pride, and started for the door. Then, to my astonishment, he said, "You may stay, Miss Wentworth, if it means so much to you."

I spun round, relief and thankfulness glowing in my eyes.

"For one month only," he growled angrily.

Whether he was angry at himself or at me, I did not know. I did not care. He had said I could stay, and that was all that mattered.

Chapter Two

Perhaps I should not have been so eager to stay. Perhaps I should have taken note of his chilly glance. Perhaps I should not have forgotten the premonition that warned and disquieted me; perhaps I should have remembered the seagulls' warnings. But gratitude and relief overrode every other thought and feeling, and I could only thank him from the bottom of my heart.

"I suggest you go to your room now and rest," he said. "You've had a long and tiring day, and you endured a savage crossing. It's no wonder you felt faint. I'll ask Carty to send your evening meal up on a tray."

"Oh, but I feel much better now." I smiled, ready to like him now that he was proving a less obdurate man than I had thought and was showing signs of humanity. He had seen my need and, without prying too deeply, had assuaged it, however temporarily.

He crossed to the door and opened it for me. Clearly, the interview was at an end. I started to go.

"What time would you like me to start in the morning, Mr. Penrose?"

"I am always at my desk by eight o'clock."

"Then I shall be, too."

I was still smiling, but there was no answering smile on his face, and my smile died away as, with a disparaging glance over my blue silk, he said, "I trust you have brought some businesslike clothing with you. There is no need to dress so finely here. There is no one to impress."

The door closed on my back. I stood in the hall, fuming with indignation, my cheeks flaming. No one to impress! He had implied that I had set out to make an impression with my appearance . . . and so I had—but not on him. Not on him! I had not known he was Mr. Penrose until . . .

I stopped fooling myself. I had known—deep down. I had blinded myself to it, but I had known. And still I had set out to impress. But not for the reason he had implied. He thought I had set out to attract him—I, who wanted nothing to do with men after . . .

On impulse, I ran across the floor of the big medieval hall where the candles burned and the fire blazed and, wrenching open the massive oak door, threw myself into the arms of the gusting glacial wind. I knew not where I was going, only that I needed to go somewhere, anywhere, away from the insufferable man who thought I was setting my cap at him. Honesty compelled me to admit that that *was* what most females would do. He was, after all, good looking, wealthy, unmarried—a prize catch. (Was he unmarried?) It made no difference, married or not, he was conceited enough to believe every woman angled for him, but to think that I should! After my experience at the hands of Ted Gibbon! I had no desire to angle for any man . . . ever!

The wind whipped my skirts into a tangle round my legs, impeding my flight and bringing me to a halt beside a giant boulder. With the sting of salt on my face, the taste of it in my mouth, I leaned back against it and closed my eyes. Listening to the wind howling round the island, the wild waves pounding against rocks that grew like a fungus out of the sea, I wondered what I had come to. I had sought a haven and had thought it found. But it was a dark haven I had reached, full of its own secret anguish. I could hear it in the mournful wind, in the

30

discontented sea—and I had become part of it.

There would be no balm for my soul here. The very air was filled with whispers, with unseen beings crowding round, chanting, "Run as far as you will. There is no escape for you. You are trapped. Trapped."

But I was being fanciful. I had a tendency to be overimaginative and in this gloom, with the sea spray flying high up into the air, the wind moaning, and the castellated house etched starkly against a brooding sky, the least imaginative person would be inclined to flights of fancy.

I shook myself angrily. I was no fey Cornish islander to be led away by strange fancies. I was a practical young Englishwoman well able to tell the difference between imagination and reality, and I was not in the least superstitious.

Nevertheless, I was conscious of a unique quality about the island, the like of which I had never encountered before.

Well, I thought, battling my way back to the dark lonely cliff-top house, I should have to come to terms with it. I had chosen to stay, begged to stay—when I could have accepted dismissal and left—because I needed to. I needed time to plan my next course of action. Therefore, I was not going to fall prey to the haunting quality of the island and leave before my month was up—even though every instinct prompted me to do just that.

I entered the hall, invitingly bright with its many candles, and held my hands out to the flames mounting the chimney in golden spirals. I was cold, cold, cold, inwardly and outwardly, not yet fully convinced it had been fancy ruling me out there on the windswept heights.

The clatter of footsteps on the staircase drew my glance. My employer was descending, a black cloak thrown over his shoulders, black thigh boots replacing the soft shoes he had worn when we took tea together. His black brows drew together at sight of me—I should have been in my room, resting— however, he made no comment, only acknowledging my presence with a slight incline of his dark head as he passed on

31

his way to let himself out of the house.

Hardly aware I was doing so, I rushed to look out of the window. He was taking the reins of a sleek, black horse out of the hands of a groom. He swung himself up into the saddle and galloped away. His black cloak flared out behind him as he rode, like the wings of a vampire.

Black, black, black. Black was his cloak, his horse, his hair. Black was the wind that roared across the island. Black were my thoughts as I watched him ride out of sight.

I shuddered and wondered what I had let myself in for, what kind of man I had come to work for. Ours would not be an easy relationship, that much was obvious. He objected to my presence. He was cold-hearted and distant—and yet, beneath that cold exterior I sensed a powerful force, passions held in check which, unleashed, could prove devastating to anyone careless enough to cross him.

Was I being fanciful again? Maybe, but I promised myself I would take care not to rouse the sleeping tiger in him. I would be meek and subservient. It would be difficult. I had never been one to submit unquestioningly to authority; instead I had always demanded reasons for obedience, always wanted to make my own decisions. Willful behavior, my mother had called it. Independence of spirit, had been my father's judgment—and I was inclined to his way of thinking.

But things were different now. I could not afford to be so independent. I was Mr. Penrose's employee, and if I wished to remain in his employ, must adjust accordingly.

"So you'm staying, after all."

I swung round. Mrs. Carthew had come up behind me. How long had she been there? I had not heard her enter the hall.

"Why bain't you resting in your room, like Master Justin said?"

"I . . . I was just going."

"Tha's right. 'Tis best."

Her voice was gentle, but terror swept through me as I read all kinds of significance into her quiet words. I edged past her and hurried to the staircase.

I hesitated. It was dark and shadowy up above. Painted figures waited silently for my tread, and I feared them, feared they might spring from their frames and attack me.

"Take one o' they candles." Mrs. Carthew removed one from a sconce and handed it to me. Then, smiling, she waddled away.

I mounted the stairs feeling foolish. How could I have thought there was anything sinister about that dumpy little body? I really was allowing my imagination to run away with me. How my father would have shaken his head at me. I could almost hear him cautioning me as he had so often done in the past. "You must learn to keep your imagination in check, Nicola. You are, I fear, over-blessed in that respect. Don't let it run away with you, or the day may come when you will rue the consequences."

It was good advice. I knew it was. And I abided by it. Or I had—until lately. Perhaps it was the uncertainty about my future that made everything appear so dark and bleak to me. Or was it something about the island, some deep disquiet in its heart, that communicated itself to me? Whatever it was, I wished it would go away.

The lamp was lit in my room. There was the faint smell of paraffin in the air. The fire burned brightly. The sheets on the bed were turned down. The curtains had been left undrawn, and I could see through the diamond panes a leaden sky, a leaden sea, its waves whipped to a frenzy by the raging wind. The Black Wind which the seamen said I had brought with me to the island.

Had I brought it? Would it stay while I stayed? Go when I went? What comes with the Black Wind, goes with the Black Wind, Mrs. Carthew had prophesied. Drawn to the window, I looked out onto jagged rocks thrusting upward like fingers from the deep. How many sailors had those sinister fingers beckoned to their deaths?

I pulled the curtains across quickly and turned back into the

33

warmth and brightness of the room. I was reminded by the writing desk standing mutely by the wall of my obligation to write to my mother. She would be waiting to hear of my safe arrival.

I picked up a pen and started to write. *Dearest Mama, I have reached my destination safely and . . .* And what? She would want to know about the island, about Mr. Penrose; and what could I say? I could not tell her the truth—that I was not wanted here—by anyone. That Mr. Penrose had sacked me on the spot and only later, reluctantly, relented, allowing me a month's grace. She would want to know what I intended to do when the month's grace was up. She would declare I must return home.

Home! My heart leapt wildly inside me. If only I could go home. I was not wanted here. Mr. Penrose did not like me, would be glad to see the back of me. Mrs. Carthew did not like me. The seamen did not like me. They all believed I had brought bad luck to their island . . . And there was that other "something" I could not put a name to, but which sent spasmodic fits of unease to my heart.

Why stay then? Why not go back home?

I threw down my pen in anger and pain. I could *not* go home. While Ted Gibbon remained in my mother's house, I could not enter it again. My mother's house? It was no longer that. It belonged to me. Under the terms of my father's will, it had become mine the moment she remarried. Had she forgotten that? Surely my father's solicitors would have reminded her? No matter. The house was hers for as long as she wished, as far as I was concerned. I could have turned Ted Gibbon out, but what good would that have served me? My mother would only have gone with him, and I should have forfeited her love.

Was Ted Gibbon aware of this? Aware that the fortune he enjoyed would become mine and not his should my mother predecease me? Probably not. Impecunious as he had been, her fortune must have played no small part in his wedding her. Friends had pointed this out to her and me, for all the good it had done them. It had lost them her friendship.

A knock came at the door. It was a young maid bearing a tray of food. She set it down on a small table and asked, "Shall I draw the curtains for 'ee, Miss Wentworth?" She glanced slyly at me.

"Yes, thank you," I said, surprised to see that it was pitch dark outside and the moon was rising. "Has the storm passed?"

"It has, Miss, the Lord be praised."

She removed the silver cover from the plate on the tray and I breathed in the appetizing smell of roast chicken.

"Mmm. That smells good," I said. I had not eaten since noon, and I realized I was ravenous.

"Yes, Miss," she said and started to leave.

I stayed her. "Oh, by the way, could you tell me where the office is? As you must know, I am Mr. Penrose's new secretary."

"'Tis through the library," she replied, her eyes sliding away from my face rather shiftily, I thought, as she hurried away.

Roast chicken, roast potatoes, and small green peas had a restorative effect on me, and the apple pie and cream that accompanied it completed the process. I then went eagerly in search of the office. I wished to be acquainted with its whereabouts so that I should encounter no difficulty in being at my desk on time in the morning. I meant to prove myself a prompt and efficient secretary. At the back of my mind was the hope Mr. Penrose would find me indispensable by the end of the month.

I tapped on the library door. I believed Mr. Penrose was still out, but it was just as well to be careful. There was no reply so I entered and, looking round the room, saw a door in the far wall. The office. I entered it and stood on the threshold in stunned amazement. In the light shed by the lamp I carried in my hand I saw a shambles—a complete shambles. Papers and books were everywhere. Open folders, contents spilling out, vied for space on desk, cabinet and floor. Drawers had been left open. Dust filmed every bit of space lucky enough to have escaped the clutter. A dried-out apple core sat dismally on the mantel above the fireplace. Crumpled pieces of paper and torn fragments littered the desk.

I surveyed the scene in dismay. What did it mean? The rest of the house, as much as I had seen of it, was spotlessly clean and well tended. Why had this room been neglected?

"I've been without a secretary for a very long time."

A harsh voice behind me caused me to swing round. Justin Penrose glowered at me. He apparently considered his comment explanation enough for the appalling state of the room. I did not.

"Mrs. Carthew should never have allowed the room to fall into such a mess," I said.

His eyes snapped angrily. I had criticized his housekeeper, and he did not like it.

"Mrs. Carthew is not to blame for it," he rasped. "I am. I will not allow anyone, even Carty, to touch my books or papers. I have discovered to my annoyance that they are invariably put away wrongly, or before I have finished with them, which is worse. So I made it a rule that other than myself, only my secretary should handle them. It will be your job to see that everything is properly filed and that any book I am using for research is at hand."

"I can appreciate that," I declared. "But the whole room needs a thorough cleaning. It's filthy."

"Then I suggest you come to some arrangement with my housekeeper about it—in the morning." He stood aside, indicating an end to the conversation.

Summarily dismissed, I returned quickly to my room. I undressed and climbed into bed, longing to bury myself in sleep, but was kept awake by an overactive brain.

All sound died away. The wind dropped. The sea calmed. A quiet stillness was everywhere. Then I heard a door slam, a deep vibrant voice, a lighter, feminine one. More doors closing. Then silence. I turned over and fell asleep.

*　　*　　*

I woke early, refreshed and eager to start the day, a completely different being from the bedraggled and fearful creature who had arrived with the Black Wind.

The day was different too, golden, bright, and shining. I looked on a world transformed: a sky of cloudless blue; a sea of sapphire silk; a carpet of green velvet patterned with the yellow, white and mauve of buttercups, daisies and clover. Bees buzzed. Seagulls soared—no warning squawks today. A lovely, lovely day.

I dressed quickly and sensibly in a skirt of navy blue wool and a white blouse with high neck and long sleeves. Having pinned my hair into neat coils round my head, I ran lightly down the stairs, my spirits high to match the day. Gone were the morbid fancies engendered by yesterday's uncertainties and gloom. Today, I was full of hope and expectation. Today, everything would go right.

Everything went wrong.

My employer was already at his desk thumbing through a bundle of letters. He looked up at my entrance and immediately two deep vertical lines appeared on his forehead.

"Good morning, Mr. Penrose," I said brightly, determined not to be browbeaten by him.

"Good morning," he grunted as if the effort to be polite cost him dear. "There's a lot of mail. We'll make a start right away. Bring your notebook and pencil, will you?"

I went to search the office for them. It took a little time, and when I returned, his brow was thunderous. He started dictating at a rapid speed.

"Do you mind going a little slower, Mr. Penrose?" I said, "I don't do shorthand."

His brows drew closer together.

"Mr. Pedlar said that it would not be necessary . . . that you wouldn't mind, under the circumstances."

His brows met in one unbroken line. "What circumstances?"

"He said you were getting desperate."

"Did he, indeed?" He sucked in his breath between his teeth

and looked blacker than ever.

I had never known anyone look so black, so thoroughly bad-tempered, and knew I should have to tread warily with him in order to keep him sweet. It would prove a difficult task. I was not best fitted to pander to ill-temper, to be meek in the face of insufferable behavior.

"Then we'll have to manage as best we can with longhand, won't we? I daresay you will find it extremely tiring, but that can't be helped."

My pencil was kept busy for well over an hour, during which time I made an extremely interesting discovery. Justin Penrose was not only the owner of Penrose Island, responsible for its administration and the lives of all who dwelt there, and the writer of Cornish histories. He was also the acclaimed author and playwright, James St. Just.

"James St. Just!" I exclaimed on learning this. "Are you he? How wonderful! I've read all your books . . . seen all your plays . . . I never dreamed I'd be working for you."

"Shall we get on?" He glowered angrily.

I bent my head obediently. It was clear our relationship was to be nothing if not businesslike. Any intrusion into his private life would not be countenanced. Well, I thought, that suits me down to the ground. The less familiarity there is between us, the better I shall like it. I had spoken out of turn in surprise. I should not do so again.

My hand had begun to ache unbearably when, at length, he kicked back his chair and rose—how tall he was, a towering giant of a man. "Right," he said, "That will do for now. Let me have them back for signing as soon as you can. I should like them to catch the next tide."

"Yes, sir," I said, in as servile a manner as I could muster.

"Then you can take the rest of the day off. I shan't be needing you again."

"Thank you, sir. I would like to go out for a walk. Explore the island."

"Take the trap, if you like," he said. "Use it anytime."

"That's very kind of you, but I'd rather walk. I like walking. I often walked . . . back home."

I was suddenly aware I might never walk my old haunts again and turned away quickly to go back to my office.

"Then I trust you have brought stouter footwear than that with you." His caustic voice reached me. "Our island terrain is not like your London streets."

"Oh, I think I can rustle up something," I returned pertly over my shoulder. "I'm not a complete idiot—"

A subtle change came over his face which stopped my foolish tongue. Bitterness and hatred were in his glance, and it sent a spasm of fear shooting through me. Yet why should he hate me? There had to be cause for hatred, and I had given him none. Perhaps I had given him cause for annoyance by wishing to stay on the island and by having persuaded him, against his will, to allow it—but hatred! His glance held me paralyzed for a moment, then he turned his attention to something on his desk and movement returned to my limbs. I fled.

Before I could start work, I had to clear the desk and dust the typewriting machine. With no duster handy, I used my handkerchief, hoping I should not need it for the purpose for which it was intended. I should have liked to have had the whole room dusted and tidied before starting work, but as the old proverb says, *When the devil drives, needs must . . .* And I could almost think he was the devil, the man I worked for.

Halfway through my first letter I heard his voice raised in sudden anger, and a moment or so later my door burst open. He glared at me from the doorway. "I shall be obliged, Miss Wentworth, if you breakfast *before* coming to work in future. Please see that you do. I will not have my housekeeper dancing to your tune." Before I could digest his words, he strode away, leaving Mrs. Carthew to set her tray down where best she might and leaving me open-mouthed with astonishment.

"Well, really!" I exclaimed at last, wincing as the library door was slammed shut.

"He be a mite touchy today," Mr. Carthew said mildly,

39

having made space for the tray on the window seat by elbowing some books out of the way. "And 'tis no wonder. He've reason enough."

"What! Because I started work without breakfasting first!"

"'Tis more'n that, m'dear."

"Well . . . whatever it is . . . he needn't take it out on me."

Mrs. Carthew glanced round the room. "I'll send Sally to help you clean up in here when you'm ready. 'Tis 'bout time. Master Justin be a stickler for order and neatness, though he'm quite incapable of being tidy hi'self. 'Tis an army of servants he needs running around after him. Lordy, lordy, the times I've said that."

She laughed and started to waddle away.

"Don't 'ee forget," she added as she went through the doorway, "Sally'll come and clean for 'ee. Don't 'ee be soiling your hands with such work. And," her face assumed a stern expression, "don't 'ee be startin' work without breakfast inside 'ee again. 'Tis not good for 'ee."

"I didn't want to be late on my first morning," I said humbly. "Mr. Penrose told me he likes to be at his desk by eight."

"Glory, m'dear!" she expressed horror by throwing her hands up in the air and slapping them down against her snowy-aproned thighs. "There be no need for 'ee to start so early. Miss Clunes never did."

"Miss Clunes?" I enquired curiously.

Her face had grown sour. "'Er never made a start till after nine. 'Er'd leave his mail on his desk the night afore so's he could look through it, and arrive when she saw fit. And being an easygoing gentleman, he never complained."

"Easygoing!" I sputtered incredulously.

"Well, p'raps not so much now. . . . 'Tis different when he be working on a book, mind. He become a slave driver then. You won't have a minute to call your own. So don't 'ee be over-working yourself till you have to."

Her glance had become analytical and she gave a reflective

sigh . . . finding me wanting?

"I'm not afraid of hard work," I said. "In fact, I'll welcome it."

"Aye, well," she continued, sizing me up, "probably t'won't come to that. 'Ee won't be here long enough. Luncheon at one o'clock in my parlor."

"Where?"

"I'll send one of the maids to show you the way."

I munched pensively on my toast and drank my coffee, pondering all she had said. Who was Miss Clunes? His previous secretary, I presumed. But a woman? He did not like women secretaries. He believed a woman's place was in the home, not in the world of business. So why had he hired her? It couldn't be another case of mistaken identity, that would be too coincidental. Why had she left? Had she resigned or been dismissed? Probably the former—because of her employer's cold, harsh, and taciturn ways. I had discovered early on just how well those adjectives fit him, and since had discovered a few more. He was prone to anger, easily irritated, critical, and sarcastic. Yes, he had probably driven her away with his harsh tongue and brusque manner. And yet, Mrs. Carthew had called him easygoing.

Well, he might have been easygoing in the past, but he most certainly was not now. He would drive me away if he could—before my month was up—but he did not know how stubborn I could be. I would stick it out to the last day, and maybe even longer.

I laughed at myself suddenly. As if I would have any choice in the matter. He had allowed me a stay of "only a month." He had been emphatic about it. I knew he would not change his mind.

Did I want him to? Yes, I did. At this present moment in time, there was nothing I wanted more than to stay on this island, way out in the Atlantic, far away from the world at large, safe and secure, where no one could trace me—Ted Gibbon loomed large—yes, I wanted Justin Penrose to change his mind.

41

Somehow I must make him do so. Penrose Island was to be my haven.

I settled down to work. I could type well and at a good speed. I was able to set out a letter neatly. He liked neatness; I would show him just how neat I could be. With luck, I would have his letters finished and waiting for his signature before he returned to the library. I would prove myself an efficient secretary. I would give him no reason to complain of my work—or tardiness.

But it was not long before I heard the library door open. He was back already. Would he require me for more dictation? Where was my notebook? In my anxiety, I dropped my pencil on the floor. It made a great noise on the floorboards. It couldn't drop onto a rug, of course! I scrambled down to pick it up. I was jumpy and nervy, not at all the efficient secretary I would have him recognize. I prayed he would not come in . . . but the door opened.

"Justin, is that you? Oh, my God! *Caroline!*"

A young man halted on the threshold, his stunned expression exactly matching the tone of his voice. When I rose from my place on the floor, he shook his head vigorously, as if trying to rid himself of a bothersome gnat, and came forward.

"Please forgive me. I thought for a moment . . . I was looking for Justin. I heard something . . . I thought he was in here."

"I'm afraid he's out." He still appeared slightly distraught. Who was this Caroline he had mistaken me for? Miss Clunes? Had he thought for a moment, seeing a female in the office, that she had returned? It was a reasonable assumption. "I'm his new secretary. If you'd care to leave a message, I'll see he gets it the moment he comes in."

"Thank you, it doesn't matter," he said. "I'll wait to see him. Er—new secretary, eh?"

"Yes. Nicola Wentworth. I started today."

"Well, I'll be. . . ." A smile came over his face and he shook his head in bewilderment. "Justin vowed he'd never hire

42

another woman as long as he lived."

"He didn't know I was a woman when he hired me," I explained. "I'm afraid the cable failed to make that clear."

"He didn't know you were a woman?"

"Not until he saw me."

"And he let you stay?"

"Yes." I was amused at his bewilderment, and was going on to explain it was only a temporary arrangement when a smile of singular beauty illumined his face and quite took my breath away.

"I'm glad," he cried warmly stretching out to grasp my hand in his. "I couldn't be more happy to meet you. You'll brighten the old place up a bit. It's been like a morgue for far too long."

It was the friendliest greeting I had received from anyone since setting out from home, and I responded happily. "I'm glad to meet you, Mr. . . . ?"

"Trevelyan. Dr. Trevelyan. Justin's best friend. We'll be seeing a lot of each other from now on—Nicola."

His familiarity was not offensive and his blue eyes, thickly fringed with long curling lashes any girl would be proud to own, dwelt lingeringly, admiringly on my face.

I had made a conquest and, despite all I had suffered at the hands of one of his sex, a feeling of pleasure ran through me. But I was still not ready to accept his, or any man's, admiration, and I tugged my hand away.

He let it go with apparent reluctance and I felt my cheeks redden. My heart began to thud like any seventeen year old's.

He was handsome, this friend of Justin Penrose—very handsome, and very charming.

But so was Ted Gibbon a handsome and charming man.

Yet was I to look upon all good looks and charm as if they were a cloak for evil desires? My friends had been at pains to point out to me the wrongness of such a course, and I knew they were right—but still I wished Dr. Trevelyan would not look at me with such open admiration. It discomfited me.

"If you wouldn't mind telling Justin I called and that I'll call again later. . . ."

The sound of excited barking interrupted him, and we both went to the window and looked down across the sloping lawns. My craggy-faced employer was throwing sticks for his dogs to retrieve. He was laughing and appeared carefree. For a moment I could not think he was the same man.

"I'll go out to him," Dr. Trevelyan said, "though I can't say I am looking forward to the encounter."

"Why not, Dr. Trevelyan?"

"He won't be pleased with what I have to tell him. And please, the name's John."

Again his blue eyes came to rest approvingly on my face, and I looked out of the window in sudden confusion at Justin Penrose and his dogs.

"He appears to be in a good mood," I murmured.

"It won't last," John remarked drily.

I stayed looking out of the window after John had gone. Justin Penrose was still laughing and calling encouragement as the dogs dashed to retrieve the sticks he threw, as if he had not a care in the world. Why couldn't he always be like that? I asked myself. Why couldn't he be like that with me? I saw him raise his arm in salute and a moment later John Trevelyan came into view. His voice rose clearly on the still air.

"Good morning, John. Good to see you back. How was the trip?"

"Fine, Justin. Fine. Can I have a word with you? There's something I must tell you."

"Tell me over coffee," Justin said and, placing an arm around his friend's shoulders, directed their footsteps toward the house.

"Miss Wentworth."

My employer called me as he entered the library and I hurried to present myself. He did not smile as he looked at me, but was his usual stern and forbidding self.

John Trevelyan smiled—hugely. "Hello again, Nicola," he said with pleasure in his voice.

His friend whipped around, scowling dangerously. He was not a handsome man—not in the conventional sense, in the way John Trevelyan was handsome. He was more the eagle than the swan, and, like the eagle, proud and cruel. It showed in his face. Like the eagle, he was possessed of a fierce power, held in check, but ready for use at the slightest provocation . . . and he was provoked now.

"You know each other?" It erupted like a growl from his throat.

"We met this morning. It was a pleasant surprise. I never expected to see a woman in your office again."

John Trevelyan seemed completely unaware of his friend's glowering visage as he focused his eyes on me and kept them there. I was very much aware of it, and was glad to accede to the brusque request for coffee to be brought in.

"Can't Carty bring it? She usually does," John said. But I was already going through the door.

I closed it quickly behind me and followed the rich aroma of freshly percolating coffee to the kitchen. Mrs. Carthew was pouring steaming brown liquid into a tall china coffeepot. A maid I had not seen before was putting the finishing touches to a tray.

Mrs. Carthew looked up and smiled.

"Mr. Penrose has a visitor," I announced. "Dr. Trevelyan."

Her face darkened at the doctor's name. "What's he come for?" she frowned.

I did not think she required an answer. She had simply been reflecting out loud. Nevertheless, I gave her one. "There's something he wants to discuss with Mr. Penrose."

"Humph!" She sniffed disparagingly. "No sooner back from foreign parts than he . . ." Without bothering to finish her sentence, she addressed the maid. "Another cup, Mary."

"Oh, no," I cried quickly, "I'll have mine with you, if I may. I think Dr. Trevelyan wishes to speak to Mr. Penrose alone."

Mrs. Carthew gave another disparaging sniff. I felt she did not care for the doctor very much.

"Where has he been?" I asked curiously. "You said he'd been to foreign parts."

"London," she said. "He'm always gadding off there. And he always brings trouble back with him."

London, foreign parts! I shook my head in bewilderment as I took the tray to the library. *He always brings trouble back. . . .* I could not imagine Dr. Trevelyan bringing trouble to anyone. And yet . . . He had hinted to me that he had some disturbing news for Mr. Penrose, news he would not best like to hear. What was it? I wondered—but it really was not any of my business.

I took the coffee in to the two men. They were arguing forcibly.

"But Justin," John was saying, "Clara's your—"

"I said I didn't want to hear any more on the subject."

"But she's far from well."

"I've heard it all before."

"It's true this time."

"I don't believe it. I've said all I'm going to say on the matter. She's not coming here, and that's final."

Justin Penrose was blazingly angry, and he made no effort to hide the fact.

"Then you'd better get a message to her before she sets out," John returned with tightly set face.

"Blast the woman!" Justin Penrose roared.

I left them together—I don't think they even noticed I had been in—and went back to the kitchen, eager to question Mrs. Carthew.

"Who is Clara?" I guessed she must be Justin's wife.

Mrs. Carthew paused in her task of cutting into a dark fruitcake.

"What you know 'bout her?"

"Well, it's just that I heard Dr. Trevelyan telling Mr. Penrose that she wants to come here, and . . ."

"'Tis no concern o' yours."

"No, of course not." I blushed to the roots of my hair at her well-warranted chastisement. It was no concern of mine. But I sensed a mystery and was intrigued.

Just then, a fluffy black and white cat strolled in through the open kitchen door, made straight for me, and jumped up onto my lap. It settled down contentedly beneath my stroking hands.

"What's its name?" I asked.

"Fluff."

"He's lovely."

"You like cats?"

"Yes, I do. I . . . had two at home. I miss them."

Mrs. Carthew passed me a cup of coffee and nodded sagely. "I alus says, them that likes cats can't be all bad, and them that cats like is a sure sign of . . . Well," she turned back to the table to pick up her own coffee and finished sternly, "'tis all the more reason for not staying on the island."

"Why?" I asked, again puzzled.

"You'm too nice a girl to waste your life here," she said, and changed the subject before I could question her further.

When I returned to the library, the two men had gone. I breathed a sigh of relief and settled down to finish my work. It was almost one o'clock by the time I placed the neatly typed letters on the big mahogany desk to await Justin Penrose's signature. I was to lunch with Mrs. Carthew at one o'clock, but judged there would be sufficient time to wash my hands and face and change into something cooler than the thick woolen skirt and long-sleeved blouse I was wearing. The day had warmed up considerably.

The clock in the hall was striking one as I ran down the stairs. As I crossed the hall to join Mrs. Carthew in her parlor just off the kitchen, I glanced through the open door of a room I had not yet seen and, arrested by its magnificence, entered and gazed round in admiration. The walls were papered in crimson silk and were hung with fine portraits and landscapes and gilded mirrors. Windows opening out onto a terrace overlooking formal gardens were draped in crimson brocade. A

47

gleaming mahogany table stretched endlessly in front of me, covered at the nearest end by a white, damask tablecloth, and set with fine crystal and heavy silverware. The fireplace was of white marble and the mantel displayed an elegant French clock and beautiful porcelain statuettes.

I heard the front door open. I had lingered too long. Before I could leave the room, I came face to face with Justin Penrose and John Trevelyan.

John beamed. "Hello, again, Nicola."

Justin Penrose scowled. His glance raked over me in disdain, and his earlier admonishment that there was no one to impress by fine apparel had me hastening to explain the light summer garment I had changed into.

"You said I could have the rest of the day off, Mr. Penrose. I changed into something cool. It has grown so warm."

His glance left me.

I swallowed nervously and muttered, "If you'll excuse me, Mrs. Carthew is waiting for me to join her for luncheon."

"You mean we're not to have the pleasure of your company?" John exclaimed. "This can't be allowed. She must eat with us, mustn't she, Justin?"

"She may stay, if she so wishes," Justin grunted.

"Mrs. Carthew is expecting me."

"She won't mind." John propelled me to the table and drew out a chair for me.

Justin Penrose despatched a maid with a message for the housekeeper, and another prepared a place for me at the dining table. I felt most uncomfortable, very much aware of Justin Penrose's disapproval.

"I hear you arrived yesterday in the storm," said John, conversationally.

"Yes."

"You should have waited a day. I wouldn't have risked setting out in a gale, particularly with the Black Wind gathering her skirts around her."

"It was fine when I set out."

Soup was served to us in fine, white china bowls.

We ate in silence for a while, then, "You must allow me to show you round the island," said John.

"Thank you. That's very kind of you."

"Nonsense. My motive is purely selfish. I can think of nothing I should find more gratifying than spending a few hours in your company. Unfortunately, I shall be unable to join you this afternoon. A baby is due to put in an appearance and I must be there."

"Of course. You are the doctor."

"But there'll be other opportunities."

Poached trout, new potatoes with butter soaking into them, and fresh green salad were brought in.

"You'll find the slate quarries most interesting. Won't she, Justin?"

"It's possible." Justin Penrose spoke for the first time since we had sat down to our meal.

"Slate is the island's biggest source of revenue—or it was, till Justin shut it down. Now there's only fish."

"You're forgetting the income from my writing," Justin rasped.

"You shouldn't need to use that for maintaining the island."

"What else should I do with it?"

"I can think of lots to do with it. Now, if you were to open up the quarries again. . . "

"I'm not prepared to do that."

"Then there's the copper and the silver . . . rich veins of it. . . ."

"Haven't I made it perfectly clear that I'm not prepared to extract copper and silver from the island? Penrose has been scarred enough by the slate. And we don't need the revenue. I've got more than enough."

"Your father was all set to—"

"My father is dead."

Those four words dropping like ice from Justin's lips

silenced John Trevelyan. I deduced this argument had long been a bone of contention between the two men, but though John's expression was mutinous, he forebore to continue it now.

However, it was not long before he was in full spate again. I wondered if anything could depress his spirits for long.

"Where do you hail from, Nicola?"

"London."

"Oh. What part?"

"Kensington. Not far from the palace."

"What a coincidence! Justin's—" He broke off, the glance he had sent in his friend's direction having been returned ferociously, and changed his tack. "Whatever made you forsake London for this remote island? Aren't you afraid you'll be bored? There are no theatres here, no bright lights."

"Miss Wentworth's not here for the bright lights. She's here to work."

"But you're not expecting her to work all the hours God sends, are you?" John reacted sharply to my employer's terse comment. "She'll have time off. I'm just wondering how she'll adjust to our quiet way of life after—"

"If she can't, she can always leave. In fact, it would be better if she did."

Any idle hope I had entertained about being allowed to stay if I proved an efficient secretary was killed stone dead. Justin Penrose did not want me to stay even for the month he had promised me. I almost rose from my seat to pack my bags and leave on the next tide, but defiance prevented me. I would stay in spite of him. Besides, I needed the month to formulate new plans.

"How do you think you'll like working for this bad-tempered spinner of tales?" John asked now. He spoke lightly, but I thought I detected a sneer behind his words. Yet I must have been wrong; one did not sneer at one's best friend.

"I . . . It should be very interesting," I said, far from spontaneously, for I doubted the accuracy of it. But how could

I say what I really thought under the scrutiny of those caustic dark eyes at the head of the table? How could I admit that I did not think I should enjoy it at all?

John laughed. "A very diplomatic answer. You've got a gem here, Justin. Take care you don't lose her—like you did the last one."

If looks could kill, John Trevelyan would have died on the spot.

"I'm only here for a month," I said, hoping to discharge the ugly atmosphere that seemed to be developing between the two friends.

John's eyebrows rose in surprise. "But a month is no time. You must give yourself a little longer to become adjusted. You might find you like it here."

"Well, I . . . I'd like to stay longer, but . . ."

"This is no place for a woman like you," Justin Penrose rasped harshly.

"Why not?" I faced him boldly, encouraged no doubt by John's presence. "What's wrong with it? What's wrong with me?"

He stared back at me coldly and steadily, and said not a word.

"It's because I'm a woman, isn't it? That's no good reason. I'm a good secretary. As good as any man. I'll prove it to you."

"You are at liberty to try. It will not alter my decision either way." He rose from the table. "A word with you, John."

"Aren't you going to stay and have a dish of these luscious strawberries that have just come in?" John protested with raised brows.

Justin Penrose glared at him.

"I'll join you in a few minutes, then. I can't resist strawberries."

Justin Penrose stalked away in disgust.

John helped himself to strawberries. I had indicated that I did not require any. Even the sight of their ripe redness could not bring back the appetite I had lost in the past few minutes. John ate heartily.

He dismissed the maid waiting at the sideboard and, when she had gone came round the table, placed a sympathetic hand on my arm.

"You're upset. I can see you are. It doesn't surprise me. Justin has a vicious tongue. He can be so thoughtless. And where women are concerned . . . He doesn't like women and he makes no effort to hide the fact."

"He doesn't like me, that's plain."

I was on the verge of tears now that Justin Penrose had gone and John's sympathy held sway.

John sighed deeply. "Why did you come here? Did you need the money so desperately?"

"No, it wasn't the money that brought me here. I have plenty."

"Then what was it?"

He was puzzled, but I could not enlighten him. Even if I had wished to, my throat was so hot with unshed tears I could not continue.

He rose from his bending position. "I'd better go. Nicola, please don't take this amiss, but may I give you a bit of friendly advice? Don't stay here. Not even for a month. Justin's not the sort of man . . . and you're too nice, too vulnerable. . . . Go back home. Now. Before it's too late."

Chapter Three

They all wanted me to leave the island. Justin Penrose, Mrs. Carthew, now John Trevelyan.

"Leave now, before it's too late."

John's words had carried a warning. They had held a sinister quality that implied I had reason to fear Justin Penrose. I knew that I feared him a little already, and it caused my heart to stumble in its beat.

Yet why should I fear him? I had no fear he would turn out to be another Ted Gibbon. He did not like women, was not attracted to them. Women might chase after him, but he did not welcome their attentions and treated them disdainfully. Had I not experienced his disdain myself? So I need not fear him on that count. He was of a cold, harsh, distant, unfeeling disposition—scornful, too, and unjust. Perhaps that was what John had been warning me about. I was vulnerable, he had said. But was I so tender a plant that I should wilt beneath such treatment?

"Just off for your walk, Miss Wentworth?"

Justin Penrose came in at the door just as I was about to go out. His expression was scornful. I refused to wilt.

"Yes. I thought I'd take the letters down to the post."

"A worthy thought. However, there's no need. Thomas always collects and delivers."

53

"Then I'll save him a journey," I said pertly.

Craggy brows, already lifted high above sarcastic orbs that had not been slow to notice I was not wearing the stout shoes I had led him to expect I possessed, rose higher.

"Well, take the hill path," he advised. "It's less steep than the coastal road, which you would be wise to avoid. Turn sharp right once outside the boundary wall. It's a well-worn track. You can't miss it. It will lead you down to the village where—"

"I am not a weakling, Mr. Penrose." I interrupted him with asperity. "I am very used to walking. Steep roads hold no terrors for me."

A thin fragment of a smile cracked his lips. "As you will," he said, standing aside to let me pass. "But I think you should heed my advice."

He remained at the door watching me go. I could feel his eyes boring into my back, and deliberately turned left instead of right as I went through the gates. The contrary streak in my nature had always reacted adversely to anything that smacked of autocracy—and he was an autocrat if ever there was one. But I could not subdue the feeling that I should be punished for my contrariness, as often I had been punished as a child for my defiance of authority.

But I was no longer a child to be told what to do, where to go. I was a grown woman, twenty-three years of age, my own mistress. What punishment could Mr. Penrose mete out to me? I scoffed. He could terminate my employment, but somehow I did not think he would do that. With all his faults, I did not see him as a man who would break his given word. And he had promised I could stay—at least, for a month.

I trod the tarmacadamed coastal road which was smooth and steeply descending, overshadowed by looming, granite cliffs on my right and braced by a low, granite wall on my left, where the sea swished at the rocks below. The road soon became more steeply inclined. I found myself straining backwards, grabbing at any stray tuft of vegetation tough enough to have established itself in crevices in the soaring rockface. As I struggled to prevent what might nevertheless prove a headlong flight over the low wall into the swirling waters below, I found I wished I had not acted so hastily, but had taken Mr. Penrose's advice.

Eventually the steep incline decreased and I found myself at a fork in the road. One route led down to the harbor and the other led across open fields cropped by fat sheep and sleek brown cows. I saw pretty white cottages with slate roofs, flower-bright gardens and windowboxes. I saw a little church squatting amidst an array of gravestones, and a building with a little bell tower and a collection of children outside—a school. And over all loomed the imposing battlemented presence of Penrose House. Only today, in the bright sunlight, it did not look menacing. On the contrary, it wore a smiling protective air, benign on its promontory.

In the other direction, down by the harbor, were more cottages clustering together. There were shops and an inn, The Ship Inn, by its sign, a ship in full sail on a painted blue ocean. This was the path I should take.

The tide was in and fishing boats were sailing into the harbor. Women were gathered together in small knots waiting for the boats to land. I would have liked to join them there, but as I neared, their apparent suspicion and resentment froze the smile on my face, and I hurried past them. I entered a shop where the sign read A. TREVOSE & SON, CHANDLER & GENERAL STORE. It was also the post office. There was a red pillarbox outside.

I greeted the apple-cheeked woman behind the counter cheerfully.

"Good afternoon. I've brought the mail from Penrose House."

She took the bundle from me, wordlessly mistrustful.

"I'm Nicola Wentworth," I explained. "Mr. Penrose's new secretary."

"Aye, I know that," she said and cast a sly look over my shoulder. "There's nought can be kept secret on Penrose Island."

I became aware of a shuffling of feet behind me and, turning slightly, saw a number of women grouped there. There was something sinister in the way they eyed me with silent hostility; something sinister in the words the woman behind the counter had used. Sinister. How often that word kept cropping up in my thoughts.

"I have no wish to keep my occupation secret," I said, assuming an air of bravado, and made a move toward the door.

The women blocked my way and my heart beat wildly, fearful of their intentions. Then they drew apart and let me through.

A hiss of whispering marked my going.

"'Tis true." "She'm like 'er." "'Er could be 'er twin."

I swung round abruptly. I knew they must be talking about me. I resembled someone they knew. Miss Clunes? They shuffled about nervously and avoided my glance when I asked them if I reminded them of her. But the woman behind the counter was more forthcoming.

"Oh, you know 'bout her." Her eyes widened as she prepared for a good gossip. "Well, there be no 'arm in telling 'ee . . ."

"Hush you, Dora Trevose!" a gaunt, thin-lipped woman reprimanded her. Then the women rapidly dispersed.

I started to question Dora Trevose again, but she scampered away and hid herself behind a door leading from the shop. I waited a few moments, but it was obvious she was not going to appear for me again, so I left.

The incident disturbed me a little. There seemed to be some mystery about Miss Clunes . . . Caroline . . . Were they one and the same? I wondered. I was intrigued, and decided to question Mrs. Carthew on the matter when I got the opportunity—although she had not been eager to answer my questions about Clara, I remembered glumly.

I put the incident behind me. It was a beautiful day and I was going to enjoy it. I had the whole afternoon in which to enjoy my freedom. And I did feel free—free from everything that had darkened my life for weeks past. It was this island that had done it. This beautiful, wonderful island that I had feared last night, but loved today.

I decided to be sensible and make my way back to Penrose House along the hill path rather than the punishing coastal road—but not just yet. First I would wander about the hills, perhaps visiting the little squat church.

I struck out across the daisied fields. Ahead, dominating the skyline, was Penrose House, no longer the grim, forbidding bastion of the night before, but the protective guardian of all it surveyed in the brightness of the day. I soon discovered the well-worn track Justin Penrose had told me about, but I turned away from it. I would keep going in that general direction—I did not want to lose myself, after all—but would let my footsteps tread the green grass of the sloping hills inland and discover more about the island.

Up, up I trudged, past the white cottages, the grazing sheep and cows. I stopped now and then to gather buttercups and clover. The sun grew hotter, the hill grew steeper, I grew wearier and wearier with every step—and I was hungry, too. My fob-watch told me it was half past four. I was dying for a cup of tea.

I looked round for the house. It was a long way away; I had strayed farther than I had intended. My feet were sore and I was exhausted, yet I must tramp still farther before I could relax, staunch my hunger and quench my thirst.

But I must rest awhile.

I flopped down on the springy turf, surprised the grass was not longer, for there were no animals up here. I looked about me with sudden wonder at the flat table-like tract of land high above the sea, the harbor, the busy life of the island. It was remarkably quiet up here away from everyone and everything. I lay back and closed my eyes.

"You'll freckle, Nicola."

I heard my mother's voice and quickly opened my eyes. But of course she was not there. Yet still I heard her.

"You should have covered your arms, my dear. You'll peel in this heat."

57

"Oh, Mama, Mama . . ." Tears trickled down my cheeks in an extremity of longing . . . for her . . . for home . . . for everything I had ever known and would never know again. Yet only a short time ago I had been happy, carefree. Now I felt only misery and despair. I had nothing to look forward to. I might never see my dearest Mama again. The tears became a flood. I abandoned myself to the despair of homesickness.

But homesickness was a luxury I could not afford to indulge in. There was nothing to be gained from harking back to days gone by. I had to look forward. I must make a new life for myself.

I blew my nose hard and dried my eyes. Despite my protesting limbs, I rose to go. Yet, curiously, I felt loathe to leave this quiet place where all was peaceful. Something held me back from starting out, something . . .

I stood atop the breezy prominence and wondered what it was that kept me there. Not a sound reached me on the dizzy height. There were no wildflowers growing among the grass, therefore no bees to buzz, no insects of any kind to make a noise. No birds sang, even the ubiquitous gulls gave this place a wide berth. Nothing existed up here on this flat piece of land. Only I, I alone in all the world. And yet I did not feel alone.

Suddenly I knew I was not alone. Someone was with me in this high place. Someone—or something. It was tugging at my dress, whispering in my ear, urging me to stay—forever . . . forever . . .

Aches and pains forgotten, I plunged into action and went racing down the hillside. There was something up there on that strange hilltop, something not of this world. And I must escape from it or be lost.

I ran into something hard and unyielding. A rock.

"Whatever is the matter, Miss Wentworth? Has something frightened you?"

Justin Penrose's voice was the pleasantest sound I could ever wish to hear, the haven of his arms the safest place I could ever wish to be. I did not even think it strange how one man's arms could fill me with dread while another's offered such peace and security.

Mumbling incoherently into his chest, I was contentedly aware of the warmth of his body through the fine linen of his shirt, of the safe enclosure of his embrace—then I was thrust away from him, not roughly, but firmly, and it was as if he had abandoned me to all the forces of evil. I started to shiver. My teeth began to chatter. I felt cold beneath the hot June sun.

His hands were gripping my arms, biting into my flesh. "Steady. Steady," he was saying. "Calm yourself. Tell me what has happened. Why are you so frightened?"

"I . . . I . . . It was . . . was . . ." But how could I explain to this man whose eyes had become twin pieces of granite, that which I could not explain to myself?

"Something's scared you," he said grimly. "Stay here. I'll take a look around."

"No, don't go!" I clutched at his arm, fearful of being left alone, then let it go at the frown he gave. "I-it was nothing."

"Nothing? You come hurtling down the hill as if all hell were after you and you say it was nothing?" he scolded.

"I just thought I heard something. . . . Sounds . . . whispers . . ."

"So," he said softly, "'twas the piskies sent you skeltering into my arms, was it?"

"Piskies?" I squeaked.

"This hill belongs to them. There is a fairy ring up there. You must have stumbled into it and disturbed them."

Yes. Yes. I wanted to agree with him, but his eyes were mocking. He was treating my fear as a joke.

"I don't believe in fairies. Such creatures don't exist," I said.

"Miss Wentworth, hush!" he cautioned. "Do not let them hear you say so. The little people do not take kindly to unbelievers."

A stab of fear ran through me and I swallowed nervously. I did not believe in fairies, but on this island I felt anything might be true. There might well be such things as piskies dwelling here. But, "Tush!" I said. "I don't believe such foolishness."

He shook his head sadly at me. "Oh, Miss Wentworth, I should not have thought you so undiscerning. Do you honestly expect me to believe you felt nothing up there, after your headlong flight down the hill? You admit you heard sounds, whispers. . . . Who do you think made them if not the little people?"

I swallowed again and said nothing. But I did not believe in such things. *I did not.* They existed only in the imagination.

"Did you notice how flat it was up there?" he continued.

"Yes. As flat as a table top."

"How prosaic, Miss Wentworth. A table top indeed. It is a plateau. The Plateau of Love we call it . . . because of the legend attached to it."

Interested in spite of myself, I said eagerly, "Legend? What legend?"

"In days of old," he said, "long before King Arthur or Merlin, this island was the stronghold of my ancestor, Penn. He was a giant of a man, wealthy and warlike. He fell in love with Roselle, the beautiful daughter of Zill, his implacable enemy who ruled all of Cornwall from Pendeen to Penzance, and she with him. They were constantly at war with each other, Penn and Zill, but when Roselle stole his heart, she begged Penn to make peace with her father. Zill, however, spurned his overtures. He did not want Penn for a son-in-law. He wanted his lands, his wealth, his death. So Penn made a deal with the piskies. He promised he would give them the High Plateau, which they had long coveted, in return for their help.

"The next time Zill came marauding, the piskies haunted and bedeviled him to such an extent that he fell into a swound at Penn's feet, whereupon Penn lopped off his head and set sail in triumph to claim Zill's domains and the beautiful Roselle.

"The piskies meanwhile turned Zill's body and head to stone and set them side by side on the High Plateau as a constant reminder to Penn that he owed his victory to them and must keep his pledge."

"What a fascinating story," I breathed.

"You may have noticed the stones up there—one large, one small, worn by the ravages of time, but still resembling the head and torso of a man. The legend says the piskies will remain on the plateau as long as the stones stand."

"Yes." I was carried away by his storytelling. "They are still there. I felt them all around me."

His eyes began to crinkle at the corners. His lips took an upward turn. He burst into laughter.

I blushed hotly. He had been leading me on. "You certainly know how to spin a tale," I declared bitterly.

His mood changed suddenly. Laughter departed and granite returned to his eyes. "Come," he ordered. "We'll ride back together."

It was then I heard the neigh of a horse and saw his black stallion standing a little way off.

"I'll walk," I said, the long trek back to the house seeming infinitely preferable to sitting in close proximity to him on that high, black back.

"You've done enough walking for one day," he retorted tartly. "I don't think you realize how far you have walked. Too much in one day. You'll suffer for it afterwards." A shadow of a smile crossed his face. "Admit your limbs are beginning to ache already."

He was right, but I refused to admit it and fell into step beside him. My heels shrieked with pain and found expression in my voice.

"What's wrong now?" he asked irritably.

"I've got blisters," I snapped.

"Serves you right. Perhaps in future you'll not be so quick to ignore my advice."

"Thanks for your sympathy."

"I've no patience with stupidity."

"You've no patience with anything, it seems to me."

We were glaring at each other, snapping away, when I was suddenly swept up with an exasperated grunt and carried in his arms to the waiting horse. He deposited me in the saddle and jumped up behind me. His arms came round me and my heart leapt to my throat—but it was only to take the reins in his hands. At a given command, the aptly named Ebony transported us swiftly and easily back to Penrose House.

I had perforce to submit to being held in his arms again as he lifted me down from Ebony's back, but when he would have carried me indoors, I demanded indignantly to be set down.

Without argument, he set me on my feet. I winced in agony. With an impatient click of his tongue he swept me up again, silenced further protest with an angry "Be quiet," and did not set me down again till we reached the door of my room. He threw the door open, said, "I'll send Carty to you," and abandoned any further interest in me.

My heels were red raw and bleeding profusely when I finally managed, amidst moans and groans, to separate them from my stockings. I was trying to staunch them with my handkerchief when Mrs. Carthew arrived. She carried an armful of towels and was followed by a maid holding a bowl full of steaming hot water smelling strongly of antiseptic in her hands.

"Master Justin says you've walked blisters on your heels," she said. Her eye taking in the situation, she added, "He said 'ee'd be needin' salves and bandages."

"I foolishly walked too far," I murmured. "But there was no need for Mr. Penrose to bother you."

"Put the basin down, Susan," she said. "You may go. I'll tend Miss Wentworth."

Mrs. Carthew lifted my feet with gentle hands and immersed them in antiseptic water. I immediately withdrew them, crying out in agony, as it seemed flames lapped the water.

She pressed them back in again and held them down. "'Tis painful, I know, but 'tis necessary. 'Ee'll suffer worse if blood poisoning sets in."

So I clamped my teeth together and suffered her ministrations in silence. Then she was dabbing my feet dry and spreading soothing salve over my heels, and the pain gradually eased. I gazed down at the graying head as she bandaged them with skill and thought how kind she was. Then I thought about the man who had sent her to my aid. That he should have bothered showed evidence of a streak of thoughtfulness in his nature.

"He's a strange man," I murmured, involuntarily speaking aloud.

The gray head came up. "Master Justin?"

"I can't make him out. He's harsh, cold, taciturn, yet thoughtful and—kind."

"Aye, 'ee be all those things."

"I thought he was a hermit, you know. I thought he'd be old and—"

"Hermit! Master Justin!" The idea seemed to amuse her. "He likes his privacy, I'll not deny, but he'm sociable enough. Hermit, indeed!"

"He doesn't like women though, does he?"

She shrugged and rose from her knees. "There!" she said, "Treat 'em kindly and the'll soon heal."

"Thank you, Mrs. Carthew. They do feel much better."

She took the bowl of water into the bathroom.

I called out to her, "Is there a Mrs. Penrose?" and hardly knew why.

There was some hesitation, then she appeared in the bathroom doorway, her eyes grown cold. "There be Master Justin's mother. But that bain't what you'm askin'—be it?"

I squirmed beneath her astute glance.

"You want to know if there be a wife. Well, there bain't, nor never likely to be. Women 'ev no interest for him since . . ."

"Since Caroline?" I asked quickly.

A frown was her only reply.

"Who is Caroline?" I insisted, hoping at last to discover something about her.

Mrs. Carthew's eyes gleamed like live coals and I received

63

the impression that, whoever Caroline was, she had stirred hatred in this little woman's soul.

"You ask too many questions," she said, and closed the bathroom door.

With the empty bowl in her hands, she crossed the room. Before leaving, she turned to me again. "I'll give 'ee a bit of advice. Don't 'ee be poking your nose into things that don't concern 'ee. And don't 'ee go making up to Master Justin, neither. 'Twill do 'ee no good."

I stared at the door after she had gone. Her words, their implication, had taken my breath away. As if I had any intention of making up to him—or any man. It was the last thing on my mind.

But who *was* Caroline that her name should bring forth such advice?

I sat at my window overlooking the cliffs and the sea, with all that had occurred during the past two days occupying my mind. My arrival on a June afternoon turned dark and cold by the Black Wind which I had been accused of evoking. My meeting with Justin Penrose, a man as grim and hard as the rocks that met the sea. My dismissal from a job I had not even started, and my reinstatement. My meeting with John Trevelyan this morning, when he had mistaken me for the mysterious Caroline. Hearing about Miss Clunes from Mrs. Carthew. The women in the shop. Their behavior when I mentioned Miss Clunes. Was Caroline Miss Clunes? It seemed likely. And what had she done to earn Mrs. Carthew's hatred?

There was a knock at the door.

"Come in."

It was Mrs. Carthew bringing me tea on a tray. She enquired solicitously after my "poor sore feet."

"They're fine, thanks to you," I said.

She nodded and turned to go.

I stopped her, saying, "That's a beautiful yacht out there."

It had come into my view just before she had entered—a gleaming white boat with sleek lines, sails billowing in the breeze. I could not help commenting on it.

"Oh, aye," she said, joining me at the window, "that's the Justinia."

"The Justinia? Does it belong to Mr. Penrose?"

"Aye. Named it after his grandmother, he did. She loved the sea every bit as much as he."

She went on to tell me what a great beauty his grandmother had been and of the great affinity between them. "'Tis a pity she died afore he could take her out in the boat he named for her."

"Does he do much sailing?"

"As much as he can. He'm never so much at home as when he'm standin' at the helm. Look at him, ridin' afore the wind. 'Tis a lovely sight, to be sure."

I thought back to my one and only experience aboard a sea-going vessel and shuddered. I should have to endure another in the not-too-distant future, and although it was unlikely the Black Wind would accompany me on that journey, I was not looking forward to it. Particularly as I did not want to make the trip, anyway.

I wanted to stay here. On the island. This mystical, magical island. It might be full of dark secrets, but at least it offered a kind of refuge—and I could live with the secrets. I had one of my own.

I had not written to my mother yet. I sat down at the writing desk and hastily repaired the omission, withholding my address. All my mail, I had decided, should be addressed to me care of Mr. Pedlar's agency in High Holborn. I would write Mr. Pedlar to that effect in the morning, making it clear no one, *no one,* was to be given my address under any circumstances whatsoever.

Darkness fell, and I prepared for bed. I drew back my curtains and looked out, telling myself I was not looking for the Justinia, yet feeling a keen disappointment when all that met my gaze was an empty sea silvered by half a moon and a few stars.

I was about to turn back into the room when I was arrested by a movement farther along the cliffs. It was a man striding

65

along at a great pace. He came to a halt. He stood legs astride, arms akimbo, and looked up at Penrose House.

My heart somersaulted. He was watching the house! Watching me!

I drew back quickly. I saw him turn and gaze out across the sea. I edged forward again. I saw him raise his arms heavenwards and throw back his head. He shouted something into the night sky—or laughed—I could not be sure which, I caught no sound of his voice, only saw the action. And as I watched, he seemed to grow in stature, assuming gigantic proportions.

I started to tremble, and a haunting fear dried my mouth. Was it Penn out there? Was he planning fresh assaults on the mainland? Was there another maiden he wished to carry off? Had the warlike Penn returned to Penrose?

But what was I thinking of! I was allowing myself to be carried away by the stories Justin Penrose had told me. And that's all they were, stories. There were no piskies, no Penn, no Zill. They were all products of Justin's writer's mind. He was a storyteller. He had made them all up. He had laughed at my gullible belief in them. How he would laugh at me now if he could know how I was reacting to the sight of that man out there. It was probably Justin Penrose himself taking the air, perhaps pondering a book taking shape in his head. Or it might be a shepherd looking for lost sheep . . .

But I knew it was no shepherd and I was far from sure it was Justin Penrose. Justin Penrose was a tall man of powerful build, but this man was bigger, heavier—or was my vision distorted by the night clouds as they passed over the moon?

While I watched and wondered the man walked away, disappearing into the distance.

I turned back into the room and went to bed.

It must have been Justin Penrose. Who else could it have been?

Chapter Four

I woke from a sleep haunted by piskies and hobgoblins; by
ogres climbing in at my window to wrench me from my warm
hide; by unseen beings chasing me through dark forests, deep
caverns. Fear had shared my bed through the night. It shared it
still.

But it was morning now, and bright sunlight streamed across
my bed in place of the shadowed moonlight that had ignited
fancies, chasing away the last clinging vestiges of my dreams.
They withdrew farther and farther from my grasp, till I could
recall them only vaguely.

It was not so easy to forget my vision of Penn on the edge of
the cliff. It was still etched on my brain. I sprang out of bed and
ran to the window to convince myself he was not still there.

An arc of blue sky reigned over a calm sea, soaring golden-
beaked seabirds the only creatures in sight. Peace and light
were everywhere. It was preposterous to feel afraid on a day
like this, to dwell on thoughts of Penn and fairy folk. I told
myself to put them back where they belonged—in the realms of
fancy. The man I had seen last night had been Justin Penrose,
not Penn, a creature of his imagination fostered by mine.

I went to breakfast on scrambled eggs and bacon, toast and
honey, and rich, aromatic coffee. I breakfasted alone in the
dining room, where two places had been set at one end of the

huge dining table, and was finishing my last mouthful when my employer made his appearance.

"Good morning, Miss Wentworth," he said.

"Good morning, Mr. Penrose," I replied, rising quickly. "I was just going."

His eyebrows lifted slightly. "Don't hurry away on my account."

"I'm not. I-I've finished."

He set about the task of supplying himself with food from the chafing dishes on the sideboard. I left him to it and went to sort out the mail. I had it all ready for him by the time he arrived at his desk. He gave no indication that he was pleased at my efficiency, or that he had even noticed it.

We worked solidly for almost an hour. I began to develop my own form of shorthand, an abbreviation of words, which I was to perfect as time went on, and this enabled me to keep up with his sometimes rapid dictation.

I had been sent into the office to fetch a file when, a few minutes later, I heard him bellow, "Miss Wentworth, come back in here will you, please?"

About to enter the library, I halted in my step. The library door had opened and Justin Penrose was saying, "John! Good morning. What brings you here so early?" He sounded less than pleased by the interruption.

"I was just passing and thought I'd drop in for a coffee."

"Passing?" Justin's voice was caustically sarcastic.

"Well," John gave a careless laugh, "perhaps I just wanted an excuse to see that bright-eyed secretary of yours again. How's she shaping up?"

"Well enough, I suppose," was the ungracious reply. "She's much too young. I'd have preferred someone older . . . and of a different sex. Can't think what Pedlar thought he was up to. I distinctly said I wanted a male secretary this time."

"Oh, come now, Justin. Because you had an unhappy experience once doesn't mean—"

"If you don't mind," his friend cut him short, "I have some work to do. Carty'll give you coffee if you go along to

68

the kitchen."

I had been considering closing the office door and waiting until John Trevelyan left, but as he had been dismissed, I waited a moment longer.

John did not take the hint, however. "You really ought to try to put it out of your mind, you know," he said. "It's no good dwelling on the past. It's over and done with." After a slight pause, he continued, "Have you thought any more about what I said?"

"About Mother, you mean . . . I wrote to her last night. I have to go to London to see my publisher. He wants me to meet some American producer who is keen on my work, and there's my new book to discuss. I'll take the opportunity of calling on her, and see for myself the state of her health."

"You'll find it's as I said. When are you leaving?"

"Friday, maybe."

"But that's days away. You can't leave it that long. She . . ."

I closed the door. The conversation between the two men seemed set to continue and it was wrong of me to stand listening, however much I might want to.

And I did want to. I was intensely curious about Justin Penrose and his relationship with his mother. Why did he harbor such bitterness toward her? It almost amounted to hatred. He seemed adamant about not wanting her to come to Penrose House.

Also I was curious about the "unhappy experience" John had referred to. And whose was the "pretty face about the place"? Caroline's? Miss Clune's?

It was all very intriguing and I longed for some answers.

I felt irritated when I thought of how Mrs. Carthew had deliberately avoided answering my questions about Caroline and Mrs. Penrose. She had told me, in as many words, to mind my own business. But how could I, under the circumstances? She had whetted my appetite with her evasions and obvious dislike of both ladies. And then there was her warning not to set my cap at Mr. Penrose.

As if I would . . . or could.

69

With my experience at the hands of Ted Gibbon still large in my mind, there was not the remotest possibility of my setting my cap at anyone, and if, *if*, by some unlikely chance I might wish to do so in the future I most certainly would not choose a man as dour, taciturn and bad-tempered as Justin Penrose.

But bad-tempered as he was, I was glad he was so. I might chafe beneath his brusque, uncharming manner, but I welcomed it. It blunted any vestige of liking for him I might be persuaded to indulge in. At the same time, I was happily aware that, with his dislike of women, and particularly of me, I had no cause to fear any unwanted sexual harassment from him.

Occupied thus by my thoughts as I stood by the window, I had observed, without it really registering, two black Labradors come bounding into view, but when their master followed immediately on their heels, the whole scene took on a remarkable clarity.

He had gone out! I had not heard him leave the library, yet there he was, striding away, heading for the cliffs with his pets! How long would he be gone? John was not with him. Had he left also, or had he taken his friend's advice and gone to seek a cup of coffee in the housekeeper's kitchen?

I took a peep into the library. It was empty. I settled down to type the letters already dictated to me.

I neither saw nor heard anything more of Justin Penrose for the rest of the day, though the letters I had left on his desk were signed when I went back for them after a luncheon shared with Mrs. Carthew.

During supper, also shared with Mrs. Carthew, I said, "I can't think where Mr. Penrose can be. I haven't seen him since early this morning."

I was hoping she would be able to enlighten me, though if she could, I doubted she would bother. I was delighted when she said affably, "He's up along, I 'spect, with his dogs."

"Up along?" I was caught by the unusual term.

"Did 'ee not see him go striding off this morning? I thought then we'd not be seeing any more of him for a few hours."

"What makes you say that?"

"I knows the signs," she said, nodding her head wisely. "There be a book takin' shape in his noddle. I can alus tell."

A tingle of excitement coursed through my veins at her words. A new book! A Justin Penrose history or a James St. Just novel? Either way, it was an interesting prospect.

"'Twill mean more work for 'ee. Like I said, he'll slave-drive 'ee. Have you working all hours he will. 'Twill likely prove too much for 'ee 'fore long."

Was there hope in her hard stare that it would lead me to leave the island? I said, as I had said before, "I'm not afraid of hard work. In fact, I shall welcome it."

She fell quiet then, but by persevering with questions about the island and its way of life, I succeeded in loosening her tongue again.

"Do many people live on the island?" I asked.

"A fair number. Three hundred and twenty-six at the last count."

"All fisherfolk?"

"No. There be farmers and shopkeepers and the like."

"I suppose you remember the slate quarries being worked."

"Aye, I do."

"There must have been many more people living on the island then. Men who worked the quarry."

"Aye, but they've all gone now. All imported, they were, from the mainland. No honest islander would do such work. Harvesters of the sea they be, mostly. They want no truck wi' hacking the soul out of the island."

"Justin—Mr. Penrose stopped the quarrying, I believe?"

"To his everlasting credit. 'Tis the one thing I could never forgive his father for—tearing the heart and soul out of Penrose. But 'twas common knowledge he needed the money it could bring."

"Dr. Trevelyan says there's a rich vein of silver running through the island, and copper."

Mrs. Carthew's face soured and she gave one of her disparaging sniffs, so I decided it was time to change tack.

"It's all so different from what I expected. I thought I was coming to a deserted island, that Mr. Penrose was a hermit. The last thing I expected to find was a house as beautiful as this, a thriving community."

She smiled again. Fluff jumped onto her lap. She stroked the furry body.

"I suppose you were born here?" I murmured.

"Born and bred, m'dear."

"Mr. Penrose, too?"

"Where else would the Master of Penrose be born?"

"But he doesn't spend all his time here, does he? He doesn't strike me as a man used to living the simple life. I mean, there's such an air of sophistication about him. . . ."

I broke off and bit my lip as her smile faded. I was being too inquisitive, too familiar. However, she answered me readily enough.

"His work takes him away from the island more than he'd like. There be times when we see nothing of him for months. Though these last two years've been different."

A closed look came over her face and, afraid the conversation would dry up, I said quickly, "He owns the island, doesn't he?"

"A Penrose has ruled this island for as long as anyone can remember. As far back as—"

"Penn and the piskies," I laughed.

"Don't 'ee be laughing at the fairy folk. 'Tis not proper. And if they be alistenin' . . . 'Tis wrong to laugh."

She was serious, almost angry.

"I'm sorry," I apologized. "I meant no disrespect."

She sniffed. "Like all foreigners, ye see no further than your nose."

I saw I had fallen out of favor again, and no longer felt welcome in her parlor. I made my excuses and left.

"Is that you Miss Wentworth?"

I was passing the open door of my employer's private parlor. His voice stopped me in my tracks.

"Yes, Mr. Penrose?"

"Come in here, will you, please?"

Betsy and Winnie, the two Labradors, ran forward to greet me as I entered, and were immediately chastised and ordered back to their positions on the heart rug. Notwithstanding, they thumped their greeting with their tails, the bright light of welcome in their gentle brown eyes. I paused to pat their heads on my way across the room.

Justin Penrose was near the window. He was in his shirt sleeves, and his hair looked as if he had been running his fingers through it. He held a sheaf of papers in one hand and a pencil in the other. In the middle of the room in lonely state, a wastepaper basket was full to overflowing with crumpled sheets of paper.

"Will you be so good as to type these out for me?" He handed me the sheaf of papers. "I know it's late, but I can't make head or tail of them as they are."

My eye was traversing the pages. The handwriting was appalling. There was much crossing out. Many words were overwritten, and sentences were squeezed in above and below several lines. It was clear why he could not make head or tail of them. Neither could I.

"They are in a mess, aren't they?" I opined, but I was excited. Did I hold in my hand the beginnings of a new history, a new novel?

"If you think you can't manage . . ." He moved to take the papers from me again.

"Oh, I'm sure I can," I returned brightly. "I was only agreeing with you."

His glance was crushing. I was not supposed to give comment. But then he smiled suddenly, surprising me with the warmth of his expression.

"The trouble is," he said, "my hand can't keep pace with my ideas."

I smiled back, the excitement I still felt at the prospect of working on his new book lighting up my eyes. It seemed to annoy him. He turned away and said tersely, "Let me have

73

them back as soon as you can."

I hurried away, hardly able to contain my impatience to start deciphering what he had written.

It was some three hours later that I handed him my neatly typed copies of his notes. I was not sure I had deciphered everything correctly. Much of the time it had not made any sense to me. But they were, after all, only notes. Perhaps they weren't meant to make any sense.

He was still in his private parlor listening to a Beethoven symphony on his gramophone. "Finished already?" he asked in surprise. "You needn't have rushed. Tomorrow would have done."

"I thought you needed them urgently," I said with a twinge of annoyance, thinking he might have shown some gratitude.

"Well, thank you," he said, setting the papers aside and stretching his long legs out as he settled down to listen to the music again.

I had been dismissed and oh, how I longed to be asked to stay. To be cosily ensconced with him by the fireside with Betsy and Winnie, too tired now to do anything more than give me a desultory thud, thud of a greeting with their tails on the floor at his feet. To listen to the symphony, with him, seemed to me the most desirable thing in the world at that moment.

But I had been dismissed. I had to return to my lonely room. Excitement drained away from me and a lump came to my throat. I knew I should never be welcome here—no matter how long I stayed. I should never be made welcome here, either by him or by the islanders. They all resented me and wanted me gone for one reason or another.

It was hard to accept. I had never in all my life experienced difficulty in making friends, but, possibly apart from John Trevelyan, I knew I should make none here, where I so desperately needed to. And I dared not become too friendly with John Trevelyan. I had read in his eyes a certain admiration of me. It had warmed me even while it had disturbed me—but I could not allow myself to succumb to his charm, innocent though I felt it to be. Ted Gibbon had a lot to answer for. He had destroyed my trust in men. He had destroyed my life.

Each day followed a pattern. I would sort the mail, Justin Penrose would dictate for an hour or so, then he would disappear. I would catch no further glimpse of him for the rest of the day—yet his letters were always signed when I went to collect them.

He gave me no more notes to type out for him, and I wondered if he had found the others unsuitable. He had not commented on them. I knew he was still working on his new book. Though I never saw him myself, Mrs. Carthew told me he "tired they animals out with his walking," and complained that she never knew when to expect him in to meals now that his mind was so full of "characters and situations."

I took to going for walks myself. I bought myself a pair of stout shoes from the general store. Mrs. Trevose served me. She was a little reserved with me at first, but as I steered clear of anything that might prove controversial, she unbent toward the end of my visit, even going so far as to tell me of the many pleasant little bays to be found.

"But they're all on the east side, mind. Don't 'ee be trying to find any over by Penrose Light. 'Tis not safe."

The island terrain held no terrors for me now and, as I grew more used to the ups and downs of the hills, my calves grew stronger and I could stride out with no fear of aches and pains. I grew tanned. I had never felt so full of life and vigor.

I discovered many new places, but never went anywhere near the High Plateau—The Plateau of Love, as the islanders called it—for fear of crossing the wee folk again. It was foolish of me, and I tried to laugh myself out of it, but a growing belief in the fairy folk Justin had told me about was taking hold of me. On this island, I felt, there could well be such fey creatures abroad.

It was a magical island, fresh and green and lapped by waves of deepest amethyst. It was a jewel-bedecked island—by day and by night—its landscape a palette of sapphires and amethysts, emeralds and pearls, all strung with silver and gold. It claimed my heart with its beauty. And yet, in spite of all the peace and serenity, I sensed a deep, hidden anguish that I could not ignore. Perhaps it was only an echo of my own unhappiness, but there was a convincing, abiding reality about it.

I was growing to love the island. I loved to potter about the harbor and watch the ships come and go. I pestered the fishermen mending their nets with questions about their work. At first it was difficult to provoke a response, but my stubborn refusal to be defeated won through in the end, and the fishermen became almost affable. As the islanders grew accustomed to seeing me around, smiles and words of greeting began to come my way.

I met Dr. Trevelyan once. He reined in alongside me.

"Hello," he called. "How are you? How are you getting on with Justin? Is he treating you all right?"

"I'm beginning to feel quite at home here," I smiled, happy to see him.

"Good. You're finding your way about the island?"

"Little by little."

"Good. I've been feeling somewhat guilty. I promised I would show you round the island. But I reckoned without the islanders. Quite a few of them have chosen this very time to fall sick, and Mrs. Tregallis's third decided to cause a bit of trouble. Oh, she's all right now. Just needed helping into the world, that's all. However, I will take some time off to show you round. There are lots of hidden away places you will not have discovered yet. I'll call on you. Now I must be off. Goodbye."

Once I thought I saw Justin Penrose. He stood outlined against the sky for a brief moment, then disappeared beyond a rise in the hills. But I did not see his dogs—so I could have been mistaken. It set me thinking about him, however, wondering where his ramblings took him, how his book was progressing, wondering whether I should have any more to do with it, or if

76

he would wait till I had gone and been replaced by a new secretary—a male secretary.

I met Ruth Norman.

Ruth was the schoolteacher; thirtyish, pleasant, and friendly. She saw me talking to some of the children as they left to go home at four o'clock, and came out to introduce herself and invite me into her cottage, which was right next door to the school.

The cottage was as immaculate as Ruth herself. I never saw a speck of dust or an ornament out of place during all the times I visited her, just as I never saw a crease in her skirt, a hair out of place. Her pins defied the stiffest of breezes. I asked her once how she managed it: two minutes in the lightest of breezes and my hair was tumbling about my ears.

"My hair is coarser than yours," she said. "It's difficult for the pins to escape from it. Yours now, yours is so fine, I wonder it stays up at all."

"Yes. It's the bane of my life. It starts off well enough, but as the day progresses, strands begin to slip and my pins fall out. I could spend all day at my dressing table."

"Have you ever considered cutting it?"

"Cutting it!" I stared at her in astonishment. "Good heavens, no. My mother would have a fit."

"It would be better than letting it fly loose like that."

"I know it's a bit of a mess at the moment; that's because I've been out in the hills for a couple of hours. But usually I tie it back and it keeps reasonably tidy."

"It still hangs down your back."

"You don't really expect me to cut it?" I asked with a chuckle. "How would you like to cut your hair?"

She shrugged and laughed with me. "I shouldn't be lecturing you on something I would not do myself, should I?"

She made tea and brought out some dainty little cakes that first day.

"So," she said, "you're Justin's new secretary. How are you finding it?"

"It's an interesting job," I replied, "but I can't quite make him out."

"You haven't been here very long. It takes time to get to know someone. I've been here for eight years. . . . After my father died, I was penniless. I had to go out and earn my own living. He was a clergyman, a parson in Hertfordshire. It was not his fault he left me without a shilling to my name. It was not a very good living, and he was ever and always sharing what he had with others less fortunate than himself."

"Eight years," I mused. "That's a long time."

"Yes, and I'm only just beginning to be accepted. You've no doubt found the islanders very reserved."

"Oh, yes, indeed. And I'm afraid I shall never be accepted."

"Why do you say that? Give them time. They'll accept you in the end."

"I shan't be here long enough for that."

"Don't you think you'll stay, then?"

"I'd like to, but it doesn't rest with me."

Her face creased in a sympathetically questioning frown.

"It's Mr. Penrose," I added. "He doesn't want me to stay."

"Why not? Oh, forgive me. It's really none of my business."

"I don't want to go," I sighed. "This is the first job I've ever had, and I love it."

"I hope you don't mind my asking, but what made you want to come here to work? I mean, it's such a lonely island . . . miles from anywhere . . . and you're so pretty. You must have had many admirers. I can't understand why you're not married."

My cup clattered onto my saucer as it slipped from my suddenly nervous grasp, and hot color stained my cheeks.

"I shall never marry," I said.

"You can state that categorically?" Her smile was skeptical.

"Yes." I placed my cup and saucer on the table. "I have no intention of becoming any man's property. There's more to life than being bound to the home like a slave."

78

"Well, I agree, up to a point, but . . . I say, are you a free-thinker?"

"I don't know. I believe every woman has a right to choose what she wants from life. If she wishes to follow a career, she should be allowed to do so. But a man will have her tied down to home and family. Her place is in the home, he insists."

"And you wish to follow a career. Is that wise? You have not the look of a career woman. I should have said you were cut out for wifedom and motherhood."

I could see where her thoughts were taking her. She'd assumed that I had been proposed to and had turned the offer down because of the man's insistence that I stay at home rather than take up a career. I did not disillusion her. Instead, I asserted in a forthright manner, "You never married. You chose a career."

"No, I did not. It chose me. I told you how my father died penniless. And I was never very attractive to men. I was past the age of marriage before my father died."

"But that was eight years ago, you said. You could not have been very old then."

"Work it out for yourself. I'm forty-four now."

"I can't believe it," I declared. "You don't look any more than . . . well, thirty-one or two at the most."

"That's what living on this island does for you," she laughed. "It's taken years off me." She leaned forward to pick up the teapot. "Would you like more tea?"

I shook my head. "No, thank you."

She poured a cup for herself, then she sat back and continued, "I was at a very low ebb when I came here. My father had been dead for four years and during that time I had done a variety of jobs. Having looked after my father since my mother died—I was fifteen when she passed on—it seemed I was only suited for a housekeeper's position. Ada Cox, a doctor's daughter, whom I had always considered a friend, had recently married and settled in the next village. As luck would have it, her housekeeper had packed her bags and left without

79

even giving in her notice. Ada asked me if I would like the job, and I jumped at it. I soon learned why the previous housekeeper had left.

"I was on my feet from morning till night. There was very little other help in the house and I was expected to serve meals—after having cooked them. Make the beds. Do the shopping. Dust and polish. About the only thing I did not have to do was scrub the floors and make the fires—a girl from the village came in to do that. And to top it all, Ada made it quite plain I was no longer to be considered a friend.

"I stood it for as long as I could, then I, too, packed my bags. I eventually found myself a post as governess to three small boys and two girls. I hated it. The family was rather bohemian. The house was always full of strangely dressed people whose behavior was, to put it mildly, unusual . . . and the children were allowed to do as they liked. Somehow I managed to instill a little grammar and arithmetic into them. But they played abominable jokes on me. And when I complained to their parents, they just laughed and said I should have a sense of humor.

"I was just about at the end of my tether when I met Justin Penrose. I had one free evening a month, and on this particular evening I had gone to hear a lecture on the history of Cornwall. For two hours I forgot my worries, carried away by the lecturer's charmismatic voice and personality, swept into a world of wonder and excitement. Cornwall, I thought. If only I could go to Cornwall. I felt, if I could go to Cornwall all my problems would be at an end. He, Justin Penrose, had that effect on me."

She sipped her tea reflectively, and continued.

"They served refreshments afterwards, and I found myself standing near him. I didn't expect him to notice me. No one ever did. But he turned to smile at me and soon I was chatting to him as if I'd known him all my life. I don't know how it happened, but I was telling him my life story, telling him how unhappy I was in my job, what little horrors the children were, how I had looked around for something else, but had so far failed—and he was listening as if he cared. I believed he did care. I think I fell in love with him then. Oh, Nicola, I would have given anything to be beautiful, to have him fall in love with me . . . to marry him."

"Justin Penrose?" I murmured incredulously. How could any woman wish to marry such a man?

"Of course, he's a lot younger than I. About ten years, I think. When I was back in my little room in the house in Bloomsbury and the scales fell from my eyes, I realized how foolish I had been even to imagine he might fall in love with me, thirty-five if I was a day. He was very young to be such a successful author and to be so erudite.

"Anyway, I stuffed my foolish dream to the back of my mind and tried to forget him. Then, to my surprise, some few weeks later I received a letter from him. The schoolmistress on Penrose Island was retiring in a couple of weeks' time; would I like to take over from her? I would be in complete charge. If I would telegram my answer, he would be obliged. He hoped it would be yes and, if so, would come and collect me himself. As you can imagine, I didn't hesitate. I wired my acceptance at once. He's a wonderful man. So kind, so sympathetic. If it had not been for him . . . He could quite easily have forgotten all about me, but he remembered and . . ."

I listened in amazement. Was she talking about the Justin Penrose I knew—the stern, forbidding, angry man who was my employer?

"I don't find him at all kind or sympathetic," I cried, and then bit my lip as I realized it was not quite true. He had shown me kindness—overlaid with cynicism it was true, but he had granted my request to stay and work for him when he need not have done so. Nevertheless he was a cold man, harsh, dismissive. I said so.

"Yes," she agreed, "he is now, but he was not always so. There was a time when he was always laughing, always carefree."

81

"What happened to change him?"

She rose and prepared to clear the tea things away. "I'm afraid I shall have to ask you to excuse me now. I've a lot of preparation to do for tomorrow's lessons."

Now why should she wish to close the conversation? She had been very talkative up to this point. I was certain there was a reason, and guessed what it was.

"Had it anything to do with Caroline?" I asked.

She held her breath, then, "What do you know about her?"

"Nothing really, but I believe there's some mystery about her. The women in the store didn't want to talk about her, and Mrs. Carthew shut up like a clam when I questioned her. She was his secretary, wasn't she?"

"Yes." Ruth sat down again. "But there's no mystery about her. It's just that . . . we don't speak of her."

"Why not? Did she do something wrong?"

"She jilted Justin Penrose. We'll never forgive her for that. It would have been their wedding anniversary this month. . . . On the sixteenth."

"The sixteenth? But I arrived on the sixteenth. No wonder he was in such a black mood. If only I'd known . . ."

"How could you have known? Anyway, it would have made no difference. One day would have been as bad as another—because of the resemblance."

"Resemblance? Are you telling me I resemble Caroline?"

"Yes. It's uncanny. You're not really like her at all. She was taller, her features were sharper . . . yet, at first glance, you are the very image of her."

My heart was beating madly. So that was it. The reason behind all the resentment I felt, the hatred I evoked in Justin Penrose, the silent disapproval of the women in the store. I was beginning to understand.

"It must have been like a knife turning in his heart when he saw you step ashore," Ruth continued. "He adored her. Fair piskie-mazed, he was—to use the islanders' phraseology."

"What made her . . . Why did she . . ."

"Jilt him? Who knows? But it was typical of her, the way she did it, leaving secretly like that. She hadn't the guts to face him and tell him openly that she'd changed her mind. He would have understood. She should have told him straight out, instead of . . . But he's well rid of her. She was the most selfish woman I've ever known, and the slyest. She wasn't true to him. There were other men. I know for a fact she and . . . Well, that's water under the bridge now, but good riddance to her, I say. She was not half good enough for him."

I listened avidly. She was clearing up much that had puzzled me. She continued.

"He went abroad afterwards. To America. Stayed away two years. He wrote *Love's Balm* there. Perhaps you've read it?"

"Yes, some time ago. It's about a woman tied to a man she doesn't love, is it not?"

"Yes. Kitty Lynton. I believe he modeled her on Caroline."

"Do you?"

"I do. But I think he painted too kind a picture of her."

"As far as I remember, Kitty was a most unpleasant character, yet one could not help feeling sorry for her."

"That's exactly what I mean. No one could feel sorry for Caroline. She had no saving graces."

"He must have loved her very much."

"Men are such fools," Ruth said bitterly.

I was thoughtful as I made my way back to Penrose House.

What was she like, really like, this girl Justin Penrose had been—was still?—in love with, who had jilted him on the very eve of their wedding day, turning him against women forever, changing him from a happy, carefree young man to the cold, embittered man I had come to work for?

She intrigued me. Any woman who could so enslave a man like Justin Penrose and cause such a powerful change in his personality when she rejected him, was a woman worthy of much thought.

Why had she jilted him? He was clever, famous, rich, handsome in a grim sort of way. He was kind and generous—

Ruth had said, and he obviously had adored her. *So why had she jilted him?*

She must have had a strong reason. I promised myself I would read *Love's Balm* again to see if I could discover it—and to see if I resembled her in more than looks. It was disturbing to think I might resemble her in character; Ruth had painted a very unkind picture of her . . . But I did not see myself in such a picture. If I had been the girl Justin Penrose loved, I would never have left him.

Oblivious of everything but my thoughts, I tramped on.

"Miss Wentworth! Miss Wentworth!"

My reverie was shattered. A horse drew up at my side. Its rider dismounted.

The man who had been occupying my thoughts said, "You were so lost in thought I could have ridden you down and you would not have noticed. What weighs so heavily on your mind that it leads you into danger?"

"Danger?" I was not wholly back to awareness yet. I was aware of him, deeply aware of him, but of nothing else.

"If you had continued on your present path you would have tumbled headlong into the sea."

He spoke lightly, but I sensed concern underlying his words.

"It seems I must thank you for saving me from certain death," I said, my heart halting in its beat as I saw how near the edge of the cliff I was . . . or was there some other reason?

"Where have you been?" he asked.

"Taking tea with Ruth Norman."

"Oh, you've met her?"

"Yes."

"And you're on your way back to the house?"

"Yes."

"Then allow me to act as your guide." He took my elbow and steered me in the other direction. "You were going the wrong way. Perhaps I'd better draw you a map of the island, in case you get lost anytime."

"There's no need," I said stiffly, irritated by the chuckle I heard in his voice—he thought me a fool. "I'm quite capable of finding my way around. I've explored quite a bit of the island."

"Yes, I know," he said surprisingly.

Leading his horse, he walked by my side in silence for a while. Then he asked, "What do you think of Ruth?"

"She's very nice. I like her."

He seemed pleased with my reply.

"A bit progressive in her views. A great believer in women's rights."

I bridled. "And what is wrong with that? So am I."

"I had not forgotten," he said.

There was a slight lift to the corners of his mouth. He was leading me on, yet I could not resist doing battle with him.

"You don't like women to be independent, do you?"

"Not if it erodes their essential femininity, which it does all too often."

"It's possible to be independent and retain one's femininity."

"I haven't seen much evidence of it."

"Because you don't want to see. You prefer women to be compliant, to always be on hand to pander to your merest whim. Well, the day is coming when women will no longer be looked upon as chattel. They are waking up to a sense of their own importance, and nothing you or any man can do will stop their advancement. They will no longer be content to sit at home waiting for their lord and master to return. There's more to life for a woman than running a home, bringing up children, and looking after a man."

"In my experience, most women are content to do just that."

"You believe a woman's place is in the home," I snapped. "You want them to be men's playthings, to kowtow. You want a woman to be submissive and meek. You want—"

"I hardly think, Miss Wentworth, that you are in a position to know what I want in a woman."

He spoke lightly, yet with an underlying hint of disapproval

85

that reminded me of how tenuous was my place here. Whatever I believed was of no consequence. He had the right to terminate my employment, and I wasn't ready for that yet.

"I'm sorry, I should not have said that," I apologized. "Nevertheless, the time will come when men will have to concede women their rights."

"You sound exactly like a tract. But you're entitled to your opinion."

"Oh, don't be so pompous." I rounded on him, my tenuous position forgotten.

"I don't think you really believe any of that stuff," he said mildly.

"I have thought very seriously about it," I said.

"Women should be soft and pliable. Feminine."

"Then you must think me completely unfeminine, for I am neither of those things."

"On the contrary, I think you are one of the most deliciously feminine women I know." He was being deliberately provocative. "Pretty, delicate, argumentative . . . exasperating."

I drew in my breath and opened my mouth to decry his words, but before I could utter a sound he added, "But I detect a core of steel in you that will be hard to break."

We had reached Penrose House and had come to a halt. I gazed up into his strong face, unable to fathom what lay behind his words and his deeply penetrating glance.

"I think you can find your own way from here," he said, swinging away from me and leading his horse toward the stables.

I watched him go, fuming yet strangely elated. I had enjoyed battling with him. But as I started to go indoors I thought of those words—*"I detect a core of steel in you that will be hard to break."*

Did he intend to break it? Break my spirit?

I clenched my teeth together. He could try. He would not succeed.

Chapter Five

I had promised myself I would read *Love's Balm* again. After supper, when I knew Mr. Penrose had gone "up along" with his four-legged companions, I went into the library to look for a copy.

There was a whole shelf given over to James St. Just novels, and to this I made my way, pausing to run my fingers over the titles before drawing out the one I was looking for.

So many. They must have taken years to write. How old had he been when he had written the first one? I judged him to be about thirty-three or thirty-four now. There were certainly a great many I had not seen before, and they offered a feast of reading for me. I had looked for his books ever since reading *Left to Roam*, chosen at random from the traveling library, and had found no more than three.

Then of course there were his histories, written under his own name. Much fatter tomes they were, on the shelf beneath. Did they include stories of Penn and Zill? Perhaps I would read one, or all, of them eventually.

But first I must reread *Love's Balm*.

I started thumbing through it searching for clues to Caroline's character, and became so engrossed in the story that I lost all track of time.

The slam of a door brought me back to the present and the heavy tread of footsteps on the floor outside. I thrust the book back into its allotted space on the shelf. I should not have been afraid to be found by Justin Penrose with any other book in my hands, but *Love's Balm* was not just any other book. It was the testimony of a man's love and betrayal, *his* love and betrayal, and I did not want to be caught with it in my hands if he came into the library—which I knew instinctively he would.

The door opened. The dogs dashed toward me.

"What are you doing here?" Justin Penrose rasped from behind them.

"I was looking for something to read."

"In the dark?"

"It was light when I came in. . . . It's not really dark yet."

He walked up to me. "Have you found anything to your liking?"

The heady scent of the outdoors clinging to his clothing made me feel dizzy—either that or the fact that I had been straining my eyes too long in the fading light. Or could it have been the searching glance from those dark heavy-browed eyes? The nearness of him?

"Not yet," I whispered. His glance stole past me to the shelf of novels no longer in regimental precision, but with *Love's Balm* slightly out of line, as if guided there by my anxiety.

"Then I'll leave you to continue your search," he said, and turned to go. His dogs flew to join him. At the door he looked back. "You could ignore my advice, but I suggest you light a candle if you intend to read in here and you treasure your eyesight."

His sarcasm was not lost on me. I hated him for it. It seemed so petty, and somehow, I did not see pettiness as part of his nature. But it was just another attempt to irritate me to the point where I would be driven to take my leave of him and the island. It would not work. I was determined to stay the month out—more so than ever now.

I returned to my room with *Love's Balm* and read well into the night.

* * *

Friday came and went. Justin Penrose remained on the island despite his promise to visit his mother. Perhaps he had forgotten all about it—and her, with his new book taking possession of his mind. I wondered if I ought to remind him. Was it not part of a secretary's job to keep her employer abreast of his appointments? Then I thought better of it. This was not a business appointment. It was purely a personal matter. He would be perfectly within his rights to tell me to mind my own business, if I mentioned it. For all I knew, he could have altered the arrangements. So I said nothing and waited on events.

On Saturday afternoon, just as I was about to go and visit Ruth, he called me into the library. That was the beginning of a long, hard grind. I learned what Mrs. Carthew had meant when she had said I would be "slave-driven." I was given notes to decipher and type, and reams of dictation. Most of it was handed back for re-typing after being altered beyond recognition.

I went to bed that night with shoulders aching and fingertips tingling with pain.

Sunday was the same. He took time off to attend church in the morning, but on his return it was work, work, work, with hardly a break for coffee or tea. I wondered if he was working me so hard deliberately—to achieve his aim of getting rid of me, but the "I told you so" expression on Mrs. Carthew's face whenever I saw her disabused me of that supposition. She had warned me I would be slave-driven.

I watched the book grow under my hands.

Round about seven-thirty on Sunday evening, I placed the last of the work he had given me into his hands. He looked down at the typescript in silent contemplation.

"Will there be anything more?" I asked, hoping he would say no. I was worn out, both mentally and physically, though I would never have admitted it to him, but would have accepted stoically any more work there might be.

I was hungry too. Tea had been slight, and nothing since. I wondered what there would be for supper and whether I should eat first or soak my aching body in a hot bath.

To my joy he said, "No. This will do. Thank you."

He raised his eyes from the papers and as I caught his glance I felt as if I became weighted down, unable to stir hand or foot, held in a time trap, in a state of breathless exhaustion . . . It was the result of tiredness, of course. It had to be.

"Thank you," he was repeating. "You are an excellent typist and have proved more than equal to making sense out of my scribbles and scrawls. What would I do without you?"

His praise, so unexpected, delighted me and I smiled broadly. It appeared to stun him for a second or two, but then his own lips parted in a smile before he nodded my dismissal.

"Have you had your supper yet?"

His question surprised me as I reached the door. "N-no," I said, turning round to face him again.

"Then perhaps you wouldn't mind if we supped together?"

"N-no."

"There are a few things I should like to discuss with you."

He nodded again, dismissing me again. I left in a daze.

As I looked for something to change into, I was wondering feverishly about his invitation, why he had made it, what lay behind it. He had said he wished to discuss something with me. Was it my departure? My month's grace would soon be up. Did he want to know what I had done about finding another position? I had done nothing. The time had flown . . . I had thought about it, but had done nothing. Perhaps he had a few ideas he wished to put to me. Perhaps he had spoken to Mr. Pedlar about me and together they had come up with something.

I dressed in white silk overlaid with lace at the bodice and short, lacy sleeves. I placed a string of pearls round my neck— my father's present to me on my eighteenth birthday. Then I hesitated. He might think I was dressing to impress. Ah well, I tossed my head. Let him think what he liked. What did it matter, anyway? I would be leaving shortly.

I made my way to the dining room and stared in dismay at the long shiny mahogany table bare of all but its large silver centerpiece and two branching candlesticks. I could not believe my eyes.

Have supper with me, he had said. In half an hour, he had said. Yet nothing had been laid out. So had he changed his mind? Forgotten? Must I sup with Mrs. Carthew as usual? Was our discussion to wait until tomorrow?

Disappointment flooded over me. I realized it was because I had been looking forward to this meal shared with him. I had been looking forward to being alone with him in a sociable climate where I might learn more about him—and he about me. I had no illusions about why he had issued the invitation. He had said, *"There are a few things I should like to discuss with you. . . ."* And I knew what they were. But all the same, the mere fact of sitting together at the same table, eating together, might elicit some social chat. Underneath, perhaps, I still cherished the hope that I might be able to persuade him to allow me to stay.

But it was not to be. The man I had categorized as hard, ruthless, and cruel on first acquaintance, was to remain as much a mystery to me as ever.

I did not like him. Who could like such a brusque, fierce and scowling man? But if one could not like him one could try to understand and, perhaps, excuse him.

And since rereading *Love's Balm*, I felt I could understand him. It had not been the heroine, Kitty, who had captured my sympathies—though she was drawn with kindness and compassion—but the hero whose pain had leapt tangibly from every page, the pain I knew now was Justin's own.

A maid appeared at my side.

"Mr. Penrose be awaitin' 'ee in his parlor, Miss Wentworth," she said smilingly.

My heart lightened as I followed her to the room I had previously entered only briefly and into which I had never expected to be welcomed as a guest. It was a bright, comfortable room with soft leather furniture to lounge in. There were lots of books, pictures, photographs. The fireplace had a mantel of richly carved wood, and Betsy and Winnie lay sprawled on the thick rug in front of the hearth where, instead of a fire laid ready to light, a mass of blooms filled the space.

They sprang up to greet me with wagging tails and shining eyes. They nuzzled into my white silk skirts and I stroked their glossy heads.

They were ordered back to the hearth rug by their master.

"They're all right," I said. "They're not doing any harm."

"They'll spoil your pretty dress," he taunted, handing me a glass of sherry. My appearance had not been lost on him.

"They're such beautiful animals." I ignored the sarcasm. "You must be very proud of them. They're so healthy and well-cared for."

"Shouldn't all animals be healthy and well-cared for?" he responded.

"Well, yes, of course, but . . . not everyone gives their pets adequate care and affection. I've seen evidence to the contrary. But I know these two get all the attention they could desire. You must be very fond of them."

"Fond? Yes, I am. Very fond. They are constant in their love. Never-changing in their affections."

Bitterness had edged its way into his voice. Was he thinking of Caroline? It was highly likely. She had proved fickle-hearted. Then he laughed, and I was surprised to hear humor in his voice.

"Although I am not so sure of them now," he said. "You seem to have succeeded in attracting them away from me."

"Only because I'm someone new," I said softly, happy there was this point of contact between us that might be put to my advantage. "Once they get used to me—" I broke off as they turned their quick brown eyes from me to him. "You see? I'm beginning to pall already."

"I can't see that happening," he said, and an odd gleam came to his eye. Something passed between us that I could not understand, but I knew it was of great import.

Supper was brought in and placed on the table beside the window.

The dogs were banished. The maid departed. Justin Penrose

held out a chair for me to sit at the table, then went to sit opposite me. He poured out some wine, sat back—and waited.

Was I to serve?

It appeared so.

He watched in silence as I spooned chicken pie and vegetables onto our plates. Then, as we began to eat, he said, "Do you like it here, Miss Wentworth?"

I said I did. Very much.

"You seem to have settled down very well."

"Yes, I—I think I have."

"Would you consider staying on?"

I squeaked in my surprise, "Staying on? Oh, yes. I should love to."

"Good," he said, and that was all. We continued eating in silence.

Did it mean he *wanted* me to stay and if so, for how long? I waited for him to make his meaning clear.

But he said nothing more on the subject.

At last, unable to contain my impatience any longer, I asked, "Am I to take it you wish me to continue in my employment here, Mr. Penrose?"

He looked directly at me. "It's what you wanted, is it not?"

"Yes . . ."

"Well then, there's no more to be said. I'm satisfied with your work, despite everything, and if you're happy to remain . . ."

"Oh, I am. I am."

He poured more wine for me and for himself and, as he raised his glass to his mouth, enquired, "Have you seen much of the house yet?"

"No. I should like to. I've often thought about asking Mrs. Carthew to show me round, but somehow never seemed to find the time."

"I'll show you round after supper, if you like."

"Oh! Would you? I should be most interested. It must hold a lot of history, a place like this. It looks like a castle. I thought it was a castle at first."

93

I knew I looked and sounded eager. I was hoping to lead him on to talk about the past, the house's past—and his.

But his eyes had grown cynical.

"History? What do you mean by history? The lives and loves of the people who lived here in the past, I suppose?"

"Isn't that what history is all about? Tracing the lives of men and women—our ancestors. Finding out how they lived, what their hopes and desires were, who married whom? You're an historian. Isn't that what you write about?"

While I spoke, his craggy black brows had drawn closer and closer above the strong bridge of his beaky nose, and I felt I was saying too much, probing too much, for behind my words lay the desire to find out more about him, about his hopes and dreams—if there were any left after Caroline's desertion—and I feared he guessed as much.

But then he laughed and said, "Yes, I suppose it is."

Hearing again that unexpected humor rise, I joined him in laughter and, for a moment, felt almost at ease with him. I thought it odd that a man of such a cold and stern nature could contain such humor, but it tallied with Ruth's description of him. I wished he could always be like this. However, I very much feared it would not be long before he reverted to his habitual self. The man he had been was no more. But I glimpsed him now, and believed I should have liked him.

We drained our glasses and commenced our tour of inspection. Betsy and Winnie joined us, trailing us patiently through the many rooms and corridors.

It was a large house, built like a castle with its battlements and twin towers. Every room had a superb view and each was beautifully furnished. I was excited and unrestrained in my comments, impulsively myself now that we seemed to be getting on so well together.

"It should be called Penrose Castle," I declared. "It's so much more than just a house."

"It was at one time. I changed it after . . ."

I hardly noticed the change in his voice. I was much too interested in the house.

"It's all very impressive. It must date back a very long way. It appears to be Jacobean in parts, but there's a lot of Tudor here . . . and the chandelier in the hall is pure fourteenth century, isn't it? Or is it a replica?"

"I don't go in for replicas," he said. "I prefer the real thing. But you are quite right, the house has been altered and added to over the centuries. The hall is the oldest part of the house. The towers were added during Elizabeth's reign to give it a more symmetrical appearance, then the battlements were added to complement them and, I suspect, to give a more impressive effect. It was then it was dignified with the title 'castle,' I believe."

"How interesting. Do go on."

He smiled and obliged. "Earlier on it was a single-story dwelling—a fortress. Before that," his grin widened, "a hut, most likely. A very large hut, of course, as befitted the Lords of Penrose."

I smiled back happily at this further evidence of a sense of humor usually kept at bay by his gruff exterior. Again I wished he would allow it to come to the fore more often. What a world of difference it would make . . . to everything.

We stepped back into the hall with its circular gallery and wheel-like chandelier suspended from the high ceiling on heavy chains. It was fascinating to think it had hung there since the Plantagenets ruled England . . . When the Battle of Crecy was being fought and won . . . When the Black Prince was rapidly acquiring his reputation as one of the greatest warriors of all time . . . When . . .

"Well, now you've seen it all." My musings were interrupted by my guide. "There are the stables . . . but they are like stables the world over. Then there are the gardens . . . but you are already well acquainted with those."

How did he know that? Had he seen me there? I often strolled through the gardens of an evening, sometimes taking a book with me to read in the small arbor sheltered from the breeze. It gave me a peculiar feeling to think I had been observed by him while oblivious to the fact.

I thanked him for showing me round.

"I'm glad you enjoyed it," he said.

His smile still lingered. He made no movement to go, giving the impression that he did not wish to leave. He appeared to be waiting for me to say something else, to continue the conversation.

I said the first thing that came into my head.

"What a lot of rooms there are, and all so tastefully furnished. Whoever was responsible has an artist's eye."

His lingering smile vanished. I saw the lines, which cut into his face so deeply they never completely disappeared, return to his forehead and cheek. "My mother's influence," he grated, as if it hurt him to admit it, hurt him even to mention her name.

His mouth set into its usual straight line. His eyes had hardened. There was hatred in his glance. Did he hate me? His mother?

But a man could not hate his mother. It was against nature. And yet . . .

I remembered he had not wished to talk to John about her. He refused to allow her to visit him, refused to treat her civilly. Why? What had she done to provoke such antagonism in her son? My curiosity was aroused. It got the better of me.

"She doesn't live here, does she?" I asked as a preliminary to the many questions I wished to ask.

I was astounded by his reply.

"No, and she never will again, if I have anything to do with it."

"That's terrible!" I exclaimed. "To deny your own mother access to her home. . . ."

"It ceased to be that the day she walked out."

"Walked out?"

"Oh, it's a common enough story. Woman leaves man. Man goes in search of woman. Man dies searching. It happens all the time."

"Oh . . . I'm sorry."

96

"Never put your faith in human beings, Miss Wentworth. They will always let you down—one way or another."

He swung away from me and I watched him go, a lonely, embittered man with only his dogs for company. I felt a wave of compassion for the man wash over me. He was a man alone. He had loved two women, his mother and Caroline, and both had left him. He was unable to forgive either of them, and it had soured his soul.

Why had his mother walked out on his father—and on him? I could only guess at the reason. But the reason did not matter. What was important was that it had resulted in his father's untimely death. I could understand that he might blame her for it, but how long could he carry on a hatred so unnatural? She was his mother, after all was said and done. How old had he been at the time? A young man? A youth? A child? Again, what did it matter? It was the effect it had had on him that mattered.

And then there was Caroline. She had walked out on him just when, in his own happiness, he might have been expected to forgive his mother's errant ways, and his bitterness had been compounded. It had resulted in the molding of the man I knew: a cold, harsh, unfeeling man. And yet he was vulnerable. Somewhere, deeply hidden within him, was a cavern of pain. I had sensed it. I had seen it plainly in the anguish behind his eyes.

Or was it simply an open sore, unhealed because he would not allow it to heal? Was I crediting him with more sensitivity than he actually possessed?

Perhaps it was only an echo of what had once been. Perhaps there was no softness left in him. Perhaps what his mother had started, Caroline, the woman he had adored and wished to marry, had finished. Perhaps he held women in such little esteem because of them. Neither of them had given him cause to view the female sex in a kindly light.

But that he should allow the grudge he bore these two women to so erode his personality that he had become a different man! I could not understand it. He was not the only one such things happened to. I myself had suffered a terrible experience. I could have allowed it to change me, to turn me against men forever. I brought myself up sharply. Was not that exactly what I had done? No, I told myself. It had made me wary, suspicious of men, and I had believed for a time they were all tarred with the same brush, but I no longer thought so. When Justin had caught me in his arms on my headlong flight from the High Plateau, I had not recoiled from him. On the contrary, I had melted against him. I had felt safe and secure in his arms. I had . . .

But that was no road to wander along.

I hurried to my room and to my bed.

The following morning there was a letter in the mail addressed to The Master of Penrose. It was unusual for a letter to be addressed so, and it was in a decidedly feminine hand. It also exuded a delicate perfume. My heart skipped a beat. Was it from a lady friend? It skipped several more. Was Caroline attempting a reconciliation?

Or was it from some other lady?

Common sense told me it was from some other lady. Many women saw themselves as one of his heroines and wrote to him in such a manner that their letters brought a blush to my cheeks as, in my capacity of secretary, I read them. Thankfully, he did not read them; early on he had instructed me to reply to them myself, using a standard reply originated by him a long, long time ago. And as I learned to recognize them, I did not bother to read them either, the name and address of the person writing and the book in question providing sufficient information. Letters of a more serious nature, of course, received attention from Justin Penrose, or James St. Just, himself.

This letter, I was certain, fell into neither category. It did not proclaim itself to be Private and Confidential, but it was addressed to The Master of Penrose, and I hesitated to open it.

In the end, I set it down unopened on his desk.

He saw it as soon as he came in. Betraying no emotion, he pushed it to one side as he sat down and started dictation. It was still there, unopened, when I went back to my office. It was still there in the same position when I returned with his letters for signature. I looked down at it with a furrowed brow. What was it? Who was it from? Why hadn't he opened it? Why was I so concerned?

A sound from the fireplace drew my attention. Unusually for him, he had remained in the library and was sitting in one of the armchairs surrounded by sheets of paper, some crumpled, some not. He rose and crossed to the desk.

"Don't go," he said. "I'll sign them straightaway."

He did not bother to read them through, which pleased me. It meant he was satisfied with my work and no longer saw the need to check it.

I watched him scrawl his almost indecipherable signature across each page and thought how familiar it had become. I looked down on his dark head, at his hair beginning to silver at the temples, at the ridged forehead. The lines seemed softer, as if some of the tension endemic within him had lessened, and his lips beneath the hawklike nose were not so tightly held together as usual. In fact, and I caught my breath in sudden emotion, they betrayed a sensual fullness, a curve rarely seen. He was like the man I had supped with the night before—before I had started asking my questions.

He had signed the last letter and, looking up, caught me off guard. I lowered my eyes quickly, afraid of what he might see there. What should he see there? Nothing that I need be afraid of. Nevertheless, my eyelids did not lift.

"Right," he said, "that's the lot," and handed them to me. "Oh, before you go . . . I've got some more notes for you to type. There's no hurry, but if you could let me have them back by this evening . . ."

He smiled. Why did my heart rock suddenly?

"Yes, of course," I said.

99

"I'm off for a walk now. . . ."

He paused, looking at me strangely. I had the feeling he wanted to ask me to accompany him. But as the pause lengthened, I grew uncomfortable and asked, "What time will you be back?"

"Late afternoon, I should think."

He started to go. I didn't want him to. Without thinking, I called out, "Oh, Mr. Penrose . . ."

"Yes?" He turned quickly, eagerly. But what had I intended saying?

"This letter," I picked up the sweetly scented envelope that had been so persistently ignored by him, and held it out. "Aren't you going to open it?"

Creases appeared on his forehead. "No. I know what's in it."

"Would you like me to deal with it?"

"No." He relieved me of it and stuffed it into his trouser pocket. "I'll deal with it in my own time, thank you. See you at supper."

My reference to the letter had annoyed him. I wondered why, but did not dwell on it. What was the point when I could not come up with an answer? Besides . . . there was supper to think about. Supper with *him*.

I made a start on the notes until the clock hands crept round to pass the hour of noon. I then set them aside and went to join Mrs. Carthew for our midday meal.

She was not in her parlor when I presented myself, so I settled down to wait, not expecting her to be long. While I waited, I glanced round the homely room. It was stocked with ornaments and knickknacks, pictures and photographs. Hitherto I had not liked to look too closely at these, but with Mrs. Carthew away, I took the opportunity to study them more carefully. Some of the ornaments were of exceptional quality: Dresden china ladies and gentlemen in fine period costume; little groups of animals, birds, and the like; carved wooden animals and little trinket boxes. Many of them were of foreign origin. Mrs. Carthew could surely not have traveled to collect

100

them. Were they gifts from her employer? Probably. I knew he had a high regard for her. This might be his way of showing his appreciation.

I looked at the pictures. They were very fine. One or two were childish daubs—framed and obviously greatly valued. Justin's?

I looked at the photographs last of all, though they drew me as surely as a snake hypnotizing a prospective victim. I was drawn to the one showing a sleek, white yacht—the Justinia, with its owner proudly at the wheel. Surrounding it were many more photographs, some faded with age. One was of a beautiful lady in the dress of an earlier age. On closer inspection I could see she was an older lady—Justin's grandmother? Most were of Justin himself: Justin much younger, Justin as a boy, a child. There was no mistaking the granite jaw and high cheekbones, the hawkish nose, in even the youngest child, though the harsh lines had not yet made their appearance on the smooth skin.

His mother had been to blame for the development of those. She had sown the bitter seed from which they had grown, and Caroline had fed and watered it. As I looked into the face of the innocent young child, I was more than ready to blame both women, and to excuse the black moods and angry silences of the mature man. If they had been less selfish, he would have been a different man. He would have been the man Ruth had told me about.

I was alerted to look out of the open window by the sound of hooves. Justin, on Ebony, was reining to a halt in the courtyard below. His housekeeper, tiny beside the magnificent stallion, raised her anxious face and appeared to be beseeching Justin to do something, or not to do something, I could not be sure which. His reply was vehement, his face livid, as he swung down to stand beside her. But she continued to argue, and he grew more and more angry. He attempted to remount. She caught hold of his booted leg. He looked down at her hand, wrathfully prepared to shake it off, then his anger seemed to collapse and he gave a rueful shake of his head. "Oh, Carty," I heard him say, for I was half out of the window by now, "if only . . ."

My gaze was fixed on his face and suddenly, as if grown aware of it, he looked up at me. There was no point in drawing back, as instinct prompted me to do; he had seen me quite clearly. So I braved it out, smiling and waving, trying to appear as if I had only just that moment looked out of the window and had seen nothing of their strange encounter.

I received no answering smile from him, no salute, only a dour, dark look. Mrs Carthew, who had followed his gaze, assumed a look as black as his own.

I drew back, my smile grown tight on my face. They immediately discounted me. Justin leapt upon his horse and rode away, Mrs. Carthew's renewed exhortations in his ears. He shot off across the daisy-dappled fields, anger in every line of him.

I could not keep pace with his moods. Only a short time ago, he had been calm, easy, and, though annoyed by my reference to the scented letter, he had more or less invited me to sup with him again. Did that invitation still stand? I wondered. If the mood he was in persisted, I thought it would not. Ah well, it was no more than I could expect. I might make excuses for his moods, having learned something of his background, but the fact remained that, whatever he might once have been, he was now an irascible, flint-hearted, bad-tempered misogynist. I would forget this at my own peril. I had seen the hate in his eyes as he had looked up at me just now, and I did not think it was solely on account of my resemblance to Caroline, which was slight anyway, according to Ruth. It was because I was a woman—and he hated all women.

I was being stretched two ways. On the one hand, I wanted to stay on the island and work for Justin Penrose because it was as far away from Ted Gibbon as I could get, and because the work was interesting. On the other hand, there was an unease in me that I found hard to suppress, so that I sometimes thought I should be glad when the time came for me to leave.

I was worried about so many things. I worried about the resentment of the islanders. I believed it had lessened, but it was still there. I worried about my employer's wildly seesawing moods, his hatred of women, his bitterness toward his mother, and his inability to forgive her for inadvertently causing the death of his father. Or did, perhaps, his antipathy stem from a different cause? Did the fact that she had left *him*, her only child, weigh more heavily than the death of his father? Did he use his father's death as the excuse for not facing up to the truth, that his mother had loved someone else more than him?

Then there was Caroline. He hated Caroline for jilting him. I remembered something Ruth had said to me. *"He's a man who does not love lightly,"* and the truism, *Love is akin to hate*, sprang to my mind. Did the strength of his hatred betoken the strength of his love? I hoped I should never love so strongly.

I hoped I should never be put to the test.

Then there was John Trevelyan's warning to me. Overheard snippets of conversation that had seemed full of threat. Mrs. Carthew's mysterious hints and deliberate evasion of my questions. All things to worry about.

Then there was the island itself. The lovely, lonely island of Penrose, which seemed to carry in its heart an anguish I could identify with, yet felt threatened by.

Was I being fanciful?

My father would have said I was.

Perhaps I was.

And yet . . .

Oh, how I longed to be safe at home with my mother—only Ted Gibbon was there, and he was a greater evil than any I might face here. Evil? What evil? That something I sensed but could not put a name to?

Before I was carried completely away on the wings of fancy, the housekeeper's homely little body walked in. She did not refer to the scene I had just witnessed, and we ate our meal in almost total silence, I very much aware of the tension. I escaped from her as soon as I could.

103

I took the dogs for a walk as Justin Penrose had, for once, left them behind. It was nearly four o'clock. I had finished the work he had given me and I thought, as school would soon be out, Ruth would be free to talk to me. Mrs. Carthew had made a mystery out of Mrs. Penrose, and I wanted Ruth to clear it up for me. She was a down-to-earth Englishwoman, not given to mystic fancies like the fey Cornish islanders—or like me, blessed, or cursed, with an imagination I persisted in allowing to run away with me. From her I would learn the truth about Clara Penrose. I would discover why she had left her husband, and reach a firmer conclusion concerning Justin's bitterness toward her.

But Ruth knew no more about Mrs. Penrose than I did.

"It all happened long before I came here," she said. "I was curious like you, and made enquiries. But they're a closed-mouth lot, these Penrose Islanders. Even Dora Trevose kept silent on the subject. Perhaps there was nothing to tell."

"Or perhaps it was too scandalous to talk about."

"You think she ran off with another man?"

"Don't you?"

"It's the most likely explanation."

She gave me tea while Betsy and Winnie rested just outside the open door, wearied by their exertions chasing rabbits, birds, and each other. Then, leaving her to mark a pile of exercise books and prepare the following day's work, the three of us started back across the hills toward Penrose House.

I was hailed by John Trevelyan riding his chestnut mare.

"Hello, Nicola."

"Hello, John. How nice to see you again."

"Yes, it's quite a while since we've seen each other, isn't it? And I promised to show you round the island. But I've been so busy. It's amazing, I can go weeks without seeing a single patient, then all at once everybody seems to have something wrong with them."

"I've seen quite a bit of the island already. I have a lot of free time."

"Yes, I've noticed you running across the hills like some fairy sprite with those two bitches of Justin's dancing around you like a couple of familiars."

"Oh, John," I laughed, "only witches have familiars."

He smiled down at me, a curious stillness about him. "Well, I do believe there is something of the witch in you, my dear, with your eyes of captivating blue and your hair like strands of silver. Oh, yes, I think there is a lot of the witch in you."

A sudden shiver ran down my spine. He had been teasing me earlier, but now a disturbing element had crept in, and I felt our easy friendship tremble.

But then he sat up straight on his horse and looked out to sea.

"I see the *Justinia*'s going out."

"The *Justinia*?" I followed his gaze and saw Justin's gleaming white yacht leaving the harbor.

"Beautiful, isn't she? Named after his grandmother, you know."

"Yes, Mrs. Carthew told me."

"Has he offered to take you out in her yet?"

"No. I'm not sure I'd want to go if he did."

"Why not?" He subjected me to a long hard stare. "Don't you like sailing?"

"My last encounter with the sea was not a very pleasant one," I said wryly.

"Ah, yes, I was forgetting. You came with the Black Wind, didn't you? But look at the sea today. Calm as a millpond. And Justin's too good a sailor and judge of weather ever to set sail when a storm is brewing. However, I doubt he'll even invite you aboard his precious boat, let alone take you out in it." Again there was in his voice that certain criticism of his friend which I found repellent. It might show how well he knew his friend, but it also showed a flaw in his nature and I was sorry to see it there. "Well, I must be off. I've got another call to make before I can relax. What about meeting tomorrow? I'll call for you. About ten o'clock?"

"No, I'm sorry. I can't. It . . . it's too short notice."

"Oh." His face creased into an uncharacteristic frown. "I'm disappointed. I was looking forward to—"

"It's just that Mr. Penrose has started work on a new book, and I'm not sure when I'm going to be free."

"Oh." He still looked disappointed.

"Perhaps . . . you'll ask me again."

"Yes, I'll do that."

His face cleared. He spurred his horse and waved goodbye. I watched him ride away, in a topsy-turvy state of mind. I would have liked to go out with him. I knew he was attracted to me . . . and I liked him . . . The danger of the situation added a certain spice; I was surprised to find I was not afraid of that. He sat his horse well. I loved the way the breeze rippled his hair. But, as if drawn by an invisible string, my head was jerked away from him back to the *Justinia* riding the waves, and John's words ran through my brain. *"Has he offered to take you out in her yet?"*

What would my answer be if he did? It would be yes, no doubt about it. Calm or wild the sea, I would go with him.

My answer disturbed me. I thrust it away from me. I had not meant it. I would never go with Justin Penrose anywhere. Never.

I strode across the hills to Penrose House and turned my thoughts to John. If only I could go out with him tomorrow. But how could I? I had work to do. Justin Penrose was working on a new book and I must be on hand.

Hot and dusty, I headed straight for my room. The dogs flopped down in the hall. I wondered what I should wear for supper that night. Something less severe than my everyday secretarial garb. Nothing too elaborate, of course. Nothing that would lead my employer into thinking I was trying to impress him. I had a pretty lemon-colored cotton dress which . . .

I caught my breath in dismay and went weak at the knees. My room was empty, swept clean of all my possessions. I might never have been there. What did it mean? What had happened to all my things? Seized by a sudden panic, I lunged out of the room and went racing down the stairs calling out excitedly.

"Mrs. Carthew! Mrs. Carthew! Mrs. Carthew!"

She came hurrying into the hall. "What is it, m'dear? What be wrong?"

I almost fell into her arms. "Oh, Mrs. Carthew, thank goodness. I had begun to fear you did not exist. That this was all a dream."

"Calm yourself, m'dear, and tell me what's wrong. 'Tis piskie-mazed 'ee be, to be sure."

"Oh, Mrs. Carthew, all my things are gone. My room's empty."

"'Tis nothin' to fret over, m'dear. They've been moved, that's all."

"Moved? Where to?"

"Master Justin says to move 'ee to a room more fitting for a lady—as you'm staying."

Her round brown eyes censured me. She had not wanted me to stay in the first place. She did not want me to stay now.

My heart still beating anxiously, I followed back up the stairs and round the gallery, not at all certain she was not leading me to my doom. But when she opened a door and bade me enter, my heart assumed a different beat.

I walked into a room as elegantly furnished as any I had ever seen. Not that this was the first time I had seen it; Justin Penrose himself had shown it to me on our tour of inspection and I had enthused over it at the time. The color scheme of ivory, pastel green, and rich apricot had delighted me. And I knew that beyond a white door with golden filigree was a bedroom all white and rose, with a canopied four-poster bed and a dressing table covered with flounces of white lace. Beyond that lay a bathroom, pink and white to match, with shell-shaped accoutrements.

I had commented ecstatically on the apartment when he had shown it to me. He had given no sign that he had taken particular note of what I said—but he must have.

What a strange man he was. How complex, how contradictory was his nature. He could be harsh, boorish, tyrannical, and at the same time kind, thoughtful, caring. These latter qualities he had shown Ruth in abundance in his dealings with her, and she loved him for it. He was kind to his housekeeper and she obviously adored him.

But I could not feel that way about him. He had shown me far too much of the dark side of his nature for me to feel anything other than animosity toward him.

Yet was I being fair to him? He had shown me kindness by acceding to my request to stay on the island despite reluctance on his part. He had allowed me to stay because he had seen my need for it. Later he had offered me permanent employment— for his own convenience. I was not fooled on that score. But now there was this, a beautiful apartment given to me for my own use.

For how long? I wondered, reluctant to give him too much credit. For as long as it pleased him and no longer. I only hoped it would be long enough for me to recover from the trauma Ted Gibbon had inflicted on me. Only then could I face the world with equanimity again.

"Susan has unpacked for 'ee. Everything's as it should be."

There was still censure in Mrs. Carthew's eyes. She did not approve of this further evidence of my continued residence at Penrose House. Would she ever accept it? Would she ever accept me? Though her attitude had changed since that first day, it was still tinged with reserve. She still gave me the impression she would rather I were gone.

However, in spite of her, in spite of everything, I was to remain, safe and secure, on this enchanted island, for the foreseeable future.

Chapter Six

I did not sup with Justin Penrose that night for the simple reason that he had sailed away from the island. Even now, the *Justinia* was carrying him over the waves on the first lap of his journey to London to visit his publisher . . . and his mother.

It annoyed me that he had not seen fit to inform me of his plans, but then Mrs. Carthew told me how he had asked for me. When I was not to be found, he had left instructions for me to deal with his correspondence during his absence.

"'Anything you can't manage,' he said," Mrs. Carthew said to me, "'Leave on one side till my return.' He has every faith in your capabilities, m'dear. He says you'm turnin' out to be a treasure."

I went to bed with a light heart and a feeling of irrepressible joy. A treasure! Surely that meant I was here to stay!

I missed Justin Penrose. Like him or not, it was impossible not to be affected by his personality. His absence left a void. Everyone felt it. Betsy and Winnie, after moping for hours, attached themselves to me and became my constant companions. I had a lot of time on my hands after dealing with the mail, and spent a great deal of it tramping the hills with them.

But I could not spend all my time traipsing round the island. I needed something more to help me fill the hours, some task to occupy myself with.

I decided to give the library a spring cleaning.

"Can I have Susan or Sally to help me?" I asked Mrs. Carthew.

She threw up her hands and slapped them down on thighs in her characteristic manner. "Lordy, lordy," she protested, "there be no call for 'ee to soil your hands with such work." Her lips tightened with aggravation.

"But I'd like to. . . ."

"'Tis not necessary. Things is regularly dusted and polished in 'ere. I see to that."

"But you're not allowed to touch his papers or books."

"Your job be to keep his books tidy and do his secretarial work. Housekeepin', cleanin's my responsibility."

I could see I had trodden on her toes and tried to explain, but the more I apologized and tried to make amends, the tighter her lips drew together in unconscious imitation of her master's.

There was no point in arguing further. I went for another walk.

Betsy and Winnie raced ahead of me, joyously carefree, creatures living for the moment. I started to run, joining them in their carefree abandonment to the soft pure air, till out of breath, I came to a halt beside the little Celtic church.

From where I stood, I could look down on the harbor, the cottages, the little knots of people chatting together, others busy in their gardens, some just sitting by their doorsteps soaking up the summer sun. Nets were being mended on the quayside. I could see piles of baskets—they looked tiny from this height, but I knew they were quite large and were used to trap the lobsters and crabs which abounded in the surrounding waters. Suddenly, children swarmed out of the schoolhouse. Lessons were over for the day. I toyed with the idea of visiting Ruth. It would be pleasant to take tea with her, and she was always glad to see me.

"Hello. Where have you been hiding yourself these past few days?" she called out when I appeared in her open doorway.

"Mr. Penrose has gone to London and I've been left to deal

with all his mail," I said proudly.

"He's gone to see his mother, I believe?"

"Yes . . . and his publisher. But how did you know? Oh, of course, don't tell me. . . . Nothing can be kept secret on this island for long."

"As a matter of fact, John told me."

"Oh?"

I did not know why I should be so surprised. John was Justin's friend and, as such, would be privy to his doings. Perhaps I was surprised he had not thought to mention it to me when we had seen the *Justinia* sailing away. Perhaps I was surprised he should tell Ruth and not me. But then, he and Ruth had been acquainted for a long time. It was only natural he should tell her. So why should I be so surprised?

"He's worried about her health." Ruth put the kettle on and busied herself with the teacups. "He thinks it would do her a tremendous amount of good if she could spend a few weeks on the island."

"Justin won't have her here."

Ruth smiled. "He may say that, but I'm sure he'll give in in the end. Once he sees her, he won't be able to hold out. She can twist him round her little finger."

"How do you know? You said you knew nothing about her."

"John told me." She turned from me to reach for the tea caddy, and as she scooped tea into the pot, the smile still played around her lips. "Anyway, he's such an old softy. He's incapable of turning his back on anyone in trouble."

The kettle boiled. She poured the water onto the tea and placed a woolen cosy over the pot. She said abruptly, "John likes you. How do you feel about him?"

"I . . ."

Her bright eyes were on me. "You could do a lot worse, you know, than to take him."

"But—"

"Oh, I know you want, or think you want, a career, but as I said to you at the start of our friendship, I think you'd be

111

happier as a wife and mother. And when all's said and done, isn't that what we all want, deep in our hearts? In any case, John's not the sort of man to keep his wife chained to the kitchen sink."

"Has . . . has John been talking to you about me?" I frowned, annoyed to think I might be the subject of such a discussion.

"He didn't need to. I saw it plainly enough, and when I tackled him about it, he admitted it. Oh, Nicola, don't let life pass you by. Grab at happiness with both hands. Don't finish up like me."

"But I thought you were happy teaching."

"Oh, yes, teaching other people's children. But where are *my* babies? The ones I'll never have? Where is the man to cherish me for the rest of my days? Look at me, Nicola, an aging spinster. Look at me and be warned."

I returned to Penrose House by way of the church. I felt I needed to go in there, to sit in its quiet interior and sort out my thoughts. There were so many questions in my mind to which I could find no answer. Perhaps if I knelt and asked for guidance . . .

"Nicola."

I had heard the footsteps coming along the aisle and when they stopped beside me, my heartbeat had quickened and I was afraid to look up. Now, at the sound of John's voice, I gazed up in relief.

"Oh, John, it's you!"

"Forgive me if I startled you, but I was worried. I saw you come in here, and waited outside, not wishing to disturb you, but when so much time went by . . ."

I glanced at my watch. "Good gracious, is that the time? Betsy and Winnie must be worried to death about me."

John gave a mirthless laugh. "You don't really believe them capable of worrying, do you? That requires thought, and dogs have no such power at their command."

"How do you know?" I responded teasingly. "How does

anyone know?"

"Don't grant them qualities they don't possess, Nicola."

"They have senses, instincts more finely tuned than any human's."

"Granted. But they're not human beings. They're animals. They were wolves in the wild, hunted and shot by man. They're just the same underneath. Living in close habitation with man has not changed them."

"It has." I was arguing seriously now. "Betsy and Winnie are nothing like wolves. They *are* different. They are household pets. Justin loves them."

"Oh, well, in that case," he said with sarcastic mien, "there's nothing more to be said."

We had reached the doorway and the animals in question rushed up to us, barking excitedly.

"Down!" John snapped angrily, but they were not interested in him. It was me they were eager to greet with loving tongues and wagging tails.

"Damn nuisances!" John declared forcibly.

"I can see you're not a dog-lover," I said.

"No. I prefer cats. They're more dignified. I have two at home."

Home! I felt a twinge of the heart. "I had a cat," I said. "I miss her."

I was aware of him looking at me for a few moments in silent contemplation. Then he said, "Come and have dinner with me at Peacehaven and I'll introduce you to mine."

"Peacehaven? What a lovely name."

"It's a lovely house. Built for the sister of an eighteenth-century Penrose to inhabit. She and his wife did not get on, and their incessant quarreling nearly drove him out of his mind. So, despite her protestations that she could never live away from Penrose House, which had always been her home, he had Peacehaven built at the other side of the island. He sent her to live there with instructions never to set foot in Penrose House again. She died within three months of taking up residence

113

there—of heartbreak and loneliness, the islanders say."

"What a sad little story," I murmured.

"Probably not true. Not completely true, anyway. You know how time and telling can distort truth. Come, you can meet my cats and I'll show you the house."

"No, I can't. I'd love to, but Mrs. Carthew will be wondering what has become of me. And she," I added mischievously, "*is* a human being."

"Are you sure about that?" His tone was serious.

"What do you mean?"

"Well, don't you think she has the look of a pisky? An elderly pisky? An elderly, wicked pisky?"

"Oh, John! You're teasing!" I laughed, but it was a shaky laugh, for I had thought of Mrs. Carthew in very much that same way, on more than one occasion.

"Am I?" he said. Then he laughed too. "Well, if you won't come with me now, meet me tomorrow and we'll make a day of it. A picnic by the sea, a drive round the island, and dinner at Peacehaven with music to follow. I have a fine collection of gramophone records."

"It's very tempting," I said. "But I can't possibly spend the whole day with you. I've work to do."

"Nothing that can't wait, surely. Come on, Nicola, be a devil."

The temptation was strong.

I succumbed.

The day dawned bright and sunny. I dressed coolly in blue and white striped cotton, and breakfasted in a lighthearted frame of mind. I was looking forward to my outing with John, and was eager to see his house, Peacehaven, with its sad, but romantic, history.

There was nothing romantic between John and myself. I did not wish there to be. But I liked him and knew he liked me. I was very aware that he admired me; still, he never did or said anything out of place. He was my friend and I trusted him. But, as I waited for him to arrive and saw the minutes tick past the time he was due, building beyond that time to add an hour, two hours, and more, I realized he would not come. He had forgotten our arrangement.

On a wave of disappointment, I attacked the mail which I had set aside to wait for the morrow and pounded the typewriter keys with savagery. I had been looking forward so much to seeing John again, to sharing his company. I dashed away the angry tears that sprang to my eyes as Mrs. Carthew knocked on my door and entered with a tray of coffee and biscuits.

"He 'ent come, then?" she said with a quick, penetrating glance.

"No."

She gave one of her disapproving sniffs. "I knew 'ee'd be disappointed. He'm not to be relied upon."

She would have continued if at that moment a cheery voice had not hailed us from the doorway. "Hello. I'm sorry I'm late."

"Only by about two and a half hours," I said coldly.

John grimaced sheepishly. "Forgive me, Nicola. I should have sent a message, but to tell you the truth, I never gave it a thought. I've been so busy getting Jackie Prudoe off to hospital—"

"Jackie!" I knew Jackie Prudoe. He was a dear little lad of about seven who ran up to take my hand whenever he saw me. I was immediately concerned. "What's happened? What's the matter with him?"

"Scarlet fever. He had to be isolated. Then I had to see about the fumigating of Mrs. Prudoe's house and call in at the school and examine all the children. Can't be too careful with scarlet fever. It's highly infectious."

"Oh, the poor little mite!"

"Don't worry about him. He'll be all right. But am I forgiven?"

"Of course. Need you ask?"

"Well, what about a cup of coffee then? I'm parched."

"Oh, Mrs. Carthew, will you bring another cup, please?"

Mrs. Carthew's eyes narrowed and her lips compressed. She was not impressed by the doctor's explanation. She departed to carry out my wishes, her plump little body registering complete disapproval.

I did not know how to look at John, for he must have been aware of Mrs. Carthew's disapproval. It was almost as if she did not believe his excuse. Then I heard his chuckle and wry comment. "A *cross*, elderly pisky."

I laughed in spite of myself. John could always make me laugh.

"She doesn't like me, you know," he said then.

"Oh, I'm sure she does," I murmured uncomfortably, for I felt he was right.

"It's true. We don't hit it off. Never have. She knows I see through her."

"What do you mean?"

He hesitated for a moment and I thought he was not going to answer my question, but then he gave a short, derisive laugh and said, "She's jealous of me."

"Jealous? Why?"

"She sees me as a threat."

"To what?"

"To her power over Justin."

"I can't believe you're serious."

"I am. She'd have me off the island, if she could."

The conversation was getting beyond me. But he *seemed* serious.

"Justin and I have become very close over the past couple of years, and she can't accept it. She resents me. Looks on me as an interloper. I'm Cornish, as Cornish as she, but I wasn't born on the island and anybody not born on Penrose . . . Well, you know how it is."

We shared a few moments of reflective silence together.

116

"The trouble is, she's worked at Penrose all her life, as far back as anyone can remember, and she behaves as if the place belongs to her. Runs it as if she owns it—and Justin lets her have a free hand. I think he's wrong to do so. I've told him so, and she knows it. But she was his nurse and he adores her. She still treats him like a small boy. Tries to order his life. And he lets her get away with it."

I could not imagine anyone ordering Justin Penrose about, but then I remembered the scene in the garden. She had certainly seemed to be giving him orders then, and he had appeared to defer to them. True, he had swung away from her and ridden angrily away—but that had been because he had seen me watching them from the window.

Mrs. Carthew sent Mary with the extra cup. John gave me a significant glance. "See?" it said.

"Where did you live in Cornwall, John?" I asked him as I poured out the coffee.

"I was born in Truro, but I was brought up in London. We used to visit Cornwall often, my mother and I. My father couldn't be bothered. He died before I was ten. I didn't miss him. I didn't really like him. He wasn't good enough for my mother."

He broke off and I searched for something else to say, something to take his mind off what appeared to be unhappy memories. But then he spoke again.

"I remember she took me to Port Zennoc, I can't have been more than about five at the time, but I remember it clearly. We stood on the cliffs looking out across the sea. There was a great mound in the distance. 'That's Penrose Island,' she said to me, and as I looked at it, it seemed to cast a spell over me. . . . I could not get the sight of that island out of my mind. In later years, I came as often as I could . . . just to stand there looking at it rising out of the sea like . . . like . . ."

"Like some gigantic slug," I breathed, quite carried away.

His eyes, which had taken on a faraway expression, came to rest on me in astonishment.

117

"That's what it reminded me of when I first set eyes on it," I explained.

"Nicola! How could you! A slug! Of all things!" I could not make up my mind whether he was amused or angry. Then his eyes took on that faraway expression again. "To me it was a magic land. As a boy, I believed all the Knights of the Round Table lived there, with King Arthur presiding and Merlin forever casting spells. I used to imagine I was one of those knights. I had been sent out on a quest and was not allowed to return till I had succeeded in my quest.

"You smile. A childish fancy, you think. But I'm Cornish, you see, and we Cornish know that the past is ever-present. It is here with us now, in the future, always. And we believe in King Arthur. We don't believe he is dead—only sleeping, waiting for the day when his people will need him again. On that day he will rise in all his power and wisdom, and fight for them as of yore."

"You sound exactly like Justin—Mr. Penrose—telling a story," I declared.

"That's not surprising," he laughed, "seeing as I lifted that little flourish from one of his histories—*Arthur, King of Cornwall.* You should read it sometime. It's well worth it."

"It sounds fascinating," I said. "I thought history as dry as dust at school, but this—"

"You must have been unlucky in your teachers," he said.

"How did you . . . ?" I hesitated, afraid I was being too nosy again, but he picked up my unfinished question and answered easily.

"Come to be here? It was all Justin's doing. We were introduced at a party. The fact that we were both Cornishmen in a roomful of English drew us together, and we were soon in conversation. We hit it off at once. You know the way people do sometimes. The way we did, Nicola. And he's such a good listener. . . . Have you found that? I was soon unburdening myself of all my troubles. It did me good.

"I was at a low ebb at that time. Everything seemed to be

118

working against me. The woman I had proposed to had turned me down. I had been by-passed for a consultancy at the hospital where I worked. In consequence of that, I had applied for a number of posts higher up the scale at lots of other hospitals, without any luck. I was considering emigrating to America, the land of opportunity—I needed an opportunity, and there was one for me here. I told him this, and more besides.

"I poured everything that had been festering inside me out to this man I had just met and who listened so sympathetically. When we parted, I didn't expect we should meet again. He was one of those ships that pass in the night. A stranger. If he had not been, I doubt I should have opened up to him the way I did. However, I received a telephone call from him the following day asking me to meet him at his club. He said he had something which might be of interest to me.

"We lunched together, and I found him as easy to talk to as I had the night before, but he didn't touch on that 'something which might be of interest to me' till the meal was over. Then he staggered me by offering me a doctor's practice on Penrose Island.

"Apparently Walter Pengelly, the island's doctor for many years, was getting old. His eyesight was failing and he was becoming more and more troubled with arthritis. Would I mind going as his assistant with the idea that, as soon as he could be persuaded to retire, I should take over? And, as if that wasn't enough, there was a small hospital.

"Of course I jumped at the offer. I would have accepted any job he had offered me, no matter how menial, if it meant living on the island that had mesmerized me from childhood. This was the end of my quest, and it had come about in the most casual way. It never ceases to amaze me that he, of all the people I could have met and unburdened my soul to, should turn out to be the Master of Penrose Island. *My* island, as I had grown used to thinking of it since a very small boy. He was King Arthur and I was his knight."

"Isn't it strange how things happen?" I said. "Just when you were in desperate need of help, you met Mr. Penrose. It was the same with Ruth Norman. She was in a similar situation when she met Mr. Penrose. The schoolteacher on the island had retired, and he offered Ruth the job. I . . ."

"You?"

"I needed a job too. He was in need of a secretary and, after a bit of persuasion, he gave the position to me. It's odd, isn't it? It's as if there were a guiding hand somewhere."

"A divine guiding hand, you mean? Yes, you could be right. . . . I'm sure you're right."

There was silence between us for a while as we pondered these things. Then he laughed and cried out, "How serious we are. And on such a lovely day. We should be out having fun. Come. Let's go."

He caught hold of my hand and ran with me to the door. We were in high spirits as we dashed into the hall. Mrs. Carthew glowered at us as she descended the stairs. I called out to her my plans and told her not to expect me back for supper as I would be eating at Peacehaven.

She glowered more fiercely than ever, and I couldn't help thinking that she must have been taking lessons from Justin Penrose, whose line in scowls was not to be beaten.

"See, I told you she doesn't like me," John whispered loudly. "She probably thinks I'm about to abduct you."

"Hush!" I hissed. "She'll hear you." But I smiled nevertheless. His humor was so outrageous. I did not think he cared if she did hear. He probably meant her to.

A pony and trap waited outside the door. We boarded it.

"We really ought to go on horseback," John said as the pony broke into a trot. "You see the island much better that way. A horse can go where a vehicle cannot."

"Oh, I don't mind," I responded. "In fact, I'd rather travel this way. I must confess, I don't care for riding. I was put in the saddle when I was very young, and I was terrified. It seemed so far from the ground. I started to scream and the poor animal, frightened by it, promptly threw me. I fractured my arm. I've had a fear of horses ever since."

"Really? What a pity. You should have been made to mount again at the earliest opportunity. There's nothing in the world to touch the thrill of sitting a high-stepping horse. The feeling of freedom and power it gives one, riding high above everyone and everything. It makes you feel like a king. Or, in your case, a queen."

He urged the pony to a faster pace and I thought, as I glanced at him sitting beside me, straight-backed and proud-headed, *and you look like a king—or at least a prince, with your head held high; your handsome head.*

It was a handsome head. He was a very handsome man, with his thick, black, wavy hair and large blue eyes fringed by their long, curly lashes. He was nice, too, and very amusing.

He became aware of my observance and turned to me with a quizzical smile.

"Where are you taking me?" I asked, hiding my embarrassment by gazing airily about me.

"Don't you recognize anything?"

"No."

"I told you there was a lot you hadn't seen."

"Yes. But where are we?"

"Nearing the west coast. There's a little cove, sheltered from the wind. Safe for bathing. We'll picnic there."

"Oh, good."

"Afterwards we can bathe together."

I gaped at him in sudden alarm. "We can't bathe together. I haven't brought a swimming costume."

"Well, there'll be no one around to see."

"John!" I was scandalized, bitterly disappointed in him. I had never expected this of him.

He grinned at me wickedly. "Relax," he said. "I was only teasing."

"Oh." I swallowed my anxiety. "I'm sorry, I . . ."

He looked suddenly concerned. "You didn't think I meant it?"

"No. No, of course not."

121

"You did! Oh, Nicola, forgive me. I have the damnedest sense of humor. I thought you must have realized that by now. I promise I'll try to be more circumspect in the future."

But he could not remain serious for long—already his eyes were twinkling and the corners of his mouth were reaching upward. I began to laugh. I could not help myself. He laughed with me.

"I thought we'd picnic on the sands," he said, happy again. "Then I'll take you to see . . . but I shan't tell you. Let it come as a surprise."

We trotted on. I thought how silly I had been to credit him with unworthy thoughts. How ready I was, still, to think the worst of men.

"You obviously know the island well," I said. "How long have you lived here?"

"Three years come September."

"You knew Caroline Clunes then?"

He looked at me strangely. "I didn't know you knew about her."

"Ruth told me about her."

"Justin won't thank her for it."

"Why not? What does it matter? In any case, he'll never know. I shan't tell him. . . . Will you?"

"No." He laughed a little at my accusing stare. "You were bound to find out about her sooner or late."

"That's what Ruth said."

"Did she—tell you the whole story?"

"Yes."

He looked hard at me. "Everything?"

"She told me Caroline left Justin Penrose on the eve of their wedding."

"And?"

"And that none of the islanders liked her very much."

"And?"

"That everybody, yourself included, tried to warn him against her because she was no good."

"She's informed you well. Did she also tell you that she

122

was his secretary and that you resemble her to an uncommon degree?"

"Yes. I was glad to hear it in a way. It explained so many things that had been puzzling me. . . . The resentment the islanders held against me. Mr. Penrose's reaction when he first saw me, his antipathy towards me. I could not understand why they disliked me so much when they'd never seen me before. Ruth's explanation cleared that up for me."

"You're not really like her at all," he said, after a moment's silence. "It's only a superficial likeness. After the first glance it's hardly noticeable at all."

"Yes, that's what Ruth said. Why do you think she walked out on him—Caroline?"

"I don't know, unless it was because . . ."

"Because?"

"Well, there's no great mystery about it. She didn't care overmuch for life on the island. It was too quiet for her. It was all right for short stays, holidays, but she liked the bright lights too much to be happy cooped up on a lonely island where every day is the same as the last."

"I can't understand anyone not liking it here."

"She didn't. She tried to persuade Justin to take up residence in London, permanently. But he wouldn't agree to that. There are times when he has to be away from the island, but it's never by choice. He always returns as fast as he can. She came to realize this, and their quarrels about it became more frequent, till at last she couldn't stand it, I suppose. Anyway, whatever the reason, for Justin, it was the best thing that could have happened. But now," he changed his serious mien, "let's stop talking about it. It's ancient history. Let's concentrate on enjoying ourselves."

And we did.

We ate our picnic on the golden sands of Senta Cove— named after one of Justin's long-dead ancestors, John told me. His housekeeper's pastries really were delicious, and with a green salad accompaniment, fine white wine, and little lemony cakes to finish, it was a meal fit for a king.

I had thought I would never again feel at ease alone with a man after Ted Gibbon. Yet here I was in a quiet little cove far from any other person, lying side by side with John Trevelyan, gazing up at the sky completely relaxed, perfectly at ease.

"It's lovely here," I breathed.

"Yes," he said jumping up and pulling me up with him, "but we can't spend any more time idling. There's more to see, much more."

Back in the trap, we climbed higher and higher. The air was heavy with the scent of wildflowers and I drank it in delightedly till, almost surreptitiously, it changed and an acrid pungency had my nose wrinkling in distaste.

"What's that smell?" I asked resentfully.

John laughed. "Wait and see."

A little farther on, he halted the trap and helped me down. We were high up, very high up, on a headland, and the wind blew strongly around us. But it was a warm wind and, although it flapped my skirts and tousled my hair, was not unpleasant.

"Look!" he said. "You can see halfway round the coast from here; all along the west coast and the south coast right to the east where Penrose House proudly stands. It's a sight, isn't it?"

It certainly was a fantastic sight. All along the south coast were little coves and bays, each with a strip of golden sand fringed by lacy foam. I could see the harbor, the little square, people as small as ants. There appeared to be relatively easy descents from the cliffs to the beaches.

The west coast was a different proposition altogether. Here, the cliffs fell sheer and jagged into the sea, and every inaccessible ledge, it seemed, was home to a thousand sea birds. Every spare inch was occupied by squealing, squawking terns and guillemots, and yet the air was filled with flying birds—on the lookout for an empty space? The sea below was turbulent, different from that which lapped the south coast. It pounded at the rocks, eroding them still further, throwing fountains of spume in a vain attempt to wash away the appalling mess made by the birds, but they built too high for the water to reach. The water flowed and eddied, revealing now and then the sharp points of submerged rocks, and I shuddered, wondering how many were hidden just below the surface waiting, lurking, greedy for a diet of ships and men. I was glad Penrose Light stood sentinel.

I turned to John, ready to comment, and was surprised at the elation on his face. His eyes glowed with excitement. He was in his element up here, at one with sea and soaring rock.

Sensing my observation, he swung his gaze to me. "Lovely, isn't it?" he shouted above the noise of wind and birds.

"But treacherous," I declared. "I was just imagining it in a storm. Any ship looking for safe anchorage would never find it here."

He sobered. "You're right. It's a magnificent but vicious coast. There have been many ships wrecked here. There was a terrible incident last year. A passenger ship . . . blown off course. . . . It was dreadful. Women and children screaming. . . . There were no survivors."

He was silent. As a doctor, it must have affected him greatly.

"There was a storm the day I arrived. The Black Wind was blowing, and it was so dark it could have been nighttime, yet it was the middle of the afternoon," I said.

"Ah, yes," he said thoughtfully, "the Black Wind."

"Mrs. Carthew says it's a 'whirly wind.' I think she meant a whirlwind. But that can't be, can it? We don't get whirlwinds in England."

"Not in England, maybe, but in Cornwall . . ."

"But Cornwall is part of England."

He smiled and did not take issue with me, though I could tell he disagreed. To him, perhaps to all Cornishmen, Cornwall was a country of its own, as different and separate from England as Africa or Asia. And he could very well be right.

In fact, he probably was right. From all I knew of the people on this Cornish island, it could very well be so.

"It's strange that you, a newcomer, should have experienced it. I never have. I've heard a lot about it. I'm told it never actually hits the island, just passes it by, but it always presages death or disaster of some kind. The nearer it comes to Penrose, the greater the disaster."

A shiver ran through me. "You surely don't believe such nonsense?"

"Is it nonsense, Nicola?"

"Island superstition, surely?"

"You forget, I'm a Cornishman."

"Well, what about the storm that you were telling me about? That brought death and disaster. Yet it was not the Black Wind that brought it—you said you've never encountered it. So what do you deduce from that?"

"Logic doesn't enter into it," he said.

The pony, rested, greeted our return with a gentle whinny. John helped me to my seat and resumed his. "I suppose you'll be leaving us shortly," he said as he urged the animal forward.

"Oh, didn't you know? It's all been changed. Mr. Penrose wishes me to stay. I thought he might have told you."

"No, he didn't." He kept his eyes on the road, his face set stiffly, as he tried to assimilate the turn of events. Then a smile transformed his features and he said with an admiring glance, "But who can blame him? Certainly not I."

We trotted on apace. "Where to now?" I asked, not recognizing the countryside.

"Peacehaven."

I sat back contentedly, eagerly anticipating my visit to the house that had stirred my imagination.

"I suppose," John reverted back to the subject of my employment, "you'll join him on his business trips abroad?"

"You mean, when he goes to London?" He turned to me with a frown. "Mrs. Carthew considers London 'abroad,'" I explained quickly.

"Mrs. Carthew considers anywhere away from Penrose 'abroad,'" he sneered. "No. I mean, foreign lands. Justin's books and plays are translated into a variety of foreign languages, and he's often required to go on sales tours."

"I see. But I don't think he'll wish to take me with him."

126

"Why not? I should, in his shoes."

I blushed at the open admiration in his eyes, but then he looked back at the road again. A subtle change came over him as he continued, "And his shoes fit me perfectly. I've worn them often."

"I—I don't understand," I said.

"Whenever he's away from the island, I wear them. Then *I* am king."

"King?"

He laughed and turned back to me again. "Regent, then. Justin is King of Penrose, forever and always. Only when he's away, he leaves me in charge. The people have to turn to me in their troubles, turn to me for guidance. I take on Justin's mantle of leader and protector." His smile faded and his eyes grew angry. "It's not quite the same, of course. They do not revere me as they do him. He's a god to them."

I thought this very high-flown, and said so. "That's going a bit far, isn't it? I've noticed they like him tremendously, but—"

"Like him!" John interrupted me angrily. "They worship him. There's not one man, woman, or child on this island who wouldn't go through fire and water for him if asked."

"You're exaggerating," I said tremulously and a little afraid, touched by something I did not understand.

"You think so? Wait till you've been here a bit longer. You'll see it for yourself and will probably end up feeling the same way. I'll tell you this much, there's not much I wouldn't do for him, either."

I laughed somewhat shakily, for there was that in the air which cautioned me to beware of being too skeptical. There was something about this island, these people, that set them apart. Something that set Justin Penrose apart. John knew it. Ruth knew it. I was beginning to know it too. But was it for good—or ill?

It was very late when John drove me home after another delicious meal and an evening of music at the piano. I played,

127

and he sang—he had a fine, melodious voice. We also played records on the gramophone. He had a fine collection of Melba and Caruso.

It was a lovely, starry night with the moon's beams dancing on the water. As we turned up the road leading to Penrose House, John said, "I often wonder as I pass this way how much longer it will be before the sea erodes these cliffs right away and the road vanishes completely."

"That's a long-term prospect, surely?" I shivered as I recalled the west coast's eroded rock face.

"Oh, assuredly," John was quick to reply. "I was just pondering what might happen one day—in the future. Justin has some old maps of the island. He showed them to me once. It's amazing how the coastline has altered over the centuries."

He had now gone back to Peacehaven, and I was facing Mrs. Carthew in the hall. She was glowering, just as she had been when I left her hours ago.

"You'm late," she said.

"I said I would be," I countered. "I said I would be having supper at Peacehaven with Dr. Trevelyan."

With a disapproving sniff she said, "Don't 'ee get too thick wi' that one." She went to bolt and bar the big oaken door.

Chapter Seven

I was asleep, then I was awake. What had awakened me? Carriage wheels? A door banging? I raised my head and listened, nerves taut, heart stilled, ears strained. Voices filtered through to me. High-pitched voices—feminine voices. I recognized a deep, reverberating one which set my heart beating again, loudly into the night's dark.

Justin Penrose had returned.

But who was with him?

Driven by curiosity, I slipped out of bed and out of my room. From the shadowed gallery, I looked down on a little group of people standing in a pool of light. Mrs. Carthew, a white linen nightcap on her head, a voluminous dressing gown tied around her ample middle, was holding aloft a branched candlestick. Justin Penrose, looking bigger and broader than I remembered him, was supporting a small fur-clad personage on his arm. He was saying, "You should not have come down, Carty. I could have seen my mother to her room."

"'Tis my duty," she replied. "'Twouldn't be right, Master Justin, to let Mrs. Penrose fend for herself."

"I had intended returning on tomorrow's tide, but . . ."

"'Tis no matter sir."

I heard censure in both comments. So had the small, fur-clad figure who now spoke up.

"I have been ill, Mrs. Carthew. Very ill. I know Justin doesn't believe me. . . . He never believes anything I say. But Dr. Thornley managed to convince him that I need a long period of convalescence and—"

"What better place to get it than here." Justin finished her sentence for her with a heavy lacing of sarcasm.

A deep sympathy developed inside me for the frail creature on his arm as her plaintive voice reached my ears.

"Oh, dear. I knew I shouldn't have come. I knew you didn't really want me, only you said—"

"You're here, Mother," he snapped irritably. "What are you grumbling for?"

"You're so unkind to me. . . . I don't think I'd better stay. I'll leave tomorrow. . . ."

"Don't talk rot. You know you'll stay now you're here."

Her son's voice, though still harsh, had grown weary. It gave the impression he had said the same thing, or something very like it, many times during the past few hours. But it did not lessen my contempt for him. I thought his treatment of his mother deplorable.

They started to ascend the stairs, and I drew back by the side of a tall, lacquered Chinese cabinet, unable to withdraw completely without drawing attention to myself. I hoped against hope they would not pass nearby and notice me there, eavesdropping.

Mrs. Carthew led the way, candlestick held high, a grim cast to her face. Next came Justin with his mother on his arm, and there was no doubting the grim set of his features. I could not see his mother's face. A chiffon scarf had been tied over her hat to keep it in place and it shrouded her looks from my view. She was tiny and frail, drooping with weariness. She seemed hardly able to climb the stairs, even aided as she was by the strength of her son's arm. My sympathy for her increased. I thought he might at least have carried her up to her room.

Her room was almost directly opposite mine on the other side of the gallery. The door was left open as they went in, and I was able to observe Justin as he set her down on the sitting room sofa—for this was a suite of rooms identical to mine, apart from the furnishings—and the way she fell back against it, exhausted by her long journey.

"Goodnight, Mother. Goodnight, Carty," I heard him say as he left the two women in the room together.

He closed the door behind him and stood there for a few seconds, drawing in breaths so deep that when they were released it was like the sound of a rushing wind emerging from his mouth. They spoke volumes of the resentment he felt at his mother's arrival—but that his face should suddenly acquire so ravaged an appearance, I could not understand. His bitterness against her went deep.

He moved and started back to the head of the staircase. I pressed myself flat against the wall, praying he would not look across and see me. I need not have worried. He was far too taken up with his own thoughts to notice anything. He made his way downstairs to the library, which he entered like a man in a dream, finding his way by long accustomed use.

I went back to bed, but it was a long time before I fell asleep again.

I was awake early the next morning, in spite of my interrupted night, and at my desk long before my employer.

"Good morning, Miss Wentworth." He made his greeting with a smile when he put in his appearance.

I could not return it. I was still blaming him for his harsh treatment of his mother, for making it so plain she was unwanted here. I knew how it could hurt. I had been hurt in the same way when I had first arrived—and I had been a stranger with no claim on anyone. But she was his mother. She had every right to expect to be made welcome. The fact that she appeared to know there was no welcome for her made it all the more poignant.

"Good morning, Mr. Penrose." I acknowledged his greeting coldly. "I trust you had a good trip."

"It served its purpose." His smile faded. "I brought my

131

mother back with me. I trust you were not disturbed by our late arrival?"

"No," I lied. I did not wish him to know I had observed his return and his cruel treatment of his mother. He would think I had been snooping—which was not *quite* the case.

"She'll be staying for a week or two. She's been very sick, and needs a period of peace and quiet to recoup her lost energies."

"That will be nice for you—having her here," I said wickedly.

His eyes narrowed. His lips tightened. "How have you got on during my absence? Any queries?"

"No. I've managed to deal with everything. There has not been a great deal of post, to be truthful. I've had quite a lot of free time on my hands."

"And what have you done with it? Explored the island, I suppose?"

"Yes. With John. He took me to the top of Polern Head yesterday to see the seabirds nesting there. It was a fantastic sight."

I paused for him to make a comment, but he made none and, as he appeared to be listening with interest, I continued.

"It's so wild up there, isn't it? He told me there have been a great many shipwrecks off that coast. It didn't surprise me. All those submerged rocks stretching far out into the sea."

I paused again for his comment. He said nothing. I continued.

"Afterwards, he took me to see his house, Peacehaven. Such a lovely name for a lovely house. But there's a sad history attached to it. You'll know all about it, of course, seeing as it concerns your ancestors."

He still made no comment, although I thought I saw him give a little start and waited for him to speak. I began to feel self-conscious, but was driven on by his seeming interest in what I had to say.

"Mrs. Hawkes cooked us a superb meal and we sang songs at

132

the piano and played records. Then he brought me home. . . ."

I became aware that what I had thought of as interest was cold boredom, and said no more.

He smiled, a thin forced smile, "I'm glad you've been so well entertained."

He went to sit at his desk. "What about the mail?"

"Quite a bundle arrived yesterday. I've sorted it all out."

"Yes, so I see. We'd better get started then."

He was terse, very much his habitual self. We worked quickly together. I had perfected my abbreviated writing techniques and found it a great help. When he sat back in his chair, I rose to go. I was halfway across the carpet when he stopped me.

"I've had an offer from an American film company. They want me to adapt *Love's Balm* for the silver screen."

I held my breath. *Love's Balm*? That document of the betrayal of his love? I could understand a film company wanting to film it. It was a dramatic, poignant love story. But would he do it?

"It might prove interesting." It was almost as if he had picked up the thread of my thoughts. "I've never done anything like it before, but I shouldn't think the technique is very far removed from that needed for writing a play. And moving pictures are the up and coming thing. In twenty odd years or so, there'll be a picture house in every city, every town. I shall have to give it serious thought, shall I not? It will mean going to America, of course, living there for a while. But that is in the future. I have enough on my plate for the present, with Ralph clamoring for my new book. When you've done those we'll start on it again."

I started for my office door. Again he stopped me.

"What do you think of *Green Sorrel* for a title?"

"It—it sounds marvelous." Was he really asking my opinion?

"Yes," he said, nodding in agreement.

I reached my office at last, and all the time I worked at the

133

typewriting machine, at the back of my mind was a niggling worry. What would I do when he went to America? Would he take me with him? Would he leave me here to look after his mail while he was away? Would he terminate my employment? It was in the future, he had said. But time had a way of passing very quickly, and I wondered what my future would be.

At last I could bear it no longer, and left my desk to confront him with the question.

He was lounging in one of the leather armchairs. His long legs were stretched out in front of him, his hands were folded behind his head, and he gazed up at the ceiling with a smile about his lips. He was looking forward to the future with enthusiasm.

As well he might. His future looked bright indeed. There was his new book almost ready for publication, and then the chance to work in America on a film script—all the excitement of working in a new medium to look forward to.

His eyes were ashine as he looked at me. I asked my question.

"What will happen to me when you go to America, Mr. Penrose?"

"*If*, don't you mean, Miss Wentworth?"

But I could tell from the look in his eye there was no "if" about it. He would go. He would not be able to resist it.

"Will you require me to stay here and look after things till your return?"

"No, no. That won't be necessary. John looks after things for me when I'm away for any length of time."

"Then he'll need a secretary?"

"I shouldn't think so. He's never needed one before."

"So my employment will be terminated?"

"Why? Do you wish it so?"

"No. I should be sorry to leave."

"Good, for I shall need you with me."

"To go to America with you? You wouldn't wish to hire a secretary out there?" I questioned, unable to believe my luck.

134

"Why should I when I've got you? I've grown used to you. You know my ways."

I rejoiced inwardly. My future was secure. He had grown used to me and did not want to lose me. Why, I could live the rest of my life out on Penrose Island—my haven at last.

Mrs. Carthew came in with the coffee tray. She was smiling a secret smile.

"Your favorites, Master Justin," she said holding the tray out for him to inspect.

"Carty!" he yelled, making me jump. "Doughnuts!"

Beaming now that her secret was out, she said, "Thought I'd give 'ee a bit of a treat your first day back."

"Carty, I love you," he grinned, relieving her of the tray and settling it down. Then, to my utter astonishment, he planted a smacking kiss on her rosy cheek, lifted her off her feet, and swung her round and round.

Blushing with pleasure she cried, "I'll make 'em for 'ee more often, m'dear, if I can look forward to this each time."

"'Tis a bargain I'll hold 'ee to, m'dear," he responded, with a Cornish lilt to match her own.

I watched in astonishment this display of affection between them. I knew she had been his nurse, his nanny, before becoming his housekeeper, and there was always a special bond between a nanny and her charge, but I would never have believed Justin Penrose capable of such a show of emotion. Where had he dredged it up from? How had he managed to find it beneath all those layers of bitterness in the cold, dark depths of his soul?

Betsy and Winnie, the sleek black Labradors, rushed into the room to lavish their own brand of affection on Justin, and then swamped me with their wet, adoring kisses.

"I can see who's been taking my place while I've been away," Justin remarked pointedly.

"Aye. They've taken to Miss Wentworth. Hardly been able to make a move without 'em, 'ave 'ee, Miss?"

Mrs. Carthew was smiling at me. Justin Penrose was smiling

135

too. The dogs continued to display their affection for me. For the first time, I felt I was accepted in Penrose House. I was part of the household. The happiness it gave me must have shown in my smiling face. Their smiles broadened.

Suddenly, we were all laughing together. I could not have said why, unless it was because we were all at once at ease with each other. The dogs grew boisterous as we laughed, bounding from one to the other of us in their excitement. Then a blight was cast over the proceedings.

The entrance of a tiny, dainty lady, dressed in mulberry red silk with a string of pearls reaching down to her waist and pearls like huge teardrops hanging from her ears, wiped the gaiety from our faces. As her querulous glance settled on each of us in turn, even Betsy and Winnie fell silent.

"Why wasn't I told coffee was being served?" she asked in hurt tones.

"We thought you would wish to lie in after your late night. Carty said you asked not to be disturbed till you rang," said her son.

"Well, I didn't feel like breakfast so I didn't bother," came the pouting reply.

Mrs. Carthew smoothed her crumpled apron and departed, saying she would fetch another cup and more doughnuts. The dogs left with her, sensitive no doubt, to the tension that had seeped into the room.

Silence ruled momentarily, then, "Aren't you going to introduce us, Justin?"

With a visible effort Justin roused himself from the black mood he had settled into. "My secretary, Miss Wentworth," he said. "My mother, Miss Wentworth." Then he betook himself to the far end of the room, took a book down from a shelf and started flicking through the pages.

How quickly he had changed back into the man I knew— curt, brusque, dismissive.

"You never told me you had a new secretary." Mrs. Penrose darted a resentful glance after him.

"Didn't I?" His manner was extremely offhanded. "It must have slipped my mind."

I felt for her as her small, even teeth came out over her bottom lip. He had hurt her. He was rude in the extreme. He might wish her anywhere but beneath his roof, but did he have to make it so obvious? She was only here for a short while. He could at least try to put a good face on it. She was his mother, for heaven's sake. She deserved some respect.

"Won't you sit down, Mrs. Penrose?" I pleaded. "I'll pour you some coffee."

"Why, thank you, my dear." She turned to me gratefully. "That is most kind of you."

"Do you take cream?"

"I do. Thank you."

I poured a cup for Justin, acutely aware of her blue eyes upon me. It made me feel restless, edgy. But then she said, "Would you mind passing me the sugar bowl, Miss Wentworth? I can't drink coffee without sugar."

I breathed with relief. So that was what it was. She had been waiting till I finished pouring Justin's coffee before she asked me for the sugar.

"Of course. Forgive me. I wasn't thinking."

"That's quite all right, my dear." She helped herself to three lumps.

Mrs. Carthew returned with the extra cup. She did not speak, did not look at Mrs. Penrose, but she exchanged an odd glance with Justin. I read in it annoyance at his mother's presence. No—more than that. I read condemnation there, blame. Did she blame Mrs. Penrose for the death of Justin's father also? She did not like her and made it plain. Was that the reason? Did she follow Justin's thoughts on the matter? He was a god in her eyes. Perhaps what he thought, she would think. This troubled me. It seemed all wrong.

I poured coffee for myself automatically, vaguely unhappy at the whole situation. I heard Mrs. Penrose speak, but did not catch her words.

"I'm sorry, Mrs. Penrose. What did you say?"

"I said, come and sit beside me and tell me all about yourself."

She was sitting in one of the capacious fireside chairs, looking hardly bigger than a child in it. I half expected her to tuck her legs up underneath her and snuggle into a corner to allow me to sit next to her there. But of course she did not, and I went to sit in the chair opposite her.

She smiled sweetly. "How long have you been working for my son?"

I saw Justin turn over a page of his book with an impatient movement. But why should it annoy him that his mother should ask me such questions? She was only showing an interest in me, which was more than he had done.

I answered her readily. "Nearly a month."

"And you're not bored?"

"No."

"Don't you find it rather lonely?"

"No."

"But how do you pass the time? There's nothing to do here, no entertainment. . . . Where do you come from?"

"London."

"That's where you should be. A lovely young girl like you should be in some big city, meeting young men, enjoying yourself."

I had noticed Justin set aside his book and take up his coffee. He was facing toward me, and I could see his brows drawn in a thick black line across his forehead—a sure sign that anger was getting the better of him. Now his cup crashed into his saucer. His eyes were blazing.

"Miss Wentworth is perfectly content here, Mother," he rasped.

She twisted her neck to face him. "I can't believe that, Justin. Every girl likes to enjoy herself, and there's no chance here of—"

"Change the subject, Mother," he snapped, and she lapsed

into silence.

Her lower lip trembled and I thought she was going to cry. Don't, don't cry, I pleaded with her silently. Don't give him the satisfaction.

I was mortified to have witnessed such a scene. It was most embarrassing for Mrs. Penrose. I looked hard at my employer, criticism I would dearly have liked to voice in my eyes. But it was not my place to take him to task. And I must remember my place; his glowering glance told me so.

So I berated him with my eyes. *You might have cause to be bitter,* they said, *but why must you be so cruel, so unforgiving? You can't go on blaming her for your father's death. It's not fair to hold her accountable for something that was, after all, an accident. She must have suffered a great deal of remorse. No woman wants a man's death on her conscience. Yet here you are, setting yourself up as judge and jury, condemning her to perpetual misery. How are you to know what led to her decision to leave your father? Who knows what goes on between a man and his wife? The fault may not have been all on her side. Yet you blame only her, and you have let your bitterness against her warp your personality, cause still more grief and pain—for everyone. It's all so unnecessary. If only you could forget the past . . . come to terms with it . . .*

Of a sudden he stalked from the room and slammed the door behind him, as if he read my thoughts and could not be easy with them.

While I stared at the door I heard the sound of a sob. Mrs. Penrose was weeping.

"I shouldn't have come," she sobbed over and over again. "I shouldn't have come."

Overcome by a desire to comfort her, I fell to my knees and took her hands in mine. They lay soft and still, like little dead birds, within my grasp.

"You . . . must . . . have gathered, Miss Wentworth, that my son doesn't want me here. My son . . . doesn't want me . . . here."

"Oh, please," I begged, "please don't cry. I'm sure that's not so. I'm sure he . . . he . . ."

"You cannot say it, can you?" Her voice rose on a triumphant note. "You can't refute my statement because you know it's true." She leaned forward to pat my shoulder. Her tears seemed to have dried magically. "You are a dear thing. You mean well. But my son hates me. Oh, he does." She prevented me from making further protest. "One day I'll tell you all about it. But not now . . . not now. . . ." She sighed deeply. "I had hoped it would be different this time. John insisted Justin would wish me to come, under the circumstances."

"John did? John Trevelyan?"

"Yes. The last time he was in London. He always visits me whenever he's there. Keeps me in touch. Tells me all the gossip. He didn't tell me about you, though."

"He didn't know. I came while he was away."

"Oh, I see. Will you pour me another cup, dear?"

I took her cup and, as I poured, she went on, "What is your Christian name, Miss Wentworth?"

"Nicola."

"Nicola. What a pretty name. And so unusual."

"It was given me because I was born at Christmas, I think. My parents were hoping for a boy and had decided to call him Nicholas—because of the time of the year. When I came, they simply shortened it to Nicola."

"Hm. My name's Clara. You may call me Clara. And I shall call you Nicola."

We smiled at each other. We were getting on very well together, Justin's mother and I.

"What do you think of my son?" she asked with a sudden shrewd glance.

"I . . . I . . ."

"Do you like him?"

"Well, I . . . I find him difficult at times, but on the whole I like working for him."

"Difficult. Yes, he's that all right. You don't find him—attractive?"

"He's—quite good looking, I suppose. He has a very forceful personality."

"You're not thinking of falling in love with him, are you?"

My answer was forceful. "No! Certainly not! Whatever put such an idea into your mind!"

"Oh, please don't be offended, my dear. I didn't mean anything by it. I'm just a prying old woman."

I looked at Mrs. Penrose, so elegantly clad with her two small feet, shod in the softest kid, resting side by side on the carpet, at the faint silvering of hair at the temples, and skin as clear as any girl's. I could not help crying out, "You're not old, Mrs. Penrose. You look hardly older than I."

She gurgled happily. "How sweet of you to say so, but I'm turned fifty, you know, although I may not look it. How could I have a son Justin's age else?"

We talked a little longer and then I excused myself. I still had plenty of typing to do, and Justin had intimated his wish to resume work on his new book as soon as possible.

My morning's work done, I presented myself for luncheon with Mrs. Carthew as usual, only to be told I was to join Mrs. Penrose on the terrace leading off the dining room.

"Ah, Nicola," she called to me gaily as I stepped out. "Come sit down. We won't wait for Justin. I doubt he'll join us, anyway."

She rang a little silver bell and almost immediately we were served a cold collation of various meats and salad.

"Well, now," Clara said spreading her napkin over her knees, "tell me more about yourself."

I told her about my background, slowing down when I came to my mother's second marriage. I did not find it easy to talk about, even mention, Ted Gibbon.

"I suppose you left home because you didn't get on with your stepfather," she observed, with remarkable perspicacity.

"Yes."

"And how long do you intend to stay here working for my son?"

"For as long as he'll let me. I enjoy working for him. I find it

141

most interesting."

"That's what Caroline said—and look what happened to her."

My heart stumbled in its beat at the mention of Caroline's name.

"But hers was a different case from mine," I said. "She left because—"

"Because she fell in love with my son," came the sharp interruption.

"Yes—but then she jilted him because . . ."

"Because she found out in time that he was stringing her along, just like all the others."

"Others?"

"Oh, there were lots of them. He's a man with a man's needs, and women are necessary to satisfy those needs, but he has no intention of ever cluttering up his life with a wife. I have heard him use those very words, 'cluttering up.' He has a poor opinion of women."

Oh, yes, I knew his opinion of women. But he had proposed marriage.

"He was going to marry her," I cried.

"No, no. He had no intention of marrying her. That was simply the bait to lure her into his bed when all else failed. Luckily, she realized this and jilted him before he could jilt her. It infuriated him. He never forgave her for making a fool of him. He wrote a book about her—*Love's Balm*—in which he made her out to be everything she was not—shrewish, cruel, selfish. . . . You should read it sometime. It's quite an eye-opener. An insight into the author's mind. I found it most unpleasant."

I felt bemused. This was a view of Justin Penrose I had not considered. It did not tally with Ruth's view of him. She had not even hinted that he might be promiscuous—quite the opposite in fact. And her view was that he had been too kind to Caroline in *Love's Balm*. Yet here was his mother saying quite the opposite. Whom was I to believe? Who was right? Could it

142

be that Clara was prejudiced, unconsciously taking revenge on her son by blackening his character, payment for his harsh treatment of her over the past years? I decided this must be so, for John, also, had intimated that Caroline was not a very nice person and that Justin had escaped, by the skin of his teeth, a marriage he would have regretted. Clara had got hold of the wrong end of the stick. It had been Caroline who had been stringing Justin along, not the other way round.

"No, Caroline was not as bad as he painted her," Clara was continuing sadly. "I quite liked her. We became great friends. We used to meet quite a lot in London. Justin never knew of our meetings. He wouldn't have approved. Remember what I've told you, Nicola, and don't become too attached to my son. Don't give him any encouragement. . . ."

She started to yawn, wearying of the conversation, and indicated to the maid that she was finished with her food. I indicated that I had finished too. In fact, I had quite lost my appetite.

She removed herself to a padded and cushioned garden couch, stretching out luxuriously on it, and waved an arm languorously at the cushioned chair nearby, to which I made my way.

"It's lovely here in the summertime," she breathed, drawing the scent-laden warm air deep into her lungs.

"Yes. You should get well quickly here. It's the perfect place for you to convalesce. I've only been here a short while, and already I feel like a new woman. I never felt so vitally alive in London."

"But you must miss London," she said.

"No, I don't. Not at all."

"I hate it here in winter," she went on. "It's killing in the winter. I always wanted to spend the winters on the Continent, somewhere warm like Italy, but Trim—Tristram, my husband —wouldn't hear of it. He never wanted to leave the place. I met and married him in London. I never dreamed that after bringing me here he would never want me to leave again. It was

143

with the utmost difficulty that I persuaded him to allow me a few days in London every year to renew my wardrobe, and if I should overstay my allowance by one second, he was after me, bringing me back.

"We quarreled incessantly. I had always been used to a life of excitement. Balls, concerts, the theatre, ballet, opera, racing at Ascot, riding in Rotten Row, all were the breath of life to me. Visits to Baden-Baden, Venice, Rome . . . Suddenly it was all denied me. I missed it all so much. If I'd known how unsociable Tristram was, how attached to his precious island, I should never have agreed to marry him. Never. But I was very young. I was in love. I looked no further than that. But I was never happy here and, in the end, I could not take any more of the loneliness . . . the boredom . . . the terrible, terrible weather. I had a constant cold right through from November to April. So, I'm afraid—I left him."

I began to understand now. This was probably the very core of the matter. Her husand had contributed to the break-up of their marriage through his blind neglect of her. He had neglected to provide her with even an iota of the things she had been used to and had neglected her health by insisting she stay through the long winters on a cold, storm-tossed island. Had he been unable, or unwilling, to see how the harsh winters undermined her health? If he had been a little more understanding of his wife's needs, everything might have been different. She would not have left him. Tristram would still be alive. Justin would not have become the embittered man he was.

The summer sun beat down warmly upon us now, making the island a golden island. She was happy now. Her eyes were closed, her face relaxed. Such a delicately chiseled face, with fine cheekbones, a small, slightly upturned nose, beautifully shaped lips. Tiny, and frail as the finest porcelain, she was someone to be cherished, cosseted and cared for.

I thought she had fallen asleep, and was about to rise and go indoors to see if Justin was waiting for me to take notes, when her eyes flew open.

"Justin's just the same," she said looking directly at me. "He can't bear to be away from the place, either. There are one or two occasions when he has to leave, of course, being a playwright and author, but he's back as soon as the opportunity presents itself. You should go back where you came from, before it's too late."

My heart gave a convulsive bound at the echo of John Trevelyan's words. But she was only referring to the weather, not to Justin's character.

"You won't want to spend the winter here," she confided. "It's wild and rough and stormy. You won't be able to stand it. It will grind you down, down—like it did me."

Her eyes closed again. Whether she slept, I don't know, but as the minutes passed, it became apparent she had no wish to talk any more. I left her to go in search of my employer, after leaving a message for Mrs. Carthew to keep an eye on her. It would not do for Clara to catch a chill if the wind should change.

Chapter Eight

I was not successful in locating Justin Penrose. I hung about the library and the hall waiting for him to appear. When he did not, I noted that Betsy and Winnie were also missing, and realized he must have gone on one of his long "thinking" walks.

By the time he came back, he would have another chapter or so in his head, and I and my typewriting machine would be pressed into service, probably into the late hours. The prospect did not disturb me. I was looking forward to finding out what happened next to the characters he had created. However, I thought it might be a good idea to go for a walk myself, making the most of the free time left to me.

Perhaps if my mind had not been so taken up with thoughts of Clara Penrose, Justin, and the rest, I might have noticed where I was heading. As it was, I did not realize I had climbed up to the High Plateau—somehow I could not bring myself to think of it as The Plateau of Love, the islanders' name for it— till I was conscious of the high wind in my ears, my hair blowing about my face.

I realized it with a sudden inrush of breath. I had deliberately avoided this place since my last encounter with the piskies—and Justin Penrose. I knew there were no such things as piskies. At least, I didn't think there were. A part of me was not quite so sure now, since coming to Penrose.

All of a sudden I became aware of an almost imperceptible change in the atmosphere. Again I heard the whispering of unseen beings, felt them tugging at my skirts . . .

But it was my imagination running loose again. There was nothing up here but me and the wind. It was the wind tugging at my skirts, whispering in my ears . . .

But there were the two stones, drawing my attention, holding my gaze; the head and torso of Zill, King of that part of Cornwall between Penzance and Pendeen . . .

But that was one of Justin Penrose's tales; it was not true. I would not be swayed by his story-telling.

Denying the urge to run from this place, I stood firmly atop the flat expanse, defying the wind's attempts to blow me over, eventually bowing before it by squatting on my heels and, finally, by sitting down.

I had a lot to think about. My conversation with Clara Penrose had forced me to open a door—a door I had been keeping firmly closed, a door behind which I had confined a growing awareness of Justin Penrose not only as my employer, but as a man, and a potentially attractive one at that.

Attractive—and dangerous, I now realized. Not in the way Ted Gibbon was dangerous. Justin Penrose would never force his attentions on the unwilling. He was dangerous because he was a man one could not ignore, no matter how hard one tried. One whose harsh exterior hid a character of great complexity and, therefore, of great interest. Any woman worth her salt would wish to unravel it.

I wished to unravel it in spite of myself, even though I had sensed the danger that had now become clearer to me. And now that it had become clear, could I draw back from further investigation?

Why was I so interested, anyway, in finding out more about the man who was my employer? I was grateful for my job. Why not leave it at that? It would be the wise thing to do.

Was I so wise?

I was not aware that my thoughts held any great significance. I was interested in him, but I did not like him. I liked John Trevelyan much more.

I rose to continue my walk and as I did so, a figure came into view. He was some distance away, but it was impossible not to recognize the well-built figure of Justin Penrose. He had been so much in my thoughts that, for a brief moment, I thought I had conjured him up. But he had seen me. He seemed to hesitate. Was he thinking of coming over to me? I waved to him. He waved back and continued on his way. He had no desire to approach me. He wanted to be alone. To think? To work out the intricacies of his new novel?

I was still trying to discern the motives behind his actions.

I returned to the house. John Trevelyan was there taking tea with Clara Penrose. They invited me to join them.

"Do you know where Justin is?" John asked me.

"He's out walking. He's been out for hours. I thought he'd probably called on you and had a meal with you. He did not come in to luncheon."

"No, I haven't seen him. I didn't even know Clara had arrived till I came here half an hour ago."

He sounded put out—angry. I said, "He's very much involved with his new book. I expect everything else has flown from his mind."

"You could be right," he said.

But he still looked annoyed, and I could not help wondering why he should feel so. It was not beholden on Justin Penrose to inform him of events that took place within his household, even if they were friends.

John stayed for the rest of the day. Justin did not return, and the three of us had supper together. I felt anxious and uneasy. I did not know why. Was I afraid something might have happened to Justin Penrose? But what could happen to him on the island that he knew so well, among the islanders who loved him?

I left John and Clara together and went to write a letter to my

148

mother. Afterwards, as it was a balmy evening, I went out and sat in the garden for a while. Then, when I could not sit any longer, I started to walk about the garden. I wandered over to where the lawns reached out onto the cliffs. I went out onto the cliffs, rather nervous and ill at ease. I could not get it out of my mind that something might have happened to Justin Penrose—something bad.

I stood on the cliff top and looked all around; at the sea, the sloping hills, Penrose House. Outlined against a dying sun's blood-red shroud, the house stared back at me, its many leaded windows dark and reproving. What are you doing here? they seemed to say. You have no right to be here.

I gave myself a mental shake and turned to face the sea, which was busily soaking up the dying sun's blood, relieving the night sky of the task.

I shook myself again for having such morbid thoughts about an innocent sunset. But it was a measure of the unease I felt.

The sun lowered. The moon rose, red to begin with, then silvering. The dark mass of Penrose House, battlemented, grim-looking, caught my attention again. It was my home now, and it would be for—as far as I could see into the future. It no longer repelled me as it had done at first. But it held secrets. I knew it did. Secrets it would not share with me.

Someone was coming up toward me. My heart started bumping, then settled as I saw it was only John. He sat down beside me on the springy turf.

"Lovely up here, isn't it?" he said.

I agreed that it was.

"You don't mind my joining you? You seemed wrapped in contemplation as I spied you from the house."

"Of course I don't mind."

"Were you admiring the house—or just dreaming?"

"A bit of both, I think."

"It is an impressive house, is it not?"

"It's like a castle," I said.

"Exactly like a castle," he confirmed, awe in his voice,

149

intensity in his gaze.

He seemed to hold his breath for a moment, looking at something visible only to himself, but, though I strained to see what had attracted his attention, I could see nothing unusual, not even someone standing at one of the windows.

"Justin's not back yet," he said suddenly. "It's too rude of him to go off like that without a word to his mother, leaving her the whole day when she's only just arrived. Don't you think so?"

"It—does seem a little unkind."

"I knew you'd agree. It's not surprising that she likes you."

"But she hardly knows me."

"It doesn't take anyone long to realize what a kind and generous soul you are. She saw it at once. Just as I did the first day I met you. Remember that day? I admired you then. I admire you now."

His eyes left my face to take a stroll over the rest of me, and returned shining with admiration. I looked away quickly. I knew John was not like Ted Gibbon, but I dared not give him any encouragement. Would I ever recover sufficiently from Ted Gibbon's advances to accept admiration willingly?

"Thank goodness you're here to give her your company. Justin never gives her more than the time of day, and she needs someone to talk to. She was feeling very depressed this evening. She knows he doesn't want her here. I'm almost sorry I persuaded her to come."

"*You* persuaded her to come?"

"I thought she needed a break. She was looking so peaked when I saw her in London. She'd been very ill."

"Why didn't she let Justin know she was ill?"

"She said she didn't like to worry him. In any case, I told him she wasn't well on my return. He didn't thank me for it. Said he didn't believe it, that she'd made out she was ill before so that she could come and stay at Penrose. I was so aggrieved at his attitude, I wrote her suggesting she come anyway. I thought surely he would not turn her away if she actually

150

arrived on his doorstep."

"But he brought her here himself. She had written him a letter. . . ."

"I suppose he must have some atom of feeling for her somewhere," John said grudgingly.

"I wish . . ."

"What?"

"I wish he didn't hate her so much."

"I don't think he hates her exactly, but he is very bitter towards her. If only . . ."

"What?"

"If only they could be brought closer together. I wonder . . . could we bring them together, do you think?"

"But how?"

"I don't know. But there must be a way. It's not right that a mother and son should be so estranged."

"Oh, I do agree. If only we could—"

"Let's try," he said. He took my hands in his—and I let them stay there.

"It will be a difficult task," he continued. "Perhaps I'd better tell you the story behind it all."

"There's no need. I know he blames her for causing his father's death."

"How do you know that?"

"He told me."

"*He* told you? That's very strange. Now if you'd said Mrs. Carthew told you, I could have understood it, but he usually keeps it secret."

"Secret?"

"He keeps a discreet silence about it, anyway. After all, it's not a very pretty story. I suppose he told you she ran off with another man?"

"More or less."

"It's all ancient history. It's about time he got over it, came to terms with the situation. She would be only too ready to let bygones be bygones. Why can't he do the same? She admits she

151

was to blame. She should never have run off and left him—a young child—in the care of an ignorant island woman."

"Mrs. Carthew?"

"Mrs. Carthew."

"She brought him up then?"

"Yes. After his father died, I believe she had sole charge of him."

"She doesn't appear to have done a bad job of it."

"She probably helped poison his soul against his mother. He's a fine man, but weak—but aren't we all weak in one way or another? Still, Clara's such a warm, caring person. . . . It breaks my heart to see her so unhappy."

"How long have you known her?" I asked.

"Justin once asked me to look her up on one of my trips to London. We got along famously from the start. She's such a charming person. Well, you've seen for yourself. Till I met her, I'd heard only Justin's side of the story. Afterwards I found—"

"You found you believed hers against his," I said sharply, surprised to feel anger.

"You think me disloyal," he said, reacting equally sharply to my tone. "I assure you I'm not. But you don't know the whole story. There's a lot more to it than meets the eye."

I turned away from him. "Well, it's none of my business," I muttered, angry with him for his seeming disloyalty, angry with myself for caring.

"Oh, I think it is." His voice was quiet, almost sinister. "You've made it your business by talking about it the way you have. Whether you like it or not, Nicola, you are part of life here now. What occurs on Penrose Island affects you as it affects us all. You can't help being involved. All who set foot on the island and choose to stay are caught up in its affairs. There's no escaping it."

I swallowed nervously. His words seemed to fall like ice crystals, cooling the warm air around me so that I found myself shivering.

"You're here for a purpose. You might not know what that purpose is—but the island knows, and its voices will lead you where you have to go. Can't you feel its tentacles winding around you to keep you here till your purpose has been fulfilled? Writhe as you may, there is nothing you can do to free yourself from its hold."

"Stop it, John!" Already I was beginning to feel suffocated by those tentacles, which I knew did not exist. He was leading me on—as he had led me on with his tales of King Arthur and his Knights, his suggestion that he himself was one of those knights. I refused to allow myself to be so misled. "What are these voices? Do they belong to the pixies? I've already told Mr. Penrose I don't believe in them."

"Piskies, m'dear," he corrected me in the Cornish lilt. "And don't 'ee be talkin' about 'em so lightly. They be alistenin' and awatchin'."

"I'm going in," I cried, rising abruptly.

He rose with me. "I'm sorry. I was only teasing."

His hand was on my arm. He stood very close to me. Suddenly, I knew he was going to kiss me. Jerking myself from his grasp, I ran back to the house.

Justin was still absent. I grew more and more anxious about him, and voiced the fear that he might have had an accident to Mrs. Carthew.

"He knows the island like the back of his hand," she said. "He won't come to no harm."

"But he's been out so long—and it's getting so late."

"'Tis no cause for worry. 'Tis his habit to take long thinkin' walks."

"Yes, but . . ."

"Betsy and Winnie be with him. They'd have raised the alarm by now if anything be wrong."

"But what if he went out in his boat and—"

"Sea's as calm as a mill pond, m'dear, and he's at home on the Justinia as much as in Penrose House. Don't 'ee fret. He'm a good sailor. In fair weather or foul, 'e'll come to no harm."

I tried to hang on to her words as the house settled down for the night and he had still not returned. I did not know why I should feel so concerned about him—but I was. I had the feeling, a feeling I was to experience time and time again, that danger threatened him. It was an irrational fear, but I could not rid myself of it.

I lay awake for hours worrying about him. Every little sound jerked my head from my pillow. Was it Justin coming in? But each time I knew it was not so. The sounds I heard were the sounds the house made as it eased its old timbers to rest.

Impatiently I kept reminding myself that Mrs. Carthew had not been disturbed by his long absence. If she could be easy about it, then so should I. He was a grown man, well able to take care of himself. It was preposterous to feel danger menaced him on his own island, among his own people.

I drew the sheets up over my ears and fell asleep at last.

It was a fitful sleep, and when I finally rose from my bed and hurried down to breakfast, my heart was still full of anxiety. Would he be there in his usual place at the table? My heart fell when I saw he was not, but then I spied the empty coffee cup, the plate bearing toasted crumbs of bread. All my worry had been for nothing. He had come home. I had missed hearing him, but he had returned sometime during the night.

He was sitting at his desk when I reached the library. He looked up with a smile—that slow, sweet smile that appeared all too rarely and which transformed his face from that of an eagle's, cold and cruel, to that of, if not a dove's, a considerably less formidable creature's.

"Good morning, Miss Wentworth," he said.

"Good morning, Mr. Penrose."

"Is anything the matter?" he frowned. There was a graze on his forehead, and I was gazing at it in dismay.

"Your head . . . ," I murmured.

"Oh, that." His hand went up to touch it. "It's nothing."

"Have you been in an accident? I thought you might have been when you didn't come home last night."

154

"Didn't come home? Of course I came home. What are you talking about? Not that it's any of your business, but I'd like your explanation."

"I'm sorry." His smile had disappeared; the eagle had returned. "Of course it's none of my business." I had been a fool to be concerned.

"As a matter of fact, I did have a bit of an accident."

"I knew it," I breathed. "What happened?" I was not such a fool, after all.

"I'd gone for a long walk, and found myself close to Peacehaven. I thought I'd call on John and invite myself to luncheon. He wasn't at home. Mrs. Hawkes said she didn't know when he would be back, but she gave me a meal and fresh water for the dogs. Tired out, they then dropped off to sleep. John still hadn't returned by the time we left."

"He was at Penrose House. He was having tea with your mother. I . . . I . . ."

My voice faded. He was looking at me curiously. He continued softly. "I saw you on the High Plateau. You seemed to be very deep in thought. I called out to you, but you did not hear me."

"I saw you . . . I didn't hear you."

"No."

We were silent for a few moments. There was a contemplative look in his eye which I could not understand.

"I decided not to intrude. . . ."

"I waved."

"And I waved back. Yes. But there was something about you that suggested you wished to be alone with your thoughts. I certainly wished to be alone with mine. Instead of going home as I had intended, I pushed on, walking farther and farther, till I found myself in the vicinity of the slate quarries. It was then I had my accident. Or rather, it was Betsy who had the accident."

"Betsy?"

"She fell down a gaping hole and could not get out. I should

155

have gone for help, but she was looking up at me so pitifully, so trustingly. If I had gone away, she would have thought I was leaving her. I thought I should be able to manage by myself. I could get footholds on the slates jutting out at the sides . . . but as I scrambled down to her, Winnie following me in spite of my order to stay behind, there was a slide."

"A slide?"

"Loose slate becomes dislodged and starts tumbling down—like a rockfall. As I glanced upwards on hearing the first loose slate fall, I was struck on the head." He touched his forehead. "Hence the graze. It knocked me out for a while."

"You could have been killed," I breathed.

He regarded me in silent speculation for a few moments and asked, "Would it have bothered you if I had?"

"Yes, of course it would. I . . ." My voice ran out again. I would have been utterly horrified—but I could not tell him so.

"It was dark when I came to," he continued. "Betsy and Winnie were curled up beside me. They stirred when I did. I peered about me, thankful there was a moon, searching for some way out, and as I did so, I thought I saw someone looking down from above the rim of the quarry. I even called out—but of course there was no one. It was only an aberration of the mind. However, a little investigation showed that the slide had settled into a sloping stairway and that, with care, I should be able to climb. But what of the dogs? I had no need to worry about them. They found their way up more easily than I did."

"That was very fortunate. You might have been trapped all night if . . ."

"Well, I wasn't, and 'all's well that ends well,' as Shakespeare says. Now, we'd better attend to the business in hand. We'll leave the correspondence for the present. I've a couple of chapters inside my head bursting to get out."

"I'll get my pad," I cried, rushing off for it.

He had just started dictating when Clara came in. His face hardened at the sight of her dainty little figure in the doorway.

"What do you want, Mother?" he demanded testily.

156

"I wondered if Nicola could come for a walk with me."

"No, she can't. She's working. You must go by yourself."

Her Dresden china face crumpled. "But you know I must not go out alone, in case I have one of my blackouts."

"You won't black out, Mother. You are not ill now. You will come to no harm if you go out by yourself. Stay within the confines of the gardens and call if you feel faint. Somebody will hear you."

He was being very unpleasant, and I began to feel a growing impatience with him. There was no need for him to be so rude, so unfeeling.

"But I'm afraid, Justin. I *have* been ill. *Extremely* ill. They say I'm better, but I'm not so sure. I still get headaches." She turned her anxious blue eyes in my direction, explaining, "I used to get such severe headaches that I'd faint right away with the pain. The doctors thought it might be something ... something ... It's very frightening ... and I *do* still get headaches."

"If you could wait a couple of hours, Clara," Justin Penrose gave me a quick glance as I spoke his mother's Christian name, "I shall be able to come with you. At this moment I'm afraid I am rather busy."

"There! You've heard what *Nicola* says." The emphasis he gave to my name brought the blood rushing to my cheeks. It was full of his usual sarcasm, and indicated his annoyance at my familiarity with his mother. "She will accompany you later, when she has the time. But she is my secretary, not your companion, and I need her here when there's work to be done."

"Yes. I understand, Justin," Clara said meekly. "I ... I'll go and sit in the garden, as you suggest."

"You were rather unkind to her," I found myself criticizing him aloud after she had gone.

"Indeed! And do you think it's any business of yours?"

I swallowed, but refused to be cowed.

"She's afraid of you."

"Nonsense."

"She is. It's obvious to anyone. You are too harsh with her."

"Am I?"

"I think so. After all, she has been ill, and if she is still getting bad headaches . . ."

"If."

That "if" exploded heavily into the air.

"Don't you believe her, then?"

"She has been ill, I'll grant you that, but nothing like as bad as she would have us believe."

"But John said—"

"John!" He raged with contempt. "John takes her at her word. A foolish thing to do with a woman who can bamboozle most people into believing anything she says. She has two powerful weapons, my mother, charm and an air of fragility, which she uses all the time."

"She certainly appears to be delicate, and I know she can be easily hurt."

"She's as tough as old nails."

"Aren't you being a little unfair? After all, she is your mother, and she has been ill. . . ."

"Do you think I didn't check up on her health while I was in London?" he demanded angrily. "Her doctor said there was nothing wrong with her. Her headaches are purely imaginary, her blackouts fictitious. When I confronted her with his report she said she had not been satisfied with him for a long time and was seriously considering finding another doctor. She said John had advised it. Meanwhile, he thought it would do her good to get away from London for a while. Fresh country air was what she needed. Sea air. Island air."

"It was only natural she should think of coming here." John and I had agreed to try to bring about a reconciliation between Justin and his mother, and I began to look upon this conversation as a preliminary to that reconciliation. "It is only natural she should want to be with her son."

An angry snort erupted from his mouth. But I was determined not to allow this opportunity to pass by.

"Don't you think you could try being a little more pleasant to her?" I ventured boldly. "I'm sure she would react accordingly."

My courage wavered as his face grew more stormy, but then I hit upon an idea that might appeal to him.

"Her stay would pass all the quicker for it," I said quickly.

I could see he was swayed. "It would be difficult," he growled. "Damned difficult."

I felt a glow of triumph. I felt I had achieved something, no matter how small. I had headed him in the right direction. Elated, I decided, for the present, not to pursue the object further. I had planted the seed and would leave it to grow. I would nurture it later.

I poised my pencil in readiness for his dictation.

"Nicola. . . ."

His soft mention of my name surprised me. I raised my eyes with a little flurry of excitement. There was a strange expression on his face. I tried to read it, and failed.

"Don't . . . don't let my mother . . ."

His dark eyes roamed my face. His forehead was creased into thick furrows. I stared at him, puzzled. What was he trying to say?

"Don't let her what?" I prompted.

But his eyes fell. "Never mind," he said, and started dictating.

"*Chapter Five. Paragraph. There was no intention on his part to . . .*"

Clara and I were not able to commence our walk till well into the afternoon.

"I'm sorry to have been so long," I apologized. "There was more to do than I had anticipated."

"It doesn't matter," she said with an air of resignation. "It's no more than I expected. Once Justin knew I wanted you to

159

come out with me, I knew he would place obstacles in the way."

"It wasn't like that," I explained quickly. "It's just that his new book . . ."

"If that hadn't been his excuse, he'd have used something else," she responded sulkily. I let the matter drop.

We had hardly stepped through the door when Justin himself came up to us. He announced that he was coming with us and gave a short, sharp whistle which brought Betsy and Winnie bounding into view.

"You're not bringing them!" Clara objected strongly.

"Why not? They won't bother you."

Clara tutted with annoyance and said to me, hardly bothering to drop her voice lest he hear, "He's doing it deliberately. He knows I don't like dogs."

I was soon to learn dogs were not the only thing she did not like. She did not like rain. She did not like wind—the slightest suggestion of a breeze gave her cause for complaint. She did not like sun and must always carry a parasol. She had a delicate stomach and must take great care with the food she ate. She did not like duck. She did not like ham. She could not abide cheese. Certain vegetables were anathema to her. Tarts and pies gave her the most frightful indigestion, and Cornish pasties—ugh! Poor Mrs. Carthew was often at her wits' end devising dishes that would please her and not offend her delicate stomach.

As her health improved, she grew more demanding. The servants learned to keep out of her way, for she was most adept at finding "little" jobs for them to do at that very moment, no matter what errand they might happen to be engaged upon.

I was not exempted from performing these little duties. I was prevailed upon to fetch her sweets from the village shop, her bag, her shawl, her embroidery—anything she had forgotten to bring downstairs with her. Nothing was ordered. Everything was *requested*. And all with such sweetness and charm of manner it was impossible to object—on my part, anyway.

But all this was in the future. At present, I hardly knew her.

The dogs ran on ahead of us, stopping every now and then, looking back, waiting for us to catch up a little, before bounding off once more. Justin stayed close to his mother, engaging her in a somewhat stilted conversation. I counted it a small victory. I was certain he was putting himself out to be pleasant because of what I had said to him earlier.

But before long, Clara was complaining.

"I can't walk much farther. I'm beginning to feel tired."

"We're almost at the church," Justin said, "and there's Parson Bryn at the gate. He's seen us. We'll have a word with him and then turn back."

Clara frowned. "Must I speak to him?"

"Of course you must."

Her footsteps had slowed, and I sensed in her a great reluctance to meet Parson Bryn—but he had opened the gate and was coming toward us.

"Good afternoon to you all. 'Tis a bright and beautiful day, is it not?"

He bent down to pat the dogs, who were fawning round him, but his quick, shrewd eyes were on Clara's face, I noted.

"It is indeed," Justin agreed.

Parson Bryn came forward to take Clara's hand in his. "Ah, you have come back to see us, Mrs. Penrose. And will it be a long visit this time?"

"That depends on my son, Parson." Clara's eyes seemed to be looking anywhere but at the parson. I felt she was a little afraid of him. "My fate lies in his hands."

"I think not, Mrs. Penrose. Your fate, like that of us all, lies in the hands of our Maker." His glance fell on Justin.

"Are you saying no one of us is responsible for his actions?" Justin shot out. "Were we not given free will to choose the paths we tread? The deeds we commit? Are you saying we are at liberty to shovel off our actions because our fate is already mapped out for us?"

"No, no. That is not what I am saying at all." There was a hint of irritability behind the parson's reply. "What I am saying is that ultimately we will all be brought to account for our actions. We will stand before our Lord God on the Day of Judgment, and there will be no escaping His wrath. We will all have to pay for our misdeeds."

His glance passed from Justin to Clara and back again. Justin's lips tightened to invisibility and a throbbing vein stood out on his temple. Clara's lips trembled and the look on her face was one of abject terror, as she turned to gaze at her son.

She had done wrong. She knew she had done wrong. And here was the parson rubbing it in, implying that dire punishment awaited her on that dreadful day when all sins would be revealed. And here was Justin, her son, punishing her now, day in, day out, for her—in his eyes—heinous crime of being the cause of his father's death.

"Good day, Parson," Justin said frostily. He had not taken kindly to the criticism of himself implicit in Parson Bryn's tone.

The incident occupied my mind for days afterward. Had the pastor's words been chosen as chastisement for both? He must be aware of how things stood between them. He had been blunt with Clara, making it clear that she would be brought to account for her wrongdoing in the Lord's own good time. He had been equally blunt with Justin, making it plain his treatment of his mother was blameworthy and that he, too, would be brought to account for his actions.

Parson Bryn, I believed, had chosen his words deliberately, targeting them toward a better understanding between mother and son. Would he achieve his aim?

Chapter Nine

As the days passed, hardly knowing how it happened, I found myself accompanying Justin Penrose on his long walks round the island. Pleasant, summer-perfumed days were spent in the open, with Betsy and Winnie romping around us or resting at our feet as we sat together on the cliff tops working on his novel.

He would dictate to me while looking out across the sea, his eyes crinkled against the sun. I forced my pencil to keep pace with the flow of his sentences, which grew into phrases, phrases into scenes, scenes into chapters, with the most astonishing speed. It was as if the chapters were already written in his mind and only needed to be put down on paper.

But of course I knew there was much more to it than that. There were the hours of thought he had spent on creating his characters as he tramped the long, lonely miles round the island; the reams of notes he had made—many of which I had had to decipher and type; the research involved; the massive alterations he made to work already done—sometimes scrapping whole chapters, which appeared to me excellent, but to him had not attained the quality he aimed for.

Back at my desk, I typed the work that had been done beneath the blue Cornish sky. Long, long hours I worked, and I had never been happier in my life.

Clara complained bitterly.

"I never see anything of you these days. I had thought when I first arrived that we would be able to spend a lot of time together, but Justin monopolizes you the whole time."

"I am his secretary," I reminded her. "There's lots of work on hand at the moment. He's deeply involved with his new book, and I'm needed to—"

She frowned angrily. "Be careful, Nicola. Don't let him take advantage of you."

"I'm his secretary," I said again. "He has every right to expect me to work as hard as is necessary."

"That's not what I'm talking about, and you know it. Or are you really as innocent as you pretend to be? I've told you what sort of man he is. I thought you understood. He has a way with women—a kind of magnetism that draws them to him like flies. He has a list of conquests as long as your arm and, given half a chance, he'll add you to it."

There had been a time not so very long ago when I should have laughed to think women were drawn to Justin Penrose, a man as harsh and cold and cruel as the sea round Penrose Island could be. But since working so closely with him these past few days, I saw him in a different light—almost in the same light as Ruth Norman—and I had to admit there was a magnetism about him. I had felt it myself, even on that first day's meeting, though I would never be attracted by it. But I could see that Clara might be right; he might have a list of conquests as long as my arm.

When I saw Ruth, during one of my brief periods of respite, and told her what Clara had said, she curled her lip. "Don't take any notice of her," she said. "She doesn't know what she's talking about. No woman has any need to be afraid of Justin Penrose. He is no philanderer."

I should have remembered he was Ruth's idol and that she would not hear a word said against him. But I forgot, and when I handed him the neatly typed final chapter of his novel and he said, "Thank you. Done in record time. We work well together,

I think," I glowed with pleasure.

We smiled at each other in mutual satisfaction. We had done a good job together, with hardly a cross word between us. It was hard to remember he was the same man who had greeted me so harshly, resolved to turn me away, on that first January-in-June day of my arrival.

I had no qualms about going with him when he said, "Come. I think we've earned ourselves a break."

"Where are we going?" I asked as we left the house.

"I'll take you to see Lovers Knot Copse. I think it will interest you."

I was intrigued. The Plateau of Love, Lovers Knot Copse, Penn's love for Roselle . . . So much on the island seemed to be connected with love and lovers.

I caught sight of Clara waving frantically to us from her window.

"Perhaps I'd better go and see what she wants," I said.

"No," he said callously. "She'll only want to come with us, and I'm not about to include her in our outing."

"It might not be that. She might need something."

"Oh, Nicola," he frowned, "my mother's always in need of something. She likes to have everyone dancing to her tune. I tried to tell you once before—don't let her batten on your good nature. You do, you know. I've seen you running little errands for her, performing little duties."

"I don't mind."

"*Nicola!* Will you not listen to what I say, and take notice? She'll use you in any way she can, if you allow her to. She'll treat you as her personal servant, just as . . ."

He hurried me away and did not finish his sentence. I felt he thought he was saying more than he ought, and puzzled over what he had been going to tell me.

The incident seemed to have disturbed him, and he spoke curtly as he took me by the arm and led me to the stable block.

"We'll ride."

"I don't ride," I admitted, and he looked coldly at me.

165

"We'll take the pony cart then."

He kept the pony trotting briskly till we reached the ascent to the High Plateau. We skirted the hill at walking pace—it was a slightly downward slope, and we soon found ourselves in a narrow valley hemmed in by gently sloping hills. When we reached the farthermost end of the valley, we turned sharply to our right.

"There!" Justin pointed straight ahead. "Lovers Knot Copse."

I eyed the small scattering of trees without enthusiasm. There was nothing special about them.

"There's a legend attached to it," he added.

"Another legend?" I scoffed.

"The island's full of them." He glanced at me with a twinkle in his eye. "Would you like to hear it?"

"I can see you're dying to tell it."

"Just as much as you're dying to hear it."

"Well, you're such a good storyteller."

"I make my living from it."

We were bandying words good-humoredly, and I was thoroughly enjoying myself. I had never felt so at ease with him—with anybody. Perhaps Ruth was right about him. When he let himself go, forgot to be bitter and unkind, he was extremely pleasant to be with.

"Go on then," I said. "Tell me the legend."

"Legends have their roots in truth, you know that don't you? You scoffed when I told you about Penn and Roselle, but I promise you I didn't make those stories up. They've been handed down through the ages. Aren't you willing to agree there might be a grain of truth in them?"

"Possibly. A grain. No more. But do tell me about the legend of the copse."

"Very well. But let's get down. I want you to go into the copse, to feel the atmosphere there. . . . It's different from anything else on the island. It might help you to understand the legend and how it arose."

We walked toward the trees and he began his tale.

"It is said that Joseph Penrose, an ancestor of mine, fell in love with a pisky princess and she with him. But under pisky law it was forbidden for a pisky to marry a mere mortal. But their love for each other was so great that Princess Vanora—the name means White Wave—defied her people and ran away with Joseph. They did not get very far. They were captured as they entered the copse.

"Once more she was entreated to give up her lover, but she refused. Then she must give up her pisky immortality, they told her. She said she did not care. Her only wish was to be with her lover, tied to him forever.

"The piskies took her at her word. Her immortality was taken from her, and she and Joseph were tied together and bound to a tree with a strand of Princess Vanora's own hair, a strand which could never be broken. They were left there, helpless, to die."

We had reached the copse and I, once more, was spellbound by his storytelling. As we entered, there was a change in the atmosphere. It was achingly sad within that small enclosure. The sadness seeped into my heart. It was dark, strangely dark, when there were so few trees to cast any shade. And it was quiet . . . very quiet . . . eerie . . . Somehow my hand found its way into his.

"Afraid?" he murmured, giving my hand a reassuring squeeze. "Don't be."

"I'm not afraid . . . here . . . with you. . . ." I turned to face him and strange emotions were unleashed within me as I met his gaze.

His arms went round me and I melted into them. With no thought to the future, I gave myself up to the sweet delirium of his kiss. It enveloped me completely, my heart, my mind, my body, my soul.

His hands and voice caressed me. "Vanora, Vanora, my little pisky love." A thousand devils danced around us singing, "Give. Give. Give."

And I gave. I gave back kiss for kiss, reveling in this timeless moment of ecstasy.

Then I heard a voice, a warning voice, from somewhere deep inside me chanting, "Remember. Remember. Remember."

The devils danced and sang, "Ignore it. Ignore it."

And I listened to them.

His lips strayed over my cheeks, my eyes, my hair, then claimed my lips again, forcing me to surrender.

"Resist! Resist! Remember! Remember!"

The warning voice rose to a scream, cutting through my ecstasy, and vaguely I began to perceive what it was I had to remember.

But I was tied to my lover with a silken strand of my own hair. I could not free myself.

I cried out in panic, "I can't. I can't. I'm bound to him forever."

"Nicola! Nicola!" A different voice came through to me. "Nicola!"

I stirred. The silken strand snapped. I was free.

Through a swirling mist I saw a face close to mine. "Justin?"

"Thank God!" he said. "Thank God! You fainted. I was so afraid."

"I thought . . . I thought I was . . . you were . . ."

"I know. I know." He groaned softly and gathered me up in his arms. "I'll get you out of here. I should have known better than to bring you here, knowing how sensitive to atmosphere you are."

He carried me out into the bright sunlight, and with the sea breezes fanning my face, I finally woke from the weird thralldom in which I had been the Princess Vanora and Justin my lover, Joseph.

With the awakening came fear. Had he kissed me? Had I given him more than kisses in return? Had I dreamt it all? How could I tell?

I demanded breathlessly, "Did . . . did you kiss me?"

"You know I did," he said softly.

He had set me down, but his arms were still round me. He tightened them and tried to draw me closer.

I pulled away from him. "How dare you!" I gasped. "How dare you!"

He smiled. "I just gazed into those large forget-me-not blue eyes of yours and surrendered to your sweetness."

"You . . . you . . . ," I almost choked on his teasing tone, "you are despicable! You took advantage of me!"

"No, Nicola, my sweet Vanora. You wanted me to kiss you. Your eyes begged me to. Just as they are begging now. . . ."

He reached out for me again—Justin Penrose with a list of conquests as long as my arm—unable to believe I was repulsing him, smiling, supremely confident . . .

I struck him. I brought my hand up and struck him a stinging blow on the cheek. The sound ripped through the quiet air as I yelled, "You took advantage of me! You tricked me to going into the copse with you so that you could . . . you could . . ."

His expression changed, his smiling confidence giving way to surprise. I was glad, glad I had shaken him out of his complacency. How dare he think I wanted him to kiss me? But the devils were still around and they started singing, "You did. You did." I wanted to stamp on them, to drive them away, knowing them to be wrong. It had not been I who wanted his kiss, it had been Princess Vanora.

But now I grew afraid of him, of the cold anger that had gained control of his features, of the contempt in his eyes, of the gravel in his voice as he took up my unfinished sentence.

"Rape you? My dear Miss Wentworth, what do you take me for? An unwilling female is not to my taste. Forgive me if I misinterpreted your glance. And do not fear for your virginity. We were not in there long enough for anything more than an exchange of kisses to occur."

He turned from me abruptly and headed back to the pony and trap. I followed, completely demoralized. I had accused him of behavior as lewd as Ted Gibbon's, and he had treated me

169

with the contempt I deserved.

Why had I reacted as I had, when I knew in my heart of hearts he was an honorable man who would never take advantage of an innocent girl?

Because, in my heart of hearts, I had desired what I denounced?

No, this could not be. I was not a wanton female. Was my brain still affected by the strange atmosphere of Lovers Knot Copse?

I had been carried away by the strange belief that I was the pisky Princess Vanora and he, my lover. I had wanted to be kissed ... Princess Vanora had ... and had shown him my desire. How could he have not responded? He was a man with a man's needs. He would take what was offered. I had offered him my lips ... would have offered him more ... Vanora would have offered him more ... Would he have carried our lovemaking to its logical conclusion if I had not fainted? I knew he would not have, knowing I was under a pisky spell.

I knew I had maligned him and longed to apologize, but my tongue was stuck to the roof of my mouth, glued there by anxiety and disgust at myself. I looked at his stern, eagle-like profile, and wished with all my heart we had never gone into the copse. Now the old easy friendship would never return. I had killed it with my Ted Gibbon-haunted imagination, which led me to believe the worst of all men. Even men like Justin Penrose.

Was I to be forever tormented this way? Would I never learn to trust men again? I trusted John Trevelyan. I trusted Justin Penrose—at least, I thought I did. Yet even as I thought it, doubts crept in to nag at my brain. Could I really trust any man? Could I trust him?

I could not find it in my heart to snub Clara when she requested me to do little things for her, as Justin had suggested. She treated me as her friend, seemed to rely on my friendship.

"If it were not for you, I don't know what I'd do," she said. "You make my stay here worthwhile. But I shall have to be going soon. Back to London and my friends. I'm not wanted here. Justin doesn't want me here."

It was quite true. He made it perfectly plain he did not want her here and would be glad when she was gone. His earlier attempts at pleasantness had not come to anything. I believed I was to blame. Since the incident in Lovers Knot Copse, not a word had passed his lips that was not harsh and cruel. Most of the time he took himself off alone and kept a cold silence. I could not blame him for his attitude toward me—I felt I deserved it; but his mother was faultless, and blame should not be laid at her door. But then, he was not the man to concern himself with such distinctions.

I felt a certain satisfaction at finding things in him to dislike. For a while these things had been hidden beneath a veneer manufactured by him to fool people, but he had found it impossible to sustain. The bitterness inside him had become too great. It had eroded everything that was good in him. He might try to revive his good qualities, but he would never completely succeed. I had been fooled for a while, but no longer.

But now I longed for the man he had, for a little while, become to return.

Mrs. Carthew noticed the change in him and blamed Clara for it.

"Why do she stay to torment him?" she muttered to me one day. "Why don't she go back to London?"

"She doesn't torment him," I said. "Rather, he torments her."

She threw me a chilling glance which made my skin crawl.

"Anyway," I added, "she is going. Soon. She told me so."

But as the days passed, Clara had still not left Penrose House, and she made no further mention of going home. Justin snapped out of his morose mood and, though he continued tactiturn in speech, gradually became more amenable. Over all this time he had continued to accompany his mother and myself on the short walks we took together, "for her health's sake," she said. Many a time she had hinted that his presence was not necesary, that we would not go far and would not get lost. But he had persisted. To me it seemed almost as if he did not wish me to be alone with his mother. This could not be, of course; we were left alone together often enough in the house. Still, I thought it strange.

John came over to visit us. We were still endeavoring to bring about a better understanding between Justin and his mother, an uphill struggle though it was, and I doubted we would ever succeed.

"He's so very bitter," I said on one occasion. "I can't see us ever overcoming it."

"Unconscionably so," he agreed. "For a man of his age to go on harboring a grudge against his mother is, well, to put it mildly, bordering on the unstable. There's a kind of—madness about it."

Unstable, yes. Unstable was a word one could use about Justin Penrose reasonably, with his wild changes of mood— but madness? Surely that was going a bit too far.

"We must try to get him on an even keel," he said.

And I agreed that we must.

Was there madness in Justin Penrose? I asked myself. I had not thought so till John had mentioned it. Now there were times when I thought I could see it, and it made me more wary of him than ever.

But then something happened that made me change my mind about him yet again.

I had been thinking for a long time about tidying up the library. The room was cleaned regularly, as much as it could be, by the maid, who had to circumnavigate piles of books occupying space on the floor and various pieces of furniture. But the time had come for the books to be replaced in their positions on the shelves. Justin had finished with them, and I had time on my hands now that the new novel was finished. I went to ask Mrs. Carthew for the loan of a duster.

She reacted as usual to any request I made that she considered unsuitable to my position, throwing her hands up in the air and slapping them down on her thighs, crying, "Lordy, lordy, 'tis no work for 'ee to be at. Sally be the one to 'tend such things."

"But Mr. Penrose doesn't like anyone to touch his books but me."

"As long as you'm there to oversee, m'dear," she said complacently, "'twill be all right."

"But it's so unnecessary. I only wish to dust a few books. Please let me. I've had my mind on it for ages, and now I have the time . . . Sally is busy in the dining room and I would like to make a start. Please, Mrs. Carthew."

"Oh, very well," she agreed after a moment's hesitation. "But don't 'ee be gettin' yourself in a mess. Master Justin won't like it."

"Master Justin's gone to see Dr. Trevelyan and won't be back till late. I'll have plenty of time to make myself presentable again."

She sniffed. "And what about Madam—Mrs. Penrose?"

"She's resting."

With another sniff, she placed a yellow duster in my hands. I went off happily to make a start not only on the books littering the floor and furniture, but on all the books on all the shelves, which had collected a fair amount of dust. Naturally, I dipped into many of them. I enjoyed myself thoroughly, and the afternoon passed all too swiftly.

I began to realize it was a bigger job than I had anticipated. I should have to leave most of it for another time if I were to wash and change in time for supper, but there was still time to finish the shelf I was working on. There were three spaces left to be filled by three great tomes, and I had already ascertained which were the three.

I nipped nimbly down the library steps, wondering why the biggest books were kept on the top shelves. I picked up one—

173

which was as much as I could manage on one journey up the steps—placed it in position, and turned to descend again.

And then the door opened. My heart started thumping. Justin Penrose came in.

"What are you doing up there?" he said.

As if he couldn't see. "I'm tidying the bookshelves," I said.

"Hm," he grunted. I could see his eyes had missed nothing of my disheveled appearance. "Well, I should be obliged if you will call it a day now. I want to do some work in here."

"Do you wish me to take dictation?"

"No. It's something I have to do alone."

"I see."

"I must say," he added with a touch of self-mockery, "I find it damned difficult to get any time to myself these days, what with Mother and the need to chaperone you."

"Chaperone me!" I cried indignantly. "I have no need of a chaperone. You took that duty upon yourself. You can't blame me for—Ah-h-h-h!"

My words were lost in a shrill scream as everything seemed to disintegrate beneath me and I hit the floor with a sickening thud.

"Nicola!" Justin was on his knees beside me almost before I realized I had fallen. "Are you all right? Are you hurt? What a damn fool thing to say. I can see you're hurt. No, don't try to rise."

My face must have been contorted with pain as I tried to move. My left leg was tucked underneath me, and an agonizing pain shot through it.

"I think I've twisted my ankle," I whispered faintly.

"Broken it, more likely," he said grimly. "What happened? Did you slip?"

"No, I didn't slip. The ladder just gave way."

"Gave way?"

His eyes followed my glance. The ladder was still standing, but one of the rungs was hanging loose, broken off completely at one end, held on by a thread at the other. The breaks were

174

clean. Too clean to be accidental? My head dizzied at the thought. Did he think so too? I waited for him to remark on it—but he didn't.

Instead he said, "You'd better not move, in case you have a fracture. I'll send for John at once. He'll come in an instant."

A few moments later he was at my side again. I had straightened my leg from beneath me, not without a great deal of pain, but at least it proved I had not broken it. Justin whistled through his teeth as he saw the puffy swelling above my shoe.

"It is just a sprain," I said. My voice sounded a bit wavery, probably from shock.

"Better get this off," he said, and with great gentleness proceeded to remove my shoe.

I looked down at his bent head and noticed strands of silver among the black. Ridiculously, a disturbing swell of tenderness rose up in me and I felt my hand lift to stroke his head.

"There!" he said. As he looked up at me, I brought my hand swiftly back to my side and tried to control my breathing, which had unaccountably quickened.

He stared at me for a moment, a look of puzzlement flying across his face. Had he noticed the rush of feeling I had tried to quell? How had he interpreted it? Then his expression changed. What did it show now? Doubt?

I moved slightly, wincing with pain.

"Keep still," he commanded. "I'll be back in a minute."

He hurried out and returned with a cup of sweet tea, which he ordered me to drink.

Mrs. Carthew bustled in behind him, full of sympathy and concern.

"Lordy, lordy," she cried when she saw me. "What a to-do! What a to-do!"

"She's in great pain, Carty. Show Dr. Trevelyan in the moment he arrives," Justin said.

"But you can't leave her on the floor like that," she cried.

"No," he agreed. He picked me up and deposited me on one

175

of the leather armchairs.

I felt not a flicker of pain he was so gentle.

"What is it? What has happened? I thought I heard a scream."

Clara had appeared, all of a flutter, in the doorway.

"Nicola's had a fall," Justin said.

"What? Oh, my dear child. Have you hurt yourself?"

"Of course she has, Mother. Why do you think—?"

He was being short as usual with his mother, and I saw her face pucker as it did when he spoke to her harshly—which was often.

"I think I've sprained my ankle, Clara," I came in quickly, before he could finish.

"Oh. I won't stay then. I can't stand to see people in pain."

She turned to go and almost fell over Betsy, who, with Winnie, had been alerted by the noise and had come to see what was going on.

"Get out of my way, you silly creatures," she spat at them. "Take them away, Mrs. Carthew. They shouldn't be in here when Nicola is in such agony. I don't know why you keep such big, lumbering animals, Justin. I really don't. I don't know why you have to have dogs about the place at all. If you must have them, they should be kept outside in kennels, not allowed to roam the house at will."

She went out grumbling, leaving behind her an atmosphere you could cut with a knife. Then Justin said, "You'd better take them out, Carty."

Dutifully, Mrs. Carthew shepherded the animals out. Not long afterward, she shepherded the doctor in.

"What's happened?" he said on entering. "I was told that Nicola had fallen."

"Yes. She slipped and fell down the library steps."

I stared at Justin in amazement. His reply had been quick, glib, and untruthful.

"I didn't fall," I declared resentfully.

"Of course you did. You sprained your ankle. How did you

manage that if you didn't fall?"

"Let's have a look at it," John said, falling to his knees and taking my foot in his hands. "Hm. Yes, it is only a sprain. You were lucky, young lady."

"Lucky!" I gasped, wincing with pain under his examination. "Yes, you could say that. I could easily have been crippled, which is what the person responsible for sawing through the rungs of the ladder seems to have had in mind."

"Sawing through . . . Justin, what have you been up to now?"

"Don't talk like an idiot!" Justin growled.

"Sorry, old chap." John hurriedly erased the fatuous expression from his face. "Ill-timed humor."

He was not taking me seriously. "Look for yourself," I cried. "You'll see."

He got down on his haunches to look. His sensitive fingers stroked the broken end of the rung and, with a snap that made us all start, the whole thing came away in his hands. He rose, cradling the rung, and frowned. "It certainly looks as if it had been sawn through."

"Rubbish!" Justin's repudiation was swift and firm. "How could it have been? Who would do such a thing? And for what reason? The whole thing's preposterous!"

"Preposterous or not, it's true!" I flared.

Why did he not admit it? He had seen the break the same time as I. I was certain I had caught a look of fear in his eyes as he had come to the same conclusion. But here he was, denying it vehemently.

And now John was agreeing with him. "Of course. It's nonsense. No one would do such a thing. The rung must simply have become weakened with age. I believe the steps date back a long way, don't they, Justin?"

"A couple of generations, at least."

"Yes, I thought so. Now don't worry, Nicola, just rest your ankle and you'll be as right as rain in no time." John picked up his black medicine bag. "Hot and cold compresses are the order

177

of the day. I'll instruct Mrs. Carthew as I go out. She's a fine nurse. I'll come and see you tomorrow. The swelling will have gone down by then, I can assure you. But don't try to walk on that ankle till I've had another look at it. If you must move about, use a cane. Justin will let you have one—he has plenty."

"But . . ." I protested, still concerned about the sawn-through rung.

"I must go now," he smiled. "Mrs. Tremayne's expecting her first. I think she might have a bit of trouble. I ought to be there."

There was something behind his eyes which I could not quite fathom. It might have been concern for Mrs. Tremayne, but somehow I thought his concern was for me—not for my ankle—for me personally. For my safety. I started to tremble.

Justin followed his friend from the room after giving a brief, backward glance in my direction and a curt, "I'll be back."

As soon as the door closed, I stood up, intending to take a closer look at the ladder, and the rung, which had been set down on the desk. I fell back immediately as searing pain shot up my leg, causing me to squeal in agony. Once in control of myself again, however, I strained forward to see if I could examine the breaks. No matter what they said, I was *certain* the rung had been sawn through. Why? I did not know. For what purpose? It was perfectly clear—to effect just such an accident as I had sustained.

But who would do such a thing? Who could possibly wish to harm me?

But had it been meant for me? I never used the steps. Today had been the first time.

So had it been meant for Justin? Justin, whom I had seen climb those steps many a time . . .

Justin returned, swinging a silver-topped cane. "It belonged to my grandmother," he said. "I think it will support your small frame. You're no bigger than she was."

"Thank you," I said. I tried to rise with it, but the slightest pressure on my ankle caused such excruciating pain I could only fall back again, teeth gritted to smother my moans.

Almost immediately, I was scooped into his arms. He strode with me into the hall and up the staircase, calling for Mrs. Carthew on the way.

"Nicola's in agony," he said when she came running. "I think she'd better keep to her room till her ankle's healed. Have all her meals brought up to her. Have a maid in constant attendance upon her."

"'Twill be just as you say, Master Justin."

"Have you got the compresses ready?"

"I have."

"Good. Bring them up at once, will you?"

"At once, Master Justin."

It was exactly as it had been when I first arrived here, decisions being made for me, orders given for my welfare. It irked me now as it had done then.

"I don't want to have my meals in my room," I declared irritably. "I don't wish to be kept in my room. I'm not sick and dying, for heaven's sake. I've only sprained my ankle. After a brief rest I shall be up and about. I have a cane to use if I need it. I shall be able to fend for myself."

Mrs. Carthew had opened my sitting room door, and Justin had carried me inside while I said my little piece. They had both heard me out in silence. Now, as he lowered me onto the sofa, he said, "Let's see how it goes, shall we?"

Then I was left alone—my cane just out of reach. Fuming at my inability to retrieve it, I awaited Mrs. Carthew's ministrations with the compresses.

Chapter Ten

I had to admit I enjoyed being pampered. Susan was sent to look after me, and she fussed round me like a mother hen. Visitors came and went in rapid succession. After the first evening, when I was content to lie in bed, my foot raised on a cushion in between hot and cold compress sessions, I lounged on the sofa, waited on hand and foot, and received my visitors right royally.

My first visitor was Justin Penrose. He came even before John did. It was not a lengthy visit, but it showed his concern for me, and I was grateful. Again I pondered the contradictions of his nature.

John came next and pronounced himself satisfied with my progress.

"The swelling's gone down nicely," he said. "We'll soon have you up and about again."

"It still hurts when I put any weight on it," I told him.

"It will for some time yet. Don't be overeager to walk on it for another day or two. You might have torn a ligament, in which case, I'm afraid, it will take somewhat longer than that."

"Oh, I hope not!" I exclaimed.

"Well, we'll see. Don't fret about it. And now, what about a cup of coffee? Do you think that wicked old pisky woman downstairs can be persuaded to send some up?"

180

"Shush!" I hissed. "Susan's in the bedroom, tidying up. She might hear you."

"Should I care?" he asked lightly, then whispered. "Get rid of her."

"Oh, John!" I shook my head sadly at him. "You're incorrigible."

I called Susan and asked if she would bring us some coffee, which she agreed to do with pleasure. She liked Dr. Trevelyan as, indeed, did all the servants at Penrose House. Mrs. Carthew seemed to be the exception that proved the rule.

"Nicola," he said when Susan had left us, "that ladder . . ."

My breath caught in my throat. "Yes?"

"I've been mulling it over all night, and I think you could be right. The rung was deliberately sawn through."

"But you said . . . You agreed with Justin. . . ."

"Yes, I know, but . . ." He frowned and bit into his lower lip, unsure of himself. "Oh, I'm probably on the wrong track . . . being overcautious because you are concerned . . . but do take care, Nicola. Be careful!"

"I've been thinking about it, too," I said. "What if it wasn't meant for me?"

"You mean—Justin?"

"Well, I don't normally use the steps. Justin does. Suppose he were the intended victim, not I."

"Oh, no. Surely not. Nobody would take such action against Justin."

"Nobody would take such action against me. Why should they?"

He shrugged, nonplussed.

"It must be somebody who has a grudge against Justin."

"Nobody has a grudge against Justin."

"His mother has."

"Clara?"

"She's as much as said so. She knows he doesn't want her here. He makes no attempt to hide how he feels about her."

"But you're not suggesting that she . . . ?" John burst out

181

laughing. "That's carrying supposition too far. Perhaps we'd better forget all about it if that's where it's leading us. It was probably wood fatigue—or woodworm. Anyway, Justin's sending the steps away to be repaired by an expert. He should be able to clear the mystery up for us. We'll probably find that's what it was—woodworm boring away unnoticed."

I agreed he must be right. I had allowed myself to be carried away by the fact that Clara was the only newcomer to the island—apart from myself—and that, since her arrival, danger had threatened Justin twice, first in the quarry and next in the library. But they had both been accidents. They could have happened to anybody. The fact that the one in the library had happened to me, proved it. No one would set up an accident designed for a certain person when anyone might be caught by it. And his mother . . . How could I have entertained the idea that his mother wished him harm? It was—I unconsciously provided the word Justin had used earlier—preposterous.

Clara herself was my next visitor, and I hated myself for thinking such awful things about her as she talked and laughed and cheered me up.

"You need cheering up, my dear," she said. "I know what it's like to sit all alone in your room with no one to talk to."

"I'm not alone," I said. "Susan's always with me, and I'm having lots of visitors."

"That's good. How is your ankle, my dear?"

"I think it's improving."

"You mustn't start walking on it too soon. John says you've torn a ligament."

"He says I *might* have. Another day or two will tell."

"Ah, well, see that you rest it then."

I was touched by her concern.

Ruth came to see me. The school holidays were in progress and she was able to come early. She had heard from John about my accident and had come over straightaway. She stayed to take luncheon with me.

Parson Bryn called too. All in all, I had a thoroughly

enjoyable day.

They all called on me again the following day, except Parson Bryn and Justin.

I missed Justin.

He was brusque, discourteous to a degree, the harsh, distant man of my first acquaintance. Yet I had known many pleasant days of companionship with him, and I had had to reevaluate my conception of him continually.

He was a dual personality, difficult to understand, a man of black and dangerous moods. Yet he possessed charm which, when he chose to exert it, altered him completely. But he used it only to achieve his own ends and, when unsuccessful in so doing, quickly reverted to his true nature, which was cold and mean-spirited.

Did I really believe this? I did not think so. There was so much evidence to the contrary. Ruth's testimony. John's. The love he seemed to inspire in his fellow islanders. Carty's adoration.

But what about his mother? His treatment of her? I considered it reprehensible, but understandable, under the circumstances.

But why had he turned against me after being so friendly? All I had done was repulse his advances. Surely he could accept that, a man of his mature years. Perhaps it had been a blow to his male ego. If so, I must be glad he had not reacted in the way Ted Gibbon had. Not that he ever would have. There was no comparison between the two men. I knew that as surely as I knew anything. In time he would recover from his wounded pride and become an amenable friend again.

So I argued with myself as I sat in the rose-scented arbor sheltered from the wind, the cane I no longer really needed propped against the rustic walls, Justinia Penrose's cane that, somehow, I could not bring myself to part with. But underneath it all, I was aware of something else—something that was eating away at the very heart of him. Was it his thwarted love for Caroline?

183

I believed this to be so. That she had jilted him hurt him more than his mother's defection, which had led to his father's death. This, I felt, was the answer to the dark despair that showed itself in his black moods and helped feed his anger against his mother.

And so I continued finding excuses for this man whom I really did not like.

"Hello, Nicola." Ruth was coming across the lawn, waving to me with something in her hand.

I thought how attractive she looked, with the sun lighting up her brown hair and the pretty dress molding her trim figure.

"Justin gave me this for you."

So that accounted for the light in her eye, the spring in her step. She had been talking to Justin Penrose. I had noticed that whenever he was in the vicinity, she sparkled. It was evident she was in love with him. She knew it was a hopeless passion, that she must worship him from afar—but did she nourish the faint hope that, one day, her love might be requited? If this were so, I felt she might as well hope for the sun never to set, for all the good it would do her. Caroline Clunes had left his heart a shriveled husk that no other woman would ever be able to penetrate.

She put a letter into my hand. My heart jumped when I saw the handwriting. "It's from my mother. Do you mind if I open it now?"

"Of course not," she said, seating herself beside me. "I know you are always eager for news from your mother."

Eager because I was always worried about her; I could never be otherwise while she lived with Ted Gibbon. With each letter I received from her, I expected some mention of unhappiness, of regret. There was never any, of course. She was still blind to his faults. I told myself this was all to the good—it prevented her heart from breaking. But this time, as I started to read, my heart sank.

"My mother's not well," I whispered.

"Then you must go and see her."

184

"No, I don't think that will be necessary. She's not desperately ill. She just says she's been feeling off-color lately, but that it's nothing to worry about."

"Then why mention it?"

I gave a puzzled shake of my head and sighed unhappily. My mother was not one to complain unduly.

"It worries you. I can see it does," Ruth said. "Why not ask Justin for a few days off and go and see her? Set your mind at rest."

"I . . . I . . ."

"What's the matter? Why do you hesitate? You'd like to see her, wouldn't you?"

"Yes, but . . . Of course I would, but . . ."

"But what?" She would not let the matter drop, and began to probe more deeply as I kept silent. "Nicola, exactly why did you come to Penrose? It can't only have been because you wished to be independent. You could have taken a job anywhere and achieved that. There was no reason to choose a place like this, where it would be difficult, if not impossible, to get away. So why? Did something happen that made you want to leave home? A quarrel with your mother?"

"Oh, no, nothing like that."

"What then?"

"Don't ask me to explain, Ruth. I might tell you about it one day, but not now."

I felt sure she would have pursued the matter if Justin had not approached, greeting us from a short distance away. The concern she had displayed for me vanished in a glow of pleasure at seeing him. But then it faded as he said, "I'm sorry, Ruth, but I've come to steal Nicola away from you. I need her to help me start work on my film script."

"You're doing it, then," I cried breathlessly.

"Yes. It's a challenge—and I never was one to resist a challenge."

"And you'll go to America?"

"*We'll* go to America," he said with emphasis. "But that's in the future. Right now, I want to get something on paper, and I hardly know how to begin. The cinematograph is a new medium for the arts and demands a new approach, a technique different from the theatre. Ralph says he doesn't think so. His view is that a play is a play whether for the stage or the screen—but I'm not so sure."

"Well if Ralph says so . . ." Ralph Tegwood was Justin's publisher and would know, I felt, what he was talking about.

But Justin was continuing with hardly a break.

"He called me last night. Bert Kleinberger, of Kleinberger Films, will be arriving in London in a day or two, and he wants me to meet him. He thinks, rightly, that I shall want a say in things right from the beginning. I'm not sure what he expects in the way of a script, but I want to have something ready to show him, so we've got a couple hard days of work ahead of us. Do you feel up to it?"

I nodded, but my head was awhirl. He had made up his mind to allow *Love's Balm* to be portrayed on film for all the world to see, and I could not believe it. That poignant love story, that document of betrayal, surely touched his inmost soul more deeply.

He must have seen the perplexity in my eyes. "Is anything wrong?" he asked.

"No," I said quickly. I felt a movement at my side. It was Ruth. I—we?—had forgotten all about her.

"I'd better go," she murmured.

"Oh, Ruth, I'm sorry. . . . I'll call on you as soon as I can."

"Do that," she said, and my heart ached to see the sadness in her glance as she made a swift exit across the lawn. I knew Justin was the cause of it.

Justin, completely unaware, said, "Come, Nicola," and handed me my cane.

But I knew Ruth had been hurt by his careless attitude. She adored him, let it show in her eyes, and he did not notice—or if he did, gave it no thought. I felt deeply for her. She was a good, kind friend to me, and I did not like to see her unhappy.

186

Evidence of her kindness, her thoughtfulness, was given to me the following day, though at first I was angry at what I considered her interference in my affairs.

Justin and I were taking tea together during a break from work, munching contentedly on a dish of Mrs. Carthew's delicious little cakes, when he said, "I shall be going to London tomorrow to see Ralph and this Kleinberger fellow. I thought you might like to come with me. You can stay with your mother while I deal with my business. I'll pick you up when I'm ready to leave."

I sensed Ruth's hand in this, and experienced a moment of anger. I did not reply to his offer.

"You'd like to see your mother, wouldn't you?" When I remained silent, he continued, "Ruth stopped by this morning and told me about the letter you received. She said your mother was ill and that you were worried about her, but that she doubted you would ask me for time off to go and see her." His glance sharpened. "Why should she doubt that, do you think? You're not afraid of me, are you? You do not give me the impression you are. You didn't think I would deny such a request from you?"

"I told Ruth it was not important. My mother only said she had been off-color for a few days," I muttered.

"But you'd like to see her?"

"Yes . . . I'd like to . . . but . . ." Panic began to grow in me. I longed to see my mother. But I was afraid to go home. "If it were only my mother . . . But there's Ted Gibbon!"

"Ted Gibbon? Who is he?"

His persistence unnerved me. He wanted to know why I was so reluctant to go home, and gave the impression that he would not be satisfied till he had wormed it out of me.

"My . . . my stepfather," I whispered.

For a moment I thought he had not heard me, but then he said, very quietly, "I see," and a moment later, "Something happened between you. What was it?"

I kept silent and looked down at the shoes on my feet.

187

"It's obvious to me that you're afraid of going home, and he's the reason. What happened? What did he do to make you so afraid to return?"

"I . . . I can't tell you."

"You mean, you won't."

"I can't."

He said no more, but he observed me closely. He knew something had happened between my stepfather and myself, and was turning over every possibility in his mind. Eventually he would settle on the right one—and would blame me for it. He would not see me as the innocent victim of a man driven by lust, but as a coquette, deserving of all I had received. Yet it had not been my fault. I wanted to tell him so, to explain. Only, knowing his opinion of women, I knew he would not believe me. Believe of my stepfather such gross indecency? A man newly married to my mother? No, he would say, whatever had happened between us must have been my fault. I must have led him on.

I knew this was what he would think because of Caroline Clunes, because of Clara Penrose, who, between them, had turned him against all women.

Suddenly tears were streaming down my face. There was nothing I could do to stop them.

He rushed to kneel at my side. "Don't, Nicola. Don't cry," he begged.

"I'm not crying." I brushed my hand angrily over my eyes.

"Something's troubling you. Is it me? Have I caused you pain by probing into your past? Won't you tell me about it? Perhaps I can help. I've raised memories you were trying to forget. I had no right to do so. But now that I have, can't you tell me about them? It might help if you talk about them." He was persuasive, but . . .

"There are some things one cannot talk about," I whimpered.

"With the right person it's easy to talk about anything. It doesn't do to hug things, painful things, to yourself."

I stared at him. The right person. Did he see himself as the right person? He was the last, the very last, person I could talk to about it.

"That is what you do, isn't it?" I countered to steer him away from my troubles, afraid I might say more than I wished.

He stiffened. "What?"

"Hug painful things to yourself. You can't, or won't, unburden yourself of the anguish in your soul. Why should you expect me to be able to?"

I felt this whole conversation had taken a wrong turn. I had meant to say none of this. He would spurn me now, and I did not want that.

"I can't think where you got hold of that idea. But if there is 'anguish in my soul,' as you put it, don't let it concern you. You are the one who is suffering. I'd like to ease that suffering, if I can."

Tears spurted from my eyes again. There was so much kindness in this man. I could see it now. His own suffering was great, yet he put it aside as being of no account. He only wished to ease the suffering he saw in me. Or perhaps that was what I wished to believe.

"Oh, Justin," I murmured weakly, "you're so kind."

"Nicola," he responded, clasping me to him, "I want to help."

In the comfort of his arms, I rested my head against his chest and felt the pressure of his lips on my head. I felt I could have stayed there forever. But Clara came in, and he released me quickly.

I detected anger in him as he rose to ask, "Yes, Mother? What do you want?"

Clara's blue eyes flashed at us, reading more into the situation than was actually the case. "Young Arthur Trevose and his fiancée wish to have a word with you. They are waiting in the hall," she said.

"I'll see them at once," he said. Turning to me, he added, "Don't worry. Nothing's so bad it can't be helped."

189

Then he was gone. The door had hardly closed on him when Clara started berating me.

"What can you be thinking about, letting him kiss you like that?"

"It wasn't as it appeared," I said.

"No?" Her tone was full of disbelief.

"No. He was comforting me, that's all. I'm worried because I've just heard that my mother is ill, and . . ."

"He put his arms round you and kissed you—to comfort you," she voiced scathingly. "Oh, Nicola! You don't believe that, any more than I do."

"It's true. He's taking me with him to London tomorrow so that I can visit her."

"Well, if you'll take my advice, you'll stay there and not come back."

"But I must come back."

"Why?"

"I . . . I . . ."

"I should think again, if I were you. You've already had one narrow escape."

"What do you mean?"

"Your accident in the library."

"You're not suggesting that Justin was to blame for that?"

"I'm not suggesting anything, only warning you to think again about coming back. Remember Caroline? I told you about her. She fell in love with Justin. He promised to marry her. She thought he meant it. Luckily, she saw through him before it was too late and left, never to return. Now you are being given the same chance. Take it, I beg you. Don't let Justin . . ."

I could not take her seriously. Whatever it was she was hinting at—and I could not be sure whether it was that he would try to seduce me or that he might injure me in some other way—I did not believe it. I thought I had the measure of Justin Penrose. But I began to see a certain futility in trying to bring them to a better understanding of each other. With such thoughts as these in her mind—did she really believe them?—

where was the basis for it?

And what about him, the bitterness against her that bit deep into his soul? How could it be overcome? I had seen on first acquaintance that he was a man who, once having made up his mind, would never change it. Though I had slightly modified that judgment later, it was, in essence, true. He had made up his mind that Clara was to blame for the death of his father, and he would never forgive her for it.

So were John and I butting our heads against a brick wall? Yes, I answered myself, we were.

"I'll drop you at your home before going on to my club."

Justin Penrose and I had sailed in the *Justinia* to Port Zennoc on a quiet sea, crossed Bodmin Moor in a rattling old carriage, boarded the train for London, and were now sitting in a hansom cab in that great metropolis.

"I'd rather book in at an hotel," I cried after he had ordered the cabby to drive to Kensington.

I steeled myself to answer the questions he was bound to put to me. However, he betrayed no more curiosity than a puzzled glance.

"Brownings is a good hotel," he said. "You'll be comfortable there."

"Yes. Brownings will do fine," I agreed.

He redirected the cabby, and I sat back against the worn leather, glad of the respite I had acquired. My visit to Kensington could be put off until tomorrow. As I sat there it dawned on me that there was no reason why I need go to Kensington at all. I could avoid the prospect of meeting Ted Gibbon by arranging to meet my mother somewhere in town— I had only to telephone her from Brownings. Why hadn't I thought of it before? Now I could relax for the first time since receiving the letter that had brought me here.

Justin kept the cabby waiting while he escorted me into Brownings and saw me safely registered and installed in one of their best rooms.

After dispatching the pageboy with a tip that brought a huge smile to his face, Justin asked me, "You'll call on your mother in the morning, I suppose?"

"Yes, I should think so."

"Would you like me to collect you and take you there?"

"Oh, no, thank you. That won't be necessary."

I was aware that I sounded ungracious, but as I did not know what my plans were, and was still slightly fearful that I might yet have to visit my mother at home, it had to suffice.

"You will probably wish to spend the whole day with her?"

"No . . . Yes . . . Maybe . . . I don't know. I'm so tired I can hardly think straight."

He was immediately contrite. "Of course you are. It's been a long day. And here I am pestering you with unnecessary questions. Just one thing more . . . Will you dine with me tomorrow night?"

"Yes. I should like to."

"Good. Eight o'clock?"

"Fine."

"If you change your mind—you might decide you'd rather stay and dine with your mother—will you leave a message for me at my club? I'll understand."

We said goodnight, and I ordered a light meal to be sent up to me. I picked at it desultorily, anxiously wondering what the morrow would bring. I wanted to see my mother, of course I did—but I was reluctant to go home. How strange it seemed, being in London and not going home! A wave of homesickness washed over me. I longed to see my mother, to hear her voice. Well, I could ring her up now and speak to her. How surprised she would be to hear from me—but she would want to know where I was, why I had chosen to accommodate myself in a hotel instead of going home, and I felt I could not cope with such questions now. I would wait till morning when I was fresh.

Unexpectedly, when I did ring, she seemed unsurprised to

hear my voice and made no comment on learning where I was. She did not sound overeager to see me, either, and refused to meet me somewhere in town. She even left it to me to suggest I should call round to see her. I could not understand it, and it worried me.

Hartley, butler to my father before I was born, opened the door to me. His face lit up. "Miss Nicola!" he cried. "You've come home!"

"Only visiting," I said, and his face dropped. "Didn't my mother tell you I was coming?"

"No, Miss Nicola. But it's good to see you. We've all missed you. Cook, Polly, William—everybody."

"Thank you, Hartley. I've missed all of you, too."

He stood before me and an awkward silence grew between us.

"My mother *is* in?" I said, an odd little flutter of panic starting within me.

"Oh, yes, Miss. She's in the drawing room. If you'll come this way."

He led the way, as if I were a stranger, across the hall with the orange and white tiles so familiar to me, past the curving staircase carpeted in Indian weave. How often had I slid down that fat, shining banister and been chastised for it? I smiled at the memory and looked up to see my father's portrait, which hung on the first landing wall. I felt my heart stop.

It wasn't there. Why? By whose authority had it been removed? I needed no one to answer me. I knew Ted Gibbon had ordered it.

Had my mother objected at all to its removal? I doubted it. It would have been sufficient for her that he wished it taken down.

What else had changed since I had been away? I wondered, and saw to my horror, as I stepped into the drawing room, that my mother had.

She had always been rosily plump, fresh-faced, and smiling, very much in command of herself and those around her. Her will had always been my father's command. He had indulged her every whim. I had followed his lead—albeit with occasional rebellion, which as I grew older had led me into conflict with her. Yet she reigned supreme in her household and among her circle of friends. No one flouted her wishes. Even Ted Gibbon gave way to her and hid from her that which he knew would grieve her. I believed it his one saving grace.

But the woman I looked at now was hollow-eyed and thin-cheeked. She looked crushed, incapable of saying boo to a goose.

"Mama!" I rushed across to her. "You *are* ill."

She raised thin arms to hug me, and I felt her bones through the silk of her dress.

"I thought you were only a little off-color," I gasped.

"Yes . . . off-color. . . . That is all."

"It's more than that. You look so . . . so . . . Have you seen a doctor?"

"No."

"But you should. I'll call Dr. Bragg. He must come round at once."

"No. It's not necessary."

I looked at her thin frame, her darkly shadowed eyes. "I think it is," I said, lifting the receiver from the hook.

"Put that down!" Her voice suddenly became sharp, authoritative. "Do as I say. I'm not sick. No doctor has a cure for what ails me."

And she burst into tears.

I had never before seen my mother cry, and for a moment all I could do was stand and gape at her in amazement. Then I ran back to her and hugged her to me.

"Mama! Mama! Please don't cry. Don't cry. Don't cry."

I said it over and over again, not knowing what else I could do, only wanting her to stop the dreadful sobbing which brought back memories of her abject sorrow at the death of my father.

"He's left me, Nicola."

My blood ran cold, then started to pound. "Ted Gibbon?"

"It was my own fault. If I hadn't complained about being left alone so much . . . But it was the headaches, Nicola. They were so bad. They made me do and say things I wouldn't have dreamed of doing normally."

"Headaches? You've been getting headaches?"

"Migraines, I think they were. Ted said that's what they were. He was very understanding, Nicola. I shouldn't have complained. It's one thing he could never stand, and as he explained, he couldn't spend all his time with me. He had things to do, people to see . . . but I began imagining things. I had heard rumors. I began to think they were true. It was the headaches. . . . They made me think this way. . . . I asked him, 'Are you tired of me, Ted?' 'Of course not,' he said, 'What a thing to ask. But I'm a man who needs some time to himself. I can't be forever dancing attendance on you.' 'But I'm your wife,' I cried. 'Yes, and I love you,' he said, 'but . . .'"

She had stopped crying and was staring ahead of her, seeing it all again, trying to understand how it had happened.

"You can't blame yourself," I said.

"I did terrible things," she said. "It was the headaches, you see. I asked him if he'd got a mistress. He grew angry . . . so angry. . . . No, he said, he hadn't got a mistress. Whatever put such an idea into my mind? I told him I didn't believe him. I knew he had a mistress because I'd seen him with her. I'd followed him one day and . . ."

"Mama!" I was horrified. I would never have believed her capable of doing such a thing. She had always looked with disdain on such practices.

"I followed him when he said he was going to his club one night. He didn't go there. He went to a music hall and waited at the stage door after the show and . . . and . . ."

She broke off gulping. It was all too much for her.

"You needn't go on, Mama," I said gently. "I can guess what happened. I've known for a long time the kind of man he is. Your friends have known. They tried to warn you. You wouldn't listen."

"He was so angry when I told him." She hadn't been listening to me at all. "I've never seen him so angry. I thought he was going to hit me. He didn't, of course. And there was a perfectly ordinary explanation for what had happened. He had met the woman for a friend."

"Oh, Mama!" I began, ready to repudiate his story. I knew it to be false.

But she was running on. "His friend had been unavoidably delayed and had begged Teddy to meet this girl for him and take her to his house to wait for him till he arrived. Teddy did this and then went to his club—as I would have seen if I had continued to follow him and not gone home as soon as I saw him with her. And he said . . . he said, 'If you can't trust me, perhaps it's best we part.' I said I was sorry. I begged him not to go. I went down on my knees. . . . But he left the house, and I haven't seen him since."

"Hush, Mama," I said, drawing her close as the tears flowed afresh down her wasted cheeks. "Don't upset yourself so. You're better off without him."

She pushed me away, her face contorted with rage. "How can you say such a thing? I'm not better off without him. I love him. And he loves me. I know he does. He'll come back. He will come back, won't he, Nicola? He must come back. If he doesn't I'll have nobody . . . nobody. . . ."

"You have me, Mama. I'll come home. I'll look after you."

"No!" Her voice was strongly assertive again. "I don't want you to come home. He'll never come back if he knows you're here."

"But you can't really want him back. He's untrustworthy."

"Don't say that. He's not. And I do want him back. How can I live without him? I've wronged him so."

"No, it is he who's wronged you. I'll stay now that I'm here, and—"

"No! Go away. Go back where you came from."

I gazed at her unhappily. She did not mean what she was saying. She could not wish to turn me out of the house. She had never wanted me to leave in the first place. It was her misery over losing Ted, the man she loved and in whom she could see no wrong, despite all, that made her say these things to me.

"Go quickly," she was continuing. "He mustn't know you are here. He hates you and never wants to see you again. I don't know why. He says it's something you've done. . . . What have you done, Nicola?"

"Nothing, Mama. He hates me because . . ." I tried to tell her the true reason, but, looking into her eyes, could not. "Because he knows I don't like him. He knows I left home because of him. . . ."

"You'd better go," she interrupted me. "If you're here he won't come back."

I felt sick at heart. There was something seriously wrong with my mother. Her mood kept changing rapidly. She now seemed to believe Ted Gibbon was coming back, or would come back once I had gone. Was it the headaches that affected her mind still? I asked her if she still got them.

"No, not now. I haven't had them for ages."

"If they come again, promise me you'll see Dr. Bragg."

"Yes, all right, if it will make you happy. Will you stay and have luncheon with me? It's such a long time since I saw you. You must have a lot to tell me. How are you getting on? What are you doing? Is he nice, this writer you work for?"

She was suddenly quite normal. The mother I knew, with her questions tumbling from her in her usual way.

"Yes, I . . ."

But she had again lost interest. She crossed to the window and gazed up and down the street, nervously rubbing her hands together. Was she watching for her husband's return?

How could I leave her and go back to Cornwall? I kept asking myself, as I sat opposite my mother at the table. The dishes set before us were varied and deliciously tempting, but I noticed

197

she only pecked at her food. No wonder she was so thin.

How long had Ted Gibbon been gone? She had not said. But it must have been a long time for her to have grown so thin with worry over it.

Or had the headaches a lot to do with it? She said they had gone now. But was she telling the truth? I could see she was far from well; she had changed drastically from the happy, confident woman I had said goodbye to less than three months ago. Why hadn't she seen a doctor? She should have seen a doctor. A terrible conjecture entered my mind.

I decided to call on Dr. Bragg and tell him of her condition, asking him to pay her a visit despite her objections. I also decided to stay in London, if not at home, then in a house nearby, rented or bought, to be on hand if she should need me.

Formulating these plans in my head, I did not hear the front door open, nor the dining room door behind my back. But I saw my mother's face light up with a mixture of surprise, wonder, joy. I saw the splash of tears on her cheeks, her swift departure from the table.

"Ted!"

"Fanny!"

I stiffened when I heard his voice, and looked round to see my mother in his arms. He smiled at me above her head, which he stroked with the tenderness of a lover. But there was no warmth in his smile, either for me or my mother. It curled into a sneer to match the look in his eyes, and fear weakened my bones, outstripping my concern for my mother. If I had begun to think I had conquered that fear, I knew now it had only lain dormant, ready to wake anew at the sight of him.

Then he was holding my mother away from him and looking down at her with all the charm he could readily command.

"I had to come back, my darling." His voice trembled with emotion. "I couldn't stay away from you any longer. I had to see your sweet face again, hear your voice, feel your touch. I've been a brute. Will you forgive me, Fanny?"

False, false man, I wanted to scream.

"It is you who must forgive me, my dearest, dearest one. I've been so stupid. So *stupid*. Oh, I thought I should die, my love. I thought you would never come back."

She was sobbing against his chest again. Ted Gibbon's eyes held mine once more. Triumph was stamped on every feature of his handsome face, and I knew he had planned all this. He had left her deliberately, knowing he would come back, but staying away long enough to nearly drive her out of her mind with misery. Why? So that he would never have to face a challenge from her again. So that he could carry on in his chosen way of life and never again hear a word of complaint from her.

My fear was swamped by my hatred of him. I might have known he would not leave her for good. She was his bank balance.

"Come, sweetheart," he murmured with false sincerity. "Let us go to our room. We have a lot to make up for."

False, heartless man.

I wanted to run after them, to make my mother listen to me while I opened her eyes to the sort of man he was. But what was the use? She would not believe me. Ted Gibbon had won complete victory over her.

There was nothing left for me to do now, but go. I must leave the house of my childhood, where I was no longer welcome.

But it was my house. *My* house. I could evict both Ted Gibbon and my mother, if I wished. But I would never do that. It was their home, not mine. Penrose House was my home now.

I should have felt sad, but there was a core of delight in me that leavened the sadness I should have felt. My feet were not sluggish as they took me across the room to ring for Hartley to inform him of my departure. But before I could ring, Ted Gibbon reentered the room.

"So you've come back," he said, closing the door behind him. My tremor of fear could not be suppressed. "I knew you would once you knew how ill she was."

My fear gave way to anger. "You . . . you made her write

199

that letter." It was all so clear to me now.

"Clever of me, wasn't it? I knew you wouldn't stay away when—"

"She needs a doctor," I cried. "She needed one long ago, when the headaches started. Why didn't you call Dr. Bragg?"

"There was really no need. They were only migraines. He wouldn't have been able to do anything for her. Lying down in a darkened room is the only treatment for migraines."

"Well, she needs a doctor now. You must see that. Your treatment of her has weakened her considerably."

"Oh, she'll recover quickly enough now I'm back—and now that you're here to nurse her."

"But I'm not staying."

"Oh, you are. You must. She needs you."

His voice was soft, silky smooth, and my tremor of fear threatened to return.

"No, she doesn't wish me to stay. She told me so."

"She'll change her mind after I've had a talk with her."

The underlying menace I had perceived became more evident. He seemed to be saying that, if I didn't stay, it would be the worse for her. I wondered about those headaches. Were they really migraines or . . . ? No, not even he would stoop to . . . But I knew he would.

"You've been poisoning her," I accused him wildly. "Poisoning her and blackmailing me."

He looked pained. "That's not a very nice thing to accuse your father of."

"You're not my father!"

"Your stepfather then. You know I have only your mother's interests at heart."

"No! Your own! Only your own!"

"Very well," he snapped. "I always knew you were nobody's fool. Here it is then, quick and to the point. If you want to keep your mother hale and hearty, renounce your claim to your father's fortune."

"So that's it." My contempt was so great that even he

recoiled momentarily. "It's money you want. I always knew it. It was why you married my mother. You thought she had inherited everything. You didn't know how astute my father was. He loved my mother, but he was not blind to her weaknesses. He knew that she would be prey to every fortune hunter in the land—she was never a good judge of character. I'm only astonished you never did your homework properly. He arranged it so that she would never want in her lifetime, but only I inherit upon her death."

"That being the case, my dear Nicola," he said suavely, "you will appreciate my dilemma. I have no wish to be left destitute should she die before me. And it's quite likely that she will; she's eleven years older than I am. When I suggested that she make a will out in my favor, and she told me she had no money of her own to leave, I—well, I couldn't believe it at first. But then she explained it all to me. That you were the sole beneficiary. And that she could only draw large amounts out of the bank with the agreement of your father's solicitors. But I need money now. I need it right away."

"To repay your debts," I sneered.

"And other things. . . . I think you know what they are. You should have been nicer to me, Nicola, then maybe . . . But that's water under the bridge now. Come. You have no choice but to sign everything over to your mother for her use now."

"And yours."

"And mine—if you wish her to remain in good health and happiness."

"I have a choice," I said quietly.

His eyes narrowed.

"I can arrange for you to receive an allowance—a substantial one—on condition . . ."

"You are in no position to make conditions. I want more than a substantial allowance. I want everything, and once you sign over to your mother, I shall have it. Then you will never hear from me again, I promise. You can go to the devil for all I shall care."

"And my mother? Can she go to the devil too?"

He shrugged. "You needn't worry about her. She'll be happy enough with me. We'll go on as before. She'll be satisfied with that. And I'm really quite fond of her, you know, in my way."

"The trustees won't allow it," I said. "Even if I agreed to your demands, they would refuse. They would think it very strange of me to make everything over to my mother when she is amply provided for during her lifetime."

"In a couple of years you'll be twenty-five. You will then have complete control. You won't need to ask their consent to anything. Well, what's a couple of years? I can wait that long if I have to—with a little something on account."

"You've thought it all out very carefully, haven't you?"

"Oh, yes. I've thought about it constantly, ever since your precious mother told me I could expect nothing, *nothing*, after her death."

"You don't love my mother. You never have. How can I be sure you won't leave her once you can get your hands on the money?"

"I give you my word."

"Your word!" I spat contemptuously. "I would as soon put my head in a lion's mouth as take your word on anything!"

"I admit that, without the money to give her appeal, I should not have married her," he said, completely unaffected by my contempt. "She is, after all, so very much older than I. But I've given her no cause to be disappointed in me as a lover, and shall give her none in the future—it takes little enough effort. She's easily satisfied. But I need more from a woman than she can give. I need a woman like you. Someone with fire in her veins."

His voice acquired a throbbing intensity as he spoke, and I could see he was remembering that night he had come into my room. Far from being discouraged by my rejection, he would, if he got the chance, repeat it, this time, forearmed. I cowered away from him, the strength engendered by my anger deserting me in the face of this renewed danger.

"She'll inherit, anyway, if anything should happen to you."

202

He smiled, and my skin crawled. "But we don't want anything to happen to you, do we? And nothing will—as long as you do as I say. There's no reason why the two of you should not live to a ripe old age, *if* I get what I want."

"I'll go to the police," I threatened with the last vestige of my courage.

"No you won't. Think of how your mother would feel if all this were to come out. Think of what would happen were she to learn that her daughter had been my mistress."

"You wouldn't," I breathed, unable to credit even him with such a base threat. It seemed nothing was so low that he would not stoop to it.

"Try me," he said.

He had won, and he knew it.

"It will take some time to arrange," I murmured.

"I can wait. I shall enjoy waiting—with you here."

"I shan't be here. There's no need for me to stay. My mother doesn't want me to stay."

"But I want you to stay."

He took a menacing step nearer, and my throat seized up with fear. As fast as I backed away, he came forward. I started to panic. Could I reach the door before he reached me? Then I felt my knees give way with relief as my mother's voice cut through the tension in the room.

"How much longer are you going to be, Teddy? You said you'd be back in an instant."

Only I saw the blaze of anger in his eyes as he turned to face her.

"I was just coming, my sweet one. I was only having a word or two with Nicola. You'll be happy to know she's agreed to . . . Damn!" A loud knocking reverberated through the house. "Who can that be? Get rid of whoever it is, Fanny. We don't want anyone interrupting us now."

She hurried to do his bidding. I would have hurried after her, but he stationed himself between me and the door.

In a moment or two she was back. "It's a Mr. Penrose. He

203

would like a word with Nicola."

Justin? What was he doing here? "I'll go to him at once," I exclaimed, and only with the utmost difficulty restrained myself from running into his arms as he came in, close upon her heels.

"Please forgive me for barging in like this," he said, his eyes, I thought, swiftly taking measure of Ted Gibbon, whose face displayed unconcealed hostility. "I know we were not to meet till eight o'clock, but, unfortunately, I have had to change my plans and must go to the theatre. I'd like you to come with me. Not being certain you would be back at your hotel in time to receive my message, I decided it would be better if I called to see you. Could you be ready at seven-thirty?"

"Certainly," I cried, "I was just leaving, anyway."

I could not resist a triumphant smirk at Ted Gibbon as I crossed over to Justin's side, and, with an almost imperceptible shrug, he admitted defeat. With Justin here, he could not insist I stay. Besides, he was satisfied. He had achieved his aim by extracting my promise to transfer my fortune over to my mother—and therefore to him. He would have no trouble in persuading her to hand over the purse strings. A kiss, a night spent in her bed, would be all the persuasion she would need.

I could only hope he would keep his side of the bargain. But surely he could not fail to do so. He must know that if anything should happen to my mother, I would suspect him of murder and inform the police. It was in his best interests to keep her safe and well.

So I kissed her and said goodbye to her, firmly believing her safe from all harm, though my heart was heavy. I wondered when, if ever, I should see her again.

"Aren't you going to introduce me to your friend, Nicola?"

I stiffened at Ted Gibbon's dulcet tones. They were full of menace and I did not trust them, but I could not refuse an apparently reasonable request.

"This is my employer, Mr. Justin Penrose," I said. "My—my stepfather."

As I spoke, I realized the mistake I was making, the mistake

Ted Gibbon had inveigled me into making. He knew now the name of my employer. It would not take much investigation on his part to discover where he lived. My security was gone. He would be able to find me whenever he wished; and, looking into his face, I saw he was not done with me yet. He had me exactly where he wanted me, and because of my mother, I could do nothing about it.

"So that was your stepfather," Justin muttered as the hansom cab drove off.

"I'm so glad you came when you did!" Relief wrung the words from me.

"Why?"

His quick-fire question almost succeeded in wresting an answer from me, but how could I give him my reason for being glad? I longed to. Oh, how I longed to unburden my soul, to shift my worries and fears onto another's shoulders, his shoulders. But I could not do that. My troubles were my own. I had no right to saddle anyone else with them even if I could, and Ted Gibbon was capable of exacting revenge for any indiscretion on my part—if not on me, then on my mother. I could not risk that. I looked away from him with an unhappy shake of my head.

"I can't understand you," he said, a slight edge to his voice. "You're obviously worried, yet you insist on declining help when it's offered."

I remained silent.

"I know it has to do with your stepfather. Is it for the reason I think it is? Did he molest you?"

I shuddered.

"Rape you?"

"No. No. It didn't go as far as that, but . . ."

"But it might have." He ground the words out from between his teeth and continued, "There are ways of dealing with such . . . I'll see you back to your hotel, and then—"

"No, you mustn't do anything. You mustn't see him. You mustn't!"

He clasped my hand in his. "Don't be afraid, Nicola. You

need never be afraid again. He'll not be able to touch you on Penrose Island. And I'll never tell you to leave. You're welcome there for as long as you wish to stay."

"But he'll come to the island. I shan't be safe there. I must go somewhere else, where he can't find me."

I did not trust Ted Gibbon. I would never trust him. If I transferred my fortune to my mother, she would be safe. But would I? I thought not. Ted Gibbon would never give up on me. I had seen it in his eyes.

"He'll not come to the island," Justin said. "No one comes to Penrose without permission from me."

"He won't wait for permission," I cried. "He'll just come."

"No boat will carry him across without my authorization."

"Is that true?" I whispered, hope fighting fear.

"It's true," he said simply, authoritatively.

I was safe.

Or so I thought.

The following morning my fears were revived. I had been summoned to the telephone, and I heard my stepfather's voice over the wire.

"So you've found a protector. You think you're safe. But no one gets the better of Ted Gibbon. Remember that!"

I replaced the receiver with trembling hands. Justin must have gone to see him after all. Perhaps he had threatened him with dire consequences if he did not leave me alone. Oh, he shouldn't have! He shouldn't have! But as I thought about it, I grew calmer. Ted Gibbon had not been able to resist this further attempt to frighten me, but it was a bluff. I had no cause to fear him now. Justin, my protector—how wonderful that sounded—would not let him come anywhere near me.

Chapter Eleven

Penrose Island lay, no, not like a slug upon the calm waters, but like a jewel, a smoky emerald that brightened with every approaching mile. As the *Justinia* edged its way into the harbor, where waiting islanders had gathered to welcome us, my heat rose with joy at coming home.

John was on the jetty to greet us. He enfolded me in his arms and kissed me. I thought I saw Justin's eye rest speculatively upon us. But I was far too excited to consider the embrace and any implications it might have.

Then the others were coming ashore and being introduced.

John's face was alive with admiration as he was introduced to Miss Adelina Shore—as well it might be, for she was the loveliest creature imaginable. She was tall and willowy, but not thin, and her hair was black as raven wings. Her eyes were blue with a hint of violet, and she made effective use of them, well aware of their power over men. Then there was her voice, richly resonant, which could evoke any mood under the sun.

Miss Adelina Shore was an actress. A very famous one. And she was going to play the lead in *Love's Balm.*

The actor chosen to play opposite her was of equal stature in the theatre—Mr. Martin Drake. He was tall, fair-haired, extremely goodlooking. Both he and Adelina were in their mid-twenties, but off stage Martin seemed to lose his years and appeared hardly more than a boy. He was a chatterbox, full of enthusiasm.

I liked him.

I was not so sure about Adelina Shore.

Next came Bert Kleinberger and his wife Mae. He was fat and balding and wore large round steel-framed spectacles which magnified his currant eyes to the size of raisins. She was taller than he and thin as a rail. Her hair was dyed a strident blond. Her voice was loud and her laugh could be heard ringing high above everyone else's, causing heads to turn in astonishment.

When I had first met them, I had been overwhelmed by them. We met them outside the theatre Justin had taken me to for the final performance of a long-running play, one of Justin's own, which I had not seen. Adelina and Martin had the leading roles in it, and we were to join them at a party after the show.

"Secretary?" Bert had boomed. He had a very big voice for such a little man. "What a waste. You oughta be in pictures. What'd you say if I offered you the part of Cleopatra in my next epic?"

"I'd say Cleopatra was dark. I'm fair."

He chortled richly. "Atta girl! But haven't you heard about hair dyes?" His smooth white hand continued to clasp mine and his eyes twinkled merrily behind his glasses. "Say, you need educating. How's about making ourselves scarce? There's a lot I could teach a girl like you."

"Take no notice of him, honey," Mae yelled. "He's harmless really. Knows he'll have me to reckon with if he gets out of hand." Her shrill laugh rang out through Drury Lane and Covent Garden, startling the quiet citizens of London going about their business.

"Aw, she's only jealous," Bert quipped, but he let my hand go and placed his arm around his wife's waist, proving who wore the trousers.

They were both larger than life, but, I soon learned, they had hearts to match. Beneath their bluster was a kindliness and bonhomie impossible to resist. I grew to like them both enormously.

Ralph Tegwood and his sister, Mary, made up the rest of the party. They were likable people, too; friendly and warm, though Mary had a tendency to gossip. She poured into my ears tales of people I had never met, relating their life stories to me, some in lurid detail.

Ruth was in the crowd. She came to my side and embraced me.

"It's good to see you back. I've missed you," she said. "How was your mother?"

"Oh . . . fine."

"Nothing bad then?"

"N-no."

"Still was it worth the journey, to set your mind at rest?"

"Yes."

"Nicola. . . ." Her eyes had narrowed somewhat. "Are you sure everything's all right?"

"Yes, of course. Why do you ask?"

"I don't know. You seem . . . well . . . worried."

"I'm not worried. A little unsettled, perhaps, after going home."

"And finding you're not the career woman you thought you were and wishing you could stay?"

"Something like that," I laughed. Better to let her think that than attempt to explain.

But she was not satisfied. "I'm not sure I believe you. You hinted at something—disagreeable, before you went away. You said you'd tell me all about it someday."

"Yes, but not now," I said almost irritably. Why couldn't she let the matter drop? Couldn't she see I didn't want to talk about it?

"It would help to get it off your chest," she insisted. "Come and have tea with me tomorrow. You can tell me all about it then."

"Yes, all right," I agreed, as Ralph and Mary, who knew

Ruth, came up to talk to her.

Laughing and chattering, the company piled into carriages organized by John for transportation up to Penrose House. Justin traveled up with Adelina and the Kleinbergers. Adelina, I noticed, had been holding on to Justin's arm the whole time, and for some reason it annoyed me. I went up with Martin and the Tegwoods.

"See you tonight," John called out as he waved us on our way.

The irritation that had taken possession of me remained with me for the rest of the day. Justin had taken me aside and told me there would be no work for me to do. He suggested that I rest for a while. "You're looking a bit peaked to me," he said, leaving quickly to join Adelina, who had called to him from a short distance away.

I had not rested. I had gone out for a walk along the cliffs hoping the island's magic would dispel the strange mood that I could not understand. I had been irritated with Ruth when there had been no cause—she had only been showing friendly interest and concern. I had been irritated by John's open admiration of Adelina Shore, and more strongly annoyed by her monopolization of Justin, not only on the boat and the island, but all the way from London. He had not seemed to mind. Well, of course he would not mind. He would be flattered by the attentions of a woman as beautiful and vivacious as Miss Adelina Shore. And why should I be annoyed by it? It was no business of mine. I decided I did not like Adelina Shore, and knew my dislike to be unreasonable.

I took extra care with my toilette that evening and went downstairs with my silvery hair knotted high on my head. I had a long neck and good bone structure. I knew the style flattered me. I wore a white dress which showed off my golden tan. Pleased by my reflection, I told myself I would not be cast completely in the shade by the beautiful Miss Shore.

But when I saw her through the open doorway of the drawing room, black-haired and beautiful—she could have

210

played Cleopatra without the aid of any dye—looking as if she had been poured into the gold satin gown that showed off her seductive figure to perfection, and gazing up into Justin's enraptured face, I wanted to run back to my room, shatter my lying mirror, and fling myself on my bed in despair.

"A penny for them."

John had come up behind me and was whispering in my ear.

"They're not worth it," I said, turning to him with a smile.

"Has anyone told you you look adorable?" he whispered.

"Oh, John!" His words boosted my confidence. "I'm so glad you're here. I hoped you would be. To tell you the truth, I'm a bit scared."

"Of these?" He cast an incredulous eye around the room. "There's no need to be. They're only flesh and blood, like you and me."

"But they're all so famous. And influential."

"That doesn't make them ogres."

"No, but I've never met anyone from the entertainment world before. I feel a bit out of my element."

"So do I," he murmured.

I laughed up at him. "You know you're perfectly at ease with them. One would have thought you'd known them for years when you met them on the jetty."

"Well, I have met their sort before," he grinned. "And they're all the same—flamboyant and harmless. Flatter them a little and they're like putty in your hands."

"I'm not so sure they are harmless," I said, my eyes on Justin and Adelina. He was gazing down into her eyes as she spoke to him, oblivious of all else. "With their charm and looks, I should think them capable of wreaking havoc with people's emotions."

"I can see you're nobody's fool," he said, and with the echo of my stepfather's words, my blood ran cold with the chill of premonition.

A great shuddering sigh gathered inside me and burst forth before I could stop it.

"What's the matter?" John looked at me with concern.

"Nothing. I . . . It's very warm in here. My cheeks are burning."

"Shall we take a turn round the garden?"

"The trouble is," John pronounced as we left the house, "they're a worldly lot, and you are not. That's why you feel out of place with them. They're a cynical bunch. They know what life's all about."

And you think I don't, I said to myself. If you only knew!

We walked in silence for a while. The night was warm and still. Not a breeze stirred a strand of my hair nor a ripple on the sea. It was slightly oppressive, and I wondered if there would be a storm. The atmosphere seemed right for it.

"They make a good pair, don't they?" John said, breaking the silence, "Adelina and Justin? I wonder if they'll marry."

"Do you think they might?"

"If Adelina has her way, I'm certain of it. Have you noticed the way she looks at him?"

"And Justin?"

"He's not exactly blind to her allure, is he?"

"No," I agreed, clearing my throat to do so. I had been made very aware of it since leaving London. I could hardly look at Justin without seeing her draped over his arm.

Our steps had led us to the terrace, which lay bathed in a pool of light bestowed by the drawing room through the open French windows. John stopped in the shadows and cupped my face between his hands.

"Feeling better?" he asked.

"Yes," I said, attempting to draw away from him and the admiration in his eyes. "We had better go back in. They'll be wondering where we are."

"Does it matter?" he breathed, his face coming closer to mine.

"Don't, John!" I panicked.

"Don't John?" he murmured softly, his lips feathering my cheeks. "Nicola. . . ." He voiced my name on a low and throbbing note and his lips moved closer to mine. "You must know . . ." The rest of his words were lost as our lips touched.

"No!" I tried to resist, but his lips clung to mine with an insistence not to be denied.

My mind was alert, active, but after a little while my panic subsided. His kiss was nothing like Ted Gibbon's—it was not repugnant to me. But neither was it sweetly compelling like . . . I waited for the kiss to finish and knew I would never let him kiss me again. I had been flattered by his admiration, had even imagined, in time—when I had completely conquered the revulsion against men Ted Gibbon had been responsible for instilling in me—falling in love with him. Now I knew I should never feel anything more than friendship for him, never wish for more than a friend's intimacy with him.

"Dinner is about to be served, if you can tear yourselves away from each other."

We sprang apart as Justin's voice splintered the air around us. His glance was cold, at once accusing and derisive. Yet what right had he to look so disdainfully upon us? He had seen us in an intimate embrace, but it had nothing to do with him. There was no reason for such a ferocious frown. And what about him and Adelina? What about the intimacy between them? Was it as innocent as this? I doubted it. But I was trembling and unhappy at being found by him in such a situation.

John, recovering more quickly than I, took my arm. "We were just coming," he said to Justin, and then to me, "Why, you're shivering. I've kept you out too long. Forgive me."

"Forgive you?" Justin's voice was low and mocking. "I rather suspect I'm the one who should be asking her forgiveness for interrupting such a tender scene—though I doubt I should receive it."

There was a tight note of anger in John's voice as he responded. "Is it not time you stopped carrying this longing for forgiveness about with you like a double-edged sword? You keep turning it in upon yourself and doing untold damage. It will destroy you in the end."

Justin turned on his heel abruptly.

"What was all that about?" I asked John.

He did not answer me, perhaps because Martin Drake had seen us and was coming to join us. But I could not get it out of my mind. It was not the first time I had sensed something pass between the two men, an incomprehensible something that puzzled me, and I could not but dwell on it.

Seated between John and Martin at the dinner table, I had to abandon conjecture. I had come to the conclusion it was all to do with the bitterness in Justin's heart, anyway, and that his longing for forgiveness was because of it. I was soon giggling uncontrollably at Martin's gossipy snippets about people in the theatrical world, which were told with good humor and without malice.

Then we were talking about the forthcoming film.

"I read the book when Penrose got in touch with me," Martin said. "It's a tremendous love story. The sting of unhappiness permeates every page. It's not much like the other books by him that I've read—there's a lot of humor in them, but *Love's Balm* is a stark tragedy from beginning to end. Bert was saying there'll have to be a lot of rewriting. It's a bit too stark as it is, and he thinks there ought to be a happy ending."

"He won't get one," John said. "Justin won't alter a word of what he's written."

"He will when he sees those dollar signs in Kleinberger's eyes."

"They won't mean a thing to Justin. When it comes to writing, integrity is all with him. *Love's Balm* is about the tragic betrayal of a man's love. It could only end unhappily. He won't change it to suit popular taste."

"Kleinberger'll talk him round. He's got a way with authors. And I'll add my tuppence worth. I flatter myself I can be a persuasive cove when I want to be."

John just shrugged his shoulders as if to say, wait and see who's right, fully confident of the result.

My eyes sought out the subject of this conversation. He sat at the head of the table, Mae Kleinberger on his left, Miss Shore on his right. I gulped to find his eyes on me. They narrowed sternly as they met my gaze and I looked away quickly. Had he heard our conversation? But how could he have, between Mae's loud voice and the distraction of Adelina's beguiling, magical smile?

How fantastically beautiful and alluring she was, shimmering like some exotic creature from the tropics in her gown of gold, her shapely hands moving about like rare insects above the table, her jeweled bosom and fingers glittering with red and green fire. Yet behind all that tropical warmth and splendor, I felt there was a cold and calculating spirit.

Not that any man would suspect it, of course. A man, seeing only her outward beauty, would feel flattered if she should even glance his way—as Justin was flattered now. He did not see my eyes on him as he threw back his head in laughter at something she said, nor had he any idea of the pain that shot through my heart as he bent his head close to hers and spoke softly to her.

What had he said to make her eyelashes flutter so, her lips curling in a satisfied smirk?

He seemed unable to look away from her now. Was she succeeding in ousting Caroline from his mind? Would she be the next Mrs. Penrose? Would she occupy the position his mother now occupied at the other end of the table before very long?

My eyes turned to Clara, and I received a jolt at the look on her face. She was staring at Justin, hardly able to keep the anger out of her eyes—not only anger, but fear and hatred. She did not like Adelina and would not take kindly to an alliance between them, I felt. And suddenly I knew she would not take kindly to anyone marrying him. Caroline might have been the exception—the only exception. She had liked Caroline and Caroline had liked her. With Caroline as mistress of Penrose, she would have been assured of the welcome to the island

Justin withheld from her. With sudden insight, I knew that she longed above all things to be welcome on Penrose—perhaps even to settle here.

It was understandable. She was getting on in years. She was alone . . .

"Nicola, you're not listening."

I became aware of Martin's whispered censure and turned to him in self-reproach. "I'm sorry. What were you saying?"

"That you're the most beautiful girl I've set eyes on in years."

I laughed. "Nonsense!"

"No. It's true."

"What about all the beautiful actresses you meet every day of your life?"

"There are none that live up to you."

There was warmth in his glance, and suddenly I could not be so sure he was not being serious.

"You're making her blush," John reprimanded him from my other side.

"You're even more attractive when you blush," Martin whispered.

"What are you three whispering about?" Mary Tegwood called out, her curiosity raising her voice to draw everyone's attention. "Let us in on the secret."

"We were talking about you, darling, and your latest pecadillo," Martin lied smoothly, and I gasped at his audacity.

"Were you, you naughty boy?" she trilled, far from annoyed. "Oh, but I must tell you, everybody, he's the most adorable young man. French, of course. . . ."

And she went on to regale us with an enthusiastic account of her latest conquest. She was a lady, I was to discover, of vast sexual appetite, with a string of discarded lovers behind her. A slightly aging woman, she was a fine actress in her own right—though I did not realize this till later, when I learned her stage name was Leonora Bentinoni and that she too was earmarked by Bert Kleinberger for a part in *Love's Balm*. I was also to learn that her lifestyle was not unusual in the theatrical profession.

The meal progressed cheerfully, the conversation now became more general. The food was beautifully prepared and presented, and Mrs. Carthew was complimented on her cooking. The table had been set with fine china and crystal. Graceful candelabra held tall crimson candles in their arms, shedding a soft glow of flickering light upon the assembled company. The maids looked neat and crisp in their black dresses and frilly white aprons and caps. It was altogether an elegant occasion for elegant people.

Lulled by the food and the wine, I relaxed in their company and listened to their animated conversation, marveling at the tales they told each other and wondering if they could possibly be true. Some seemed to stretch the imagination beyond all belief.

"Have you ever done any pathology, Doc?"

Mae, in the middle of a lurid tale of murder, suddenly shot the question at John.

"Some," he said, and I was conscious of a stiffening in him as he sat beside me.

I thought it was because he did not consider murder a suitable subject for the dinner table, and I must say I agreed with him.

"Good," Mae continued, "then you'll be able to corroborate my story. This man claims that he can tell not only how a victim was killed, but also the kind of man his murderer was, having had so many dead bodies pass through his hands. Even when the victim has been dead for a considerable time—even buried and dug up for a post mortem, he claims he can tell. . . ."

All hung on her words, fascinated by a subject of such macabre interest. I noted their faces: Martin's, smiling, eagerly concentrating; Mary's, wide-eyed, teeth biting deeply into her lower lip; Ralph's, faintly disbelieving; Bert Kleinberger's, thoughtful and excited; Clara's . . . My heart started palpitating. Clara's face was a death mask. Only her eyes glittering in their sockets showed signs of life.

She must be ill. My eyes flew to see if Justin had noticed his mother's plight, but he was gazing at Mae Kleinberger as if she were a bat out of Hell.

My palpitations increased. There was something here I could not understand, but I felt the brush of evil, and suddenly I was fighting against a suffocating, impenetrable sea of darkness that washed over me, pulling me down, down into thick murky depths . . .

"Nicola! Are you all right, Nicola?"

Martin's voice broke through and helped me rise from the evil, cloying waves. I grasped at him.

"I'm all right. It's Clara. She's ill."

But when I looked at her, she was looking at me with compassion. Terror clutched my heart at the gentle glance of her eye. Could she have changed so quickly? She had looked like death a moment ago. Or had she? Had I been mistaken? Was I going mad?

"But she was ill," I whimpered.

"You're the one who's ill," John declared, his manner professionally speculative. He put the back of his hand to my forehead. "You're feverish. You must have caught a chill. It was foolish of me to take you out of a warm room into the cold night air."

"It wasn't cold. It's quite balmy out," I contradicted him.

"She's been overdoing it, that's the trouble," Clara pronounced. "She's been working very hard setting your books to right, Justin, and that sprained ankle won't have done her any good. I said she should have rested it longer. That's it, isn't it, Nicola? Your ankle's paining you now, and it's making you feel sick."

"No, it is not," I said. Really, she sounded as if she would be glad if it were.

"Perhaps you ought to go and lie down," John suggested kindly.

"No. I'm quite all right, really. Please don't concern yourselves about me."

"It was probably the heat. Overcame you a bit," Mae Kleinberger said. "I know it affects me that way sometimes."

"It is very oppressive tonight," Martin said. "I could do with a bit more air myself. Perhaps we can open a few more windows?"

But the windows were already wide open.

"How's about finishing out on the terrace?" Bert asked.

"Good idea. Come along, everybody," Clara picked up her wine glass and, with a sharp nod, indicated to the maids that she required their assistance with her fresh fruit salad and damask napkin.

We all trooped out with our dishes of fruit and glasses of wine. John placed himself in a chair beside me. Martin flung a cushion on the paved floor at my feet and sat on it crosslegged.

I realized Justin had not said a word.

He stood with Adelina beside him, looking out over the garden, glass in hand, as if carved out of stone. She placed her hand on his arm and he did not move. Could a man remain so still with Adelina Shore beside him if he were not carved out of stone? I looked at his granite profile—there was not the flicker of an eyelid. Had the piskies been at work? Had they brought their considerable powers to bear on the Master of Penrose and turned him into stone—like Zill?

But why should they? He had not offended them. I was the one who had offended by not believing in them. I should be the one turned to stone, not Justin. And it would be better if I were, better than to feel this—ache, deep within me.

He raised his glass to his lips and the illusion was shattered. I had been allowing my imagination play again—because I wished, against all reason, Justin stone-hard proof against Adelina's attractions.

I sighed heavily.

"Yeah," Bert Kleinberger said, sympathetically believing I sighed because of the heat, "it sure is warm, honey." He drew a large white handkerchief from his pocket and mopped his perspiring brow.

"And so still," Mary Tegwood added, using her fan vigorously. "There'll probably be a storm before the night's out."

"Will there, Justin?"

That was Adelina, tightening her hold on Justin's arm and gazing up at him, her violet-blue eyes just above her ostentatiously ornate fan, which glittered with an image of herself arrayed in a gown of golden sequins. She knew how to use it to the utmost effect.

Fluttering her eyelashes she added huskily, "I'm afraid of storms."

"Well, so am I, honey," beamed the fat, balding producer with mock surprise in his voice. "Tell you what—at the first flash of lightning you come running to your Uncle Bert. We can snuggle down together under the sheets and give each other moral support."

"Over my dead body!" Mae's shrill voice rose good-humoredly. "I'm more capable of giving *you* under-sheet support, moral or otherwise."

But Adelina's eyes were still holding Justin's own, and no one could be in any doubt as to whose bed she would rather seek, storm or no storm.

I remembered Clara's words to me about Justin being a man with a man's needs, and having learned something about the laxity of morals among the theatrical fraternity, wondered if she might not have already sought it out—and occupied it. She was extremely beautiful, desirable. How could he fail to resist her if she offered herself to him?

"Wonder when the wedding will be?" came a whisper in my ear.

I turned swiftly to Martin. "Do you think there'll be one?"

Not that I cared one way or the other. Why should I? It was of no interest to me whom Justin Penrose married.

And yet I felt the rack wrenching me apart, limb from limb,

as I saw her raise her fan to cover her face, his head bend down to catch what she said, saw them move to descend the terrace steps together and disappear into the dim recesses of the shadowy garden.

"If Addy has her way, there will be."

I looked quickly to John to see his reaction. He had said exactly the same thing to me earlier on in the evening. But he was staring out across the garden, peering into the darkness as if trying to establish the whereabouts of the departed couple. I wondered if he, too, had fallen beneath Adelina's spell and was jealous of his friend's success.

"If he doesn't marry and beget an heir, the island will go to some distant cousin," he said suddenly, quietly, almost to himself.

"He was engaged to be married once, I believe?" Martin said. "I seem to remember somebody telling me about it. Probably Mary. She knows all the gossip."

Mary Tegwood pricked up her ears. "Are you talking about me again, you naughty boy?"

"I was just remembering you told me about—oh, what's her name? The girl Justin was engaged to."

"Oh, you mean Caroline. She was his secretary. He adored her. But she jilted him, literally on the steps of the altar." She turned to Clara. "I'm still mystified as to why. I always thought she was potty about him, didn't you? Well, I mean, who wouldn't be? He's rich, famous, ruggedly handsome . . ."

"You never can tell about people," Clara broke in. "It's just possible Caroline discovered something in Justin's personality she did not care for."

"Like what?"

"How should I know?" Clara frowned irritably.

"I've always found him perfectly adorable."

"You find anything in trousers adorable," Martin said, with incorrigible rudeness.

But Mary seemed to take it as a compliment, and laughed out loud.

"She probably found someone she liked better," Mae said, and her husband agreed with her.

"Yeah. It happens all the time. Remember Nate and Cora-Lyn?"

"Do I?"

Mae seemed all set to expound on this, but Mary forestalled her.

"Whom could she find better than Justin? If you ask me, he's had a good escape from a woman who didn't appreciate him. Why, if I'd been in her shoes . . ."

"We know, old girl, we know," Martin groaned, with a knowing wink in my direction. "You'd never have looked at anyone else. Ha!"

"Well, anyway," Mary laughed again at what she took to be a compliment to her sexual behavior, though I felt sure he meant the insults he threw at her, "there's somebody who appreciates him."

We followed her gaze. It led us to the beauteous Miss Shore, clinging like a limpet to Justin's arm as they came back to join us. Every now and then a throaty gurgle of laughter erupted from between her luscious lips, and I unashamedly strained my ears to catch what was said to make her laugh so.

They came up the steps into the light and became conscious of our gaze on them. Justin appeared unconcerned, but Adelina seemed cast into confusion. She lowered her eyes, even blushed, but I could not take it seriously. I felt it was all done for effect. She was not the shy type—she was an actress.

It seemed to me these people were always acting. Even off-stage, they were all a little larger than life. It was off-putting. I could not decide whether to take them at face value or disregard any sincerity they chose to exhibit.

But perhaps the fault was in me. They were what they were—theatre people. People to whom drama was the stuff of life. But it did not mean they were insincere. Justin liked them. He must think them worthwhile. He would not be taken in by fake emotions—would he?

But he could be misled, especially by one as devastatingly handsome as the dazzling Miss Adelina Shore—couldn't he?

But why was I questioning myself like this? What did it matter what they were like or what Justin Penrose thought of them? I was not of their world. I was a plain, ordinary secretary—that was what I had chosen to be—and it was not my place to criticize them.

But how much longer would I be able to remain a secretary . . . to Justin Penrose . . . when he married Adelina Shore?

But, but, but, so many buts whizzed around my brain. Why? What was the matter with me?

"Nicola! Are you all right?"

I turned, with a startled gasp, to John. "What?"

"I said, are you all right?"

"Oh. Yes."

He was looking at me with great concern.

"Sure?"

"Yes. I'm fine. Really."

He was looking at me oddly, disbelievingly.

"You look—so pale."

"I'm *fine*," I emphasized. "Please don't make a fuss."

He was not satisfied, I could see, and I expected him to question me further. However, at that moment Clara called out to me, "Fetch me my cream shawl, Nicola dear. I'm beginning to feel quite chilled."

I sprang up at once, grateful for the excuse to get away from John's inquisitive stare.

"Sit down!" Justin's voice was firm as he swung round to face me. "There are servants to do that sort of thing."

"Oh, but I don't mind . . ."

"Do as you're told," he said, "and sit down."

I sat. In the face of the sudden anger that seemed to have taken hold of him, I could do nothing else. But I let him see my annoyance.

He scowled at me.

I scowled at him.

There was silence all around.

Then Clara whimpered plaintively, "I'm sorry. I wasn't thinking."

"That's your trouble," he turned on her. "You never do think."

Every face registered surprise and embarrassment. Justin glared at everyone, as if he knew he ought to apologize for his outburst, but was damned if he was going to. He stalked away into the darkness and was swallowed up among the fronds of the tamarisk trees.

The party broke up after that, everyone suddenly overtaken by fatigue—though Adelina stood on the terrace looking out across the garden. I expected her to go down and search for Justin, but after a few moments, she turned and followed the rest into the house.

John and I stood alone on the terrace paving.

"Is there something between you and Justin?" he asked, with a quietness I felt he was far from feeling. It seemed to me to be the quietness of some soft-footed jungle animal waiting to pounce on an unsuspecting victim.

"Of course not," I said hastily.

"Good," he murmured. "I should not like to think it was starting all over again."

My heart stumbled. "What do you mean, starting all over again?"

"Oh, nothing. Forget it. I was just thinking aloud."

But I could not forget it. It was such an odd thing to say.

"But you must have meant something by it," I cried in alarm—and then I thought I knew why he had said it. "I know what it is. You're thinking I remind him of Caroline. You're afraid he might think he's falling in love with me because of it, and that I might be flattered enough to respond."

"Something like that," he said.

"You needn't worry, John. I'm not so easily fooled."

"Bright girl. See that you keep your eyes wide open where he is concerned. I've already told you how he feels about women.

He doesn't like them, but . . ." He hesitated to put into words that which Clara had been less nice about. "Why, even Ruth—"

"Ruth?"

"Why are you surprised? She's not exactly his type, but she's a woman—and available. He sees all women as fair game, and you, my dear Nicola, are far too sweet to be caught in his trap. I should hate to see you get hurt." He placed his fingers under my chin, tilting up my face and looking deep into my eyes. He kissed me lightly on the lips. "Goodnight, Nicola. Remember what I've said."

I climbed the stairs with difficulty. It seemed heavy weights were strapped to my body, and I dragged one foot after the other from step to step, clinging to the bannister for support as I went. I saw Clara at the top of the stairs. My heart lurched. How long had she been standing there, watching and listening?

She smiled sweetly. "Come and talk to me for a little while before you go to bed, Nicola."

I was exhausted, both mentally and physically, and the last thing I wanted to do was engage in conversation. "It's getting rather late," I began. Her smiling countenance gave way to petulance.

"*Please*, Miss Wentworth." It was not a request this time, but an order.

Her use of my surname reminded me of my position, my place in the household. I was Justin Penrose's secretary. Her *son's* secretary. An employee to be ordered about.

But not now, not out of working hours. I was prepared to rebel, then, realizing it was not worth making a fuss about, bowed to her command.

"That was good advice John gave you," she said, lowering herself onto a blue velvet chair. The entire room was done in varying shades of blue, relieved here and there by touches of white and gold. "I suggest you keep it well in mind." A moment's silent observation, then, "What do you know about Caroline?"

"Only what you have told me."

225

"Ah, yes. I did tell you about her, didn't I? When I first came here. I was so surprised by your resemblance to her. Remember what I said then, Nicola. Don't get carried away by any softness my son might show for you. It's false. Pretense. Beware of it. Oh, I know it seems a strange thing for a mother to say about her son, but you look so like Caroline . . . I'm afraid for you."

"There's no need to be," I breathed, trembling at her words, so full of warning, like John's.

Did I need their warnings? Perhaps I did, for of late I had felt a softening in me toward him. Had they sensed it? Was that why they were taking me to task like this?

But I was not interested in Justin Penrose in—that way, nor he in me. Had they not noticed the way he looked at Adelina Shore? Surely she was the one they should be warning.

"I just wanted to put you on your guard," Clara was continuing. "Justin has a way with women. They seem to like his stern looks and masterful ways. They flock around him just waiting to get hurt. Well let them . . . it will serve them right. But I don't want that to happen to you. I don't want you to get yourself into a situation where—"

"I've told you, you need not worry about me. I shall not be led astray. I have too much sense for that."

"Good," she said. She rose, indicating that the interview was over. "Forewarned is forearmed. Goodnight, my dear."

Chapter Twelve

I was falling through space, through darkness, through a vacuum where nothing existed. There was nothing I could hold on to to halt my downward spiral. Down, down, I fell, into a bottomless pit of silence. I would go on like this forever. There was nothing to halt my descent. Round and round I hurtled, falling deeper and deeper into nothingness.

Suddenly into the void came the sound of thunder, growling, reverberating, roaring like a mighty jungle lion. Louder and louder it roared. Round and round I went. And suddenly I knew it wasn't thunder, but a lion in fact. I screamed and screamed, knowing it was preparing to pounce, to eat me, to crunch my bones to powder.

"Nicola! Nicola!" The lion roared my name, and the pit was not bottomless; I hit the floor with a thud and lay there, winded. The lion stood over me, jaws open, teeth bared, his hot breath on my face—again I screamed.

"Nicola!"

The lion vanished. I looked into Justin's face—my protector's face—and fell against his chest in thankfulness at being saved.

He held me close and breathed in my ear. "Thank God! You had me so worried. I thought I'd never be able to wake you from your nightmare."

A nightmare. It had all been a dream. A dream.

But Justin Penrose was not a dream. He was real. He was here in my room. What was he doing in my room? My quiet breathing changed, became agitated. I drew away from him and beat against his chest.

"Go away!" I cried. "What are you doing here? Leave me alone!"

"It's all right." He tried to draw me close again. "Don't be afraid. Your nightmare's over. You're awake now, and I'm here."

Yes, I was awake now. Wide awake, and remembering that other man's appearance at my bedside—he had drawn me close, ripped my nightgown, pinched and bruised my flesh. I screamed and lashed out at Justin.

"Get away! Get away from me! How dare you come into my room when I'm sleeping?"

"I did knock," he said, "but there was no reply. Then I heard you cry out. I thought you were in trouble and needed my help."

It was a reasonable explanation, but I was beyond reason, in the grip of fear left over from my haunted dreams and past experience.

"Get out! Get out! How dare you come in here? You're all the same! You! Ted Gibbon! The same! The same! Loathsome! Loathsome!"

"Nicola," he whispered, and I saw the blood drain from his face. "You don't believe that. You can't."

"I do! I do!" I yelled, looking at him as if I thought him every kind of fiend, as indeed I did in that moment of hysteria. "Get out! Get out!"

Through my fear I saw his face grow dark with anger and pain and bitterness. Suddenly I wanted to withdraw my wild accusations, throw myself at his feet, and beg his forgiveness for seeing in him the likeness of Ted Gibbon when every instinct told me he was fine and good and true.

But it was too late. He had turned away from me and would

never come close to me again.

Clara Penrose appeared on the threshold. White-faced and anxious, she enquired, "What's going on? What is all the noise about?" As she caught sight of Justin, she added, "What are you doing here?"

"Would you believe," he said with calculated carelessness, "I thought she was in danger?"

"What danger could she be in?" Clara's voice trembled and she eyed her son warily.

"What indeed?" he sneered. With bitterness in every line of his face he said, "I believe she thinks I was about to rape her."

My heart bled. It was true. And I hated myself for it.

Clara caught hold of his arm determinedly. "Come away," she said, and, in an undertone I could scarcely catch, "Leave the girl alone."

He allowed her to lead him to the door and then turned back to me. As if nothing untoward had occurred between us, he said, "Come down as soon as you are ready. There's a lot to be done before the Kleinbergers leave this afternoon."

"It's my day off," I cried. I wanted the day to myself in order to recover my equilibrium and scold my stupidity. Then, as his eyes became twin pieces of solid granite, I wished I had remained silent.

"May I remind you, Miss Wentworth, that, under the terms of our agreement, you have no 'day off'? You take your time off as it comes, whenever it is convenient to *me*. You may take one, two, three or four days off at a time if you wish, just so long as I do not require your services. But now, this morning, I do require them. Kindly see I am not kept waiting."

Almost weeping with frustration, I clambered out of bed, washed and dressed. Yet what had I to weep about? I had brought his cold contempt upon my head through my own stupid fault. Stupid. Stupid. *Stupid.* How could I have likened him to Ted Gibbon? How could I? How *could* I? It was useles to blame my dream, though it would be easy to do so. But I knew in my heart it was more than that, more than the remembrance of Ted Gibbon's hated lips and hands. It was something in myself. A growing awareness of Justin . . . a longing for him . . . that I could not, dare not, allow to surface. I must fight against it in every way I could.

But he had been so kind to me. Kind—and protective.

Tears started to fall. I dashed them away and dragged a comb through my hair.

We had achieved a certain amity with each other. Why could I not have been content with that? Why had I allowed my emotions to become so tangled up? I wanted his friendship. I needed his friendship. Now it was gone, dissipated by my actions, and we were back where we had started—he the cold taskmaster, I his lowly employee. And for how much longer, I wondered, after my appalling outburst and accusations? He would probably wish to tear up my contract. And who was I to blame him?

They were all in the library when I arrived there—Bert, Mae, Ralph, Mary, Martin, Adelina Shore . . . my employer.

"At last!" he said. "Will you please bring your pad quickly, so that we can get on?"

"Aw, don't be cross with the poor baby," Bert Kleinberger chided him, slipping his ever-wayward arm round my waist, "just because she overslept. We all did, after our late night."

Disengaging myself, I went to collect my pad and pencil. I returned, sat myself in my usual chair opposite Justin Penrose, and waited, not knowing whether I was to take notes or dictation. My eyes were drawn to Miss Adelina Shore. She was dressed in shimmering white organdy with scarlet trim, and I felt a twinge of envy as I noted the tininess of her waist, shown off by a broad scarlet velvet sash. Her stays must be very tightly laced for such a slender effect to have been achieved, I thought waspishly.

Then I was drawn out of my reverie by Justin's stern command to "Please pay attention, Miss Wentworth!" and his hard-eyed stare.

Certain details concerning Martin and Adelina having been settled, the two of them departed to "roam the island," as

Martin put it. When the door had closed on them, the arguments started, with Justin and Bert hammering away at each other. Bert, the businessman, kept insisting changes must be made to make *Love's Balm* acceptable to his audiences. Justin would not give an inch, just as John had said he would not. He was adamant that *Love's Balm* should remain a tragedy, unpolluted by a happy ending.

It was Bert who gave in, bowing to the inevitable.

"It's settled then," Justin declared, allowing himself a momentary smile now all had been done to his satisfaction.

"Yep." Bert mopped his brow. He had worked hard for his defeat.

"Good. And now, if you want to catch the tide . . ."

"Yeah. We'd better be going. See you in States, then. A couple of months?"

"Something like that. As soon as the film script's ready."

"And don't forget—simple, to-the-point dialogue. Our audience will be made up of kitchen maids and shop assistants, and they want something they can understand."

"So you've said." Justin's brow darkened ominously. "If you think I'm not capable, perhaps I'd better bow out now."

"Shucks, no! Can't you see what I'm getting at, Penrose? We've got to please the uneducated masses, at least to begin with. Later on . . ."

But Justin was smiling. "O.K. O.K. I follow your drift. Trust me."

"Justie! Baby! You had me going there." Bert mopped his brow again. "You shouldn't do that. My heart won't stand it."

"Your heart's as tough as old boots, and you know it," commented his wife crisply.

"It needs to be in this business," he yapped back.

"Don't worry," said Justin. "I promise that by the time I've finished, my dialogue will be capable of being understood by all. Just make sure your actors are capable of interpreting it correctly. It's not called the Silent Screen for nothing, you know."

"Are you telling me?"

Mae Kleinberger's laugh trilled out at this. It was a great joke.

"Pity you can't find it in your heart to give us a happy ending." Bert returned to his earlier argument. "It's what the world wants—happy endings. Still, I guess you're right." Justin's brow had darkened again. "In fact, the more I think about it, the more right I think you are. Adelina's a great tragedienne. She'll wring their hearts from their breasts with her sufferings. And Drake's just as good. As the long-suffering husband, he won't be slow to draw their tears. Yep. The more I think about it, the more I think you're in the right of it."

"I'm glad you think so," Justin said drily. "And now, I hate to hurry you, but the tide waits for no man."

"Yeah. Well, goodbye young lady." Bert's podgy hand clasped mine. "It's been a pleasure knowing you. If you ever want to go into pictures, just let me know, and I'll make you a star."

"And he means that, honey," Mae said shrilly, clasping me to her scrawny bosom.

Then Mary kissed my cheek, Ralph shook my hand, Justin gave me a casual nod—and they were gone.

Twenty-four hours of the Kleinbergers' exuberant company was just about as much as one could stand with equanimity. Kind, entertaining as they were, I stood watching the *Justinia* sail away, and blessed the peace they left behind.

The threatened storm had not materialized. It was still quite warm, and I could make out the departing guests lounging on gaily striped deckchairs. Justin was at the wheel, tall, dark, capable; as his housekeeper had said, he was as much at home on the deck of a ship as on the floor of his house. There was a slight breeze, enough to power the sails of the *Justinia*, yet a column of smoke curled up from her elegant white funnel—he was using steam to take them across to the mainland. Though I knew he much preferred sail to steam, he welcomed the security steam offered. With steam, he had told me, there was no need to fear being becalmed. On a journey such as this, he would not risk the sail. Perhaps he did not expect the breeze to last.

I kept thinking about him, what he thought, what he did, till at last I realized the *Justinia* was no longer in sight.

And still I could not tear myself away.

Mrs. Carthew sent Mary up to tell me luncheon was ready. I turned obediently, but found great difficulty in eating the meal served to me, in spite of Mrs. Carthew's admonitions that I should waste away. Clara, endorsing her opinion, added caustically, "You let my son drive you too hard. You should stand up to him—if you will not leave him, which would be the wise thing to do."

Yes, it would be the wise thing to do. But how could I do it? And I was not thinking of Ted Gibbon.

My food choked me. As soon as I decently could, I excused myself and went in search of the dogs. I felt edgy, at odds with myself and all around me. A tramp through the hills would do me a world of good.

I tramped till I was exhausted and, finding myself not far from the school, thought I would call on Ruth and take tea with her. As I made my way to her little, spick-and-span house, I was surprised to see a man come out of the front door. It was John. I waved, but he did not notice me. Intent on his own thoughts, he climbed his horse and galloped away without a glance.

"Gentlemen callers, eh?" I said jokily when Ruth welcomed me in.

She looked surprised for a moment, then laughed. "Oh, you mean John. He came in for a cup of tea. He'd been checking up on the children. There's been another case of scarlet fever recently, and he wants to make sure there's not an epidemic. He came to tell me that, as far as he can tell, there won't be. So, hopefully, the school term will begin on time next month."

"Another case! Who is it this time?"

"Jake Penlove."

"Oh, poor little soul."

"It's hardly surprising. He's Jackie Prudoe's best friend. They're always together."

"But Jackie recovered ages ago. Jake can't have picked it up from him, surely?"

"It doesn't seem likely, does it?"

"Is John sure it's scarlet fever?"

"Oh, yes."

The kettle was boiling. Ruth poured the water on the tea and covered the pot with a knitted tea-cosy. She replenished the plate of scones and brought fresh, clotted cream to the table. Then, the tea steaming in our cups, she sat down opposite me and said eagerly, "Now—you promised to tell me why you left home."

There was no getting out of it. I told her everything.

"Men!" she exclaimed when I reached the end of my story. "They're disgusting. Some men, anyway. But thank goodness, they're not all tarred with the same brush. Thank God, there are men like John, and Justin Penrose."

"Thank God," I said, and came to realize that, at last, I could see the truth of it. With the telling of my tale to Ruth it was as if Ted Gibbon was forever exorcised from my mind. Hetty and Dickie had said it would happen, and now it had. There were men like Ted Gibbon, lecherous, evil; but there were also men like John and Justin, good, kind, and honorable men, and they were in the majority. Thank God!

"I knew there was something," Ruth said, pouring fresh tea into our cups. "As soon as you said you would never marry—I knew. Do you still feel the same?"

"I don't know," I said slowly.

"You'll know when you fall in love." I felt the blood rush to my cheeks and saw the interpretation of it in her glance. "Or has it happened already?"

"No!" I laughed. It was an unconvincing laugh, and I added for good measure, "No, of course not!"

She smiled and I said in a rush, though it was the last thing I had expected myself to say, "I think Justin will marry Miss Shore."

"Oh," said Ruth. "Do you think so? You could be right."

Agreement was not what I had wanted from her. I added as my heart wept, "She's staying on for another week. She and Martin."

"And how do you feel about that?"

"Me? What does it matter? It's got nothing to do with me."

She did not contradict me, but there was a sly knowledge in the peculiar glance she gave me.

Did she know how I felt?

No, of course she did not. How could she? I hardly knew myself. The discovery was too new to be assimilated.

Justin returned the following day. I saw the *Justinia* steam into the harbor and watched by my window till his tall figure appeared striding over the hills. Betsy and Winnie flew to greet him before he reached the house, and he got down on his haunches to respond to their love. As always in their company, he appeared relaxed and happy. For a while he played with them out on the green hillside. Then, the dogs trotting contentedly at his heels, he trod purposefully on and entered the house.

Moments later I heard Adelina's deeply seductive voice. I heard his richly resonant reply. I did not know what they said to each other. I did not want to know.

Clara had arranged a small dinner party that evening to celebrate Justin's foray into the world's newest art form, moving pictures. His words would be seen on a large screen, his characters brought to life by actors and actresses in a way undreamed of half a century ago. It was indeed something to celebrate, and a surprise for Justin.

The guests had been asked to arrive at the hour Justin took his bath so that he should not see them come. Mrs. Carthew had been primed to keep him out of the way till all were assembled in the dining room.

Everything went according to plan, and when Justin made his entrance into the dining room, it was to a rousing chorus of "For he's a jolly good fellow." After his initial surprise, he grinned broadly, and everyone crowded round him offering congratulations—even I. Shyly, from the back of the crowd, I basked in his smiling glance.

Dancing had been arranged for later on. While the guests enjoyed their meal, servants cleared the hall of rugs, removed the center table, and arranged chairs and sofas around the walls. A gramophone and a pile of records stood on a side table. Clara was in her element as hostess. It was plain she loved parties and entertaining.

I was pleased to see Justin ask her to dance—he could hardly do anything else, after all the trouble she had gone to to make this a memorable occasion for him. I watched, everyone watched, the tall handsome figure and the small dainty one twirl round and round to the strains of a Strauss waltz. Then others joined them on the floor. Martin and John approached me at the same time to ask me to dance. John bowed and gave way to Martin. The next time I saw him he was dancing with Adelina.

My next dance was with John. I saw Justin lead Ruth onto the floor. She looked radiant. Surely he could not fail to see how she felt about him? He seemed relaxed with her, talking and smiling . . . Might he, in time, ask her to become his wife? My heart lurched with rebellion at the idea, but I knew she would be ideal for him. She was intelligent, attractive, honest—and she worshipped him.

Parson Bryn danced with me.

Justin danced with Mrs. Bryn.

Again and again, John and Martin danced with me.

Justin danced with each of the ladies in turn, but he did not dance with me.

Parson Bryn was in close conversation with Clara Penrose. Suddenly I heard her scream, "Fever? On the island? Oh, I must go home at once. I can't risk catching it. I came here to recover from an illness, not to contract another!"

"You've nothing to fear, dear Mrs. Penrose." John brought us both to a halt as we were dancing by. "Scarlet fever is a children's disease. You won't catch it. In any case, I am confident it is contained now."

"But," she clutched at his arm, "are you sure?"

"Of course."

His reassurance calmed her, and she was soon talking brightly again. As we sat down with her and Parson Bryn, I noticed Justin excuse himself from Adelina's side to go and turn off the gramophone. I also noticed how quickly she followed him over and slipped her arm through his, afterwards leading him to sit beside her on a red plush sofa. Martin and Ruth, who had been dancing together, joined them. Was I the only one who noticed Adelina's malevolent glare? Oh, I thought, if he marries anyone, let it not be Miss Adelina Shore. She can't hold a candle to Ruth.

Food was brought in, and hot chocolate for those who wanted it. Clara turned to me. "I've been thinking, my dear, about our conversation the other day. My son drives you too hard, and I wonder if you would like to go back to London with me—I'll have to leave sometime. You could stay with me as a friend or, if you would rather earn a little money, as my companion. I think you would find my remuneration generous."

"Clara, I . . ." My first instinct was to refuse. Leave Penrose? Leave Justin? Return to London with her as her companion? No. But then I hesitated. It could be the answer to something I was afraid to admit. Something that had crept up on me unawares. Something that would never be resolved happily for me.

"Think about it, Nicola. I shan't be leaving just yet. Meanwhile, I require your help in a delicate matter. I want you to help me persuade Justin to sell the island."

I gaped at her. "Sell the island? Sell Penrose? He'd never do it."

"He will. He must. Believe me, it will be best for him in the

237

long run—as well as for me. If he sells then I needn't . . . there'll be no need for . . . You must help me, Nicola."

"But I can't! He won't listen to me."

"He might. I've noticed the sway you have over him."

"I have no sway over him. And if I had, I certainly would not try to persuade him to sell the island. He loves it too much. I'd feel like a traitor if I attempted. You shouldn't even try to—"

"Oh, you talk like a fool!" Clara declared, sotto voce. "I could persuade him with your help, but if you won't . . . well, don't blame me if—"

"If what? Do you expect to share in the proceeds if he sells?"

"Lower your voice," she hissed as, in my indignation, I had raised it above our whispering level. "I'm not saying I couldn't do with a nice little windfall, but . . ."

I turned away from her in disgust and went to join Ruth, who was sitting by herself.

"Is anything wrong?" she asked. "You look so angry."

"It's Clara. She astounds me sometimes. I think she must be a most unnatural sort of mother."

"Oh?" She looked interested.

But I felt I had said too much, and refused to satisfy Ruth's curiosity.

However, when Ruth became engaged in conversation with Parson Bryn and his wife, I found it less easy to fob John off. He came right out and asked me, "What were you and Clara talking about just now?"

"Oh-h-h . . ." I shrugged as if it were of no consequence.

"It seemed to disturb you," he persisted, "whatever it was. I saw you rise from her side abruptly and hurry across to Ruth. She appeared to think something had upset you. What was it? You can tell me. I'm your friend. Perhaps I can help."

"I wasn't upset. I was angry. John!" Suddenly I was glad to share my anger with him. "She wants me to persuade Justin to sell the island !"

"What?" He stared at me, aghast. "How ridiculous! What can have got into her? She knows he'll never sell Penrose."

"That's what I said. I think . . . I think she believes she would come in for a share of the money if he did sell."

"She's barking up the wrong tree. He'll never sell."

"Of course he won't. And how she could imagine I would have any sway over Justin in such a matter!"

"It's nonsense, of course," he agreed.

We were interrupted by a question from Martin Drake, in converse with Justin and Adelina. "You'd like to come, wouldn't you, Nicola?"

"Come where?"

"For a sail with me on the *Sea Drift*."

The *Sea Drift* was a small sailboat Justin used for local trips around the island.

"Yes, I should like to."

I caught a speculative gleam in Justin's eye, then he said, "Oh, very well, I'll take you out in her tomorrow."

"No!" Martin cried out. "That's not the idea. I want to sail her myself."

"That wouldn't be wise. There are treacherous rocks and currents round Penrose."

"I'm not a novice. I have sailed before."

"Yes, but . . ."

"Mrs. Carthew told me the east coast is quite safe, and there are plenty of safe beaches there. I can haul ashore if I get into trouble. Which I won't," he added quickly at Justin's renewed scowl.

"But Martin, if Justin will take us . . ." Adelina smiled adoringly at Justin. It would suit her to bow to Justin's wishes.

"No. If I can't sail her myself, what's the point? Oh, come on, Justin, be a sport."

"I'll sleep on it," Justin replied. And with that Martin had to be content.

It was nearing midnight, and Parson Bryn and his wife took their leave. I was glad. Perhaps now they would all go. I had seen enough of Adelina's body held close to Justin's, enough of her dark head inclining closely to his. All I wanted to do was retire to my room. I would try to ease the dreadful ache that

239

attacked every part of my being in sleep.

But with the parson's departure, someone put on another record and John claimed me for another dance. Then Martin cut in. Justin was dancing with Adelina, then suddenly, he was dancing with me. I did not know how the exchange of partners occurred. I only knew I was where I had longed to be all night. My heart was pounding so loudly I was sure he would hear it.

"What's your game?"

The question came from above my right ear so casually I could not, for a moment, comprehend it.

"Game?"

"The one you're playing with Drake and Trevelyan. Trying to make them jealous of each other?"

I stumbled against him. He tightened his hold. "I don't know what you mean."

"No?" His breath was warm on my cheek. "You've been playing one off against the other all evening. What's the matter, can't you make up your mind which one you want?"

His insolence robbed me of my speech and pierced me to the soul. I tried to pull away from him, but his arm was a band of steel round my waist and I could not break loose. For a moment, I was Vanora bound to my lover with a silken strand of my hair. Then his mocking gaze penetrated the spell and I came to myself again.

"I am playing no game, Mr. Penrose," I declared haughtily, bringing my dancing steps, and his, to a firm halt. "And if I were, it would be no business of yours. You may pay my salary, but that does not give you the right to pry into my private life. What I do is my own concern, and no one else's. Have I made myself clear, Mr. Penrose?"

"I would never have believed your eyes could flash so dangerously," he said lightly, depriving me of speech again. "They have always looked so calmly out of that angelic face of yours—so calculated to entrap."

That sting in the tail of his comment loosened my tongue at once.

"If you think I'm out to entrap either John or Martin, you

can disabuse yourself of the idea. I have no wish to become involved with any man. *Any* man!" I reiterated, at the look of innocent incredulity which settled on his face.

"The dance is ended, don't you know? Could I have my partner back, please?"

I turned in surprise to see Martin beside us, and was even more surprised to see that Justin had danced me out onto the terrace without my realizing it.

Justin took my hand and gave it to Martin. "Be my guest," he said. I could cheerfully have hit him.

Martin's "sea jaunt," as he called it, took place as he had intended: he was at the wheel, and Adelina and I were passengers. Justin was left behind to fret, I thought, for he remained unconvinced of Martin's ability to captain the Sea Drift.

"Have no fear, the sea and I are soul mates," boasted the eager young actor-cum-sailor as Justin continued to voice his doubts. "A boat is my natural habitat."

"I wish you would come, Justin," Adelina sulked, with a provocative upward glance. "I should feel safe with you."

"I'd be no good as a passenger," he said, "and there's only room for one captain aboard any ship. I should not be able to restrain myself from giving advice, if not taking over, and Martin and I would come to fisticuffs."

He grinned at Martin—albeit reservedly, still not at all sure in his mind he was doing the right thing—and sent us on our way with a final warning.

"You've got a fair wind, but don't stay out too long. The weather changes rapidly here, and you could be in the middle of a storm before you realize it."

We were out longer than intended, through no fault of our own.

"You damn fool!" Justin castigated Martin the moment he stepped ashore. "What were you about? Didn't you hear what I said? I told you not to stay out too long!"

"Sorry, old man. Wasn't my fault. The old tub sprang a leak."

Martin spoke casually, but I knew it was an act he was putting on. He had been sick with worry, full of remorse at having taken us to sea, as the boat filled with water and we had to bail out for our very lives.

"He went out too far." Adelina's voice held a note of hysteria as she fell against Justin's chest, and he put his arm about her. "I told him he should turn back, but he wouldn't listen."

I heard this untruth as I stood nearby, teeth chattering. In actuality, she had urged Martin to put a greater distance between ourselves and the coast of Penrose.

I glanced sympathetically at Martin, who stood glumly while Justin berated him again. "Damn fool! I thought you knew how to handle a boat!"

"I do," Martin blustered. "It wasn't my fault. She sprang a leak. And then the wind came up and broke the mast, smashed the sails. There was nothing I could do. We drifted. We were lucky Captain Pascoe saw us and picked us up."

I shuddered as I remembered how the *Island Queen* had loomed up out of the darkness of the storm, and thanked God for the keenness of those deep-set, far-seeing gray eyes of Captain Pascoe's. We had been hauled aboard with the wind and sea spray lashing us, and were sent to huddle in the little cabin I remembered. There I suffered a feeling similar to the one I had suffered before. Martin suffered too, but Adelina was surprisingly unaffected. She scolded Martin for our predicament, complaining loudly and long, and showed no signs of sympathizing with us in our agony.

"The *Sea Drift*'s done for, I'm afraid. Her timbers must have been rotten," Martin said.

"She was in perfect trim when you took her out," Justin yelled. "You must have torn her side on a rock."

"No. There were no rocks around. I swear to you, Justin . . ."

But Justin was in no mood to listen. "You blithering idiot!" he cried scornfully. "You said you knew how to handle her. I should have known better than to go against my instincts. . . . You should stick to acting and leave boats to those who know about them." He turned to me then, as if he had only just remembered that I was of the party. "You all right?" he growled.

I nodded. I could see he was almost beside himself with anger, occasioned, no doubt, by his worry about us— particularly about Adelina, who was snuggling up against him and shivering with truly dramatic effect. No one could fail to wish to comfort her.

I shivered too, not only from the cold, but from deep, dismal unhappiness. Then I felt an arm slip round my waist. I looked up to see John Trevelyan looking anxiously into my face.

"Thank God, you're safe!" he exclaimed. "We've all been worried beyond measure. Justin was near distraction when I called round to see him after tea. He told me you'd all gone out in the Sea Drift and had not returned, though he'd expected you hours ago. He'd sent word to the coast guard on the mainland when the weather worsened, but they hadn't seen anything. An hour or so later, he was all for taking the *Justinia* out and going in search of you himself. It would have been a brave but foolish thing to do. I talked him out of it for as long as I could, but at last there was no stopping him, so I decided to accompany him. However, when we got down here, the *Island Queen* was coming in and . . . well, you know the rest. But what are we doing talking out here? Come in to the inn. I've ordered hot coffee and a meal to be prepared for you."

We followed the others, who were already making their way there. Wrapped in blankets, steaming mugs of coffee in our hands, we three shipwrecked mariners huddled close to a hastily built-up fire, willing the flames to leap higher and give warmth to our frozen bodies. Justin had gone outside again. John told us he was talking to Captain Pascoe about the *Sea Drift*. The captain had somehow managed to tether the boat and tow her back to port.

"She's in remarkably good condition, seeing what she's been through. She can be mended. So don't feel too bad about holing her, Martin. It could have happened to anybody. These waters are renowned for their treacherous—"

"I *didn't* hole her," Martin exploded. "I *didn't* hit a rock. She sprang a leak. Her timbers must have been rotten."

"One of Justin's boats? Never. He's too much of a seaman to allow any boat of his to deteriorate."

"Then," I raised my voice for a moment, but lapsed into silence as all eyes turned to me, and I grew afraid of my thoughts.

"What?" John demanded.

"Oh . . . nothing."

"You believe someone tampered with her!" he submitted challengingly.

"No, of course I don't," I responded quickly—but that was just what I had been going to say.

"But who would do such a thing?" cried Martin, visibly shocked at the idea.

"No one on this island," John reassured him.

And of course it was ridiculous to think the *Sea Drift* might have been tampered with. But if she hadn't, what was the explanation for the leak?

It was a question I was to ask myself again and again.

"The rain's torrential, and it doesn't look like it will let up." Justin came up to us, dripping water with every step. "I'll arrange for you to stay at the inn for the night. No sense in your going out in this again. Hopefully, the weather will have changed by tomorrow."

So, while he and John galloped away to their respective homes through the cold wet night, Adelina and I, in nightwear loaned to us by the innkeeper's wife, lay side by side and tried to sleep.

It was not long before Adelina's slow, rhythmic breathing told me she had succumbed to the blandishments of Mr.

Sandman. I could not be so easily seduced. Eyes staring into the darkness, I lay stiffly at her side, unable to wipe from my mind the terrifying hours we had spent fighting a losing battle against the insistent intrusion of icy water. It had risen higher and higher, till I felt sure we must all die.

How had it happened? What was the explanation of the leak? Was it possible for a stout timbered boat to spring a leak for no apparent reason? We had not hit a rock; I knew that as surely as Martin did. So had the *Sea Drift* been unsound? Knowing Justin Penrose's conscientious nature, I could not believe this possible. So what was the answer, if it were not sabotage?

And if it were sabotage, it could mean only one thing— someone bore a grudge against Justin Penrose.

It seemed ridiculous, utterly absurd, to think someone was out to cause him harm, but considering the accident in the quarry, the broken step rung, and now the leaky boat, didn't it seem more than mere coincidence? Why anyone should wish to harm him was beyond my comprehension, but the more I considered it, the clearer it became.

As far as I could see, there was only one person who fit the bill—Clara Penrose. Perhaps she had a grudge against him because of the grudge he held against her.

Yet the idea of a mother wishing to harm her own son was ludicrous in the extreme. It must be someone else. But who?

What if I were the intended victim?

No, that was even more ridiculous. Who would want to harm me? Not Clara; not anyone on the island; what reason could anyone have? I posed no threat. Besides, no one knew I would be out in the boat. It had been Martin's idea and . . . Martin? Oh, no. I had really entered the realms of fantasy if I could think Martin was in any way responsible. He had been in the boat himself.

I was tearing at windmills. There must be some simple explanation.

Yet my eyes remained wide and staring, my brain continued to revolve, till the morning light drew me out of bed to prepare myself for the return to Penrose House.

Clara and John met us in the hall, and I felt Clara's cool cheek next to mine as she enfolded me in a light embrace, crying, "Nicola, thank God you're safe. I was so worried about you."

She drew me into the drawing room and, when I was seated beside her, continued, "John's been telling me you suspect someone of tampering with the *Sea Drift.*"

"No, I didn't say that. . . ." My denial was involuntary, and I halted in the face of John's reproachful gaze, for that was what I had almost said—and what I believed, if I were honest with myself.

"What's that?" Justin had entered on his mother's words and was frowning angrily at me.

"Didn't Nicola tell you?" His mother turned innocent blue eyes on him. "She thinks someone tampered with the *Sea Drift.*"

"Oh, yes? Who, for instance?"

Justin's glance was scathing—but was there not a hint of fear behind his eyes?

"That's what we'd all like to know," Clara said sweetly.

"And just what is this—someone—supposed to have done?"

"Drilled a hole through the hull?" Martin suggested drily.

"Don't be idiotic!" Justin sneered.

"No, that's not possible," John said. "Justin has both the *Justinia* and the *Sea Drift* checked regularly. Anything like that would have been noticed."

"And he keeps an expert eye on them himself, don't you, Justin? In fact you went to look the *Sea Drift* over yesterday, didn't you?"

"No."

"But I thought . . ."

"I never left the house yesterday. Not till I grew worried over their lateness in returning home."

"It's all beside the point, anyway," Martin declared irritably. "The fact is, she was holed, and if I didn't hole her, who did?"

"It's nonsense to suspect foul play," Justin growled.

"No, you'd rather suspect me of lying," Martin shouted, growing red in the face. "Well, I'm tired of saying it and I don't care whether you believe me or not, but I'm not to blame for the leak. I didn't run her against the rocks."

Justin appeared to wrestle with himself for a moment, then he said, "Forgive me, Drake. Of course I accept your word. The blame is mine. I should have made certain she was fit before you took her out."

"Big of you to admit it at last," Martin returned resentfully. But then his smile broke out and he quoted the Bard of Avon, "All's well that ends well!" He shook off the mantle of depression that had cloaked him since the accident had occurred, and suggested, "What about going out for a picnic? It's our last day. We ought to make the most of it."

I doubt he saw the look of fury that swept across Justin's face at his words. Had anyone else noticed it? I wondered about it. Did it mean he had not exonerated Martin in his mind, despite what he'd said? Or was he simply furious at having to admit his own culpability?

Chapter Thirteen

I could not shrug off my worries as easily as Martin Drake had. But then, I had more to worry me.

I stood at my window and gazed down at the island basking in the morning sun. It was Sunday, and the ringing of church bells met my ears. The sea glistened beneath the wide blue sky. A lone seagull soared high overhead. All was so peaceful it was impossible to believe in the storm of the day before.

But there had been a storm. There had been a near tragedy. The *Sea Drift* might have sunk with the three of us in it, if the *Island Queen* had not been returning to harbor after her day's fishing.

And we need never have been in such a desperate situation if the boat had been properly maintained. Someone was to blame for that. John and Clara had gone out of their way to exonerate Justin. So who was to blame? The man Justin had hired to check them?

My thoughts were spinning and turning. I could not accept that the leak had occurred accidentally. Yet, if it hadn't, wouldn't there be some evidence of tampering in the wrecked vessel? I had to find out. I had to know, one way or the other, or I should never regain my peace of mind.

Peace of mind! What peace would there be if I discovered evidence of malpractice? Still, I must find out.

I hurried down the stairs and let myself swiftly out of the house, congratulating myself on having avoided meeting anybody. If I were turned from my purpose now, I should never achieve it. If anyone wished harm to anybody, Justin or myself, I believed the *Sea Drift* held the answer.

I ran over the hills past the little church, from which came the sound of an organ playing. With a thrill of shock, I caught sight of Justin's tall figure and Mrs. Carthew's small dumpy one on the verge of entering.

I sped onward, meeting no one, and reached the harbor breathless. It was deserted. The fishing smacks were all about their business. Sunday made no difference to them, the tides had to be obeyed. The shops in the square were closed. The Ship's doors were shut fast, and would not be opened till the church emptied and the worshippers hurried thither to slake their dry throats.

The *Sea Drift* had been drawn up on the seashore. It looked so forlorn with the tidal waves lapping around it in smug, sarcastic fashion. She seemed to beckon me, entreat me, to board her and commence my investigation into the reason behind her sad condition.

I went over to her, took off my shoes and, with no one about to see me, hitched up my skirts like the tomboy I used to be. The memory of that time, those happy, carefree days of childhood, with a father and mother who loved me and each other with a deep, abiding devotion, brought a hot ache to my throat, and I halted in my endeavors. But those days were gone. I should never see them again. I put them back in their drawer to await the time when I could take them out and look at them without this turmoil of emotion in my breast.

I clambered aboard, a difficult business achieved with a little sigh of satisfaction, and looked about me. I grew dejected as I saw the dilemma that confronted me. How could I tell if a leak had been purposely engineered? I had thought, in my innocence, that I should discover something—a hole as big as a pea, perhaps, something I could point to as being a definite

249

attempt at sabotage—yet how could I discover anything of the sort among these shattered timbers? The storm that had cracked and splintered the wooden boards had obliterated any trace of a deliberately manufactured leak.

Nevertheless, I searched for one.

Without success.

I rose from my crouching position damp and disappointed. I was no further on in my search for the truth. I had not found proof of any sabotage, but equally, I had found nothing to prove the opposite.

Stretching myself, easing my back, I saw people moving about on the hills. The church service was over. Soon, if I were not quick to get away, they would notice me and wonder what I was doing prowling around Justin's wrecked boat.

Smiling at the thought of myself as a prowler, I picked up my shoes and, unhitching my skirts as I went, hurried away in the opposite direction to hide myself from view in the folds of the hills.

My smile froze on my face and my feet rooted themselves in the sand. On the skyline above me stood a man, arms akimbo, legs astride. Justin! Had he seen me? How long had he been there? *Was* it Justin? It must be. Who else would stand like that, looking as if he owned not only the island, but all the seas around it?

Suddenly, he was gone.

I had seen him and then had not seen him, all in the twinkling of an eye.

Had I seen him? Of course I had. I could not have imagined a man as tall as that standing on the skyline, watching me; a man as tall as a giant.

A giant!

My flesh began to tingle and my mouth went dry. A giant of a man standing on the skyline, appearing suddenly and disappearing just as suddenly.

A giant of a man.

Penn!

The legendary Penn!

It was no use telling myself not to be such a naive fool, that there was no such being as Penn. No use telling myself there were no such things as piskies on the island of Penrose. I believed in them now, with all my heart and soul. I believed in their powers and I was afraid of them, certain they meant me ill for all the times I had scoffed at their existence. Perhaps they were responsible for the rising of the storm, for the buffeting of the boat, for the leak that defied discovery. I had been their intended victim.

I was unaware of my flying feet, unaware of reaching the High Plateau, till I stubbed my toe against something hard and, looking down, saw through a haze the headless torso of Penn's enemy, Zil. I heard myself scream in all my pent-up terror. My screams rose into high, blue sky as I ran through darkness, away from the place I should never have approached after my previous strange experiences on its heights.

When I came to myself I was scrambing up a cleft in the hills which had to be avoided because of the steepness of its sides and its loose scree. I looked down to see blood on my hands and staining my blue skirt, and wondered how I had come to be in such a situation.

It all came back to me, and I could not believe I had behaved so foolishly. Had I really believed it to be the legendary Penn standing on the skyline observing me so closely? No, of course I had not. It had been Justin Penrose. I had been driven to imagine it was Penn by allowing the stories he told to dwell on my mind that I had come to think them true.

I had lost my shoes. Sharp stones tore at my feet. Yet I had to keep moving, or stay where I was forever. It served me right. I had been foolish to allow my imagination to take such a hold on me. Oh, Father, you were right when you told me to curb my imagination or it would lead me to destruction—it almost had.

I entered the house by the back door, hoping to creep upstairs unnoticed and repair the ravages of my morning's bizarre adventures. Unfortunately, Justin Penrose came out of the library and gazed at me askance. "Where have you been?"

"Out," I said.

"Where to? What have you been doing?"

His eyes raked me over and, goaded by his assumed innocence, I shot back, "You know what I've been doing. You saw me."

"Saw you? I—"

"You were watching me. Don't try to deny it. I saw you watching me as I got out of the boat."

"Got out of the boat? What boat?"

"You know very well." I raised my chin defiantly. "The *Sea Drift*."

"The *Sea Drift*?" His tone and glance became accusatory. "What were you doing on the *Sea Drift*?"

I stared at him mutinously. His eyes narrowed.

"I see," he said slowly, ominously. "You were looking for this fictitious leak you've been raving about. This hole somebody is supposed to have deliberately drilled in her side. Tell me," his lip curled in a sneer, "did you find it? No, of course you didn't. There isn't one."

"How can you be so sure?" I cried, stung into indiscretion. "Only the person responsible for it could be so sure, to hide his—"

Too late, I held my tongue and wished I could retract the words at the change that came over his face. Gone was the sneer, the hard accusatory glance. These had been replaced by a look of such incredulity, such vulnerability, that I could have wept at being the cause of it.

"You can't think . . . You can't believe I would sabotage my own boat . . . drowning three human beings?"

I could not answer him. My mouth was too dry.

"Is it feasible?" he begged.

"N-no," I managed at last.

"Then why suggest it?"

"I don't know. I don't know what came over me."

"But it was in your mind, or you wouldn't have said it."

His tone was grating, his expression stony. How quickly he could change from one mood to another. Vulnerable one minute, hard and distant the next. Yet surely it was understandable after what I had said.

"I didn't mean it," I gulped.

"No," he said. His glance fell to my stained skirt, my scratched hands. "You'd better go and get yourself cleaned up. I'll ask Carty to send some antiseptic up to your room."

As we turned to leave each other, Martin Drake appeared in the hallway. "Hello, you two," he called. "You haven't forgotten we're going on a picnic, have you? Mrs. Carthew's packed a basket for us and . . . Great heavens, Nicola! What have you been doing to yourself?"

"I . . ." I was acutely aware of Justin's interest. I had given him no explanation for my appearance, nor had I given him the chance to enquire. "I had a fall," I finished flatly, and heard his indrawn breath.

"Oh, no!" Martin sounded shocked. "Do you feel faint?"

"No."

"But all that blood . . . It is blood, isn't it?"

"It's not as bad as it looks."

"Oh, good!" He was buoyant again. "It won't prevent you from coming on the picnic."

A picnic was the last thing I wanted, but how could I disappoint Martin on his last day, when he was so looking forward to it? So after I had bathed and changed, I put on a cheerful face and joined the others in the gig. I sat beside Martin while Adelina, glowing with self-satisfaction, her frilly parasol held high, sat as close to Justin's side as his handling of the reins would allow.

Keeping up a constant stream of chatter, she said eventually, "There aren't many trees on the island, are there?"

"Not many," Justin replied. "There's the copse, of course."

"Copse?"

"Lovers Knot Copse. So-called because of the legend attached to it."

"Legend? Oh, do tell. I adore legends."

"There seems to be a legend attached to everything on

Penrose," I muttered irritably to Martin in an undertone. Adelina had spent every passing mile in close contact with Justin behind her parasol, which had been lowered to obscure the view of the two of them from behind. And with every gurgle of laughter, every bend of his head to hers, every exchange of words between the two of them, my irritation had grown.

His quick ears had caught my aside, and Justin turned to glance over the top of the parasol, saying, "You should know by now that nothing on Penrose Island is as it at first appears." And though he turned back to face Adelina, a chill ran down my spine, for I felt he continued to address his words to me. "There are two worlds on Penrose. Our own everyday, recognizable world, and that other world of dark deeds, heroic men, beautiful women, and strange happenings, unseen, but self-evident. It's there, for all who can, to see, to hear."

Perhaps Adelina felt a chill too, for she shuddered behind her parasol and murmured half fearfully, "Oh, Justin, darling, you make it sound so real, as if it were true."

"He's a born storyteller," I commented with a touch of resentment.

"Tell us the legend of the copse," Adelina said.

And Justin Penrose—James St. Just—obliged.

There was a moment's silence when he had finished his tale, spellbinding as always, but then I spoke up trenchantly. "It's not true, of course. He makes it up as he goes along." And, in fancy, I heard the piskies laugh. But Justin continued, "They say they haunt the copse to this day. They can't leave until true lovers plight their troth beneath the branches of their prison. When that happens, the silken strand will break and they will be free."

"Sounds farfetched to me," Martin declared robustly.

"There are more things in heaven and earth . . . ," quoth Justin.

"Oh, come now. Don't pretend you believe it," Martin scoffed, and I wanted to warn him, "Don't scoff, Martin. Don't scoff."

"Well, I think it's all very romantic," Adelina said, "and I want to go in to the copse. With you, Justin. Take me there. Now. Please."

"No." Justin's voice was firm. "It's a dangerous place for unbelievers."

"But I'm not an unbeliever, darling. You can take me. We can leave these two doubters behind in the gig."

"No, Adelina."

"But . . ."

Something in his face must have deterred her from further argument, for she drew away from him, so that the determined set of his head and shoulders were open to our view. She sat in a sulk for quite ten minutes.

Eventually, however, forgetting to be cross, she cried out, "Look at the way the land merges with the sea. You could tread from grass to water with ease."

"If you tried, you'd soon find out your mistake," Justin told her.

"What do you mean?"

"It's a freak perspective. Nature playing tricks."

"How?"

"The sea is nowhere as near as it seems. Nor is the land as flat."

"But it is flat. Look at it."

"We're actually going uphill."

"Uphill?" Martin laughed. "Pull the other one."

"No, I mean it. You'll see when we get to the top of the rise."

"Rise?" Martin continued his derisive laughter.

"The ground appears to be level, but there's a gradient of one in ten."

Martin hooted. "I don't believe it. It's another one of your farfetched tales."

But he had to eat his words when Justin swung round to the right. Then we saw we had been trotting along a broad ridge between falling hills, and the sea, which had seemed so close, was far away in the distance. Justin halted the gig to allow us to admire the view, smiling at our gasps of astonishment.

"You see," he said laconically, "nothing is as it appears on Penrose."

We pressed on along the gently undulating ridge, the long, brown ribbon of road looping and turning, till we came at last to a huge dip. It was a crater from which all the good, fertile soil had been removed, leaving a mass of jagged stone, layer upon layer, pile upon pile of gray-blue slate. We were at the quarry.

Martin whistled through his teeth. "Did some disaster take place here?" he asked.

"You could say that," Justin replied gravely.

"It's the slate quarry, isn't it?" I said, and he nodded.

"But it's not worked now?" Martin glanced round, looking for men and machinery.

"No. And it never will be again."

"Why not? There must be tons of the stuff here. Worth a mint, I'll wager."

"I daresay." Justin's tone suggested that he wished the subject closed.

"I want to get down and have a proper look," Adelina cried. "May I, Justin?"

"If you wish. But be careful. It's dangerous."

We all gathered round the edge. "What an awesome sight," I murmured. In my mind's eye I saw Justin and his two dogs slipping and falling, a slide of slate tumbling about them. I shuddered.

"Are you cold?" Justin asked. I had not realized he was standing so close to me.

I drew away from him. "No. No. I'm quite warm."

"I thought I saw you shivering," he said. "Perhaps you're afraid?"

"No. No." I wondered why he should say that, and moved farther away. In so doing, I slipped and would have fallen, landing at the bottom of the horrendous pit in a broken heap, had he not moved with the speed of a jaguar to catch hold of me and draw me back.

"Th-th-th-thank you," I stammered, in fear of what might

have happened, in fear of being held close to his chest. "I-I-I'm all right." I strained away from him till he had to let me go or have the others think it strange he did not. As it was, Adelina looked peeved.

"Let's go!" She linked her arm in his. "I don't care for the atmosphere of this place."

"Neither do I," said Martin. Nevertheless, he demanded to know the history of the place as we departed.

"My grandfather opened it up," Justin said. "There's a rich vein of slate going right through the island. He made a great deal of money by extracting it. My father continued the process. The quarry expanded. If he had not died when he had . . ." He grew silent and morose for a while, then he picked up the thread again. "I put a stop to it once I had the power to do so."

"I've noticed the cottages here are tiled with slate. This slate?"

"That was my father's doing. He thought he was improving things by replacing the thatched roofs, which were held in place by nets and weighed down by heavy stones."

"You sound as though you didn't approve."

"I didn't at the time."

"Misled by a desire for things to remain as they were."

"Maybe."

"You can't stop progress."

"No."

"Yet you closed down the quarry."

"Yes."

"But what about all the jobs lost due to your action?"

"It was mostly imported labor."

"And that made it all right, I suppose?"

"No."

"I hope you reimbursed the workers in some way."

"They were offered jobs on the mainland. I have interests in a great many projects there."

"Oh, stop it, Martin!" Adelina exclaimed, losing patience with the argument, although I found it extremely interesting.

"It's too nice a day to talk politics. He fancies himself as a politician." This last was thrown at me. "He belongs to the Fabian Society—not that he attends any of their meetings."

"I never have the time," Martin said. "Too busy earning a living. But I support their ideals. Shaw's a member, you know."

"I'm well aware of that fact," Justin said testily.

"Politics and the theatre go together. Both demand larger-than-life personalities."

"I should have thought a politician needed to be nearer to the true size of life than that."

"Well, you know what I mean, Justin."

"We're here," Justin said.

"Thank goodness for that," Adelina cried. "Now perhaps we can forget politics and enjoy ourselves. But surely we're not going to picnic here." We had come to a stop at a point high above the ocean. "It's so windy."

"Call this a wind?" Justin chaffed her lightly. "It's only a breeze."

"But I don't like it. It's cold."

"You spend far too much of your time cooped up in the hothouse atmosphere of the theatre," he returned, unimpressed. "This will do you the world of good. The air's like wine up here. Take deep breaths of it, Addy darling."

This was the first time I had heard him call Adelina darling, and it hurt. Darlings flew about like confetti among the theatre folk, I knew—Martin and Adelina were no exception—but I did not think Justin used the expression lightly. It hurt to hear him call Adelina darling, yet I had no right to be hurt, no right at all.

"Come on, darling, give me your hand."

It was Martin calling me darling, which meant nothing at all. I gave him my hand and alighted. He put his arm round me as we walked away from the gig.

"Look at Addy," he whispered waspishly. "She hates the wind. Can't stand to be ruffled. You're so sensible tying your hair back like that. Even so," he gently flicked the errant strands back from my face with his free hand, "it escapes its bonds."

"Nothing will hold it in place for long," I murmured, my eyes on Adelina outlined against the sky, the wind molding the seductive lines of her body, showing them to perfection. I could not refrain from adding, "She's so beautiful!"

"Oh, yes." Martin's gaze followed mine. "She's beautiful, all right. And doesn't she know it! That pose is for the benefit of Lord of the Island, my dear. If she doesn't catch him, it won't be for want of trying."

Justin, busy unstrapping the picnic basket from the back of the vehicle, suddenly rapped out an order. "Get the groundsheets from under the seat, Drake."

With a quick aside in my ear to the effect that his lordship had spoken, Martin leapt to attention and gave a mock salute. "A tutti frutti, mon capitaine," he jested grotesquely, raising not a flicker of a smile on Justin's face.

"We're surely not going to eat up here," Adelina wailed. "In this wind?"

"Would I put you through such torture?" Justin scorned lightly. "Come, follow me."

He stepped over the edge of the cliff.

We rushed forward, fearing the worst, but he was perfectly safe. He descended easily to a sandy beach below by way of natural steps gouged out of the cliffside by the sea, over centuries of endeavour.

"Come on. It's quite safe," he called up to us, grinning wickedly at our anxiously peering faces, and Adelina and I exchanged looks of aggravated relief.

I made the descent with more ease than Adelina, who had flouncier skirts, a hat, and a parasol to manage. With no such encumbrances, used as I had become to the island and vigorous exercise, I set my feet on the soft sand with a smug feeling of self-satisfaction, knowing that I should have the advantage in Justin's eyes. But when Adelina reached the bottom step and held out her arms in mute appeal to him, for it required a jump to reach the sandy ground, he opened his arms for her to jump into. As she landed full against his chest, they were hidden from view behind her outheld parasol. She had had the advantage of me there. She had the advantage of me in all ways.

Mrs. Carthew had done us proud. We fed on cold chicken and pasties, fresh lettuce and tomatoes, soft rolls filled with yellow Cornish butter, followed it with thick wedges of apple pie and clotted cream, and washed it down with a sparkling wine.

We lay back on the sand-soft cushioned groundsheets after the feast, replete, contented and relaxed—all except Adelina, who maintained her sitting position beside Justin, shading herself with her pretty parasol and gazing down on him with an adoring expression.

I closed my eyes against the sight of her perfectly sculptured face hovering above Justin's ruggedly handsome one. I tried to think of something else, but all I could do was think what an atractive pair they made, and sigh with the thought.

"Why do you sigh?" Martin raised himself on one elbow and whispered in my ear.

I could not answer and was glad he did not press me to do so, but then his fingers began tracing a pathway along my bare arm and he said more loudly, "What a lovely golden tan you've got, darling." Adelina heard and rebuked me sharply.

"You shouldn't expose yourself to the strong sunlight, Nicola. It's not good for you."

"I've grown used to it," I said somewhat breathlessly, as Martin's fingers touched my cheek.

"A brown skin is so unfashionable," Adelina opined.

"But so attractive," Martin added. I shot bolt upright, as his lips brushed the upper part of my arm. He rose with me and his arm curved around my waist. My heart was pounding. I did not know what to do.

"You should always wear a hat when you go out in the sun, or at least carry a parasol. No lady is dressed without a parasol in summer."

Was she trying to make me look small in Justin's eyes? I responded pertly, "I find them so irksome. They might be all right in town, but here they are nothing but a nuisance."

She flushed and drew herself up grandly. "Are you trying to ridicule me?" she demanded in tones of sepulchral depth.

"No, no. Of course not. Whatever gave you that idea?"

Her eyes flashed displeasure, then she turned her head away from me in a gesture of such supreme disregard I almost felt like applauding. The actress in her was never very far away from the surface.

Martin started to sing, in a rich baritone voice, "Oh, my nut-brown maiden, she is so fair, with her eyes of blue and a rose in her hair."

Adelina pierced him with a frown. "What song is that? I've never heard it."

"You wouldn't have," he said with a chuckle in his voice that bewildered me. I had not realized till today that he held her in low esteem, but it was becoming more obvious to me with every word he directed her way. "I've just made it up. A tribute to Nicola, who cares not for wind nor sun. Fashionable or no, I like her just the way she is. Don't you, Justin?"

A look of fury settled on Adelina's face and she turned away quickly lest Justin see it. But he, lying flat on his back, did not open his eyes or make reply. Martin leaned forward.

"Are you asleep, Justin?" Martin enquired briskly, then with exaggerated concern, as there was still no reply, whispered, "Or dead?"

The chiseled mouth, so sensual when it forgot to hold itself in tight control, quivered.

"Hmm!" said Martin, "not dead." He fell back into his earlier supine position at my side. "That's good. What would happen to *Love's Balm* without him? We'd all be out of work." A moment's silence, then, "When do you reckon you'll be leaving for the distant shores of the New World, Nickie?"

"About the end of October."

The answer issued forth from the chiseled mouth before I could attempt to frame one. And what answer would I have given, anyway, when I knew I would not be going with him? Yet he had spoken as if he expected me to accompany him . . . as his secretary . . . nothing more. But how could I stay with him once he wedded Adelina . . . which he would . . . soon . . . probably before he left for America . . . they would honeymoon in America.

Suddenly, I could remain still no longer and, jumping up, ran swiftly across the sand to where the sea foam edged it with a broad band of lace. In the distance, the coastline of Cornwall gave me the strangest feeling that I had only to stretch out my hand and I should be able to touch it. One leap and I could be there.

The water lapped gently a few inches away from me. It was hard to believe it was the same Atlantic Ocean that surged so wildly, so bad-temperedly round the island at times—continuously, on the west coast, where the seabirds chose to nest high up on the granite ledges just out of reach of the flying spray.

How like the ocean was Justin Penrose. Calm and gentle, one minute, erupting into blazing fury the next. Did such a nature come from being born on the island? No, there was more to it than that. His anger was born of bitterness, and the island was not to blame for that.

Perhaps I was making excuses for him, because I did not want to leave this enchanted isle.

And yet leave I must. How could I stay, seeing Justin and Adelina together? It would be insupportable.

A mist of tears obscured my view and I swung away abruptly, hardly knowing what I was doing or where I was going, till I bumped unceremoniously into the man who was the cause of them.

His arms shot out to steady me. His expression was grave, yet there was a strange light in his eyes as he looked down at me. I was held by his look, rendered immobile, like a rabbit sensing danger. Then a smile lifted the corners of his lips, entered his eyes. It freed me. Spreading my hands against his chest, I thrust myself away from him and ran through the frothy wavelets, not caring that they dampened my shoes.

I could not outpace him. Without running, he matched his stride to the rate of my flight so that when the cliffs, which fell away into the sea and formed an impenetrable barrier, halted me, he was immediately at my side.

"Where to now?"

His softly mocking voice taunted me. I stared in frustration at the great granite rocks denying me further flight, and could have wept. My heart stopped in fear as his hands gripped my arms and he turned me round to face him. He tilted my chin so that I had to look up into his eyes and again I was rendered immobile, torn by fear and longing for this man who totally confused me.

Why, for instance, had he followed me down to the water's edge? Why had he kept at my side when it was obvious I did not want him there? Why did he look at me in such a strange, heart-rending way?

"Don't you know there's nowhere for you to run?" he said, his voice grown low and husky.

It filled me with dread, for I knew I must run. Run. Anywhere. Away from him. Before it was too late. *Too late. Too late.* John's warning. Clara's warning.

"Let me go!" I gasped, trying to wrench myself free.

His hold did not slacken.

"Let me go, I say! Let me pass!"

"Why are you afraid of me?" he asked, his face darkening with anger.

"I'm not."

"You've been giving a very good impression of it these last few hours. You don't still believe I tried to drown you in the *Sea Drift*?"

"Maybe."

What imp of perversity sat on my shoulder to make me say

that? An imp born of a fevered imagination, fostered by warnings against this man, who towered over me with a threatening strength? Whatever it was, it deepened his anger. He ground out my name as if it hurt him to do so, and swept me up into an embrace so fierce it took my breath away— an embrace calculated to break every bone in my body if I resisted. His face was close to mine, his expression one I could not read. Then I knew he was going to kiss me, and that it would be hard and brutal, intended to subdue and humiliate. I closed my eyes in dread, lips quivering, waiting for the hard mouth to descend and crush them.

Then, "Damn!" I heard his expletive and was released with such unexpected abruptness that, for a moment, I could not make out what was happening.

Then I saw Adelina running—no, not running, she would not do anything so unladylike—hurrying across the sands, her richly resonant voice echoing, "What are you doing over there? What's the matter with Nicola? Has she got something in her eye?"

"She's all right now," Justin replied, neither admitting nor denying Adelina's supposition. A supposition, I could see, she had used to cover her anger over what she knew had happened. Her glance at me said all.

But it was full of sweetness when turned on Justin again. "Don't you think it's time we were getting back, darling? The sun's far too hot for us to stay out in it much longer. We're not all of us determined to ruin our complexions. Besides," she tucked her arm through his and led him away as if I no longer existed, "you promised to take me to Lovers Knot Copse later this evening."

"Did I?" he murmured. "I don't remember that."

But he did not say he would not take her. So would true lovers plight their troth beneath the magic tree that night? I turned in gratitude to Martin as he reached me. He slipped his arm round my waist, and I was glad of his support as we followed Justin and Adelina back across the sands.

Chapter Fourteen

Martin Drake and Adelina Shore were about to depart.

Martin drew me to him, kissed me tenderly, and promised to do what I had asked of him, namely to call on my mother in Kensington and to let me know how she was faring. I remained extremely worried about her despite believing that Ted Gibbon would treat her kindly now he had, or would soon have, his hands on my fortune.

Adelina, her fingers barely touching mine, wished me a cold goodbye. There had grown an antagonism between us, the antagonism of rivals. For, whether I would admit it or no, afraid of him or no, I wanted to be with Justin, to stay with him, even to my life's end. She had sensed this even before I knew it myself, and her glance told me she would fight me tooth and nail. I knew it would be an unequal fight, for I could not hope to compete with her.

She flung herself into his arms. "Farewell, my dearest. I'll die till I see you again."

"Don't be so melodramatic," Justin admonished her, but he smiled as he said it, obviously flattered—or so I was inclined to believe.

The ride back to Penrose House was almost as hair-raising as the first one I had taken with Justin, and I cast an anxious frown at his grimly set profile. Now what has annoyed him? I wondered. But of course it was that he had had to part with the beauteous Adelina Shore.

This was further proof, if I needed it, as to where his desire lay.

He threw himself into his work, the morose and angry man I had first known. Not that his work could content him for long. It took him no more than a few days to condense *Love's Balm* dialogue to fit the American producer's requirements. In fact, he hated doing it, and drove himself, and me, hard in order to finish it as quickly as possible. Finally, he announced that any more work that needed to be done would have to wait till we reached America.

I saw him only briefly after this. After we had gone through the mail together, he would take himself off for the rest of the day, sometimes, but not always, accompanied by his two black Labradors.

I was thrown more and more into Clara's company. At every opportunity she badgered me to go with her when she returned to her home in London, which she assured me would be any day now. I knew this would be the sensible course to take, yet avoided making any definite decision.

As often as I could, I visited Ruth. With school in full swing again after the summer holidays, my visits took place in the late afternoon, when she would give me tea. Thankfully, there had been no further cases of scarlet fever, and John believed the scare was over. I met him once or twice at Ruth's and noticed how friendly they had become. This delighted me. Though she was older than he, she didn't look it, and with her calm and sensible outlook, could prove the perfect partner for him. True, I believed she was in love with Justin, but she realized she stood no chance with him, and I wished her good luck if she chose to look elsewhere for happiness. But when I suggested he was paying court to her, she exclaimed with a laugh, "John? Good gracious me, no!"

"But he likes you."

"And I like him, but . . ."

266

The slight shrug of her shoulders, the sudden springing of pain to her eyes, told me plainly there would never be any man in her life if it were not Justin Penrose. And she knew as well as I that the only woman capable of making him forget his erring sweetheart, Caroline, was Miss Adelina Shore. Often I wondered if even she could manage that. His bitterness still showed, and it could not all be because of his mother. And if bitterness against Caroline still lodged in his heart, it was because she was still there, because he was still in love with her, because he would not let her go.

"Anyway," Ruth cast aside self-pity as she had long been wont to do, "it's not me he's interested in. It's you. Oh, don't look so surprised. You must be aware of it. Everyone else is. He makes not the slightest attempt to hide his admiration of you. When he comes to see me, it's to talk about you. He can't hear enough about you. I think he's trying to summon up the courage to propose to you."

"Oh, no!"

The idea appalled me more than I could have imagined. I liked him, unquestionably liked him, but enough to marry him?

"He takes you about, doesn't he? Taken you to see Peacehaven?"

"Yes."

"Well, don't you think that must mean something?"

"Oh, Ruth, you haven't given him any encouragement on my behalf? You mustn't."

"Would that be so terrible? He's a very nice man, very caring. You could do a lot worse."

"Yes, I know, but I can't marry him. I can't marry anybody. You know that."

"Because of what your stepfather did, you mean. But I thought you'd got over that."

"I have—I think. But it's too soon to think of marrying—anyone."

She nodded and clucked sympathetically. "Of course, I

understand. But don't let too many months, or years, go by before allowing someone to love you. You might find you've left it too late."

She rose and went into her neat little kitchen to pour fresh boiling water into the teapot. On her way back, she stopped to glance out of the window.

"Justin's down at the harbor again, I see," she said.

"Oh?"

"I've seen him down there a lot lately."

"Oh."

She set the teapot down and placed a cosy over it.

"That's freshened it up," she said. "I'll give it a minute, then I'll pour you another cup."

"Clara wants me to go to London with her as her companion," I announced abruptly.

"You won't go," Ruth averred confidently.

"I'm toying with the idea."

"You can't. You're not serious?"

"I am."

She frowned angrily at me. "Don't do it, Nicola. She'll run you off your feet. You know what she's like."

"I know. But it doesn't worry me. I like to be kept busy. And I shall need another position to go to when I leave Penrose."

"What do you mean, leave Penrose? Aren't you staying with Justin? I thought you were going with him to America."

"No—not now."

I held out my empty cup to her. She took it with a question on the tip of her tongue. But I had set my lips and she had known me long enough to know that, when I did that, I would offer no further explanation of my thoughts or feelings. As she poured the tea, I could see her trying to work out what was behind my sudden decision to leave Justin. But when she returned the cup to me, all she said was, "Well, take my advice and think very carefully before committing yourself to Clara Penrose."

I did indeed think very carefully—and made my decision. I would not go with Clara Penrose. For all her insistence that I was her friend and that all she would require of me would be my company, I knew I should become a dogsbody, a paid servant expected to pander to her every whim. So no, I would not go with her. I would continue my employment with Justin till his marriage was imminent and then would seek employment elsewhere, in the same line of business. I had experience behind me now. It should not be too difficult to find a suitable secretarial position. Justin, I felt sure, would not deny me good references. He might even recommend me to someone of his acquaintance.

I had made my decision and thought it the right one. But then something happened to make me change my mind.

"To hell with this," Justin cried as we worked on the mail one morning. "It's like a hothouse in here. Let's go for a walk and get a breath of fresh air."

I looked up in surprise. "You wish me to come with you?" He had not sought my company for so long now, and since the day of the picnic, he had hardly said a word to me that was not in some way connected with work.

"Unless you'd rather not." He shrugged as if he could not care less either way.

But I could not let this attempt at friendliness, if indeed that was what it was, pass. After all, I told myself, I would need his good offices when the time came for me to seek another secretarial post. Besides, Betsy and Winnie, supine till now in the open doorway, indolent in the unseasonable warmth of this October day, were thumping the floor with their tails and gazing up at us in bright-eyed expectancy, alerted by the word "walk." It would be quite like old times, the four of us scouring the hills again.

"No, I'll come," I said quickly. "It will be nice to feel a bit of a breeze."

A speculative gleam sprang to his eyes. "We could go for a sail, if you like."

My breath caught in my throat. "You mean—in the *Justinia*?"

"In the *Sea Drift*."

"But she's out of action."

"Not any more. I've been working on her. She's in fine rig now."

So the *Sea Drift* had been repaired. That was why Ruth had seen him down at the harbor so often. I had believed nothing would ever get me out in a boat again after my last experience, and certainly not in the *Sea Drift*. Yet how could I tell him this without renewing past accusations, past antagonisms, just when it seemed we might be on the road to friendly terms again?

"Well?"

The harshly delivered question demanded a response.

"Er . . ."

It was as much as I could manage, and I bit into my lip in miserable silence as I saw his lips curl into a sneer.

"So you're still afraid of me," he rasped. "You still think me capable of sabotaging my own boat and attempting murder."

At the sight of the hurt he could not keep from his eyes, I cried out, "No! It's not true. It's just that—I seem to attract foul weather whenever I go out in a boat."

"You won't today." Did I detect a note of eagerness in his voice? "The wind's set fair."

"But there's hardly any breeze."

"There's enough."

Why was he so pressing? So insistent? Why didn't I trust him?

The sneer returned to his face. "Still you hesitate," he said, his voice grown harsh again. "If I ask my mother to accompany us, Carty, too, will that set your mind at rest?"

And I saw how stupid I was being. How could I believe he would sabotage the *Sea Drift*, with the deliberate intention of drowning Adelina, Martin and myself? The idea was really so preposterous as to border on lunacy—as I had told myself often enough before. Why had it taken me till now to believe it?

"That won't be necessary." I smiled brightly at him. "I shall be happy to come with you for a sail round the island. Only, what about the dogs? They're expecting to go for a walk."

"They won't be disappointed. They can come with us as far as the boat, then I'll send them back. They know their way. They won't get lost. They've done it before."

He was smiling, suddenly lighthearted, like a schoolboy released from the tedium of the classroom and ready for any adventure that might present itself.

Betsy and Winnie, catching his mood, leapt up and bounded forward in gleeful exuberance to plant their front paws against his sturdy chest and lick his face. Then they turned their attention to me. However, knowing from experience what power they had to knock me off my feet in their exuberance, I hurriedly sidestepped them and sought refuge behind the big mahogany desk.

Justin laughed cheerfully, but there was the recognizable note of authority in his voice as he addressed the joyful animals. "That's enough. Let's go." Abandoning their pursuit of me, the dogs bounded past him through the hall and into the open air with all the speed at their command, obedient as ever.

We heard Mrs. Carthew's voice of complaint as they rushed through the hall, "Lordy, lordy, what's all this then?" When she saw us appear in the library doorway, she smiled and chuckled, "What's to do? I've not seen they dogs so rumbustious these many days past. Nor 'ee, Master Justin. What be causing all this excitement?"

"We're going for a sail, Carty, Nicola and I. The dogs are coming down with us. I'll send them back before we set out."

I saw her brain working quickly behind her astute glance. She had not failed to notice that things had deteriorated between Justin and me, and had mentioned it to me once. "What be wrong atween you and the master?" she had asked. "Nothing," I had said lightly, hoping she would not press the matter. But, "Nothin' is it? 'Tis not nothin', and that I knows full well, but if 'ee be wishful to keep it to yourself, t'won't be another word I'll be uttering on the matter." Yet she referred

271

to the strained atmosphere between us again and again and, no doubt, put two and two together. "If 'ee can't be trustin' Master Justin, t'would be better for all if 'ee took yourself off back to London," she said, goading me into replying that that was the very thing I was thinking of doing. Then she had nodded and shaken her head, as if she could not make up her mind whether to be glad or sorry.

Now, as her eyes slid over me, they seemed filled with displeasure.

"Oh, aye," she said. "And when will 'ee be back, the two o' ye?"

"In time for luncheon. We're just going to get a bit of a blow, eh, Nickie? To get rid of all the cobwebs enmeshed in our brains."

Nickie! He had never called me Nickie before. Only Martin had ever called me that. Martin—and my father. I liked the sound of it on Justin's lips, and thought suddenly, my father would have liked him. Then I caught Carty's eyes on me, shrewd and darkly penetrating. She read what went on in my mind, censuring me, and I felt momentarily afraid of her again, as I had been when I first knew her. What had John called her? A piskie. An elderly, wicked piskie. I could believe, at the moment, that he was right, that she had powers far beyond those of ordinary mortals and would not hesitate to use them against me.

Then she smiled and said, "Well, enjoy yoursel's." And again I felt foolish for thinking evil thoughts about so homely and cheerful a body. I wished I could keep my imagination in check.

Riding the waves, with Justin at the helm, was an exhilarating experience. With the breeze higher than it was on land, we skimmed the waters with ease. There was a delicious sense of freedom in the air as we cut through that wide expanse of turquoise blue. It seemed no one else existed but the two of us. The air was so clear we could make out various landmarks, on both the island and mainland coasts. Justin explained them to me, regaling me with the many legends attached to them. I listened, enchanted, and accepted at last that he was not making them up as he went along, that they were all part of Cornish folklore.

"It's like a living book," I breathed at length, and he beamed delightedly, realizing my capitulation.

"Look!" he directed my gaze to the sandy shoreline of Penrose.

"Seals!" I exclaimed in wonder.

"Gray seals," he explained, adding in erudite fashion, *"Halichoerus grupus.* Very common around here."

"There must be hundreds," I breathed.

"They colonize here. It's pupping time. See those little mounds of fur? Pups."

"So many of them! Aren't they lovely? Oh, look!" I grabbed his arm in sudden agitation. "Those two big ones. They're fighting."

"The largest beasts are always spoiling for a fight. To establish their authority, their territorial rights, their mates. It's . . ."

"The nature of the beast." As I looked laughingly up at him, finishing the sentence he had hesitated over, I surprised a look on his face that caused me to suck in my breath, shaking inwardly. I felt he wanted to take me in his arm, to kiss me, to establish his authority.

Authority over me?

I looked away quickly, suddenly fearful . . . of him . . . of myself.

Then I thought I must have been mistaken in my interpretation of his glance, for he said coolly, "We'll pull in at Arthur's Cove for a while to stretch our legs."

After beaching the boat and jumping down, he held out his arms to me. A moment later my feet were sinking into the soft, silvery sand. My heart careened turbulently inside my breast as he held me close, and I saw again that look I had seen a short while ago.

273

He wanted to kiss me. And oh, how I wanted him to!

His lips were close, so close, to mine. In a moment our lips would meet.

But then I was straining away from him.

"Don't . . . ," I whispered breathlessly as the image of Adelina rose large in my mind. I knew any kiss he bestowed on me would have no meaning beyond the mere gratification of a momentary desire.

He loosened his hold on me at once.

"Sorry," he said. "I forgot your aversion to me for a moment."

He started walking along the beach. I fell into step beside him.

In silence, he sat down on the warm sand. In silence, I followed suit.

In silence, he gazed out across the sea for a while, then lay back with his hands beneath his head and gazed up into the sky.

After a few moments I did likewise.

All was peaceful.

The sun beat down from an almost cloudless sky. I closed my eyes against its glare and wished I could stay like this forever, the sun warming me, Justin Penrose beside me, no one else around, no one to part us . . . But there was Adelina.

"Anything wrong?"

I had sighed deeply, and opened my eyes to see Justin raised on one elbow, looking down at me with concern. I felt my fingers stir as a longing to smooth the wrinkles from his brow rose within me.

I smothered the urge and said, "I was just thinking how lovely and peaceful it is here. I wish I could stay forever."

"I can understand that," he said. "I feel that way about it, too. It's my favorite spot on the island. I often come here seeking . . . searching for . . ."

"For what?" I prompted gently.

"Solace. When I'm depressed. . . . When life becomes—when I need to find a little sanity, some purpose, some meaning to my life."

"But there is meaning to your life. You own this beautiful island. You are a writer. You are rich and famous."

"And you think that is sufficient? Is that all there is to life? What about love? What about marriage? What about peace of mind?"

His face darkened as he spoke, and he rose, with sudden impatience, to walk down to the water's edge.

I watched him go, longing to rise and go with him. He was in the grip of some private hell and I yearned to comfort him, to throw convention to the wind, to kiss his hurt away—but I could not. If Adelina were here, she would be able to. She would have the right to throw her arms around him, snuggle up to him, kiss him, make him forget . . .

Forget what? Whom? Caroline, his lost love? Did he still pine for her?

What was she like, this Caroline, that she could inspire such devotion in him, such a steadfast love, which endured despite all the heartache she had caused him?

Did he hope she would return to him?

Would she ever return to set him at peace with himself again?

But he knew she would not come back to him and so he was going to marry Adelina.

Poor Adelina. Did she know she would be second best?

He remained at the water's edge for a long time, as still as a statue. I rose and went to join him. His face, set in stern lines, gave no indication that he noticed my appearance at his side. His eyes were on the far horizon, but I doubted he saw it, seeing only that which lay deep within his heart.

"You said there was a legend attached to Arthur's Cove," I said throatily, attempting, in the only way I could, to draw him back from the dark place he had retreated into. "Is it to do with King Arthur? Is that why it is so named?"

He turned to face me, seeming to have trouble in adjusting to my presence. Then he nodded his head.

"Will you tell me about it?"

For a moment I thought he would not, but then he began, "Arthur knew this cove as a boy and loved it. As he grew into manhood, he continued to come here, spending his days in solitude, restoring his mind and body after the vicissitudes of war and strife. He brought Guinevere here after their marriage. He wanted her to know it too, to feel its healing balm. They spent many nights of love here, the happiest of their lives. He . . . adored her . . . and . . ."

His voice slowed, faded, and his hands lifted from his sides as if he would take hold of me.

I stepped back quickly. He was missing Caroline. Adelina was not here to give him ease, so I would do in her place. But I would not stand in for anybody.

"I think we'd better be going," I said, turning and making for the *Sea Drift*, my throat hot with unshed tears.

What use were tears?

"Nicola! Wait!"

I heard Justin's call, his footsteps crunching across the sand. I did not turn round.

But it was impossible to outpace his lengthy stride. He caught up with me and swung me round to face him.

I struggled. "Let me go!" There was no mistaking his intent.

"Nicola. . . ." His voice had grown husky with desire.

"Let me go! This is wrong! You're engaged to Adelina!" I tried to shake myself free of his grasp. It was a futile attempt.

He gazed at me in what appeared to be genuine amazement. "Engaged to Adelina?" Suddenly the puzzlement left his face. He threw back his head and laughed out loud. "Adelina! My dear, I wouldn't have Adelina if she were handed to me on a plate with her weight in gold beside her!"

My heart jumped. But there was still Caroline. And Caroline would not be so easily set aside.

"So it is Caroline," I began and got no further.

His face changed. My words had brought a terrible expression to his face—an expression far worse than any I had ever seen there.

"What do you know about Caroline?" he grated, gravel-voiced.

"That . . . that she was your secretary before I came and that . . . you were in love with her, and she . . . she . . ."

My voice petered out. His face was livid. His fingers bit into the soft flesh of my arms like pincers. I was more afraid of him than I had ever been.

"Go on," he said, "Don't stop now." His voice seemed full of menace.

Suddenly defiant, I threw at him triumphantly, "She jilted you. I used to wonder why. But not any more. If you treated her the way you treat me, it's perfectly understandable."

His face changed again. His eyes filled with a misery so intense that my heart smote me. His hands fell from my arms and, as he turned to walk away from me, his shoulders sagged—those broad, proud shoulders sagged.

What had I done?

I had humiliated him—and his proud spirit could not take it.

No. It was more than that. I had taunted him with words that must strike at his very soul, lacerating afresh a wounded heart that would never heal.

I became filled with self-loathing.

"I'm sorry," I called out after him. "I shouldn't have said that. Please forgive me. I know you were devastated by her going. She broke your heart."

His voice came back to me on a bitter laugh. "Don't be sorry. I'll survive."

We sped home through sun-dappled waters. Not another word passed between us. We climbed the hills in silence and, once we were inside Penrose House, he entered the library and shut the door upon the world—and me.

I locked myself in my room, pleading a headache and begging to be left alone. There I attempted to sort through the tangled mess of thoughts and feelings that racked and tore me apart.

How lighthearted we had been when we had started our

outing. How well we had adjusted to each other. A rapport had sprung up between us. But then, once we reached Arthur's Cove, things changed. He had made advances to me—perhaps because I reminded him of Caroline. I had rejected them, believing it was only momentary gratification he was after. Clara had said he was a man with a man's needs, insinuating that he was not averse to taking pleasures from any woman willing to accommodate him. And what had John said? *He uses women how and when he wants them.*

Oh, I had been right to resist him.

But what if I had responded? Where would that have led me? I had been under the impression that he desired Adelina—would marry her, as Martin and John seemed to believe. But Justin had denied this so emphatically that I had believed him.

So would I have stood a chance with him?

It was too late to find out now. I had ruined any chance I might have had with my spiteful taunts.

In any case, would I want a man whose interest in me stemmed from my likeness to an earlier love—a love he could never forget?

No.

All in all, I had done the right thing in rejecting his advances. At least I had kept my self-respect.

But the solace this afforded was of little worth to one whose every pore and fiber ached with longing. My heart and mind were at war with one another, each trying to convince the other of opposing views.

I spent the rest of the day and night in bitter confrontation with myself. Finally, I had accepted the facts and had made my decision.

The morning found me waiting in the library for Justin to make his appearance. Dry-eyed, cold and determined, I waited. My decision had been made. I would leave Penrose to go with Clara, to London. That was as far as I could think. Beyond that, my brain refused to function, numbed by the onset of a winter's chill that would never leave me. I had gone through the motions of washing and dressing. I had not slept, and the face that looked out at me from the mirror was pale and drawn. Uncaring, I had made my way to the library, running into Mrs. Carthew, whose face creased into an anxious frown. She asked, "You all right, m'dear? You'm lookin' peaky," and on receiving no reply, had gone on, "'Tis not to be wondered at, shuttin' yoursel' away and refusing to eat. What 'ee needs is a good breakfast to put 'ee right."

"I don't want any," I had said brusquely, without thought, without feeling. Walking past her, I entered the library and sat down in the chair I used when taking dictation, only I would not take dictation today, and this would be the last time I would sit in it.

The thought had no effect on me. How could it affect a woman whose heart had died in the night? But when he came in, the tang of the outdoors clinging to him, my senses reeled. The heart I had thought dead jumped convulsively and started thudding heavily in my breast.

He threw a package on the desk as he walked round it to face me. "The mail," he said. "I met Thomas coming up the hill."

He behaved as if nothing had happened between us. Did he expect to continue in the way we had? Perhaps he could do that; I could not. But before I had gathered up enough courage to tell him I was leaving, he said shortly, "There's one for you."

"Thank you." I took the letter he held out to me and put it in my pocket.

"Aren't you going to open it?"

"I'll read it later. First I . . ."

"It's from Drake!" he burst out savagely. "Are you sure you can wait?" Then, as a surprised frown wrinkled my brow, he said, "I recognized the handwriting," as if that made it right.

"I'll read it later," I reaffirmed.

He swung away before I could say anything more, and I was

left staring into the empty space where he had been, regretting that I had not informed him of my decision to leave. Now it would have to wait till I saw him again and, in his present mood, who knew when that would be?

What should I do now? I caught sight of the mail on the desk and automatically moved to pick it up and take it into the office. I sorted through it. There was a lot I could deal with myself. Wait a minute! I checked myself. Though he didn't know it yet, I didn't work for Justin Penrose any more. Dealing with the mail was no longer my preserve.

Stifling a rush of sadness at the thought that I should never set foot in it again, I left the office and went to my room. I remembered the letter Justin had given me. What had he thought it contained? I wondered. He had seemed very annoyed about it.

I opened it eagerly; there would be news of my mother inside. Reading swiftly through sentences devoted to how much Martin had enjoyed his stay, and my company, on Penrose Island, I slowed at mention of my mother. *". . . I called at your home in Kensington as you requested, and enquired after your dear Mama. Unfortunately, I was not allowed to see her, but was assured she was well. By the way, I thought you told me the butler's name was Hartley? It isn't, it's Larby. And he's not short and stout, but well on his way to being a beanpole, if you ask me. Perhaps you've been away from home too long. . . ."*

I could not take it in. Not Hartley—Larby. What was Martin talking about? Had Hartley been replaced? Had he fallen ill? Had he gone on holiday? With every question I grew more and more afraid, fearing Ted Gibbon's hand at work. Hartley had served the family faithfully and long. He adored my mother. He had told me he thought her the most gracious lady in the world, and he would do anything for her. He must have noticed how she had deteriorated these past months, as I had when I had called. He would also have noticed Ted Gibbon's meanness toward her, seen how he treated her, and, though it was not his place, he would have been unable to refrain from voicing his displeasure.

Yes, that is what must have happened. Ted Gibbon had probably reacted with his usual peevish conceit and would have turned him out, most likely without a reference.

And what about the other servants? Had any, or all, of them been replaced?

Had my poor Mama anyone round her who loved her?

But she was well . . . Yes, surely she was well. Although I had not signed my fortune over to her, I had instructed my solicitors not to block the encashment of any checks she saw fit to write. That effectively meant Ted Gibbon had access to all the money he could need. So . . . he would make sure she was well. He would keep her . . . sweet.

Nevertheless, I felt I should have to visit her myself as soon as I reached London. I trembled, wondering if I would have the courage.

The morning progressed. I felt hungry and I presented myself in the dining room. The table was laid for three, but when neither Justin nor Clara put in an appearance, I was served and ate in solitary state, which pleased me. However, as I rose to leave the table, Justin walked in.

"Well, has he come up to scratch?" he demanded at once.

I gazed him in puzzlement.

"Young Drake. Has he vowed eternal love? Begged you to join him? And will you? Of course you will. After all, your initial success with John hasn't come to anything, has it? Or haven't you really tried with him yet? Which one do you want, Miss Wentworth? When will you make up your mind?"

Flabbergasted, unable to believe my ears, I broke out explosively, "You are being offensive, Mr. Penrose."

"Offensive!" Oh, the sarcasm in that word. "Is it possible to offend a coquette of your undoubted abilities?"

"Coquette . . . ?" My mouth opened and closed in stupefaction.

"Oh, come now, don't be shy of admitting your powers in that department. I have had ample proof of them as I watched you at work. You might have the face of an angel and look as though butter wouldn't melt in your mouth, but you know

281

how to play one man off against another well enough."

"Stop it! Stop it!" I cried and tried to race past him.

I stood no chance of escaping him. His powerful frame blocked my way and his hand shot out to catch my wrist in a vise-like grip.

"Let me go! I won't listen to any more. You have no right."

"You'll listen to what I have to say, whether you like it or not."

"Stop and think before you say any more—"

"Afraid of the truth?"

"You don't know what the truth is."

"I'm not blind!"

"You are! Blinded by your own arrogance!"

I should have known better than to cross swords with him. It had never yet gained me a victory. It did not now. With an angry, contemptuous movement, he swung me against him, pinning me close so that I could not escape.

"Then in my arrogance," he said, "let me taste a little of your wares. Test the worth of them."

My heart threatened to burst as his lips descended on mine. Brutally, mercilessly, he imposed his will on mine, and I endeavored to resist with all my strength, for he must never know how I wanted to submit. But I felt my resolve deserting me.

Then I was thrust away. His eyes overflowed with disdain. They flickered over me as if I were some loathsome thing crawled out from under a stone. He turned from me in disgust and I was left, with legs like jelly, to stagger into a chair, where I collapsed, gulping for air.

I wanted to die. It was all so unfair. His estimation of me was lower than I could ever have imagined. He believed the worst of me. He *wanted* to believe the worst of me.

Well let him. Let him! My soul cried out in anguish, knowing that I could never show him how wrong he was about me and that I had nothing to look forward to but emptiness and bitterness.

No! I would not succumb and turn into a carbon copy of Justin Penrose, shunning the world, believing the worst of people. It would be easy to slide into that dark world, but I was a fighter and would not give way to the blandishments of self-pity. There were a great many unfortunate people in the world, people in a far worse state than I. Perhaps I could help them. Having suffered myself would enlarge my sympathy and understanding of their ills and fears. Or I could throw myself into the fight for women's rights . . . Oh, there were a great many things I could do with my life . . . if I stirred myself and bit back the anguish that filled my eyes with tears . . .

Someone entered the room, and I pressed the tears back from whence they came.

"What's the matter with my son? He just left the house with a face like thunder."

"He's in a bad temper," I answered Clara with a creditable attempt to steady my voice.

"I could see that," she said with some asperity. "I wouldn't have commented on it, only he seems to have been a lot better of late. Not so quick with his tongue. What caused his bad temper?"

I shrugged a negative response.

"Didn't you enjoy the trip?"

I shrugged again. "Yes."

A maid came in to serve her with food. She waved her away, telling her to come back later.

"Something happened," she said to me, watchfully calm. "Did Justin—misbehave?"

"No, of course not. Clara?"

"Yes, dear?"

"About—"

"Oh, just a minute, dear. I think I'd better have my meal before it gets cold."

"Mrs. Carthew will keep it hot for you."

"Yes. Well, ring the bell for me, dear. I'm feeling rather hungry."

I did her bidding, glad to find my legs had almost returned to normal, then sat down again. "Clara . . ."

Before I could get any further, the maid came in. While she set about serving her, Clara sat back, fanning herself with her hand. "Dreadful weather," she sighed.

I gaped at her in surprise. "But it's beautiful weather. It's a glorious, sunny day."

"Too hot. Unseasonal. What can one do in weather like this?"

"Go for walks. There are lots of lovely walks on the island, and there is always a refreshing breeze to make it agreeable. Then there's croquet on the lawn. I don't like playing it myself, but I'm sure John or—or your son would—"

"Oh, my dear, you ought to know by now I'm not one for taking strenuous exercise. Walking on this island with its hills and stony paths has never appealed to me. Even in the old days, when I was much younger . . . No. Give me the theatre, intimate little restaurants, Monte Carlo and the Casino. . . . Now that's exciting. Win or lose, it doesn't matter. It's being there, the atmosphere, charged with emotion, fervor, fear. No, the simple life is not for me."

With the departure of the maid, she picked up her knife and fork and nibbled daintily on a piece of meat. Then, raising her dark blue eyes, she focused on me again, shrewdly challenging.

"I don't think it's for you, either. You've never looked really happy here. It's not surprising, coming from London as you do. You must miss it a great deal—the life, the parties, the young men following you around. You must have had a great many suitors—you're a very pretty girl. You must miss their attentions."

"No, I—I like it here."

Clara's lips pinched together and her eyes, never very warm, now lost what little warmth they had.

"I wonder if you would like it as much if my son were not such a glamorous figure," she snapped. "If he were a staid married man with half a dozen screaming children, if he had a bald head and a bulbous red nose and talked about nothing but his horses and estate management, would you still find him so attractive?"

"The question doesn't arise, does it?" I managed to make it sound as if I could not care less anyway.

"No?"

"No."

"Then why are you so loathe to leave? Why won't you come back to London with me?"

"That—that's what I wanted to talk to you about. I will come with you, if you like."

"You will?" The dark blue eyes gleamed exultantly. "Oh, Nicola, you don't know how happy that makes me."

But I shan't stay with you for long, I added silently. I have other plans in mind. How was I to know Fate had already decided them for me?

Chapter Fifteen

The sun had been driven away by mounting clouds. A mist of rain was being blown across the sea by a moaning wind. I could only just make out the *Justinia* heading away from the island.

I had not seen Justin since our meeting in the dining room, when he had subjected me to his scorn and had beaten me to a quivering jelly. He had been so unfair, giving me no chance to explain Martin's letter.

Would I have explained if he had? I doubted it. My obstinacy, always ready to rise in the face of unjust censure, would have forbidden it. Besides, it was better so. Let him think the worst of me—it would make leaving easier.

Clara had sent for John as soon as she had finished her meal, asking him to come around. He had been surprised to learn that I was going to leave Penrose and live with Clara, but he had made no attempt to dissuade me. In fact, he had said, "Well, perhaps it's for the best." I had looked at him sharply, wondering if he knew about my feelings for Justin. But how could he? How could anyone? No. John was glad I was leaving the island, as he had warned me to in the beginning, because he knew Justin's faults. *"He doesn't like women . . . you're too nice . . . and vulnerable . . ."* He didn't want me to get hurt. Oh, John, I should have listened to you in the beginning.

Afterwards I had called on Ruth. I could not leave without saying goodbye to her. We were to leave on the morning's tide.

"There's nothing to keep us here now," Clara had exclaimed. Would we sail in the *Justinia*? I wondered, my eyes on the shrouded boat. Would Justin take us across to the mainland? I had not seen him to tell him I was leaving, but I felt sure Clara would have. He had not contacted me, he made no effort to make me change my mind. Why should he? He would be glad to see me go—now. I had called on Ruth . . .

"Leaving?" she had cried, devastated at my news. "To go and work for Clara? I can't believe it! I thought, after our conversation, you would have more sense. Forgive me, but I can't help thinking it is the worst thing you could do."

"I shan't stay with her long. It's only a stop-gap measure, till I can find something else."

But her mind had not been eased. "I can't understand you! Why leave, anyway? I thought you loved the island? And what about John? Have you told him? He'll be most upset. You know how he feels about you."

"John know. He understands."

"Well, I don't. Unless—it's Justin, after all."

Why pretend to Ruth any longer? I had to tell her. I would never tell anyone else, but Ruth had a right to know. She was in love with Justin herself. She chose to stay to be near him, perhaps still harboring dreams. But I could not stay, not after what had happened between us.

"I've fallen in love with him," I had told her straightforwardly.

"And he?" her face had grown pinched and white.

"Feels nothing for me."

"Are you sure?" A tremor of hope was in her voice, betraying her thankfulness that her dreams might still flourish. "I've always felt there was something . . . You attracted him. . . ."

"It was my likeness to Caroline, nothing more."

Strange how calm I had been—appeared to be.

"I shall miss you," she had said as I left. "You'll write, won't you?"

I had promised I would, wondering if I would keep the

promise. Perhaps it would be better to cut all ties with Penrose, my island haven, my dark haven. Penrose Island was an island of sadness, of sorrows plucked from the hearts of all who lived here.

Was that what the unseen beings—the piskies?—had been trying to tell me all those weeks ago, when I had first arrived? Had their warnings been given because they knew that if I stayed I should only add to the great aching sadness at the heart of Penrose?

I could not see the *Justinia* any longer. The long, slender boat had completely disappeared behind a curtain of steadily falling rain, taking with it my heart's love, my very life, my soul.

There was little sleep for me that night. The rain fell steadily. The wind moaned like a lament around the battlements of Penrose House. I lay listening to it—and for that other sound, the sound of Justin returning home. Wide-eyed, dry-eyed, I lay awake, staring fearfully into the future.

Morning came, gray and dripping. Leaden skies, leaden seas, echoed the gloom that flooded my heart. With heavy limbs I abandoned my sleepless bed, washed in cold water, dressed and finished my packing, glad the night had gone, glad of something to do. From now on I must fill every waking moment with activity to prevent myself from dwelling on that which must, *must*, be eradicated from my mind.

I rang the bell to summon a servant, something I did not usually do, but this day was different from all others and warranted the change. I did not feel I could eat anything, but I longed for a cup of tea, scalding hot and reviving.

Sally answered my summons. Her eyes took in my baggage standing by my bed. "So 'tis true, Miss Wentworth. You'm leaving us."

"Yes," I said briefly, not wishing to discuss the matter. "Will you bring me a pot of tea, please?"

"Yes, Miss." She half turned to go, but spun round again. "Must 'ee go, Miss? 'Twas thought . . . 'twas hoped. . . ."

"I shall be leaving on the tide. Bring me the tea, if you please."

"Will 'ee ever come back, Miss?"

"No, Sally." She turned away sadly. I swallowed my corresponding sigh. "Before you go, Sally . . . Is Master Justin up yet?"

"His bed's not been slept in, Miss." She replied without the least element of surprise in her voice, as if it was a usual occurrence.

My first reaction was one of thankfulness that he had not come home. He had sailed away on the *Justinia* and, with any luck, would not return till I had left. I could leave my letter of resignation for someone else to deliver, and the task of handing it to him personally need trouble me no more. I wondered where he had gone—and why. But his comings and goings were no longer any concern of mine. The thought brought a stab of pain to my heart. I ignored it. If I ignored it long enough, the pain that had rooted itself at the core of my being would wither for want of nourishment and die.

Such was my philosophy.

The tea came. I drank two cups. I gazed round the beautiful sitting room I should soon cease to occupy. I had been happy here. Sad, too; it had witnessed my heartbreak. I wished the tide would hurry. The sooner it came in, the sooner I should be gone. I felt I could not be gone too soon, now. I opened a book to make the time pass more quickly. The words blurred on the page and made no sense. Into my mind strayed thoughts of Justin, of his work, of our work, together. He had said we worked well together . . . I thought of how much we had enjoyed each other's company, how we had laughed . . . I thought of Betsy and Winnie romping ahead of us as we walked the hills . . . I thought of Ruth, of John, of so many things I should not have thought about, but try as I might, I could not keep them from invading my mind, and each one brought its own share of torture.

Ignore it.

I tossed the book aside and entered the bedroom, the bathroom, looking to see if I had left any little thing unpacked. My perambulations passed the time, but did not ease the pain.

IGNORE IT! What was the use of a philosophy if one did not abide by it?

I heard Clara's voice, a knock at the door. I saw Clara's delicate, fine-boned face appear. "Are you ready, my dear?"

At last, it was time to go. I gathered up my rain cape, my gloves, and bag. "Has John arrived?"

"He's downstairs. What a dreadful day. If I weren't so anxious to see dear old London again, I'd consider postponing the journey."

"Oh, no, we mustn't postpone it!" The Black Wind could rise again; we mustn't postpone it.

I left Clara waiting in the hall while I went to see Carty. I had no wish to see Mrs. Carthew, yet it would seem odd if I left without saying goodbye, although, after yesterday, I doubted she would wish to see me.

While I had been visiting Ruth, Clara had told Mrs. Carthew of our plans. Exactly what she said remains a mystery to me to this day, but it had put the housekeeper into a rare temper. I had never seen her so angry as when she confronted me on my return.

"So you'm leaving? 'Tis a pity 'ee stayed so long."

"I'm sorry . . . ," I began with a catch of breath at the flash of hatred in her eyes.

"For all the things 'ee said about lovin' the island? This house? These folk that've made 'ee welcome? How 'ee loved workin' for Master Justin, how grateful to him for lettin' 'ee stay, how 'ee never wanted to leave? Fine words, aye! Worth nothin'!"

"Things have happened, Mrs. Carthew, that—"

"He's been good to 'ee. Yet 'ee do have the 'eart to turn your back on him, now, when he needs you most."

"Mrs. Carthew . . ."

"'Tis shameful the way 'ee have behaved."

I could stand to listen to no more. I ran from her angry denunciations and threw myself on my bed in anguish. She did not understand! She did not understand! And she refused to listen to anything I might have to say in justification of myself.

I had avoided her for the rest of the day.

But now I would have to see her. Perhaps she had calmed down. Perhaps she would allow me to explain. Explain? How could I explain my reasons for leaving to her, even if she would listen? I would have to go on letting her believe that, for my own selfish reasons, I was leaving her beloved master in the lurch just when he needed the services of a competent secretary to help him with his American project. I knew he would have no trouble in finding someone else to accompany him to the United States. I hoped Mrs. Carthew had thought this out for herself during the intervening hours and if so, then maybe we could part on more friendly terms.

But after one look at her face, I knew this was not to be.

"I'm leaving now, Mrs. Carthew," I said stiffly, sorrowfully, because I had grown quite attached to her. "Will you see Mr. Penrose gets this, please? It's my letter of resignation."

"So 'ee lacks the decency to wait and tell him to his face, preferin' to sneak off behind his back." She attacked me at once, and the cat on her lap leapt away, affrighted at the venom in her voice.

"I can't tell him! He's not here," I cried reproachfully.

"'Twas a bad day for this house when 'ee came with your devil's tricks. I knowed 'ee was trouble the moment I laid eyes on 'ee."

Hate filled her eyes. I looked on the face of one I did not know.

I hurried back to Clara. John, who was to escort us on our journey, was overseeing the loading of the baggage by a couple of manservants. It had stopped raining, but was very cold, with the wind blowing from the north. Clara was warmly wrapped in furs beneath her waterproof cape, and I had on a warm, woolen suit beneath mine. I had tied a scarf round my neck and pulled my woolen beret well down over my ears. As we settled ourselves in the carriage John, attentive as ever, tucked a thick blanket round our legs before taking his seat opposite us.

"Let's go," he called to the groom in the driving seat, and off we went along the gray, winding coastal road hemmed in by rising granite and surging gray sea. With a canopy of gray above us, the day was as bleak as the heart which, somehow, still managed to beat within me.

Jem Pascoe's *Island Queen* awaited our arrival and sailed as soon as we were aboard. Clara went at once to make herself as comfortable as she could in the cramped little cabin, fussed over by John. Despite a fresh fall of rain, I stayed, clutching the rail with a desperate, aching sense of loss.

Farewell, Penrose. Farewell, my island. The gray hills I loved were soon lost to my sight.

London. Dirty, smelly, full of clatter and people scurrying like ants, intent on their own business, paying no heed to anyone else. Clara seemed to bloom amidst all the noise and bustle; I felt an overpowering sense of loneliness. And yet, at one time, I had been part of all this. I had not noticed the noise, the smells. But since Penrose . . .

"What's the matter, Nicola?" John's voice sounded concerned as we waited for a hansom cab to take us to Kensington. "You look sad. You're not regretting your decision already?"

"No. No. Of course not. It's just that I'd forgotten what London was like. It seems so noisy after Penrose."

"You'll soon get used to it again," he said comfortingly. "Clara will not let you pine for long. She'll soon have a line-up of concerts, parties, theatre outings and such for you. Will you not, Clara?"

"Indeed I will," she agreed enthusiastically, going on to regale me with the wealth of delights she had in store for me.

Not that these were quick in coming to fruition. More than a week passed before the first of them materialized—her own "At Home," at which I was introduced to a small, select circle of her friends. But I was kept busy. From the start Clara had me performing little tasks for her. She had me, as Ruth had foretold, run off my feet, though she employed a maid, a cook, and a handyman, who had taken care of the house while she had been away. How she managed to find so much for us to do was amazing. The maid, the cook, and the handyman complained about the extra jobs she gave them, but I was glad to be so busily occupied. It gave me less time to dwell on my problems.

I had suffered great agitation of mind as we approached her house on Church Street. It was hardly more than five minutes away from my own home, and I wondered how I should avoid running into my stepfather, Ted Gibbon. I knew I should, more than likely, run into him when I called to see my mother, but I intended to ask Martin Drake to accompany me when I made that visit. Nothing would induce me to go alone after what had happened the last time, particularly now that Hartley had gone.

I had called Martin on the telephone, and had been told he was visiting friends in Sussex and would not be back till the end of the week. I had called again after seven days, but he had not yet returned. I called again and again, and still had no luck.

I gave up trying to contact him, deciding to ask John if he would go with me. He was staying with us for another two or three days. It would mean acquainting him with my reasons for not wishing to go alone. Was I ready to do that? I was by no means certain. But I had to see my mother soon. I was worried by what Martin had told me. I dare not call her on the telephone—that would alert Ted Gibbon, and, in any case, would she even be allowed to come to the telephone? Larby was new and, unlike Hartley, owed no allegiance to my mother. He would take his orders from the master of the house, and I could guess what they would be.

So there was nothing else for it. I would have to give John

my reasons. He should understand my reluctance to go alone, and would gladly give me his protection.

I made my plans, not knowing the path I was to tread had already been paved for me.

Having made up my mind, I waited impatiently for John to return from an outing with Clara. They had not asked me to go with them, but that had not worried me. I was growing used to being left on my own with some sewing to do, or a cupboard to be turned out—whatever little task Clara had thought up for me. Perhaps it would be different when John had gone. Then Clara would wish me to accompany her wherever she went. She did not like doing things alone.

I sat with a piece of lace in my hands, mending a tiny rent in the delicate material. Plying my needle was a task I had never enjoyed, and I was glad to set it aside when I heard the door open and voices in the hall. Usually when Clara returned from an outing, she went straight up to her room to change, calling for me as she went. Usually I obeyed her call at once. This tme, however, I intended to hold back for a while so that I could speak to John alone. But things did not work out as usual.

They came into the drawing room together, and they had brought someone with them.

"Hello, Nicola, my dear. I've come to take you home."

The hairs rose on the back of my neck, and my scalp tingled at the voice, the sight, of the man smiling sardonically at me.

"You!" I breathed, my heart pounding with dread. "How—how did you find me?"

"It wasn't difficult. Clara and I are old friends. I happened to run into her and—"

"You should have told me you were Teddy's stepdaughter," Clara said reprovingly. "If John hadn't let it slip, when I introduced them, that you were staying with me, I'd never have known."

John! My eyes flew to him.

"As soon as I heard his name, I knew who he was. Naturally, I mentioned you."

294

"But how did you know?"

"Ruth told me."

"Ruth?"

"Only in passing. I'm sure she didn't think she was betraying a confidence. Did you wish your presence to be kept a secret?"

Ruth! My confidante and friend, on whom I had thought I could rely! She had told John, and John had told Clara, and now . . . now . . .

"Of course she did not," cried Clara. "And if she did, she would surely wish to know that her mother was sick."

"Sick? Mama's sick?" I looked into Ted Gibbon's face, and what I saw there made me cry, "I don't believe it. He just wants to get me into the house to . . . to . . ."

"My dear, what has got into you?" Clara's eyes widened in alarm. "Your Mama is sick and—"

"No! No! I don't believe it! I don't believe it!"

"You're becoming hysterical, my dear. The news has shocked you, but you must try to accept it. She's calling for you. She wants to see you."

"Calling for me? Is she really that bad?"

"She's giving cause for concern."

Ted Gibbon spoke anxiously. He sounded sincere. But was he? Was Mama really ill? Had Martin not been allowed in to see her because she was too ill to see anybody? Was her illness a true illness, or was it drug induced? Whatever the truth of the matter, I had to find out. I had to go with him.

The more fool I. I should have known what to expect.

"What have you done to Mama?" I turned on him angrily as we started walking the short distance between Clara's house and mine. "If you've been drugging her again—"

"My dear girl," he began, offended. It cut no ice with me.

"I know those headaches weren't normal, and you had something to do with them. You were giving her something to make her feel ill. I'm afraid you might be doing the same thing again, and if you are . . ."

295

"How can you make such wild accusations? You have an overactive imagination, my dear. But allow me to set your mind at rest. She's perfectly well—for the moment."

"What do you mean—for the moment?"

"Well, she's being rather difficult. She's started refusing to sign checks. But once she knows I have you safely under lock and key . . ."

"Lock and key!"

"It's the only way, my dear. I can't allow you to roam about loose now, can I? That would defeat the object of the exercise."

He was evil. I should never have come with him. I should have known his purpose was evil.

I turned suddenly, darting away from him to run back to Clara, John, and safety, but he thrust his arm through mine. Holding me close to his repulsive body, he muttered, with the quiet assurance of one who knew he had the upper hand, "Oh, no. You can't get away from me as easily as that. And don't think about calling for help. Your mother's safety depends on your amenity. If she won't sign, then you must."

"But you can't keep me locked up!"

"Perhaps it won't be necesary for long."

"Clara . . . John . . . will want to know why I have not returned."

"They don't expect you to. Clara is sending some of your things round. As I told her, you'll wish to stay with your Mama till she's well again."

"But they'll want to see me! They'll come round to visit!"

"And I'll be glad to welcome them . . . eventually . . . when you've come to your senses and I can rely on your discretion."

"You're mad if you think you can get away with this!" I cried.

"Not mad." His eyes glittered dangerously. "Just determined."

Still holding me in a tight grip, he steered me up the steps leading to the black front door and, with his free hand, beat upon it with the heavy, brass lion's head knocker. It was opened immediately by a tall gaunt-faced man. Larby! The new butler Martin had told me about.

My stepfather thrust me across the orange and white tiled floor to the stairs. "Go to your room, my dear. Your old room. I've had it made ready for you."

"I want to see Mama!" I cried.

"And so you shall. Later. After I've had a talk with her."

"I want to see her now!" I tried to run past him into the drawing room, where I guessed my mother would be.

He caught my arm and spun me round with such a jerk that a spasm of pain went shooting through my back.

"Upstairs with her, Larby."

He swung me roughly at the hard-faced butler, whose eyes showed not a glimmer of warmth. I could expect no mercy from such a man. He caught hold of my wrist and twisted my arm behind my back. The pain was excruciating. "Mama! Mama!" I gave a loud cry only to have it die on my lips as a bony hand covered my mouth and bony fingers clamped to my cheeks.

In this manner I was hauled up the stairs. I was pushed unceremoniously through the door of my former room, which I had hoped never to see again after my last experience there. The door closed. The key turned in the lock—*from the outside!* Ted Gibbon had made no idle boast when he had said I should be kept under lock and key. Nevertheless, I ran to try and open it, wincing with the pain that ran from my arm to my neck, down my back. I soon desisted in my efforts.

All that had happened to me during the last few minutes had had the vague unreality of a dream, as if it were happening to someone else. But this pain was no dream. This pain was real. And I knew without doubt that if I failed to obey Ted Gibbon's instructions, I should have more to suffer. Already a bruise was showing at my wrist where Larby's fingers had dug into it. Bruises were probably appearing on my cheeks too, from the same cause.

What a fool I had been to come here!

Yet what else could I have done under the circumstances? I

had thought my mother was ill and needed me. But it was Ted Gibbon who needed me—to sign his checks when Mama would not.

Biting my lip, holding my arm against me in a vain attempt to ease the pain, turning away from the door, I saw the window.

The window! I could open it and call for help. Someone passing below would hear me. The thought carried me across the room. I could have wept when I could not open it. Pain jarred through me, yet still I tried to push and pull. It was no good. The window remained fast shut. And then I saw why: it had been sealed. Ted Gibbon had left nothing to chance.

Break the glass! Yes, I could break the glass . . . but what good would it do? Someone inside the house would hear it shatter, and would be in the room before I could attract anyone's attention. And there were few people passing down below. The chances were no one would be within hearing distance. Besides, I thought now, who would believe I was in danger and needed help? If all this seemed unreal to me, how much more so would it appear to an outsider? And then there was Mama. How could I think of escaping, leaving her to the tender mercies of a Ted Gibbon thwarted and angry? Her safety depended on me, he had said.

So there was nothing I could do—for the present, at least. But I would have to think of something. I had only myself to rely on. There was no one else . . . no Justin . . . Justin would not turn up again when I needed him, as he had done once before . . . Justin had washed his hands of me.

I wept remembering that last time. I wept remembering his gentleness, his kindness to me then. I wept remembering—oh, so many things.

But what was the use of crying? Tears never solved anything. Tears would not help me in my present desperate situation. I must think. Think. Plan. Scheme.

What about John? No. He was returning to Penrose within the space of the next two days. I could not look to him for help. Clara, then. She was bound to call to see me. Ted Gibbon had

298

made it plain I should not be allowed to see her until I had shown my eagerness to cooperate. Very well, then, I would pretend to cooperate. He would then allow me freedom within the house, if not outside. If he allowed Clara to visit me, then I could appeal to her for help, could leave with her. Ted Gibbon would not dare to stop me.

But I was forgetting Mama. I could not leave without her. Would I be able to persuade her to leave with me? I had to try. This time I must make her see the danger she was in. I must force her to see Ted Gibbon as he really was—an evil monster who would use her and anyone else to gain his own ends. It would not be easy, but get her out of this house and Ted Gibbon's clutches I must.

I was left alone for hours. It grew late. It seemed no one was coming to see me, nor was I given any food. I looked at the door. It was locked from the outside. Anyone wishing to enter would have no difficulty in gaining admission. Ted Gibbon would have no difficulty in gaining admission.

Speedily, despite my aching arm, I dragged a chair across the room and wedged it beneath the door knob. That should stop anyone coming in unannounced. Hopefully, it would deter them completely. I was thinking only of Ted Gibbon, of the attempt I was certain he would try to make.

Further hours passed. I had not seen the doorknob move. Perhaps I was worrying about nothing. I lay down on the bed, fully dressed, not to sleep—I felt I could not sleep—but to rest and wait the weary night away, wait to see what tomorrow would bring.

Perhaps I did sleep, a little, for when the light fell across the room, I was surprised by it, surprised to see the sun was shining after many days of cloud and rain. My eyes flew to the door. The chair was still wedged there. No one had entered in the night. When I went to remove it, I tried the door. It was still locked.

I was hungry. I had been given nothing to eat since my arrival. Would I be fed today? Was I to be starved into submission? Had I been forgotten? Should I bang on the door, demand attention?

But of course I had not been forgotten. This was all part of Ted Gibbon's plan to bring me into line, to prove how dependent I was upon him now, for even the barest necessities of life.

However, there was water in the glazed jug on the washstand, and towels on the rail. I poured water into the basin and washed my hands and face. As I dried myself, I was startled by the turning of the key in the lock. My heart lurched as I waited to see who would enter.

It was a servant I did not recognize. An elderly woman, thin-faced, expressionless. My instinct was to dart past her and out of the door, but someone waiting outside turned the key in the lock again. The woman set down the tray of food she had brought in.

"I wish to be taken to my mother," I said.

She paid no attention to me.

"Your mistress. Take me to her."

She turned to leave me without a word, without a glance.

"Wait!" I commanded her. "How dare you turn your back on me?"

But I held no position in this house where Ted Gibbon was master now. Ignoring me completely, she passed through the door, opened at her knock, and in the next moment I heard the key turn again. She had been given her orders, and she obeyed them as Larby had obeyed his. As the rest would obey theirs.

The rest . . . Had all the loyal servants been replaced by creatures of his own, or did one, just one, remain? I threw down the towel I still held in my hands, and rushed to tug at the bell rope. If one remained, he or she would answer my summons.

But no one came. It was as I had suspected. All, all had been replaced.

Even Belle, Mama's personal maid, who had been with her for so long she knew her every mood, every thought almost? Oh, surely he could not have been so cruel to deprive Mama of

300

Belle, on whom she depended so!

But knowing Ted Gibbon as I did, I was sadly aware that such cruelty would appeal to his nature, and guessed he would not have been able to resist indulging it.

Oh, Mama, Mama; how have you managed to adjust to all the changes that have gone on since I left? Do you accept them? Are you still blind to everything he does, still so dazzled by his charm and good looks that, as far as you are concerned, he can do no wrong? But you have started refusing to sign his checks. Why? Does it mean you are beginning to see him a little more clearly? Are you waking up, at last, to his sly, vicious ways, his evil nature?

It was a slender hope, but I clung to it. If it were true, how much easier everything would be. Together, we could outwit Ted Gibbon. Together, we could evade his clutches, lose ourselves in the wilds of Wales or Scotland—even Ireland—or we could settle abroad somewhere. We could make a new life for ourselves. We could . . .

The planning, the scheming, sustained me far more than the meal I now fell upon as my hunger pangs could no longer be denied.

The planning and scheming had to sustain me throughout the day and another night—a night of fear and trembling, though the chair wedged shut the door. My eyes wide and staring, I lay, still in my clothing, trying to keep awake and failing, waking jerkily through all the dark hours. Then passed a day of hunger—for no one brought me food—and fear. Fear of the unknown. What was Ted Gibbon planning for me? Why was he keeping me locked away for so long without coming to see me? Why? Why? The questions were endless, and all on the same theme.

Then, on the third morning, food was again brought to me in the same manner as before. In the afternoon, my feared and hated stepfather put in an appearance. Behind him came a manservant with my belongings, sent on by Clara. Ted Gibbon smiled.

I greeted him angrily. "How much longer am I to be kept

prisoner like this?"

A pained look crossed his face. "Prisoner? You are not a prisoner, my dear."

"The door is locked upon me. The servants will not answer my calls."

"Ah, me!" He sighed extravagantly. "Servants are such a problem these days. They're not what they were. But a bath has been prepared for you. Come. And afterwards change into something pretty. Your Mama is asking to see you."

"She knows I'm here?" His last words drove the remark I was about to make regarding the replacement of all the loyal and good servants who used to work here, from my tongue.

"But of course," he replied with a show of surprise at my surprise. "She saw you arrive from her window."

I did not believe him. I could not believe him. My dearest Mama would not have waited so long before wishing to see me.

I took my bath, glad to get out of the clothes I had worn for so long, knowing the door was locked upon me. I had to knock to be allowed out. The thin-faced woman who brought me my meals escorted me back to my room and locked the door upon me again while I changed into fresh clothing, reflecting wryly upon Ted Gibbon's assertion that I was not a prisoner. I had just finished brushing the tangles out of my hair when he came to take me to my mother.

She was in her boudoir. Tea and cakes were set out on a table at her side. She smiled when she saw me.

"Mama!" I ran at once to embrace her.

"Darling, my gown!" She pushed me gently away from her and began rearranging the folds of her peach-colored gown, spreading the delicate chiffon skirts around her in a wide semi-circle as if to say, come no nearer than this.

Ted Gibbon walked round the dainty Louis Quinze sofa over which her skirts were spread and, bending down from behind it, kissed her cheek. She held her hand up to him. He took it and held it against his breast. She smiled up at him adoringly. I watched the whole charade in disbelief, unhappily aware that she was still besotted by him. The hopes I had cherished of

302

enlisting her aid in escaping from him—together—faded.

But she could not know how he had treated me. When she did . . .

"I've been kept locked in my room, Mama! He's kept me prisoner for days!"

"Nicola!" Her eyes were cold upon me, and her voice rang with chastisement as she continued, "How can you tell such lies?" I saw what it was about her that was different. Her eyes had been penciled round to make them seem bigger than they were. Her cheeks were rouged. So were her lips. She looked like a tart, my mother, who had never painted her face in all her life.

"I know you've been here for days." I watched the words issue from between the painted lips, frozen to the spot with astonishment. "Yet you could not be bothered to come and see me. And now, at last, when you deign to honor me with your presence, after Teddy's persuasions, you get up to your old tricks again and try to turn me against him with your lies, as you tried the last time you were here. Well, I told you then I didn't believe you, and I don't believe you now. I don't know what you can possibly have against Teddy, but I tell you here and now, if you cannot curb your tongue, please leave me. I will not listen to you slander my beloved husband."

She looked different, but she had not changed. She was as much under Ted Gibbon's influence as she had ever been, believing implicitly in all he said and did. Had he persuaded her to paint her face? I wondered now. She would do anything to please him. Or had she done it herself, believing it made her more beautiful, more seductive, more alluring to him? Was she still a little unsure of his faithfulness, still unsure about the lady he had met at the stage door?

My gaze moved to Ted Gibbon, standing so smugly behind her. The expression on his face was self-congratulatory. He had set my mother against me with his lies, and, as he had said once before, she would not believe any words of mine against his.

He bent to kiss the top of her elegantly coiffeured head,

upon which balanced a tiny scrap of lace with hanging ribbons the color of her gown. Without taking his eyes off me, he murmured into the dark curls, "Don't be too hard on her, my heart's love. She is more to be pitied than berated. I'll leave you alone together for a while. You must have a lot to say to each other after so long a time apart."

He was so sure of himself, of his power over her, that he had no qualms about leaving me alone with her, though he must have known I would continue my efforts to show him in his true lights, as I did the moment he had gone.

"Believe me, Mama, I have been kept a prisoner in my room. He brought me here under false pretenses. He told me you were ill and asking for me."

"Nonsense. Why do you insist in decrying him so? If you do not stop it at once, I shall have no alternative but to ask you to leave me. Oh, Nicola," her voice grew plaintive, "don't try to make me hate Teddy. You'll never succeed. I accept that, for some reason, you do not like him, and I know he has his faults—oh, yes, I'm not completely blind, though you may think so—I know he can't resist a pretty face. He loves me, but, charming and handsome as he is, he will always have women falling at his feet, making up to him . . . He would be more than human if he failed to respond. Only I refuse to share him, and have found a way to keep him dancing attendance on me."

"You refuse to sign his checks," I breathed, looking at her with new eyes.

"Only some of them, but it's sufficient to ensure he doesn't stray. He gambles, you know?"

"Yes," I whispered.

"I pay his gambling debts. And we have regular gaming nights here. I've discovered quite an interest in it myself—and am quite lucky. Luckier than Teddy. Tea, my dear?"

She handed me one of the cups she had filled as she spoke. I accepted it in bemused fashion. If the things that had happened hitherto had held a dreamlike unreality, how much more so did these present revelations. Was Mama really saying she was not taken in by Ted Gibbon? How long had she known him for what he was?

"Oh, yes, he has one or two faults, like any man, but he's not the demon you make him out to be. In fact, I'm surprised at you. He's very fond of you. If he's been a little harsh with you at times, it has been because you have not hesitated to show your unnatural dislike of him. He is your stepfather! Of course, you could not be expected to give him the place in your heart occupied by your dear Papa—but you've never given him a chance. Ever since I first knew him, you have tried to turn me against him. And now you come up with this cock-and-bull story about being kept prisoner in your room. Really, Nicola, admit you're making it up."

So the scales had fallen from her eyes only in part. She would never shed them all. Through the ones that remained, shielding her from reality, she looked at me coldly, calculatingly, and I did not recognize her. This woman, with her painted face, was not my Mama. She lived in the same house. She was married to Ted Gibbon. She acknowledged me as her daughter. But I did not know her.

Twice since my flight from the evil man she had married, I had returned to this house to see my mother because I was worried about her, and twice I had been received in an unwelcoming manner, as if I were an intruder, by a woman I did not recognize.

The first had been a wasted, hollow-eyed replica of the sweet-faced, softly rounded Mama I had left behind me. The second, this hard-eyed, painted lady with a gambling streak. Yet both had one thing in common—they worshipped Ted Gibbon. The wasted woman had not known how to handle him; this painted one did. She had discovered a way of making him dance to her tune.

I watched her bite into a wafer-thin, diamond-shaped sandwich, and my heart bled for the poor, deluded creature, whose defiance was already doomed. Ted Gibbon was on course to destroy her new-found complacency. By bringing

305

me back into the fold, he had provided himself with a lever to free himself from her fragile grasp.

Ted Gibbon returned to the boudoir, kissed his wife—she was more his wife than she was my mother—and hustled me back to my room. He followed me in, the key swinging in his hand.

"Do I need to use this?" he asked, mocking me, sure of himself.

"You'd better," I snapped. "You'll not keep me here otherwise."

Forgotten were my earlier plans for escape, the part I was to play to fool him into thinking I was willing to cooperate—but I was ever impulsive, and pretense never came easily to me. But fear gripped me as I saw his mocking smile widen and his eyes fill with a look of fiendish delight.

"As saucy as ever, eh? That's good. I like a bit of spirit. It adds spice to a relationship and provides a great deal of satisfaction in the breaking of it."

The smooth, unctuous tones were redolent of the evil that lay in store for me. I took a few steps backward in an instinctive attempt to distance myself from him and his evil intent.

He laughed. "Don't worry. I'm not ready for you yet. But when I am . . . you'll pay the debt you owe me, in full."

Chapter Sixteen

"He thinks your being here will make me sign his checks. It won't." I was taking tea with Mama in her boudoir, and her expression was sly as she spoke to me over the teacups. "So you might as well go back to your handsome Cornishman."

"I can't." My heart heaved as Justin's dark good looks were conjured from its depths, its deepest, darkest corner, to which I had consigned them. "I've told you, I'm kept locked up in my room."

"Nonsense!" she declared robustly. "You're not locked up now, are you? All you have to do is walk out of the door."

If it were only that simple. But I knew Larby, or the thin-faced woman, whose name I did not know and who had not uttered one word to me, but who chaperoned me whenever I was allowed out of my room, would be outside, to guard against any such endeavor. I knew from experience the futility of trying to escape from them. I had the bruises to prove it.

I had been here for over a week now, and was still under lock and key except for the half hour each day that I took tea with Mama—at her request? I had asked her once and her reply had been an ambiguous, "Do I need to request my daughter to take tea with me?" Food was brought to me regularly and, though I often felt too full of misery to eat, I forced myself to in order to keep up my strength, so that when the opportunity to escape presented itself I should be capable of taking advantage of it. I continued to sleep fully dressed, with the chair wedging the door.

Ted Gibbon had made no attempt to enter my room since that last time, when he had threatened me with retribution. But I did not trust him, and slept with an array of weaponry underneath my pillow—items from my dressing table such as my hairbrush, with its heavy handle of silver, a pair of nail scissors, a long nail file. They might not be of much help in warding off an attack, but I felt better with them there.

My mother was continually surprising me with the things she said. One minute she would be extolling her husband's virtues, sweetly, innocently; the next, a completely different woman, she was utterly contemptuous of him. Yet, when I attempted to take advantage of that contempt, she reacted with hatred toward me. It was all very puzzling, and I was more than a little afraid for her sanity.

If only I could get her away from Ted Gibbon. If only I could make her see the desperate situation we were both in. For her situation was as fraught with danger as mine. He would not hesitate to harm her, mentally and physically, if he did not get his own way. Her refusal to sign his checks might have given her power over him for a time, but from the moment I entered the house that power had been as dust upon the wind.

He had not yet brought me a check to sign, but it would not be long before he did. And when he did, would I sign it? Of course I would. My mother's safety depended on it. Mine too . . .

If only I could persuade Mama to aid me in my escape, but she refused to believe I was a prisoner. Still, I *must* escape. She would never leave Ted Gibbon, I realized that now. I would have to leave her behind to her chosen fate . . . and would that fate be so bad? I suddenly realized that with me gone, her power over him would return . . . only she would be able to sign his checks, pay his debts. Why had I not thought this out sooner, instead of wasting my time on fruitless persuasion?

Now I could concentrate all my energies on myself.

I fell back on Clara. She was my one real hope. She had not been to visit me yet, or if she had, I had not been told. I took to sitting at my window, watching for her. If she came and I could attract her attention, my troubles would be over. Ted Gibbon could not avoid letting us meet. I could make my bid for freedom. Clara would be my passport. Ted Gibbon could not take her prisoner, too. I prayed, I *prayed*, she would come soon.

She did not. But someone else did. And my whole life was changed again.

I had finished taking my bath and was returning to my room, escorted as usual by my taciturn female warder. I hugged my dressing gown around me, not bothering to do up the buttons, which were many. I would dress as soon as I entered my room and heard the key turn in the lock behind me, with its usual heart-stopping sound. I went straight across to the bed where I had set out my fresh clothing, expecting the sound, yet knowing my heart would still race momentarily with the awful finality of it.

But it did not come. I swung round in the wild hope it had been forgotten—and gasped in dismay.

Ted Gibbon stood in the doorway.

There was no sign of my chaperone. This one time when I should have been glad to see her, she was not present.

Clutching my dressing gown round me, I started fumbling with the buttons. He was coming toward me and I could not evade him. My back was at the bed.

"How adorable you look," he said softly. "I always think a woman is at her most sexually attractive immediately after her bath."

"What do you want?" My voice was husky with fear. "Do you want me to sign a check?"

"Indeed I do, my dear."

"I'll sign it later. Leave it, and go."

"What, now? Just when you are about to dress? How unsporting of you. One of my greatest pleasures in life is watching a woman dress. Though, of course, it is nowhere near as exciting as watching her undress. You are not going to deprive your stepfather of a little pleasure, are you?"

With the speed of a snake, before I was aware of his intention, he tugged my gown from my convulsive grasp, and though I struggled madly to prevent it, I could not keep it from slipping down over my shoulders. His hands slid over the smooth skin so recently washed, and I felt it grow dirty at his touch. Then, with an agility sent by heaven, I swung away from him and fled across the room. The door was closed—but it was not locked. If only I could . . .

But he had already put himself between me and the door. I backed away. He walked slowly forward.

"You're so lovely, Nicola." His voice was low, hardly more than a whisper, a silky, loathsome sound that nauseated me. "Lovelier than any woman I've ever seen, clothed or unclothed. I want to see you unclothed, Nicola. Drop that hampering garment and show yourself to me in all your maidenly glory."

"Keep away. Keep away." My own voice was hardly more than a whisper, a cracked, terrified whisper.

"I promise I won't touch. I only want to look. Let me look, Nicola, and then I'll go."

"Go now," I croaked. "I'll not sign your check if you come any nearer."

He halted in his step as I clutched at my only straw of hope. A shadow of annoyance crossed his face, then he heaved a deep sigh. "Very well. I can see I must forgo such delights. Sign this, then," he withdrew the check from his pocket and held out a pen, "and I'll leave you alone."

Could I trust him? Of course I could not. "Leave it on the dressing table. I'll sign it when you've gone."

"'Pon my honor!" he cried indignantly.

"You have no honor," I declared.

He clicked his tongue between his teeth. "Enough of this! I have no more time to spend bandying words with you. I've a dinner engagement I do not wish to miss. Look!" He put the check and the pen down on the dressing table. "I'll stand over here by the door, if that will set your mind at rest."

It did not. But I was desperate for him to go. I went to pick up the pen and regretted it immediately. As I bent to sign, he was across the room and ripping off my dressing gown, revealing my nakedness to his lascivious gaze.

"Lovely. Lovely," he whispered, running his hands over my skin, filling me with repugnance. "But that will have to do for the moment, I fear." He stood back and stared at me while I grabbed at my gown and strove to cover myself. "Or will it?" he continued in a voice grown hoarse with unslaked lust. "It might be worth risking a few paltry pounds to—"

I picked up the nearest thing to hand, my heavy silver-backed hand mirror, and struck him with it. It caught him underneath the eye, cutting the skin.

"By God!" he cried, covering his eye with his hand, looking at the blood that gathered there. "Will you never learn?" And he smashed his fist into my face.

I fell to the ground, my head spinning. He picked me up as if I were a rag doll and struck me again and again. "I'll teach you!" he yelled with each blow, cutting short the screams I made.

Then suddenly, I was free. With a yelp of pain and surprise, he went sprawling across the room. I gazed in disbelief at my deliverer.

"Justin. . . ."

I was in his arms and sobbing against his chest.

"Take me away, Justin. Take me away."

"That's what I've come for," he said. I raised my eyes at the words that sounded so sweet, so—loving, and as I did so, caught a movement behind him.

"Justin! Look out!"

He spun around just in time to evade the chair Ted Gibbon swung at him. His fist connected with the angry, blood-smeared face of his adversary. Ted Gibbon kissed the floor again.

Justin picked him up by the scruff of his neck. "Get dressed," he said to me, and marched his victim away.

I started dressing feverishly. Fear clutched at my throat when my silent warder came in. But she had come in on Justin's orders. "I'm to pack your things," she said, the first and only words I ever heard her use.

I finished dressing and went to join Justin in the hall. Ted Gibbon was slumped in a chair, no fight left in him. Larby, the cowardly henchman who had shown no compunction about inflicting violence on an unprotected female, stood nearby, cowering. Justin's persuasive means of entry were apparent in the man's swollen lips and blackened eyes.

"You'll want to see your mother before we go," Justin said gently.

"Yes." My lips trembled. Tears swam in my eyes. His dark, compassionate gaze was almost too much to bear after so much ugliness, so much fear.

"Do you want her to come with us?"

My heart leapt at the suggestion, but then I sighed and shook my head. "She won't come."

"You could try to persuade her. You might have more luck than I."

His gaze had gone beyond me and, as I swung round, I heard my mother say, "She won't, and she knows it."

I stared from one to the other of them, astonished afresh by this man's thoughtfulness. Again he had seen someone's need and had tried to do something about it. He had talked with my mother, had tried to persuade her to leave with us. Why? There was no duty placed upon him to help, no need for him to concern himself with our affairs at all. And yet he had taken the time and trouble to come to our aid. Was it simply a case of standing up for the underdog, a trait so significant in him?

How could it be anything else?

But Mama was one underdog who did not wish to be defended. She smiled as she walked up to us. Embracing me, she said, "Goodbye, Nicola. I doubt we shall meet again. It will be better that way. Ah, don't cry. And you mustn't worry about me. It will be all right now." Ted Gibbon moaned and she glanced at him with a sweet, indulgent smile. "He's not a bad man, really. He just needs keeping in check. And I can do that now, with my control of the purse strings. We suit each other, Teddy and I. Now go, go with your handsome Cornishman, and be happy."

"Will you?" Justin asked as we left the house I should never see again.

"Will I what?" I turned my red-rimmed eyes to him.

"Be happy with me?"

I came to an abrupt halt. I stared up at him with a sudden, bright, shining hope.

"Oh, Nicola," he breathed, "I love you so much. Come back to Penrose. Marry me."

All the love that was in me flowed out to him and showed in my eyes.

Then I was in his arms and he was kissing the breath out of me, and neither of us gave a thought to the world around us.

"Nicola! Nicola! Do you know what you're doing?"

Clara had followed me to my room.

"Yes. I'm going to marry Justin," I answered her blithely.

I was supremely happy, and my happiness could not be dimmed by Clara's tight-lipped disapproval, which had been evident from the moment Justin had acquainted her with our news. In Justin's presence she had offered her congratulations. Now, however, she challenged me.

"Didn't you listen to anything I told you? Did nothing sink in?"

"I know you tried to warn me against him because you

313

thought I was falling in love with him and didn't want me to get hurt. You thought that if I attracted him, it was only because of my likeness to Caroline. But it's not like that. He's not in love with Caroline. He never was."

"Oh, Nicola."

But I would listen to nothing else. I knew what Justin had told me, and I believed him.

Inside the cab, safe in his arms, I had asked him how he had known where I was. "Did Carty tell you?"

"No. When I asked her where you were, all she would say was, 'She's gone. 'Tis better so.' And so I believed, till I heard from John that you had gone to live with my mother as her companion. . . . . After all I'd told you! Then he went on to say you had gone to stay with your mother for a while because she was sick. Your stepfather had called and taken you there. I was suspicious. I couldn't believe you would go back there of your own free will. I felt something must be wrong. So I came on the next tide to find out for myself what was going on."

"How glad I am that you did. You came in the nick of time again."

"He'll never touch you again. I'll kill him if he so much as comes near you."

"He won't. Not now that he knows he's got you to reckon with. Oh, Justin, is it true? Are you really in love with me? This isn't all a dream?"

He kissed me till my head reeled. "Is that a dream? Of course I love you. I've always loved you."

"It's not because I remind you of Caroline?"

I was sorry as soon as I said it. I expected him to be angry. But he kissed me again. "I love you, only you, for yourself alone. For your information, I was never in love with anybody else."

"But you were going to marry Caroline."

"I drifted into it. To tell you the truth, I was glad when she jilted me. If she had not, I very much fear I should have jilted her."

"But I did remind you of her? My hair, the color of my eyes . . . ?"

"Only briefly, when we first met. You have a vague resemblance to her, but you're really nothing like her, in looks or anything else. Oh, my dear, my sweet pisky love, it wasn't the color of your hair I fell in love with, or the forget-me-not blue of your eyes—oh, they had their charm of course, but there was something about the little pinched, white face that looked up at me through that cold drenching rain. An irresistible attraction that I shied away from at first. But seeing you every day, watching you at your work, sparring with you . . . you'll never know how much I enjoyed teasing you, just to see your eyes flash and hear the tartness come to your voice . . . your sweet, gentle voice. And you seemed to love the island, the people, as I did, and yet . . ."

"Yet?"

"You seemed to have no very deep regard for me. Every overture I made, you rejected. It was obvious you didn't care for me. I thought it was John you cared for. Then, when Martin came . . . and I saw how he pursued you . . . I grew jealous that you did not discourage him. Then there was that letter."

"Oh, Justin, I cared nothing for either of them. It was you, always you. I'll tell you about that letter . . ."

But there was no need. I was gathered into his arms again, and lost myself in his kisses.

With all this to occupy my mind, how could I pay attention to what Clara had to say?

In the morning, we said goodbye before starting the long journey back to Penrose. Justin, his face beaming, though he rarely smiled in his mother's company, kissed her cheek and said, "I hope your aversion to our marriage will not last, Mother."

"Well, I'm not happy about it," she snapped. "How can I be, under the circumstances?"

I thought she was referring to Caroline. She found it difficult to believe that he was in love with me. But my own

315

smile faded a little at the cold expression of his eyes and the clouding of his face. Why should his mother's words affect him so? I felt a little chill of mistrust, which I banished as soon as it was born. It was his bitterness getting the better of him again.

"I hope you'll be happy, my dear." Clara's lips touched my cheek and her arms went round me. Her words were heavily accentuated, as if to aver that she did not see the possibility of them coming true. "I hope I shall be a more welcome visitor to Penrose when you are mistress there."

"Of course you will be welcome. And you'll be coming to the wedding."

"Nothing will keep me away from that," she cried, throwing a quick glance at Justin, whose face still bore the darkness of annoyance. "I want to be on hand in case you need me."

"Why should she need you?" Justin said brusquely. "She'll have Carty to turn to for anything she needs."

He hurried me away.

"Darling," I said, "was there any need to be so unkind? Your mother was only . . ."

"Dearest," he cut me short, his face serious, "promise me something."

"Anything," I said.

"Don't let my mother . . . Never let her . . . Don't let yourself . . ."

This most articulate of men seemed to be having the greatest trouble in finding the words he wanted to say. In the end, he gave a defeated shake of his head.

"You don't want her to come to Penrose, do you?" I said.

"No," he replied. "I don't."

"I wish you didn't hate her so."

"I don't hate her. I—pity her."

"You're so bitter."

"Yes. And it hurts. Damnably. And never more than when I'm with her. I can't expect you to understand, Nicola, but that's the way it is."

This admission of pain was delivered without any semblance

of self-pity, without any attempt to elicit pity from me. It was just a statement of fact. So I knew I should not be thanked for any sympathy I offered, and kept quiet. Then, hesitantly, afraid I might be taking too much on myself, I suggested something that might keep her away from Penrose.

"Perhaps if you gave her an allowance. I believe she only comes to Penrose when she is low on funds. At least, that's the impression she gave me."

"I do give her an allowance," he said. "But she fritters it away. Money slips through her fingers like water. Perhaps . . . ," his face brightened, "if I increase it, substantially . . . Darling, I think you've hit upon it. She doesn't like Penrose. She never has. It's the bright lights that attract her, the excitement of London, Paris, Rome. Yes, that's it. I'll increase her allowance. With enough money to buy as many clothes as she likes, to travel where she likes . . . Fool that I am! Why did I not think of it before? It's such a simple solution. Oh, my darling, my love, now we shall be able to get on with our lives in peace."

He was happy again. Glad of the part I had played in bringing the smile back to his face, I steered the conversation away from the controversial subject, although his last sentence stayed with me, engaging my mind, long after we reached Penrose.

The following days were a frenzy of activity. Justin wanted us to be married with as little delay as possible, and I was nothing loathe. Carty, who had welcomed me back with enthusiasm—"I alus knowed you'd come back," she said—launched into preparing for the wedding, assuming responsibility for everything.

It worried me a little. I could not help thinking it should be Clara's job. So when Justin came to me, asking for the names of any guests I wished to invite . . . "Carty wants to know how many guests to cater for. She says we can get any idea we have of a quiet wedding out of our minds. The island won't stand for it, she says. And she's right, I suppose. I shall never be able to look a Penrosian in the face again if I deny them the chance of a big

317

celebration." . . . I did not restrain my objections.

"Surely all this should be Clara's business. It's her right."

"She has no rights." Justin's anger flared. "Carty has more rights than she."

"But Carty's only your housekeeper. Clara's your mother."

"Carty has been more of a mother to me than she has ever been," he snapped, adding in only a slightly less astringent tone, "Don't try to change the way of things here, my love. You can't. Things are the way they are. You'd better resign yourself to the fact."

I knew then that any hope I still entertained of bringing about a better understanding between him and his mother, was false. He would never take his mother to his heart again. She had left him and his father when he was young and impressionable, and I now knew that he would never forgive her for it.

Ruth was to be my bridesmaid. When I had asked her, somewhat diffidently because I knew how she felt about Justin, she had accepted after only a momentary pause.

"I'm glad," she said. "You're right for him. I've known it all along. I knew it was only a question of time before . . ."

And that was the nearest she got to admitting her own bitter disappointment. We went to the mainland together to buy material for her gown, for she had said she would like to make it herself. I had already sent off to London for a gown advertized in a fashionable woman's journal, a simple gown of ivory silk, with a lace flounce at the hem and tiny seed pearls embroidered on the bodice. The long diaphanous veil would be held in place by a coronet of orange blossom and lily-of-the-valley.

It was during this shopping expedition that I asked her why she had felt it necessary to tell John of my relationship to Ted Gibbon. She had looked at me in surprise and said, "But I thought he already knew about it. He gave me the impression he did. I would never have discussed it with him if I had thought otherwise."

"He didn't know. I've never told anyone, but you—and

now, Justin. It's funny, John was responsible for bringing Ted Gibbon to the house."

I told her what had happened, how Justin had rescued me.

"If he knew all about Ted Gibbon, why did he bring him to me? He can't have known everything."

Ruth was silent for a moment, then she said softly, "I think he did. He appeared to, anyway. But he can't have known your stepfather tried to rape you. He would never . . ."

"You're sure you didn't mention that to him?"

"No . . . no . . . I don't think I did. I can't have."

"No." I agreed. "You can't have."

John was to be Justin's best man, and seemed delighted to be, although when he had a moment alone with me, he had deplored the fact that I was not marrying him.

"You never asked me," I said with a laugh, trying to make light of the remark. I hoped he would follow suit.

But he said seriously, "I would have. You know I love you. I was only waiting till I was sure you loved me enough to accept."

"I never loved you, John, not in that way. You must have known that."

He sighed. "I suppose so. But I was living in hopes. Ah, well. The best man won, eh? I only hope you won't regret it."

"Why should I?" I cried, feeling a chill pass through me.

"Why, indeed?" He shrugged it away. "I'm just concerned for you, that's all. Your happiness is very near to my heart. And Justin . . ."

"Considers all women fair game? I remember you said that to me once. I might have believed it, for a while, but now I know him. I know he loves me and has never loved anyone else. Even Caroline," I added defiantly.

"That's fine," he said. "If that's what he's told you, then believe it, my dear."

His lips smiled, but his eyes did not. He was hiding something from me. I felt this as strongly as I had felt anything since coming to the island.

319

But I did not want to know what it was.

I clung onto Justin's declaration of love and the fact that we were going to be married. We were to become man and wife. That was all that mattered. All that was real. Anything else was imagination. I had a strong imagination, and my father had warned me against using it. *"Keep it well under control,"* he had said, *"lest it destroy you."* It had been good advice. I would remember it.

"Well, I must be off. I've a patient or two to see," John said. "By the way, how was your mother when you left her? Better?"

"Oh, yes. Much better, thank you."

"Good." He turned to go.

"Oh, John?"

"Yes, Nicola?"

"Oh, nothing."

He stayed a moment longer, allowing puzzlement to alter his smile, then with a slight shrug, said "Goodbye," and left. My question had gone unasked. But I now felt that it had been unnecessary. Of course he could not have known the danger he placed me in when he had brought Ted Gibbon to Clara's house.

Chapter Seventeen

Imagination or not, the island was waiting for something. I knew it. I felt it. It had been waiting, as I had, for something to happen that would cauterize the festering wound at its heart's core, ridding it of the misery I had sensed from the first. It was hidden at times, but was there, always there, a pulsating sadness that seemed to float on the very air of Penrose.

It was not the wedding that the island was waiting for—though the wedding of the Master of Penrose was an event indeed. But I was too much in tune with the island to be fooled into that line of reasoning.

No, it was not the wedding. It was something else. Something explosive. Something I could prevent, if only I knew what it was. But how could I know? There was no way of knowing what cataclysm was in store. And would I prevent it if I did? Should I? Could I?

The island was waiting for something to happen. And so was I.

Clara came back to the island for the wedding. As usual, she brought upheaval with her. She interfered with Carty's plans, tried to put her finger in every pie. She did not have much success. Carty's strength of character was greater than hers, and she soon retired from the battle scene.

She showed me the wedding outfit she had bought for herself.

"Justin told me to charge it to him, so there was no expense spared," she cried excitedly. "And my dear, do you know, he has increased my allowance—oh, by such an amount! I shall be able to do all the things that have been denied to me for so long. He's a good son." Her voice dropped as her face clouded with a sadness I had never seen there before. "If only . . . but there," she rallied to become her old, recognizable self, "what can't be cured, must be endured. Or so they say. He's off to London tomorrow, isn't he, to collect your wedding gown? I can't wait to see it."

Most of our conversations went like this, her excited comments on the forthcoming marriage interspersed with moments of sadness when she looked at me strangely, moodily, as if her happiness was assumed.

I could have enquired about those looks. But I did not probe. I was afraid that if I did, I might hear something I would rather not.

I laughed at myself when I thought like this. It was all so silly. Prenuptial jitters—all brides had them. I remembered Hetty's. The night before her wedding to Dickie, she had wept like a lost soul, declaring she could not go through with it. And look how it had turned out. They were as happy as two sandboys together.

And so it would be with Justin and me.

I saw Justin off from the harbor, and felt lost at his going. I would have gone with him if Clara had not begged me to stay with her. "After all," she said, "you'll have the rest of your lives together. I shall only be here a short while. And he won't be gone for more than a couple of days. He's only going to pick up your wedding gown."

And to call on Mama, taking her the invitation I knew she would refuse.

It was funny how Clara had never mentioned Mama to me. She had not even commented on my wasted appearance when Justin had arrived back at her house with me. I wondered how much Justin had told her. Perhaps he had suggested to her that

I'd rather not be bothered with questions. Or maybe she felt awkward at having insisted I go with Ted Gibbon. But this was assuming she knew the sordid details behind my sojourn—and, surely, she did not, any more than John did. I must put it all behind me and stop thinking about it.

I must think about my wedding to Justin and our life together.

It was no hardship to think along these lines. Every minute that seemed like an hour, every hour that seemed like a day, was occupied in this way, till at last it was the night before the day he was due back.

I sat by my bedroom window ready for bed, but wide awake, thinking of him. Justin . . . the wonderful, wonderful man I was going to marry . . . the man I loved, who loved me. I went over the marriage service in my head. *Dearly beloved, we are gathered here together . . . To love, honor and obey . . . in sickness and in health, as long as ye both shall live . . . I now pronounce you man and wife.*

Man and wife. Man and wife. How wonderful it sounded. Hurry back, Justin. Hurry back, my love.

I gave up at the moon, rounded and full, tracking its way with a silver ladder across the black waves. The same moon shone above him far away in London town. Was he looking at it too, thinking of me, aching to hold me in his arms as I ached to hold him?

I knew he was.

Tomorrow. I would see him, hold him, tomorrow. I could hardly wait. I would go to bed and sleep, so that then night would pass quickly. About to match the deed to the thought, I was detained by a sudden movement in the garden below. At least, I thought there was a movement, but when I looked again, I was not so sure. All seemed quite still. I rubbed at the pane of glass, though it was perfectly clean, and peered out. No, there was nothing. If there had been, it had gone now. It must have been some nocturnal animal I had seen in the shadows—Mrs. Carthew's cat, perhaps.

But there it was again. And it was not Mrs. Carthew's cat. It was far too large an animal for that. What kind of animal was it? I held my breath. It was a man. He stepped out of the shadows for a moment and looked about him.

My heart pounded. Was it a burglar? Of course not. There was no crime on Penrose Island. Everyone lived in harmony, like one big happy family, and no one robbed their own family.

Who was he, then? He was behaving very mysteriously. Was he looking for someone? He kept very close to the bushes. Was he someone's secret lover that he should wish to conceal his presence. Whose? Mrs. Carthew's? I laughed at the thought. No, probably one of the maids. Sally was very pretty. So was Susan. So was Mary. Ah, well, far be it from me to spy on whomsoever it was.

About to turn away, I saw the man's hand rise in greeting. He stepped out into the full light of the moon.

It was John!

And, tripping lightly across the grass to meet him was—Clara!

They reached out to each other and clung to each other's hands.

Clara . . . and John? Lovers?

I drew back, my heart hammering at the unexpectedness of it all. Only a short time ago John had said he loved me, had wanted to marry me, yet here he was . . . with Clara, Justin's mother . . . in the garden, late at night.

Yet why should I be so shocked? I should be glad they had found each other. They were two lonely people, and though she was older than he, she was still a very beautiful woman.

But if they should marry and wish to live on Penrose, what would Justin say?

I was drawn to look out again.

Where were they?

Nothing met my eye but the open space where they had stood.

Had they retired behind the bushes? I did not think so. That

324

would not suit Clara's fastidious nature.

Had they gone into the house, then?

Had they been there at all?

My gaze became riveted to the spot where they had stood, and I knew it could all have been an illusion. This was an enchanted isle, haunted by pixies, fey. Had the two I had seen been creatures from another world, in borrowed guise?

I went to bed, trembling, wondering, longing for morning to come.

When it did, I was wakened by Sally bringing me breakfast on a tray.

"'Tis late, Miss Wentworth. Mrs. Carthew says 'tis time you were up."

"What time is it?" I enquired sleepily.

"Not far from eleven."

"Mrs. Carthew's right. It is time I was up. Thank you, Sally."

I drank the scalding tea and nibbled buttered toast, happily content to believe the events of the previous night had only happened in a dream. In the morning light it was easy to believe.

Justin would be back today, but not till late in the afternoon. Somehow, I had to fill in the long hours between. I decided to start with a long tramp over the hills with Betsy and Winnie. I could call on Ruth. Take lunch with her. By the time I returned, the tide would be coming in, and then . . .

I ran happily down the stairs. "Good morning, Clara," I called to her when I saw her in the drawing room as I passed the open doorway. "Have you seen Betsy and Winnie anywhere?"

"No."

I prepared to look elsewhere, but she called me back.

"Nicola, come here a moment. I wish to speak to you."

"What is it?" I went cheerfully to her side.

"Justin comes back today."

"Yes. I can hardly wait. I thought I'd go for a tramp with the dogs to fill in the time. You won't mind if I don't join you for lunch? I thought I might . . ."

"Nicola! Please! What I have to tell you is not easy. I'd hoped I'd never have to. I saw the way things were heading from the start. I tried to warn you. I hoped it was infatuation, that it would fizzle out . . . I should have known you're not the sort to embark upon a light affair. I've been worried ever since you told me you and Justin . . . I wanted to tell you then, but you wouldn't listen. And then I thought, well maybe . . . But now I know I must tell you. There's no other way."

"What is it, Clara?"

I hardly recognized the strangled whisper as my own. When Clara had started to speak, I had thought last night's happenings had not been a dream, that she was going to tell me about the romance between her and John Trevelyan. But, as she continued, it had become clear that what she had to tell me concerned Justin and myself, our wedding, our lives. Dread filled my heart. I heard again the gulls' warning cries, "Go back! Go back!" I felt the island's anguish and knew it contained my own. This, this, was what it had been waiting for.

Clara had taken hold of my hand. It was burning hot. Or was it only that mine was so cold? "You can't marry Justin," she was saying urgently. "You mustn't. What I have to say will tell you why."

"I am going to marry him." I managed a defiant, strangled whisper.

"No, you're not. I won't let you. I can't. Nicola, Justin . . . is a murderer."

Something snapped inside my brain. I saw Clara's lips moving, but all I could hear was the beat of my heart echoing her words. *A murderer. A murderer. A murderer.* Louder and louder it grew, the beat of my heart, till it filled every corner.

Then her words reached my ears again. "I'm so sorry, my dear. I knew it would come as a shock to you. But I couldn't let you walk into tragedy. He's a passionate man, easily roused to anger, full of dark moods. He's killed once. It will not be hard for him to kill again."

326

"It's not true! It's not true!"

"I wish it were not. How I wish it were not. But it is. It is true."

"No. No. No. No." I covered my ears with my hands.

But I could still hear her voice insisting, "It's true. You must believe me. Ask John, if you don't. He will confirm everything I've said. In fact, it was he who decided you should be told. Seeing your happiness, I might have kept quiet, hoping it would turn out all right, but John felt you ought to know."

"Was that what last night was all about?"

"Last night?"

"In the garden. I saw you from my bedroom window."

"Oh. Yes. We had to meet there. It was the only way we could be sure of privacy . . . and we had to thrash this thing out. Come to a firm decision. And now you must go. To John. He will hide you at Peacehaven till he can arrange to get you away."

"You mean, you want me to run away from Justin? Like Caroline did?"

"No! Not like Caroline!"

Her voice was sharp, threatened by tears, her expression full of fear and sadness.

"It's all lies," I said. "I don't believe anything you've told me."

Her shoulders sagged. Suddenly she looked like a little old woman.

"Well, I did my best," she said. "I can't do any more."

She left me in the room alone. At first I was glad to see her go. She was a liar. A liar! But then I wished she had not gone. All the time she had been with me, I had been able to refute her lies, denying every allegation against Justin, but with no one to shy at, doubts and questions crept in to flood my conviction.

I tried to cast them away. Of course she had been lying. But what if she had not? It would explain so much. *Oh, stop it! Stop it! Don't allow yourself to think this way.* But what if it were true? Could I go through marriage with a murderer? *He's not a murderer! He's not!* But why should she make up such a story? Because she hated him for making her suffer, because she wanted him to suffer? *No, she wouldn't want that. She was his mother.* Well, then?

Oh, don't let me be persuaded, don't let me doubt Justin, I prayed.

But how could I ever be sure of the truth? What was the truth? *Ask Justin. Ask Justin.* But how could I ask him if he was a murderer? It would be tantamount to admitting the possibility. And I did not admit it. I did not.

I had to set my mind at rest. Clara might be lying. I had to have it confirmed by one who knew the truth. John Trevelyan would give me that confirmation.

John was not at Peacehaven when I reached there, and his housekeeper had no idea where he had gone or when he would be back. I said I would wait a while, and she ushered me to the fireside and brought me something to drink.

An hour passed and he did not come. I had calmed a great deal during that hour and began to see the foolishness of my behavior. I knew Clara was lying. I knew Justin was not a murderer. So what was I doing here waiting for John to confirm my belief?

I left Peacehaven to return to Penrose House, lighter in mind, happy again. Justin a murderer? It was laughable. He was the kindest, sweetest, dearest man in the world. A defender of the underdog, protector of the weak. How much proof I had of that. Without him, without his concern, I shuddered to think what might have become of me.

The air was fresh as I walked over the hills. A strong breeze billowed my skirts and fronded my hair. I gloried in its cleansing strength. It blew away the last of the evil thoughts spawned by Clara's corrosive tongue.

I stopped and looked out over the sea which would soon carry Justin back to me. He was on his way back even now, with my wedding gown in his keeping.

The wind was growing stronger, and the sky was darkening

above the horizon. I hoped there would not be a storm to delay Justin's return.

I listened to the wind. It had an eerie sound, as if a million tiny voices all clamored at once to be heard. I remembered all the tales Justin had told me about this pisky-haunted island, and saw how easily legend could grow. It did not take much imagination to believe in unseen creatures on a day like this, with the wind heightening and the sky growing darker, and . . .

A strangled scream was loosed from my lips and carried away by the wind.

It was not my imagination. *He* was there. The man I had seen before. The stranger who stood, arms akimbo, legs apart, straddling the earth as if he owned it. Outlined against the graying sky, the darker gray of the sea, he looked to be ten feet tall. A giant! Penn!

He started to come toward me. I turned to run in blind panic, not noticing where I was going, just running, anywhere, to get away from this man, this creature, who had dogged my path with such determination. So far, I had managed to evade him. I must evade him now. I knew he boded me ill.

I ran, my cheeks set on fire by the onslaught of the keen wind. I fought to allow common sense to overcome my fear. It was not a demon who pursued me. It was not anyone, no one of flesh and blood. It was an illusion. If I turned round, I would see that the giant had disappeared.

But I ran on, afraid to look round, afraid he would still be there.

My breath was running out. I could not go on much longer. Where was I? I did not know. I daren't look round to see. I ran on, puffing, panting, slowing.

"Nicola!"

I heard my name called from behind, and the blood in my veins turned to ice.

"Nicola."

It was Penn. I was lost; I could run no more. I sank in a heap on the ground and buried my head in my hands.

"Nicola."

I knew that voice. I raised my head. Through a spring of tears I cried thankfully, "John! Oh, John! It's you! I was so afraid. . . ."

"Thank God I found you," he said. "My housekeeper told me you had been to Peacehaven asking to see me, but had since gone home. I sent a man to Penrose House and, when I learned you had not returned, I became worried. You should have reached there long ago. So I decided to look for you. I had a strange feeling you might be in trouble."

"Oh, John, I thought I saw . . . Oh, it's nothing. I'm all right now."

"What did you want to see me about?" he asked.

"Oh, nothing. It was just a silly whim. . . . Something Clara said. It doesn't matter now."

"But it must have worried you at the time?"

"Yes, it did, but—"

"Tell me about it, anyway."

"It's all so ridiculous, but—"

I went on to tell him what Clara had said, then waited confidently for his repudiation of her lies.

He remained silent.

Then he said, "Clara's a fool. I told her not to interfere. I said I would handle it."

My heart jumped. "But there's nothing to handle. You don't believe her lies, surely?"

"Suppose I told you they weren't lies, that she was telling you the truth, that Justin is a murderer?"

"I wouldn't believe you, any more than I believe her."

"Then why rush over to Peacehaven to question me about it?"

His voice was scathing, and it made me feel ashamed of myself.

"I don't know," I said. "I think I just needed to hear from someone else that my convictions were correct. Oh, John, I'm so ashamed. But I've come to my senses now. I'm not confused anymore. Take me home, John."

"No."

His answer surprised me.

"Please, John."

He laughed softly and I saw something in his face that set my heart thudding against my ribs. For a moment I looked into the face of a stranger—an evil stranger. Then the moment passed and it was John's face I saw.

"Please, John, take me back to Penrose."

"I can't," he said with a gentle quietness that held more menace than had shown in his face—the stranger's face—a moment ago.

"Please, John."

I was almost in tears.

"I can't, Nicola. You must see that. I can't let you go."

Fear coursed through my every nerve. I could not understand his reluctance.

"Please, John."

"How prettily you beg," he said. "If only you'd turned to me sooner. I could have made you happy. Happier than Justin. But it's too late now, just as it was too late for Caroline."

"Caroline?" I squeaked.

"Caroline. Justin's victim."

"No. No, it's not true. Justin didn't murder Caroline."

"Why do you find it so hard to believe?" His voice was harsh, his expression condemning.

"Because . . . Because . . ." Suddenly the truth illuminated my brain. "Because it was you. You murdered Caroline."

I shrank away from him as his soft laugh crossed the small space between us. His laugh possessed the power to freeze my bones, so that, no matter how much I wanted to obey my instincts and flee from him, I found it impossible to do so.

"How clever of you, my sweet," he said, "to have stumbled onto my little secret. But it won't do you any good. It's too late. You have no one to watch out for you. Your watchdog isn't here. You'd have done better to stay with your stepfather in

331

London. At least you'd have been alive. Now, I'm afraid . . ."

"My stepfather? You arranged for him to find me . . . on purpose . . . knowing . . . ?"

He smiled. "Of course. I wormed your secret out of Ruth. I'm good at that sort of thing."

"You're . . . evil."

"Oh, Nicola." His voice was reproachful in the way Ted Gibbon's had been reproachful—with a sarcastic edge lent by the knowledge of power over his victim. "You won't suffer. Your death won't be painful, I promise you. Just a little pressure of the fingers in the right place. I'm a doctor, I know exactly where to apply it. And when your body is found, Justin will take the blame. They will believe he killed you, as they feared he killed Caroline. They closed ranks behind him then, but they won't be able to again. The death of two intended brides is too much for anybody to stomach. No, they won't be able to keep quiet a second tme, particularly when the victim is someone they have grown to love, particularly when the island's doctor will refuse to sign a second death certificate stating accidental death."

"You're mad," I whispered.

"I'm not mad!" he screamed at me. "Not mad. Not mad. Angry. Angry that Penrose belongs to Justin when it should belong to me. It's mine by rights."

"How can it be? The island's not yours. It will never be."

"But it will, once you are out of the way and Justin is hanged for murder. When he dies, the island will become the property of his mother. *My* mother. And then it will be mine. *I* am that distant kinsman I told you about. Only not so distant after all, eh?"

"You are mad. You'll never get away with pretending to be Justin's brother."

"I am his brother. His half-brother. His mother married the man she ran away with after Tristram's death, and bore him a son. So you see, I am in line for Penrose Island. My father's dead. He died when I was young. But I was never interested in

332

him. *He* wasn't rich. *He* didn't own an island . . . Ah, the tales my mother told me about Penrose, about the slate quarry, the rich veins of silver and copper, about my half-brother who was king of it all. I hated him then and I hate him still. He had everything. I had nothing. I grew up hating him, vowing that, one day, I would walk in his shoes.

"I spent all the time I could in Cornwall standing on the shore, looking out across the sea to Penrose Island. To look was all I could do. We were never allowed to visit the island. Justin has an unforgiving heart, where his own mother is concerned."

He was speaking conversationally, as if it were the most natural thing in the world, as if there was nothing wrong between us.

"After my father died, she wrote to tell him she was destitute. She might have mentioned she had a son, I don't know. I've never asked her. It didn't matter, anyway. He wouldn't want to see me—he wouldn't even see his mother when she begged to be allowed to do so. He refused her request, but he arranged an allowance for her, to be drawn every quarter. She has expensive tastes, my mother. It hardly kept her in handkerchiefs. But by dint of continued supplication, she persuaded him to allow her more and more, and soon she was able to travel abroad and do all the things she had never been able to do while married to my father, a feckless man, if ever there was one. I was sent to school, and spent my holidays there more often than not. She was not one to give up the social life she loved for the sake of a child."

His voice had changed. His bitterness showed through, and I could not help thinking Clara had a lot to answer for. In both her sons she had inspired bitterness and warped personalities.

"But I was telling you about my brother." He picked up his theme again. "I made up my mind to meet him, somehow, somewhere. I thought, if I could meet him, make him like me, he would let me live with him on the island and share his inheritance. It was a schoolboy dream. As I grew older, I knew

333

it would never happen that way. Yet I was determined to live on the island one day, perhaps even own it.

"I planned and schemed, but there seemed to be no way to meet him." He gave a brief laugh. "I even stood outside stage doors hoping to catch him leaving the theatre, but either he never attended rehearsals of his plays, or . . . well, I never caught sight of him. Then some friends of mine invited me to a party and my luck turned. He was there. I made it my business to speak to him. You'll admit I have my fair share of charm. I could always impress anyone I wanted to. In next to no time, we were great pals. . . . Well, you know the rest. I've told you about it before."

"And you never told him you were his brother?"

"No. But I will—before he dies. I must see the look on his face when I tell him how I shall start up the quarry again, and yank the copper and silver out of—"

"You'll never get away with it!"

He laughed out loud. "Who's to stop me?"

"Clara. She'll stop you. She won't let Justin hang."

"She won't be able to do anything about it. She believes Justin murdered Caroline, just like everybody else, and she won't defy the authorities a second time to save his neck. Why should she want to, anyway? He's never treated her very well."

I let this pass, but to keep him talking—if I kept him talking, there was a chance somebody would pass by and I could call for help—I asked, "How did you manage to get away with murdering Caroline? Why did no one suspect you?"

"Why should they? What reason could I have?" His face broke into a smile, a foxy smile, full of self-congratulation. "It was very cleverly done, the way I planned it. I made her fall in love with me. Whenever Justin went away, I was there to . . . well, you know what happens between lovers." He leered. How like Ted Gibbon he was. Why had I not seen it before? "The long and short of it is," he continued, "we concocted a plan. She would marry Justin so that she could lay claim to the island after his—fatal accident, which would occur shortly after the wedding. Only, she changed her mind. She found she had scruples, and they didn't allow for murder. Anyway, she found she liked the life Justin could give her. She liked mixing with famous people. Once they were married, she thought, she could persuade him to spend more time away from the island—the way my mother had thought she could persuade Tristram to do the same, before realizing her mistake. Caroline would find out her mistake, too, I told her, but she wouldn't listen. So there was only one thing for me to do. I couldn't risk her bearing a child, yet another encumbrance to deal with on my journey to becoming King of Penrose. She had to die. And it had to be made to look as if Justin had murdered her. That way all obstacles would be removed in one fell swoop.

"I began pouring poison in his ears. I didn't like doing it, of course—he was my friend. But as his friend, I could not let a gold-digging tart pull the wool over his eyes, could I? As it happened, it turned out he was not as enamored of her as I had believed, and he jumped at the excuse for breaking off the engagement. But she would have none of it. She threatened to sue him for breach of promise. And she played right into my hands.

"When her body was found it was easy to make it look as if Justin had killed her in order to prevent a lawsuit against him. He denied it vehemently, but then he seemed to lose heart, and he became morose and silent. Then, just when I was congratulating myself on the success of my plan, the whole island put up a united front. Before I could call the police, they pressed me to sign a death certificate stating that Caroline had died from a heart attack. It was marvelous the way everybody suddenly remembered how she used to complain about pain in her chest and how short of breath she used to get. Oh, they're a fine bunch, these islanders. When a Penrose has his back to the wall, they'll do anything to help him. I, of course, had to go along with them. I didn't see what else I could do at that time.

"But now, it's different. There'll be no sudden remembrances this time. They won't clamor for a false death certificate for your death. And if they did, I should not sign it. He will hang for your murder. Clara will inherit the island, and I shall walk in the shoes of the king—and the islanders can go to hell."

While he had been talking, I had been edging away from him and now, summoning all my strength, I lunged at him, knocking him off-balance and sending him sprawling sideways, cursing as he fell. Then I was up and away, running through a mist of rain, sheer fright speeding me on.

The rain grew heavier. I slipped and slithered as I ran. I heard him panting behind me. Near to despair, I forced myself to a faster speed. I stumbled and fell. The icy rain fell like nails intent on fastening me to the ground.

Thunder boomed. Lightning zipped. My mind grew numb. My limbs moved automatically. The scream of the salt sea wind battered ceaselessly in my ears, its tartness slashing at my skin. Terrified, only my spirit drove me on, and soon even that could not prevent a slowing of my legs, their final crumpling when they could bear me up no longer.

I waited for the end of my life to come.

Chapter Eighteen

The rain fell in a soaking sheet. The wind screamed around my ears. But I was still alive. John had not found me. Somehow I had managed to evade him, and I thanked God for it.

But had I rejoiced too soon? I held my breath and listened. Someone, or something, was nearby and coming nearer, nearer . . .

I screamed as monsters pounced and began to devour me. And then I was laughing and crying all at once as I flung my arms round the soft, furry bodies. "Betsy! Winnie! Betsy! Winnie!" I cried over and over again between their excited wet kisses.

"She's here! The dogs have found her! Good girls! Good girls!"

"Justin!" His beloved face shone in the lantern light that pierced the gloom.

"Nicola! Thank God! Thank God!"

I was lifted up in his strong arms, and I buried my face in his chest and sobbed. Through my tears, I tried to tell him about John.

"Hush, darling," he said soothingly. "Don't try to say anything now. Wait till we're home and you're safe and dry."

As far as I was concerned, I was already home, safe and dry in his arms, but I was content to obey him. This was not the time to make him listen. He could hardly hear me, anyway, with the wind raging in his ears, and I was burden enough for him to carry. He had no intention of setting me down, though I indicated my willingness to walk.

Penrose House welcomed us back.

"Justin, I must tell you—"

"Later, when you have rested."

He carried me upstairs and handed me over to the care of an anxiously waiting Mrs. Carthew. Fussing over me like an old hen, she prepared a fragrant bath for me and set out fresh clothing, though if she had had her way I should have retired to my bed.

But I had to tell Justin about John. I could not rest till I had warned him.

I ran into his arms as he stood waiting for me in the drawing room.

"John tried to kill me," I cried at once. "And he's going to try to kill you."

I heard someone give a little repudiating scream. It was Clara.

"You're overwrought, my love," Justin said. "You don't know what you're saying. Here, drink this. It will calm you down. Though God knows, after losing yourself in this weather, it's not surprising you are . . . ."

"It's true, Justin. John was going to kill me. If I hadn't managed to escape . . . He killed Caroline. He tried to kill you. He's going to try again. You must do something. You must stop him."

"She's rambling," Clara snapped. To me, she said, "Why, he's been as worried about you as everyone else, searching for you all hours."

"That's right," Justin confirmed. "He met us while we were out searching for you. You were not waiting to greet me on my return—I thought that was strange, you had been most insistent that you would be there as the *Justinia* sailed in—and then, when I discovered no one had seen you since early morning, I got up a party and went looking for you. We met

338

John on his way back from seeing a patient. He immediately joined us."

"He wasn't seeing a patient," I cried. "He was with me, telling me why he was going to murder me, why he was going to murder you. He's mad, Justin. Mad! He's a murderer. He murdered Caroline. She didn't jilt you, Justin. He murdered her."

"No!" Clara's voice rose in a panic. "John's not a murderer! He didn't murder Caroline!"

"He did! He told me so!" I looked into her ravaged face, remembering something else he had told me, and I felt great pity for her. Nevertheless, Justin had to be informed. "And Justin, there's something else . . ."

"John didn't murder Caroline!" Clara said again. "Justin!"

She turned with a plea to her son. The answering look on his face frightened me.

"He did," I murmured faintly. "He did . . ."

"No, Nicola," Justin said. "He didn't. John didn't murder Caroline."

He sounded so sure, my own certainty foundered. And yet it had not been a dream. All that had occurred during the last few hours in the hills of Penrose had been horribly, horribly real.

"John murdered Caroline," I said firmly. "You must believe me."

"Tell her the truth, Justin." Clara clutched frantically at her son's sleeve. "You must. Can't you see, you must speak up now."

Justin hesitated. He heaved a deep sigh and said, "I can't . . . I can't."

"But you must. Nicola can do untold damage if she is allowed to continue to think this way. Can't you see it will be better, if she is told now?"

"Oh, Mother, how can I?" His voice broke on a groan.

Fear was with me again. Fear that John had been playing with me. Fear that the man I loved was the real murderer, after all.

"Well, if you can't, I must. I can't keep quiet any longer and

339

let John take the blame for something he didn't do." Clara's voice was firm and strong. Her face betrayed unhappiness at what she had to say, but also revealed her determination not to be deterred by it. "I've covered up for you, Justin. You can't say I haven't. And I would have gone on with the deception, but now . . . No. Not anymore. You might be willing to let John take the blame, but not I. Not I."

Justin was staring at her in bewilderment. "Mother! What are you saying? I don't understand."

"Oh, Justin." She sighed wearily. "Don't let's pretend anymore. I know. I've known from the beginning you murdered Caroline. But you were my son, and I'd have done anything to save you from the gallows . . ."

"But . . . But . . . I didn't murder Caroline! You know I didn't."

"'Course he didn't."

Perhaps I was the only one who heard Mrs. Carthew speak. The other two were still in combat.

"Why go on denying it," Clara cried. "Can't you see? It's too late to hide the truth any longer. Why don't you admit it? I doubt not Nicola will still agree to become your bride. She's besotted enough. Tell the truth, my son, and be done with it."

"But, Mother, you, of all people, must know that I can't."

Justin looked just about as unhappy as any man could.

"If truth's to be told, 'twould be better coming from yourself, Clara."

Mrs. Carthew spoke up again, and we all stared at her. Such familiarity was overmuch, even from her.

"The truth is," I cried, my patience cracking, for I *knew* the truth. "John murdered her!"

"No!" Mother and son denied it together with equal vehemence.

"It was Justin," Clara continued alone.

"It wasn't." I cried. "I know it wasn't. He wouldn't . . . couldn't . . . It was John. John!"

"'Tweren't neither of 'em," Mrs. Carthew piped up once

more. She looked at Clara. "Well, Clara, will you tell them, or shall I?"

"Tell them what, for God's sake?"

"That YOU are the murderer."

"Me?" Clara was thunderstruck. "You must be mad!"

"'Tis true. Admit it. Master Justin's been the one covering up. For you. And I've kept quiet for his sake. If I'd had my way . . ." The housekeeper's voice was cold and hard as steel, all her dislike of Clara rising to the surface.

"You're a fool!" Clara spat angrily at her.

"A fool, am I? Well, let me tell 'ee something . . ."

"Stop it, both of you!" Justin ordered the two women to be quiet.

"It's not true, anyway," I cried. "Justin!" I had to make him believe me. I had to make them all understand. They were blaming each other, hating each other, and all the time the real murderer was out there among the hills, waiting . . . waiting for the chance to . . . "Listen! Clara told me you had murdered Caroline, because she was afraid for me and I . . . I almost believed her. I . . . I went to see John, to ask him. I knew he would tell me the truth, the truth I believed in my heart, that what Clara said was a lie. Oh, darling, forgive me for considering for one moment that she . . . that you . . ."

He took me in his arms again. There was no need to say anything more of that. He understood.

But I still had to convince him of John's guilt.

"But Justin, you must believe me when I tell you that this is the truth—John murdered Caroline. He bragged about it to me. Told me it was because he could not risk an heir being born to you. You see . . ." I glanced across at Clara. "He believes himself to be the heir."

"But that's—"

"Impossible? No, Justin, it's not, because—Clara, your mother, is his mother, too. She married again after your father died. John is your half-brother, Justin."

Many things happened all at once. Clara's face went dead

white, her eyes, full of terror, gazing up into Justin's incredulous face. Mrs. Carthew's long drawn-in breath hissed like a kettle of steam. Justin murmured, "I don't believe it!" And a voice said, from the doorway, "You'd better believe it, brother."

John swaggered into the room. His hair was awry, his eyes wild. His lip curled in a sneer. I shivered at the sight of him. How long had he been standing in the doorway? What was he doing here? Had he come to murder us all? He looked mad enough for such a deed.

He started to move into the room and I thought I would faint.

"He's a murderer!" I cried hysterically, cluthing at Justin's sleeves. "He murdered Caroline. He tried to murder me. He wants to murder you."

"Yes. Yes." Justin caught hold of my hands and tried to calm me. "I know. I can see that now." His voice, tightly controlled, trembled slightly.

"Well, aren't you going to do something about it? Aren't you going to get the police and have him locked up?"

John's laughter lurched through the room. "He won't do that. Lock up his own brother! Think of the scandal that would bring. Every newspaper in the world would get hold of the story. I can see the headlines now. 'Unsavory past of famous author uncovered.' 'Famous author's bride-to-be murdered by brother he never knew.' Oh no, my brother wouldn't like that at all. He shrinks from publicity. And what a stink this would make. How it would sully his name, his reputation. Mud sticks, you know, and it matters to him what people think. See how well I know you—big brother. No, he won't turn me in. His pride won't let him."

He swung away with a jeering laugh and went to stand by the mantelpiece, surveying us with arms akimbo, legs apart—the stance I recognized only too well.

I could not take my eyes off him. Nor could anyone else in the room. There was a weird fascination about him that held each one of us spellbound.

Justin's arm was round me, and it was like a steel band encircling my waist as the tension in him pervaded his every nerve, every sinew. I guessed how he must be suffering. John Trevelyan was a friend he had loved and respected, now he had found he was a brother and a murderer. It must be heartbreaking for him to learn such a truth.

"And I'm still heir to Penrose. It's not too late for something to happen to the two of you . . . the three of you . . . the four of you."

The smile on his face froze the blood in my veins as his glance ranged over us all.

"You see? He's mad," I whispered to Justin.

"Murder the lot of us, 'twon't do 'ee any good."

A clear, confident voice rang out, and we all stared in wonderment at its owner, Mrs. Carthew.

"You'm not heir to Penrose. You never was."

John flushed, looked disturbed. "What are you saying, woman?" he croaked, his voice seeming to dry up inside him. But then it issued forth with its earlier decisiveness. "You don't know what you're saying. What are you doing here anyway? You have no right to be here."

"More right than either of you!"

John spluttered angrily searching for words to put her in her place and, not finding them, took a step forward.

"Carty!" Justin's voice was sharpened by anxiety for her. "Be quiet!"

Mrs. Carthew faced him squarely. "No. 'Tis time for me to speak out." She looked round at everybody, and we were silenced by the authority in her voice. "You was never married to Tristram Penrose, Clara. Justin's not your son, he's mine. I was Tristram's true wife."

No one spoke, but Clara trembled and, grasping for a chair, fell into it. Suddenly so much that had puzzled me became crystal clear. The quiet assurance, the obsessive affection, the genuine concern she felt for Justin—and the pride she took in

343

all he did—it was so much more than any servant's, no matter how attached and loyal.

Mrs. Carthew gazed upon Clara slumped in her chair and was pitiless.

"Tristram and I fell in love when we was hardly more than children. 'Twas only natural we should become lovers. We knowed 'twas impossible to wed, but nought could stop the love between us from growing and flowering. He was sent away to a place called Oxford, but alus when he came back things carried on the same between us. Then I found I was with child, and all at once my life took a turnaround. I'd been content never wantin' for a marriage bed, happy just to love and be loved. But now it was different. I was carrying a child, his child, and I didn't want him growing up to be a bastard. 'Twould be a boy. The piskies told me. The future Master of Penrose.

"So I knowed we had to wed. Tristram's father was dying by this time and we both knowed we couldn't blight his last days with the truth, so Tristram arranged for me to go and live in Penzance, and we were married there. I knowed he couldn't stay with me. He had to get back to his father's bedside, but he gave me money and said he'd be back as soon as he could. But as the months passed . . . I knowed he wouldn't come. I would have to settle down in Penzance and bring my son up alone. But when the time came round for my lyin' in, I knowed 'twould not be right. My son would be Master of Penrose, and he must be born there.

"So—I comed back. Told folk I'd been ravished by a sailor in Penzance once I knew Tristram was in London and married to the woman picked out for him by his father. He had to do it. It was a promise made to his father on his deathbed. I hadn't been back more'n a week when he returned with his wife, a dainty, raven-haired beauty, heavily pregnant like myself, and I knowed it was the end between Tristram and me.

"But he didn't turn his back on me. He installed me as housekeeper here and, as the piskies had foretold, my son was born where he should be born, where every Master of Penrose down the centuries had been born. I was grateful for that. It was as much happiness as I could expect."

Mrs. Carthew halted in her narrative, and the deep sigh that welled from the very depths of her being eloquently expressed her love for the previous Master of Penrose, a love that had never died. I felt a deep sympathy for the plump, motherly, little woman who had once been the passionate, loving, loyal girl she spoke about.

"Her son—your son, Clara—was born a few days after mine, but whereas mine was strong and healthy, yours was frail and weakly, with his little bones jutting out through his delicate skin, and I knowed he wasn't long for this world, and I seed the chance for my son to take his proper place as Master of Penrose.

"'Twas simplicity itself to exchange babies and later pretend 'twas my son that died. 'Ee never knowed, did 'ee, Clara, how clever I'd been? Never realized the sickly babe 'ee'd given birth to, who grew up to be the fine specimen Tristram grew so proud of, was mine."

The silence that followed her last triumphant words was intense.

"Then . . . ," Justin broke the silence, but could not finish.

"I'm your mother, Justin. 'Twas never my intention to tell you, but 'twas taken out of my hands."

"Did . . . did my father know about the . . . switch?"

"I think he did. In the end."

"I don't believe you! I don't believe a word you've said!" Clara seemed to come to life with her shrill denunciation. "You're lying! Lying! You've always hated me. This is your way of—"

"Every word is true, as God's my judge," Mrs. Carthew—no, Mrs. Penrose—said. "I've my marriage lines to prove it."

"They only prove you married Tristram, not that you bore his child."

"Justin's birth certificate proves that. Tristram seed to it

345

'twas all done proper. And there's a letter, written in Tristram's own hand, declarin' Justin's true parentage. 'Tis in a solicitor's office in Penzance. Any time I wish it opened, I have only to ask. He told me he'd done it after one of your escapades. 'Twas a form of revenge, I think. He showed it to me, afore he sent it off. 'Tis all written down, just like I telled it. He said to me, "'Tis insurance against her installing someone else in my place after I've gone. I'm damned if I'll allow her to lives as mistress here with another man.'"

"Lies. Lies," Clara sobbed, without conviction. There was a ring of truth in Mrs. Carthew's words.

"'Tis not my intention to open it, but 'twill be beholden on me if I'm forced."

A strange rumbling from the throat of the man by the fireplace erupted, like the roar of a wounded lion. He hurled himself at his mother.

"You bitch! You bitch! You said I was heir to Penrose. You said if Justin died without issue, the island would be mine. You promised!"

"I thought it would. I didn't know about . . ." Her voice gurgled in her throat as his fingers closed round it.

I screamed. Justin threw himself across the room and wrenched John away. John turned on him, black hatred on his face. "I'll kill you!" he screamed. "I'll kill you!"

But Justin was bigger, stronger, and he soon had John down on the floor, writhing helplessly to try and free himself from Justin's hold.

"Don't hurt him! Don't hurt him!" Clara begged.

Justin had his knee on John's stomach. "Send for the police," he said to me.

I flew to the door.

"No! You can't! Not the police!" Clara waited.

"We must. It's the only way. He's a murderer. Good God! He even tried to kill you just now."

"No. He didn't. He wouldn't. Please, Justin. He's my son. I'll take him away from here. You'll never see him again, or me.

We'll get out of your life forever. Please, Justin. Please."

"I can't. I know how you feel. Dear heaven, he was my friend, but . . ."

"Your friend!" John's venom was unabated. "I hated you! You had everything I wanted. Even Nicola. Yes, I fell in love with you, Nicola. I would have married you, if you'd played it my way. But you're like all the rest. When I saw which way the wind blew, I knew then I'd have to kill you. Kill you, and then him, after I'd watched him suffer. Blast you all, I've been denied even that."

"You would have killed Nicola," Justin said incredulously, "just to see me suffer?"

"What better means had I at hand?"

"But *Nicola*. She's never done you any harm."

"She turned me down in favor of you, and that was harm enough. I tried to make her turn to me. I didn't want her to die. I wanted her to rule Penrose with me. So I devised ways to make her suspect you of making attempts on her life. I sawed through the ladder rung, and meddled with the *Sea Drift*. Of course, I thought you'd be on board, and I thought I could prevent Nicola from joining you. But the piskies must watch over you. You evaded every trap I set for you. Even the slate-slide I engineered."

John spoke with gathering momentum, till by the end, his words were running into each other.

He was mad. There was no getting away from it.

"The police, Nicola," Justin said quietly, sadly.

Perhaps his sadness caused him to lose his concentrated grip on John, for suddenly John was up, dislodging Justin, who was knocked to the floor.

"The police won't get me," he cried. "I'll see you all dead yet."

Quickly, Justin got up again, but John was gone.

"Stop him!" shrieked Mrs. Carthew.

We rushed after him, all except Clara, who had collapsed into a chair, but John was swallowed up in the darkness.

347

"Let him go," Justin said. "He can't get far. There's nowhere for him to go. He can't leave the island—the tide is out and won't be in again for another few hours. By that time, the police will be landing. They'll soon find him. Once the islanders know what he's done, there'll be no hiding place for him."

We waited for the police to arrive. Mrs. Carthew—I still thought of her as Mrs. Carthew—made tea.

"How did you come to be known as Mrs. Carthew?" I asked her.

"'Twas as good a name as any," she said. "After I—"

We were interrupted by a shriek from Clara. She had been standing looking out of the window, still as a statue, not joining in the conversation, eschewing all attempts to sympathize with her.

"Look! Look!" she shrieked, her face ashen.

It was dark, but the moon was full, casting its brightness through the parted clouds. It was easy to see the tall figure, outlined against the sky, standing with his arms outstretched, his legs widely placed, in an attitude of triumph. He appeared to be shouting at the sea, at the sky. I had seen him in just such an attitude once before, and had imagined that it was the giant, Penn.

The wind raged around him, lifting his hair, ballooning his coat.

"Good God!"

Justin's loud cry was a prayer of alarm. He left the window and raced out of the house.

"'Tis the Black Wind," Mrs. Carthew gasped, and I shivered as I saw the funnel-shaped mass whirling across the sea. "'Twill take them both!"

"Justin. JUSTIN!"

I went racing after him. If the Black Wind took him, it would have to take me, too.

I could hear him shouting. "John. John! For God's sake, man, get down. Get down!"

The wind was so strong I literally trod air, raised from the ground by its force. Terrified as it lifted me along, grappling with the air, I screamed Justin's name.

I did not think he could possibly hear me above the awful screech of the wind, but he did. Somehow, he did.

He came running back toward me. "Get down! Get down!" he cried.

The wind would not let me obey. It raised my skirts above my waist, ballooning it as it ballooned John's coat, and I knew any second it would pull me into the dark funnel of its mouth.

But then Justin reached me. He grabbed hold of me, dragging me down to the sodden earth with him. Still the angry wind tried to rip me away, tugging at my hair till I felt it would be torn from my scalp.

Justin covered me with his body. He started shouting again. "Get down, John. Get down! The wind! The wind! Oh, my God!"

The weight of his body shifted as if he wanted to get up, but he did not move any farther away from me. There was no point.

I raised my head as he moved, and my heart stopped beating. I could not believe what I saw. John was floating upward into the air, coat and trousers billowing. For a moment he looked like some monstrous bird of prey. Then he was gone, lost to sight, below the cliff's edge.

The Black Wind wound its terrifying course away from the island, heading across the Atlantic toward the coast of some distant land. The noise abated, the wind left behind only a breeze. Justin helped me to my feet. He drew me to him.

In silence we gazed upon the disappearing whirl that had left tragedy in its wake.

"Perhaps it's better this way," Clara whispered through bloodless lips. "Now no one need ever know the truth. We can go on as usual."

I stared at her, aghast. Shattered as she was by John's death, it should be Justin's happiness that concerned her now. Justin's reputation among his own people needed to be restored. He had carried John's guilt on his back for too long.

"You can't expect Justin to go on taking the blame for Caroline's murder," I said.

"But nobody outside the island knows about it, and nobody here blames him."

"Nevertheless, the truth must be told. It would be immoral to withhold it."

"Tha's right. Justin's suffered enough. 'Twould be downright wicked to keep quiet now."

"Yes," Justin said. "Things cannot be left to go on as they were. For one thing, Carty must take her rightful place as my mother. For another, I have no intention of continuing to take the blame for a murder I did not commit. If I had not thought I was protecting you . . ."

"Me?"

"Like Carty, I thought you had murdered Caroline. That was why, when Nicola came, I didn't want you here. I didn't want you anywhere near her, and when you came, I suffered agonies every time she was out of my sight. I hardly dared to leave her alone with you."

"I'd never have harmed Nicola. You know that, don't you, Nicola? I'd never have harmed you."

"Anyway," Justin said, with a great sigh, "it's all over now. You'll never know what it cost me, masquerading as a murderer before all my friends on the island, wondering what they really thought of me for allowing them to cover up."

"They didn't mind. They were glad to do it."

"I minded! Do you think I'd have allowed it if I had truly committed murder? Do you have so little regard for me that you can believe I would not be prepared to take my medicine? Truly, you are not my mother, or you would never have held me in so little esteem."

She flinched under the anguished whiplash of his tongue.

"Forgive me, Justin. Please forgive me. And you, Nicola. You must forgive me, too."

Tears were streaming down her face, but, in all conscience, I did not think I could forgive her for all the lies she had told. I remained silent.

She seemed to crumple then, and would have fallen if Justin had not been quick enough to catch her.

"Of course, we forgive you," he said gently. I had thought this man harsh, cruel and uncaring, when all the time it had been staring me in the face just how kind and self-sacrificing he was.

"Nicola doesn't," she wept.

"Yes, she does. Don't you, my darling?"

I gulped. "I . . . I . . ."

"She was trying to protect you, believing I had murdered Caroline. But it's all behind us now. We can start our lives afresh."

Clara sobbed wildly. "You don't hate me anymore, Justin?"

"I've never hated you," he said gently, perhaps hiding the truth.

"You have. You have."

"No. I resented you. Bitterly. I was hurt and angry when you went away, and when Father died, I blamed you for his death, even though logic told me I was wrong, but . . . Ah, come now, no more tears. Everything has a way of righting itself. You're unhappy now because of John, but time heals and . . ."

Clara bawled more loudly than ever. "You've never spoken like this to me before, Justin. Kindly, sympathetically . . ."

"No. Perhaps I should have," he said, condemning himself needlessly.

"And I'll have no more worries? You won't stop my allowance?"

A wry smile tilted the corners of his mouth. "No. I'll see you have all the money you need to keep you happy."

"I don't deserve such goodness," she said.

Indeed you don't, I said to myself. For a moment, I thought she had changed. Now I saw she would remain the same shallow, selfish woman she had always been. Now that he had made it clear she could go on enjoying her foreign travel, her theatres and concerts, and could spend what she liked on gowns and jewels, her tears were drying.

"I think I'll go and lie down now," she whimpered. As she turned to go, her figure hunched and bent, Mrs. Carthew heaved a sigh and made to follow her.

"Aw, she'm a poor thing. Not an evil woman, just weak. I'll jus' go and look after her. Just like the old days," she said, with a sad little shake of her head.

We watched them leave the room. Then Justin turned to me. His smile bespeaking a world of love, he held out his arms.

I went into them without a sound.